Bearer of Light

Bearer of Light

FROM JESUS TO THE NEW AGE OF ENLIGHTENMENT

PAUL DESLAURIERS

NRG

𝒩𝑅𝒢 Publishing
P.O. Box 533
West Stockbridge, MA 01266-0533

Library of Congress Control Number: 2005932162

ISBN 0-9771833-0-0

1. Spiritual Adventure
2. Personal Growth
3. Religion/Spirituality

Printed in the United States of America, September, 2005

Paul Deslauriers is also author of *IN THE HIGH-ENERGY ZONE: The 6 Characteristics of Highly Effective Groups.*

CONTENTS

PREFACE

This book began on the top of Mount Shasta. I had just published my first book and was reflecting on a new direction. While I was on the mountain, a clear message came: "Write a book that focuses on the 'Highest.' Listen, it will come."

Bearer of Light did not begin in a conventional way, and the story is not conventional either. Above all else, it is a spiritual historical novel of a Truth whose time has come. Spanning over two thousand years, and situated in three locations and three time frames, the chronicle includes a message carried by the Light Bearer to a time when the world is ready to receive the Light.

PART ONE

Meetings with Jesus

It was in the city of Capernaum where Jesus' ministry first ignited. The roughly fifteen hundred residents lived on the northern shore of the Sea of Galilee, about two miles west of the Jordan River. It was removed from the religious influences of Jerusalem, and a large number of its residents were Gentiles.

The Via Maris, the "way of the sea" leading from Damascus down to Egypt, touched Capernaum. For thousands of years, travelers from Africa to Europe, from Asia to Syria and Mesopotamia, passed along or through Capernaum. Jesus could not have picked a better city in all of Israel to symbolize the worldwide implications of his Truth.

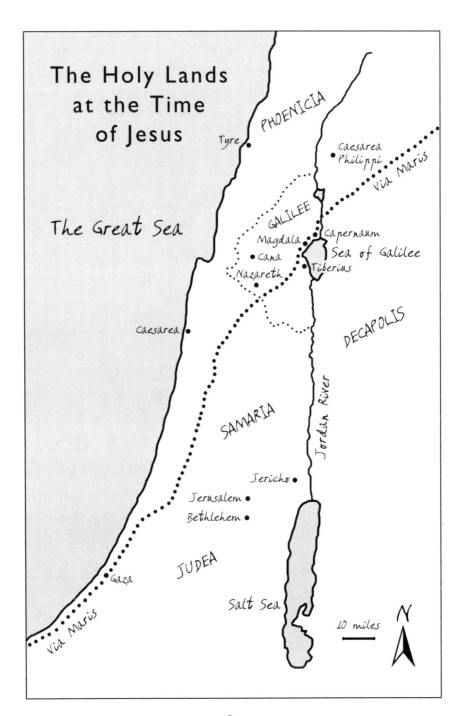

The Holy Lands at the Time of Jesus

Tyre

PHOENICIA

The Great Sea

Caesarea Philippi

Via Maris

GALILEE

Magdala

Cana

Nazareth

Capernaum

Sea of Galilee

Tiberius

DECAPOLIS

Caesarea

Jordan River

SAMARIA

Jericho

Jerusalem

Bethlehem

JUDEA

Gaza

Via Maris

Salt Sea

10 miles

N

CHAPTER 1

Orion the leathersmith leaned on his broom at the entrance of his shop, watching the main street of Capernaum come alive. As children darted in and out of the alleys, women passed, shouldering stately urns as they walked back from the well. Basket-laden men and women shuffled past on their way to the market, their sandals raising puffs of dust. Now a cart loaded high with firewood lumbered along, the driver walking beside his sweating donkey. The driver raised his hand in greeting. Orion tilted his chin and lifted an open palm, then scratched the underside of his tightly trimmed black beard. The first fires of the day were just now sending up smoke from every house on the crowded strip, filling the air with pleasant wood-smoke incense. Shortly after dawn the street was already getting hot. Orion could feel the early warmth radiating from the town's dark lava-stone walls. This was a day for staying indoors, in the shade.

"Especially the Jews," thought Orion. "It's their do-nothing day."

On their day called Sabbath, the Jews, according to strict rules, couldn't walk farther than four ells—barely enough to get to the well and back. Today, half the town would be idle. Anyone out and about or open for business was probably a Gentile. Orion looked down the street to his friend Jude's place, the pottery shop where Alexander, his son, apprenticed. As expected, shut tight. Jude would be at the synagogue, where he was the cantor. Orion understood that 'lead cantor' was something special with these people. He did have a beautiful voice. But Orion knew little about such things. He always told Jude, "Even though you're in the synagogue hierarchy, I like you anyway."

Now the tapping of stick against stone drew Orion's attention to the other side of his shop door. The old blind man, Philip, was feeling his way along the street, knocking with his stick against the walls of the houses. As always, Philip carried his head tilted at an odd angle. His useless eyes were open to the horrified stares of passersby. One of his clouded pupils was moored just below his eyelid in the far corner, and the other shifted and jerked when he blinked. Orion watched as Philip's stick touched the edge of his shop door, then tapped forward and struck Orion's broom, then Orion's ankle.

"Orion!" said the blind man and smiled.

"How did you know it was me, old man?"

"I can smell you."

Orion straightened his back and narrowed his eyes. "What do you mean, smell?"

"The leather," said Philip. "I like that smell."

Orion smiled slightly. "I like it, too. Always have. Yesterday I picked up a bundle of skins from Damascus." Letting the broom rest against his chest, Orion cupped his hands to his face and made a great inhaling sound. "It was the earth made into incense. You would have enjoyed that smell, my blind friend. It put a spell on me. I had to buy them."

"And that's why you are the best."

"The best what?"

"The best leather man in Capernaum. So I hear."

"Do you, now?"

Philip's strange face was now a blinding grin. "Yes. And I hear everything, don't you know. You would be amazed. People say anything around a blind man. Just because I can't see, they take me for an idiot." He cackled, "Hee hee hee."

"Tell me what you hear, Philip."

"Oh, I hear who's cheating who, who wants to murder who, whose wife is playing bad games."

"Any news for me?"

"Oh yes," said Philip, nodding his head. "I have news for you. Listen, for a Gentile, you are an amazingly good man. But your wife...."

"My wife, yes?"

"Your wife is much better. She is better than any

man deserves, even you."

Orion laughed out loud.

Philip said, "And I can hear that horse, coming toward us from the Roman garrison."

Orion turned quickly and sharpened his stare at the far end of Capernaum's main street. By the flashing of reflected sunlight, the bright sweep of the red cape, and the high-stepping energy of the white steed, Orion could tell that this was the centurion himself, Publius.

Orion muttered an obscenity.

"Oh well!" said Philip, cackling again. "That kind of attitude won't get you very far in a world owned by our friends from across the sea."

"Bastards," said Orion, and he spit.

It was indeed Publius himself who rode toward them and then, to Orion's surprise, reined in his horse at the door of the leather shop. Orion had never been this close to Capernaum's top military authority. The centurion was a huge, muscular man with a long, arcing nose and shaven face. He looked perfectly comfortable in his metalized gear, his plumed helmet, the dazzling scarlet cape, all astride the magnificent white charger that snorted and side-stepped, dust exploding from its hoof beats. Orion, unmoving, continued to lean on his broom.

From horseback, hand on hip, Publius said: "Leathersmith! I understand your name is Orion, just like the old hunter who moved his bones up there...." Publius jerked his thumb toward the sky. "With the bull and the bear."

Orion said nothing.

"That's not a Jewish name. Judging by your curly black hair and features, I would say that you are a Greek."

"I am," said Orion.

"Can you fix my tack? The leather is wearing thin."

Orion regarded him with a cold stare. "Can't help you."

"Look here. I'll get right to the point," said the centurion, his horse dancing and back-stepping. "I've been asking around. Word is that you're the best craftsman in town. My garrison could use your services. As I'm sure you know, Rome will pay you far better than these Jews do."

With a defiant stare, Orion said, "I have all the work I can handle."

Publius considered this comment for a moment, then he shrugged his shoulders. "All right, be that way. There are others who will be glad for the offer."

Then blind Philip called out: "You should ask Bishmehoth, the cousin of our beloved Pharisee Isaac. Bishmehoth is always looking for customers."

Publius answered with a grin, "And I know why. I've seen his work. A blind man could do as well."

"Hee hee hee," said Philip.

Publius looked at Philip. "Tell me, old man. How is it to be sightless in Capernaum? How does the world treat you?"

"Not so bad," said Philip. "Not so good."

"I'm surprised to see you walking about on the

Sabbath. Aren't you a Jew?"

"Oh, I am a Jew. But I was born blind. People get the idea that I have sinned somehow—although when I ever had so much fun as to actually sin, I can't recall. But they let me do what I want because I am such a filthy sinner."

"Filthy sinners are we all," said the centurion, "and each of us blind in our own ways. Good day to you both." And he sped away.

"Publius is a good man," said Philip.

"He's a Roman soldier."

"Yes, but he cares about the people. He feeds the hungry. He even built the new synagogue. I'm surprised you are so rude to him."

"It's not him," said Orion. "I know he is a good man. It's the uniform and the abuse I endured in my youth."

Philip laughed. "I know a lot about abuse. People have beaten me, and for what?" He swung his stick till it struck the doorway. He took a couple steps forward, then stopped and tilted his ear toward Orion. "A little abuse now and then won't kill a man. But anger will. No place to hold that anger. Good day to you, leathersmith."

"Good day, Philip," said Orion thoughtfully. The aroma of baking bread drew his attention within, to his shop and to the living quarters behind that. He unlatched the heavy shutters on one of his shop windows and swung them open. Morning sunlight fell on the shelves full of tack and sandals, his projects for today.

For a minute, he simply enjoyed the sight of his

working place—two racks of cured leather against the back wall, his work bench waiting for him, the anvil and a variety of tools laid out in easy reach, the dirt floor hard-packed and smooth, free of clutter. For twelve years now he had been promising himself to pave this floor. He knew that Jude would make him the clay tiles and no doubt help him lay them. "Maybe this year," he thought. But he was in no hurry. Truth is, he loved this shop in its humble simplicity. He had built the benches and stools himself, and they were good. His leatherworking tools—the knives, awls, hammers, the foot-shaped molds—were his familiar friends, almost as dear to him as his own wife and two sons. He still liked the heavy, hand-loomed curtain that separated the shop from the covered porch courtyard within. He had picked it up about ten years previous from a caravan that passed through Capernaum from Egypt, heading to Damascus. Its bright blue-and-white pattern gave light and color to the shop, which was otherwise rather shadowy and unornamented. This was his domain and he enjoyed it.

The curtain moved and there was Elizabeth, his wife. Orion also enjoyed the very sight of her—her large brown eyes, full lips, and smooth bronze skin were framed by thick wavy black hair that draped her shoulders. Anyone with eyes could see her beauty.

"Are you all right?" she asked.

"Yes. Why?"

"While I finished the baking, I heard you talking with that soldier. I thought you might be upset."

"Not too bad."

Elizabeth walked to his side and slipped her arms around his waist. Her touch soothed him. "We could get the boys up and go to the lake early." She then moved her right hand to his heart and any remaining tension vanished.

"Now I'm all right. I need to finish these sandals for a merchant whose caravan is leaving this afternoon. Besides..." he smiled, "I'm a Gentile. I work on the Sabbath."

"Shall I open the curtain?"

"Yes. Thank you."

During warm weather Orion often worked on the back porch that extended from his shop. He would position himself so customers could see him there when they walked in. This way, he could overlook his family compound from the elevated porch. Within their private U-shaped courtyard was the home he shared with Elizabeth and the two boys, Alexander and Julian. At the center was the fire pit, oven, and flour mill. Two other buildings, each with its own porch, framed the central courtyard. At the far end of the compound was a well-tended garden that bordered a wall separating them from their neighbors. He and Elizabeth slept in one of these buildings. Alexander and Julian slept in the one across the courtyard, except during the warmest nights when they all slept under the stars.

By late morning Orion set down his tools. He looked to Elizabeth, who was sitting on the porch of their bedroom, mending some clothes. "I finished those sandals." It was time for the family outing. Orion quickly cleaned the leather scraps while Elizabeth gathered the lunch she had prepared earlier.

"Let's go, boys. It's time."

Alexander came bounding out of the boys' house, the fishing poles and tackle already in hand. "I've been waiting all day. Let's go!" Tall for an eleven-year-old, he had his father's look—a thick mat of curly black hair, a sinewy strength, an eager energy.

"Where's your brother?" she asked.

"Back in the garden."

"What's he doing?"

"I don't know. I think he's collecting bugs."

"No, I'm not," said Julian, who had slipped quietly into the scene. Three years younger, he had his mother's brownness, straight hair, and expressive eyes.

"So what were you doing?"

"I was helping them get organized."

The older boy laughed out loud. His mother cautioned him: "Alexander…."

Alexander caught himself and said, "Well, look, Julian. Why don't we go organize some *fish* so they land in our *basket*?"

"First I have to wash my hands."

"Come on, hurry up.

"Alexander…."

It was a short walk through Capernaum's streets to the shore of the Sea of Galilee, where Orion kept a long skiff tied up for these family outings. Orion and Alexander walked in front, side by side, carrying the pack and the fishing gear. Elizabeth walked close behind, holding Julian's hand to keep the family together. On the main street they passed a solid wall of shops that lined both sides of the street. Today Julian was full of questions. "Why are the rocks black?" he wanted to know.

"The stones in the buildings?" said Orion.

"They're all black."

"It's lava stone. It comes from a quarry up in the mountains."

"What's a quarry?"

Alexander said, "A place where they get rocks."

"Can we go to the quarry?"

"It's a long, long walk," said Orion. "And not very pretty."

They stopped to wait for a while as a passing company of merchants filled the street with two dozen camels and at least that many donkeys, all heavily burdened with baskets and casks. The strange dark-skinned men who sat astride the bobbing camels wore turbans and brightly-colored robes. "Where are they going, Dad?" asked Julian.

"North. At least to Antioch. Perhaps all the way to Macedonia."

"Why do they carry swords?"

"Protection from bandits. They'll probably join a larger caravan once they are outside of town."

"I want to go on a caravan," said Alexander. "I want to go to Macedonia."

They next took a narrow side street that led away from the travelers to the beach.

A little later Julian asked: "How can grass grow on the roof, Dad?"

"What?" Orion looked up at the flat house-tops, where as always a few dry weeds clung in patches. "I guess the seeds blow up there. They grow in the clay."

"There's clay on the roof, Dad?"

"Yes. Clay and gravel. It gets rolled flat and tight to keep out the rain."

"Why is there clay on top of the roof?"

"Hmm? It's easy to get and put on. And it makes the house cool, like living in a cave."

"I see the boat!" shouted Alexander, dancing. "Come on, Julian." The boys took off instantly. Alexander quickly outdistanced his brother, but Julian didn't seem to mind. Instead he got interested in digging his toes into the muddy sand of the lake shore. The lake was flat and glistening, and it ran to the horizon under the cloudless sky. The breeze was pleasant now that they had left the crowded town behind them.

Orion took in a deep breath and felt his intuition about the safety of the lake. The weather could change rapidly, and he didn't want to jeopardize his precious passengers. His instincts told him it was safe.

By the time Orion and Elizabeth reached water's edge, the boys had already untied the boat. But it took Orion's strength to push the craft, which was nearly three body-lengths long, into the water. Julian climbed in first, saying, "Dad, I wanna go waaay offshore." He sat in the front with one hand on the bow, pretending he was captain. Alexander steadied the boat while Elizabeth and Orion hoisted themselves in. Orion took the middle seat, holding the oars in one hand, while Alexander pushed offshore and hopped in the stern seat with Elizabeth. When Orion pointed the boat offshore, Julian cheered and pointed far out to sea.

"How do you know when it's right to go out, Father?" asked Alexander.

Orion rested his gaze on his lanky son, the boy's thatch of hair shifting ever so slightly in the breeze. He took in his long face and fine features and inquisitive look.

"It's about listening. It's about being still and open to the guidance that is always there for you."

"What about Zebedee? His boats always bring in the biggest catches. They say he is the best. How does he do that?"

"It's listening, just like I said. He listens for where the fish are. He listens to their rhythms and behaviors, and to the weather, and to the water. It's the same with the work I do. I listen to the leather I am working with. To do anything well, you have to listen to your instincts."

Alexander asked, "What do you mean to listen to your instincts?"

"That's hard to say. You become still. Listen to your feelings. An inner knowing, I guess. A good fisherman knows where and when to let down the net."

Alexander was silent taking in his father's response. No one else spoke as the water churned around the oars and slapped the bow, making rhythmic sounds as an occasional cool spray of water struck their warm skin. The air had a fresh moist smell that filled Orion lungs as his heat increased with the exercise. Then Alexander said, "It's like when I know someone is interested in buying a pot, I can sense it."

"Yes, that's what I'm talking about," Orion responded with a smile. "Your mother and I are very proud of the apprentice work you're doing. Jude tells me that you're a good worker."

"I like getting the money and meeting the people."

"That, too."

Jude and Orion broke the mold of Jewish/Gentile relations. They were neighbors; they frequented each other's shop. Jude and his wife Sarah were childless and used to love caring for Alexander when he was a baby. The close relationship continued as the boy grew and became Jude's apprentice. It was as though Alexander had a second family, making Jude a brother to Orion.

Further offshore the wind picked up slightly. Small wind-induced waves splashed along the boat as it began to rock, and Julian met each motion with a wave of his hand for balance. Orion pulled back hard on the oars. He enjoyed the exercise after bending over his work for hours. The boat jerked forward with each thrust. Once he had worked up a good sweat, he laid the oars down and gazed back at the town. The three-quarter-mile stretch of homes and shops looked small along the vast shoreline. Julian, too, looked back to where the land met water.

"See that spot way over There?" Julian said as he pointed to a distant place about two miles from town.

"That is as far as I have explored." Then he looked at the distant landscape, "There is so much more."

Orion slowed his strokes; Julian then asked "How deep is it here?"

"I don't know, let's see if we can touch bottom," said Orion with a laugh. "Swim time!"

"Yes!" said the boys. Though they were excited, they knew from experience that they would have to coordinate their weight in the small boat. Orion waited for the boys to dive in, and he paused as Elizabeth slid into the water beside the boat. Then Orion somersaulted off the bow, making a huge splash that brought a big smile to Elizabeth's face. The boys screamed with excitement. Orion took a deep breath and dove down as far as he could, down where the pressure in his ears was strong. He liked to show off to the family. "No bottom here."

Later, Orion rowed to his favorite spot a mile from the mouth of the Jordan River. There was a little cove there, plentiful with bait fish. Two large trees along the bank provided shade.

Food was their first priority. Elizabeth had prepared fish with a sweet and hot olive oil dressing, and there was bread baked with the spices Orion got by bartering sandals. Everyone ate in silence except for sounds of appreciation. The hot spices made Orion's upper lip sweat, and the sweet dressing cooled his palate.

As soon as the boys had their fill, they ran off to catch bait fish. Orion stretched out beneath the trees, feeling peaceful as Elizabeth lovingly rubbed his scalp. He had to laugh to himself how like the neighbor's dog he felt, lying there on his back, feeling such deep contentment in that moment.

He said, "I woke up before sunrise this morning and was gazing at the stars before the light of day made them fade. I stared up into the three unmistakable bright stars of my namesake's belt."

"And what were you thinking?" she asked.

"The three stars on Orion's belt reminded me of a customer who ordered a belt. He wanted one design on his belt for each major accomplishment in his life. Each design I made was significant. One was for his marriage and a design for each of his children. Another was for his craft; he was the best stone mason in the region. So I wondered what great feats could possibly merit these blazing stars on Orion's belt. One story is that Orion was shot in his prime. He must have come back to Earth two more times to earn the stars that shine so brightly in the night sky."

"They say that the three great pyramids of Egypt were modeled after the stars of Orion's belt."

He was quiet for a moment letting these thoughts settle in; he knew he had spoken something of meaning. Then he said, "When I look into the vastness of the starlit sky, I can't help but believe there is something more to life than this earthly existence. Or is this it? Is this the peak of our existence?"

She said nothing, so he went on: "Even in this deep contentment, I believe there's something beyond this."

Elizabeth smiled. "Only the gods know, Orion."

"But I want to know what the gods know. I always

have wanted this. The great philosophers sparked this desire when I was a boy in Caesar Philippi. Have I stopped wondering and searching?"

"Perhaps you are just pausing in preparation for something even more important."

He sprang up and playfully gave Elizabeth a kiss, then ran off to catch up with the boys. They had caught five little fish and found some worms.

Back in the boat, the boys baited their hooks and threw their lines into the calm water. Orion rowed slowly back to Capernaum along the shore. Julian gave his line a little tug every once in a while, and before long he had caught two good-sized fish, enough to feed the family for the evening. Then Alexander hauled in a big one. After they had all pulled the boat up the shore, each boy proudly carried his fish. Julian wanted to know if fish feel bad when they die, but no one had an answer for him.

On the way home they passed close to the synagogue. It was a large, one-story building with three great steps up to a massive wooden door. Today, three members of the synagogue stood by the steps discussing something. As they passed, one of these figures, an overweight, balding man with a scowling expression, ceased speaking and turned to stare at the Gentiles. Orion recognized the lame elder of the Capernaum synagogue, Isaac by name. He'd heard of Isaac through Jude, the potter. Isaac was on a campaign to assure that none of the Jewish congregation would do business with Orion; instead, he urged them to his cousin's shop on the other side of town. Orion had never spoken to Isaac, but he knew of his zeal to promote his form of Judaism. Isaac also had a reputation for treating non-Jews with contempt. Now here he was, pointing a finger at Orion and his family. Then Isaac turned his head and made a comment to his son Barak, a hulking, oversized teenager. Barak was considered the bully of the town. Again Isaac pointed. All three men at the synagogue steps stared at Orion.

Orion stopped. He looked back with a steady, defiant gaze. He muttered: "The 'chosen people of God,' ha!"

Elizabeth stepped in front of Orion's gaze. She caught his arm and turned him, pointing to the boys. Orion got the message and they walked home.

"Ignorant beasts!" he said. "They probably never even heard of Pythagoras. Plato. Heraclites. Homer."

"Peace," said Elizabeth.

As they neared their street, Julian was the first to see Philip. The blind man was sitting at his customary corner, cross-legged on a small rug, spinning wool and talking to passers-by, who mostly ignored him. But the basket on the rug before him held a few coins. Julian looked at his father and asked, "Is it all right if I give Philip one of our fish?" Orion nodded, and Julian lifted the fish up until it touched Philip's hand. "I caught two, and one is for you." Philip's strange eyes swept blankly across the sky as he smiled. He touched Julian's hand, then gripped the boy's forearm and said, "Ah, it's Julian. Have you been talking with the angels again today, my boy?"

"No, sir."

Alexander cut in: "He's been talking with bugs instead."

"Hee hee hee," said the blind man. "That will do. That will do. Thank you for the beautiful fish, my boy." Then he got to his feet. "Orion," he said, "can I have a word with you?" Elizabeth turned to greet a neighbor, and the boys ran home. Orion stepped close enough that Philip could grab his arm.

"Did you hear about the new teacher in the synagogue?" said the blind man. "There is a lot of talk going on about someone named Jesus. They say he is the Messiah, a great prophet. I even hear that he has performed a miracle."

"A miracle? " Orion felt his skin tingle. "Say more."

"That's all I've heard. I thought you might know more."

"No, nothing. But I will let you know if I hear anything about this."

Orion approached Jude's pottery shop; empty shelves lined the outside wall facing the main street. The front door was ajar, and when Orion was in sight Jude burst from the door. Seizing Orion's shirt-sleeve, he started talking excitedly about a new teacher at the synagogue. "They say he is from Nazareth. Nazareth! What a place to be from! It's a little village with one stream, miles from any travel routes. No one of interest has ever come from Nazareth. But this one, he speaks wisdom. You should see his eyes, Orion! His eyes are filled with conviction. He is like no one who has ever been here before. While this man was teaching, a man who was possessed by an evil spirit cried out at the top of his voice: 'Ha! What do you want with us, Jesus of Nazareth? Have you come to destroy us? I know who you are – The Holy One of God!' Everyone was looking at Jesus. So Jesus walked slowly, coming close to the possessed man. Jesus looked him in the eye and said, 'Be quiet!' At once the entire room fell silent. No, beyond silent. There were more than a hundred of us gathered. I have never felt anything like this silence. And then Jesus spoke in a soft voice that seemed louder than the blast of trumpets—'Come out of him!' When he said that, the spirit shook the man violently and came out of him with a shriek. We were all amazed! He speaks with an authority that even the evil spirits obey.[1]

"We all stared at the crazed man, who was now calm and even joyous. He didn't have the same glaring stare. He was a different person."

Orion watched Jude carefully throughout this uncharacteristically excited speech. He knew this man, had known him for years. Jude was incapable of telling lies. Soft-spoken and hard-working, a tall man with a lean build, Jude was not at all given to illusions of miracles. He was a listener who liked to interject conversation with witty comments, word-play. Orion was startled by his friend's enthusiasm.

"This fellow Jesus, he was here today? He did this today?"

---

[1] Luke 4:33-37

"Right here in Capernaum. In the synagogue. He's staying at the house of Simon, the fisherman."

"Simon?"

Orion knew Simon by sight, not well. But everyone knew Simon—a huge fellow, like Hercules, but mild as a lamb. Always making jokes. One would have never thought him to be the good friend of a Messiah.

Near dusk, after the boys were fed, Elizabeth and Orion decided to take a walk and, purely from curiosity, chose to walk along the street where they knew Simon the fisherman lived. It was a narrow side street, and as they approached they found the entire street blocked by a crowd. People had come with their desperate ones, the sick, the lame, the dying. Every wild-shouting person possessed by spirits was here, choking the way to Simon's house. Murmurs and shouts mingled into a continuous roar. A pair of donkeys tied in a doorway began braying. People moved in a mass, gathered too tightly to move ahead.

Orion and Elizabeth explored the outskirts of the crowd, trying to see what was happening. They heard shouts and screams and wails. They heard words like miracle, prophet, Messiah, but they saw nothing. As darkness encroached, the crowd began to disperse. Orion and Elizabeth turned to head for home.

Suddenly they heard a single scream, a woman's voice, from deep within the crowd. Following that, they heard gasps and shouts of surprise. They turned back toward Simon's house. There was Philip, working his way with amazing speed through the crowd toward them. Everyone had turned toward them, not because of them but because of Philip.

The blind man was no longer hunched over his walking stick. He was walking upright. He glanced excitedly in every direction. People ducked and backed away, afraid that he might pass by too closely. Now Orion could see Philip's face clearly. The man's eyes were no longer glazed and strange. His pupils were centered and focused, and the whites of eyes were clear.

Elizabeth let out a screech, "Aiii!" like the sound of a gull, as she put her hand to her mouth.

Orion gasped, "Philip."

Then Philip's new eyes noticed Orion, and Orion called out his name again. Now Phillip had an image to go with the voice of kindness. Philip rushed to them, arms outstretched, and Orion grasped the healed man in embrace as tears of wonder streamed down their faces.

"Here are your faces! I can see your beautiful faces!"

"Philip," called Elizabeth. "Can you really see us?"

"You are even more beautiful than I believed!" Philip grabbed Elizabeth and kissed her on one cheek, then the other."

Orion was in shock. What he was seeing did not fit in the world he had known—a world that was quickly crumbling.

"What is this?" said Orion. "Explain this. What has happened? How does something like this...."

"It's a miracle," Philip sobbed. "I've been healed, brother. Jesus has the power of the Lord! Praise Jesus, I can see!"

CHAPTER 2

Orion and Elizabeth talked late into that evening. Who was in their midst? What had happened to Philip? Who had the power to do this? They could barely sleep that night—a restless sleep that woke Orion before sunrise. For the second morning in a row, he found himself staring thoughtfully at the constellation whose name he bore. The three stars of Orion's belt were shining as brightly as ever, but today the message they proclaimed was new. Perhaps the change was more like this: yesterday, the sky was mute. Today, though, Orion perceived some kind of meaning in that vastness, a message. But what message? All he knew for certain is that his sense of the universe had changed forever.

Unable to sleep, he rose, dressed, and quickly made his way back to Simon's house. Unsure what to do, he simply waited by the door. A crowd was already gathering—by sunrise, perhaps a hundred people or more congregated. Conversations, whispered at first, grew louder and merged into a murmuring roar.

Orion overheard the person next to him. "I was there at the wedding feast in Cana. There was no more wine when the celebration was going strong. Jesus turned jugs of water into wine. That wine was the best ever raised to these lips.

Finally, the door to Simon's house opened. Two of Jesus' followers stepped out and told the crowd to go away. Jesus had left already, well before dawn, to pray. After that he would be traveling to other cities in Galilee.

Deeply disappointed, Orion lingered until the bulk of the crowd had dispersed. Then he drifted back to the main street, where shopkeepers and townspeople were gathered in small groups, everyone talking about the same thing. Some groups looked like conspirators, speaking closely and occasionally scanning the street to see who might be within earshot. Orion moved from group to group, trying to get tangible information. Instead, he picked up a lot of wild speculation. "Jesus is the Messiah. He is the one foretold in the holy books; he will free us from this oppressive Roman rule and high taxes." Orion heard plenty of views that clashed.

"The Messiah? That man? Don't make me laugh!" said one fellow. "He's a carpenter from Nazareth. Do you suppose he'll be defeating the Roman army with a chisel and a saw?"

"Besides that," said another, "he won't even speak about the Romans. With him it's all 'the Father' and 'love your neighbor.' What kind of talk is that for a Messiah?"

"He's too clever to talk openly about rebellion. Not yet anyway."

"Rubbish!"

"Don't forget the miracles. How do you explain these powers?"

On that point, there was a lot of head-scratching. "I believe he is Elijah the prophet," said one.

"Elijah? Come back?"

"You're crazy!" shouted a man whom Orion recognized as a crony of Isaac and one of the Pharisee gang.

"This Nazarene you talk about, it sounds as if he is the crazy one."

"Yes!" said the Pharisee. "All of this is from a crazy man possessed by the Devil. There's no other explanation. Who can drive away evil spirits? Why, only the Devil himself!"

"That makes sense to me."

To Orion, all of this was absurd. Jesus had discovered what is beyond our earthly existence. But Orion had no rational explanation, just a feeling sense, a knowing.

Several days later, news flooded the town that Jesus had returned to Capernaum, and that he was again at Simon's house. By the time Orion and Elizabeth got to the place, the crowd in the street was already so thick that they could neither see nor hear what was happening in the building.

"Here's an idea," said Orion. "I know the man who lives next door. He's a regular customer of mine. Perhaps we can see something over his back wall."

Orion knocked. The door creaked open just enough for a man's face to see them.

"I wonder…." Orion began.

"Orion! Hush. Quickly." The man waved them inside, then shut and locked the door with a sliding bolt. He led them out the back of the building to the inner yard, where a small group of people—family, as it turned out—were standing on benches and boxes to look over the wall. The man's brother was steadying two small children who were sitting on top of the wall. The man quickly introduced Orion and Elizabeth. An old woman, his mother, offered her place. As the man helped her down from the bench, Orion could see that her eyes were shining with strange sort of ecstasy.

In fact, the view over the wall offered a bit of a reward. The two houses were almost touching. They could see, though from an extreme side angle, into an open window—there were a few men in view, crowded against the window and all looking to the interior of the room, which was not visible. They could hear voices.

"Can we see him?" asked Orion.

"No. But sometimes you can hear his voice."

As their host fetched a table and helped his mother get resituated in this shameless line-up of eavesdroppers, Orion and Elizabeth focused on hearing. One voice was clearly his—gentle not loud, but resonant as a deep bell. When it spoke, the other voices stopped. Every time they heard it, Orion pointed slightly with his finger and

Elizabeth nodded.

But a scuffing and grunting intervened, coming from above them and behind. Then gravel sprinkled their heads and necks. They looked up to their host's rooftop. Four men were scrambling along up there—no, not four but five. The fifth man was lashed to a stretcher, a paralyzed figure. Two men carried the stretcher; the other two bore shovels, pry-bars, and saws. When they got to the gap between this house and Simon's, they leaped across and helped each other get the paralyzed body over the dangerous gap. When this group was gathered on Simon's roof directly above the meeting room, one man looked down to Orion and said: "Is this the place? Is this the room where the Messiah is teaching?"

"That's right," said Orion.

Immediately the four able men bent to work, digging and gouging at Simon's roof. First the gravel came back. One spadeful must have flown into the street on the other side, because they heard a roar of shouts and curses from the street. Then the men worked at the stiff clay, peeling it back and stacking it to the side. Then they started prying up boards and cutting them away with saws. A hubbub of voices erupted in the meeting room. The few men Orion could see began looking up and talking to each other. Once the men on the roof got one plank fully cut away, they shouted: "Don't worry! We will repair this roof. We will make it better than before. We have a man here who must see the Master. Please!" Dirt and gravel were now tumbling everywhere, even into the meeting room. Orion heard laughter and shouts of dismay, followed by even more laughter. "Please!" shouted the men on the roof. "Our friend must meet the Messiah."

Orion heard the men by the window say to each other: "The Messiah! Do you hear that? I told you. That's what these people think of this man. It's madness. Dangerous madness."

Two of the roof-breakers leaped carefully into the room then reached for the paralytic's pallet as the two who remained above helped ease it down. When the two above finally released their grip, they knelt by the hole in the roof. Silence fell thickly across the entire scene.

In that stillness, Orion heard the voice quite distinctly: "Son, your sins are forgiven."

The men at the window began again, oblivious to the fact that their whispers were perfectly audible to the eavesdroppers:

"Forgives his sins? Why does this man speak that way?

"He is blaspheming; who can forgive sins but God alone?"

After this ceased, along with a general murmuring in the meeting room, Orion could hear that voice again, Jesus' voice.

"Why are you thinking these things?"

The men in the window glanced at each other, obviously disturbed that somehow the teacher had heard their whispered remarks.

Then the voice spoke again. "Which is easier to say to the paralytic—'Your sins are forgiven' or 'Get up, pick up your pallet and walk?'"

A perfect silence, an expectant silence, filled the air. Then the voice said: "But that you may know that the Son of Man has authority on earth to forgive sins, I tell you, get up, pick up your pallet and go home.[2] "

Suddenly a great collective gasp, a group cry, erupted in the room next door. The men at the window stared, amazed. Then one grabbed the other's sleeve and said loudly, "It's a trick. A magician's hoodwink." Cries could be heard; "A miracle!" The friends of the paralytic on the roof raised their arms toward the heaven shouting, "Praise God, praise Jesus."

Orion's host plucked him by the sleeve and ran back into the house. Orion and Elizabeth followed. The host flung open his front window shutters just in time to see what Jesus had accomplished. The throng in the street had pulled back to make way for a terribly thin man in tattered clothes. The fellow tottered forward with small steps, dragging behind him that same wooden stretcher on which he had been lowered, his face radiant. The crowd in the street looked on with excitement, fear, and amazement, saying, "We have never seen anything like this." On the roof, they now shouted, "Glory to God. He has sent us a prophet!"

Sleep did not come easily to Orion that night. He lay awake long after Elizabeth had fallen asleep, going over what he had seen and heard. This defied what he had been taught by the Greek philosophers. Who was

---

[2] Mark 2:1-17

this man who was in touch with powers that reigned over the earthly realm? Here was a master. Jesus understood the deeper meaning to existence that Orion had been longing for.

The following day, Orion and Elizabeth heard that Jesus was going to talk on the shores of the Sea of Galilee. Their faces flushed. They went about their morning chores. By the time the afternoon sun gleamed in the courtyard, Orion and Elizabeth decided it was time to leave. While walking they did not speak. Only the sound of the black stone of the street crunching under their sandals could be heard. Their minds were active, hoping to experience and learn truths that could open doors they could not by themselves approach.

They could hear the excitement long before they could see what was happening. When they reached the beach, there was much talking and mingling of old, young, male, female, Jews, Gentiles, and foreigners. Orion's eyes became fixed on a figure in the distance that stood out from the masses. A wave of excitement shot through his body. The man was on his knees talking with a group of children that surrounded him.

They walked in silence, approaching the crowd spread out before them. He and Elizabeth found an open spot and settled into the warm sand. Orion couldn't keep his eyes off the man with long brown hair as he laughed and made expressions to illustrate his story to the children around him. Soft golden light surrounded him where he stood bent against the last light of the fading day, glowing and graceful, in a white garment. A full beard and hair cascaded in waves, framing his face.

Behind him men were constructing a crude platform from fish racks and discarded boards. When they finished, one of the men approached Jesus and bowed respectfully. Jesus stood up and touched the children on their heads. Some of the close women disciples gathered the children. He straightened and moved towards the planking; his gate was fluid and easy. More than appearance was the radiance he projected. Orion's mind was still, so still. The moment consumed him. All of Orion's attention was on Jesus.

The crowd watched, almost breathless, as one of the teachers of Jewish law approached Jesus on the platform and asked, "Of all the commandments, which is the most important?"

"The most important one," answered Jesus, "is this: 'Hear, O Israel, the Lord our God, the Lord is one.' Love your Lord your God with all your heart and with all your soul and with all your mind and with all your strength. The second is this: 'Love your neighbor as yourself.' There is no commandment greater than these."

The man smiled. "Well said, teacher. You are right in saying that God is one and there is no other but him, and these are more important than all burnt offerings and sacrifices."

Jesus saw that he had answered wisely and said to him, "You are not far from the kingdom of God.[3] " And from then on, no one dared ask him any more questions.

In the quiet that Jesus allowed to settle over the

_____
[3] Mark 12:28-34

congregation, Orion reflected. He had been taught that there are many gods, each an inspirer of dramas. Now he was realizing that God is not a collection of dramatic tales. God radiates his Light through the cosmos without story. There is one God above the earthly realm.

The Master spoke with a full, deep voice. "So, do not worry." He paused, then said it again: "Do not worry, asking 'What shall we eat?' or 'What shall we drink?' or 'What shall we wear?' Those who don't believe in God run after all these things. But your heavenly Father knows that you need them. Seek first the kingdom and his righteousness, and all these things will be given you as well.[4] "

Orion had a realization. He had given a substantial part of his adult life to this kind of worry—worry about putting food on the table when business was slow, especially when Isaac's campaign started turning away his customers. Worrying about survival had certainly not turned him to thoughts of God. The most he had ever thought about God was during religious debates with his fellow merchants. He certainly had not put God, "the kingdom," and righteousness above all else.

As if to emphasize Orion's insight, Jesus continued. "No one can serve two masters. Either he will hate the one and love the other, or he will be devoted to the one and despise the other. You cannot serve both God and matter.[5] "

The Jews believed in one God, Yahweh, but what made the message of Jesus so different from other Jewish

---

[4] Matthew 6:31
[5] Matthew 6:24

teachers was that he spoke with such clarity and assertion. He knew the face of God. When Jesus talked about the connection with God, he spoke from deep personal experience. This matter-of-fact confidence gave Orion faith in something that he knew he was yet to realize.

Sitting on the warm sand next to his wife Elizabeth, Orion felt something shift inside him, a new direction, a new focus. Before this, he had simply been inattentive, scattered, and blind. He had been skeptical of organized religions and their claims on his salvation, yet this was a simple truth that felt right.

From within low clouds the setting sun spread a pastel glow that shined upon the motionless crowd and upon the stately figure of Jesus as he blessed the crowd with raised hands and said, "Seek and you will find. Knock and the door will be opened to you. For everyone who asks receives." Then, swiftly, Jesus left the platform, followed by men and women who were his close disciples.

Orion sat transfixed in the sand. He knew he needed to shift. He needed to seize this connection with God. How? By prayer, he supposed—develop an ongoing dialogue with God. Could he live a prayerful life?

Elizabeth rose and reached out her hand to Orion. Slowly he got to his feet and scanned the crowd. It was a diverse assembly—people from all over the region, certainly not Jews only. He spotted Philip nearby, talking with great animation to those around him. And he spotted Isaac standing with a group of his Pharisee types. Isaac was also excited, sweaty and gesticulating.

Orion supposed that these rule-making bullies were straining to condemn every utterance from the mouth of this new spiritual teacher. Just the sight of them darkened Orion's feeling of inner radiance, so he looked away quickly.

He turned to Elizabeth. "I can't explain what is being stirred within me. I want to bring God more into my life."

Elizabeth nodded. "Yes, I do too. When Jesus spoke of God, I somehow lost my doubt."

They slowly walked home holding each other's hand, silent except when they greeted neighbors and passersby. When they arrived home, they called the two boys. The family sat together on the porch behind the leather shop, and Orion tried to talk about what he was experiencing.

"Boys, your mother and I have met an amazing teacher."

He hesitated for a moment, and Julian said, "Is he the one who fixed Philip's eyes?"

"Yes. Have you been hearing about him?"

Alexander jumped in: "Everybody is talking about him. They call him the Master. People say he's a magician; he can fly through the air and make the sun stand still. People are scared of him."

"No, no, no," said Orion. "He is beautiful, with a great power of love."

"He wouldn't hurt anyone," said Elizabeth. "He's no magician."

"But he has been healing people, people with terrible problems," said Orion. "I can't explain how he does that. But there is no evil in this man. Far from it. Boys, we saw a man who was paralyzed, who couldn't move his legs or arms...."

"That's not important," Elizabeth interrupted. Orion looked at her, surprised. "His teaching, that's important."

Orion said, "He teaches about the one God. God is the source of Jesus' power and is in all that we see, hear, taste and smell." Then he took a long deep breath through his nostrils to emphasize that God is in the moment.

"What is God?"

"Not the gods we told you about. This God is above all religions, a God of mercy and love. He casts his Light upon everyone. Actually it's not a He. In Aramaic Jesus referred to God as the Source of cosmic radiance and vibration." Then he hesitated, unsure how to say what he felt.

Julian piped up. "You mean the bright Light inside?"

"You know about that?"

"I wondered why no one ever talked about it."

"Well, now we will. We will make that Light shine brighter. Every day."

"How?" Alexander wanted to know.

Elizabeth said, "We will do what the Master taught us. We will pray. We will talk to the Light; make it shine by focusing on it."

"Every morning when we wake up, we'll pray to

the Light," said Orion. "And then at night, before we go to sleep, same thing."

"And before every meal," said Elizabeth.

"Yes."

"Can we pray, too?" asked Julian.

"Yes, of course. We'll share. The Light shines brighter if we share."

"And then will I be able to fix blind people," asked Alexander.

"I don't know," said Orion as he laughed. "We'll just pray. Then we'll see what happens."

The following day Orion sat on the porch working on a pair of sandals. He had the idea to cut a design into the leather, and he wondered what sort of design would work as a simple reminder of Jesus' teaching. So he closed his eyes and focused his attention on the one God. "Jesus made me aware that You exist," he spoke inwardly. "Bring me an image that reminds me of Your presence throughout the day, an image that represents the family praying to You"

Later that evening Orion prayed with the family, sitting in a circle in the boys' room. They each offered prayer, and Orion could see all their invocations going toward the Light. That was when the first image appeared to Orion. Like the reflection of the moon on the lake, it was always pointing to its source. Each wave of light was like one of them, all of them focused together and aiming to the highest. As a family they were all on the same path, yet separate, all moving toward the Light.

After the boys went to bed, Orion began cutting this design into his leatherwork. As he worked, he printed into his mind and heart a clear intention of his connection with God.

CHAPTER 3

Absorbed in the details of tooling a new pair of sandals, he had failed to notice the arrival of his neighbor, the potter. Jude had entered the leather shop with a quiet bordering on stealth. Orion looked up.

"Jude! What's this? Middle of the workday, and no clay on your hands. Anything wrong? Alexander?"

"Your son is fine, my friend. He's minding the shop."

"That's good. I hope he's busy."

After a pause Jude said, "No, I just stopped by to talk about the weather."

"Hmm."

"I thought I should warn you about the storm that's coming."

"Storm!" Orion glanced through the shop door at the hot, brightly lit street outside. "Not much chance of a storm this time of year."

"Oh, but there is. I would hate to see you or your family get caught in it."

Orion set down his mallet and chisel. "What's the meaning of your riddle, Jude?" There was no levity in the potter's face or voice.

"Orion, did you pay any attention to the career of the fellow that people used to call 'John the Baptist?'"

"No. Never heard of him."

"He was another one of those wild-haired preachers from the wilderness. He baptized thousands of people."

"And what happened to him."

Jude made a slashing gesture across his own neck.

"What!"

"Wound up in Herod's little jailhouse. Then one night they served up his head on a silver platter."

"No one would do that to Jesus."

"I shouldn't be telling you this, but you are my friend. I've just come from a meeting at the synagogue. Senior members have banded together and launched a plot against your outlaw holy man."

"Outlaw?"

"He preaches without authority."

"You don't need a license to be wise! Jesus has done nothing but good. Not only good, but miracles."

"There's no point in trying to convince me. I have great admiration for the man. But the Sanhedrin is afraid of him. They want to silence him. They say he is threatening the traditions and laws that empower them, that he is criticizing the Pharisees. Jerusalem has a lot to say about it."

Orion stiffened and clenched his fists. "Jesus is not threatening. Not to anyone."

"They would oust me if they knew I was talking to you like this."

"The devils!"

"Orion, you know there is a controlling group invested in their powers. They fear that they'll lose their grip on the congregation. Ever since Jesus arrived, the whole town has been talking about him, nothing but him, his healings, his radical ideas. Now the congregation is divided. Many align with Aaron, the chief rabbi who supports Jesus, who keeps on allowing Jesus to teach at the synagogue. But there are just as many who oppose him. They say something should be done to stop this ministry of Jesus, even if he is a Jew."

"What can they do?"

"Both the Sanhedrin and our synagogue are sending spies to gather evidence of lawbreaking and blasphemy so they can catch him on a religious charge. Then they can turn him over to the civil authorities."

"Spies, is it?" Orion looked at Jude. "And what is your position?"

Jude tugged at his beard thoughtfully. "I am no spy. Or am I? After all, here I am, speaking of these things with my neighbor, a Gentile and a pagan."

"Where do you stand?"

"For now, I stand in both worlds. But I want no harm to befall Jesus— or any of us who look up to him."

"It is important that you stay involved in the synagogue hierarchy. We need awareness of what is happening. But I also think we should meet with others to discuss this. There is strength in numbers."

They decided that each would choose one other person to join them for a meeting. Orion selected Philip. Jude chose Marcus, the ironsmith.

"We'll meet here in two days," said Orion. "I don't know what we can do. But I don't want to see this group within the synagogue threaten Jesus and his revelations."

"I will let you know of any developments before then." Jude left as quietly as he had come.

Orion turned back to his leather. But now the work went badly. He tossed down his tools and let out a frustrated roar.

Elizabeth entered. "What happened?" she said.

"Nothing happened. Nothing."

She came to him and began rubbing his shoulders. "What's wrong?"

He was silent.

"I know the signs. You're in one of your moods again."

"This isn't a 'mood!'" he said abruptly, then caught himself. "I'm sorry."

"What is it?"

"It's Isaac and a group of religious leaders who are conspiring against Jesus. They wouldn't know a blessing if it felled them. They have to be stopped. Four of us will be meeting in two days. Is it all right to get together here after Wednesday's supper?"

"Yes, of course. I will make bread and tea, and take

the boys out. Just let me know when."

"Thank you."

"I'm frightened thinking you will get into a clash. I look in your eyes I see your intention and resolve. Don't endanger yourself."

Orion looked in her beautiful eyes. "I will do my best to stay safe."

The next day, mid-morning, Orion heard a familiar voice at his shop door, calling his name.

"Got some work for you," Matthew called out, smiling more than usual as he held a chewed sandal over his head. "That new puppy has been busy."

Orion stood up and clapped Matthew on the back and they embraced.

Matthew was one of the new rich—a publican and a tax collector for levies on fish catches and caravans. He had been one of Orion's first customers twelve years ago, and he had been frequenting the shop ever since.

"How is your family?"

"We are changed, Matthew, since meeting Jesus. Just seeing him has left both Elizabeth and me with—I don't know, a whole new awareness of life. We pray together, and we are all closer for it. His teachings inspire us. But seeing him there, on the shore, against the setting sun, it was God coming through him. The miracles.... This man is truly amazing, isn't he?"

"Amazing enough for me to leave my business and follow him."

"What?"

"I've handed it over to my brother. Jesus has asked me to travel with him. I am giving up my wealth to be with the Master."

"What a sacrifice!"

"It doesn't feel like a sacrifice at all. There is so much more than business and possessions." His broad face beamed. Then he looked Orion right in the eyes, and he said, "I have always wanted to know these things that Jesus is showing me. Without them I am incomplete."

"Yes, Matthew. I know what you mean." And Orion clapped him on the back, "I rejoice in your good fortune!" Then he gripped Matthew's upper arm and lowered his voice. "I wonder if you realize that this could be a dangerous choice."

"Ah, yes. Danger."

"I hear there's a conspiracy against Jesus. Three oppositions have sent out spies to follow him, to accuse and persecute him. I have great concern for the Master."

"I have heard some of this. I am also concerned."

Then Orion gave Matthew the details, and he responded, "I'll tell Jesus what you said." Matthew set the chewed sandal on Orion's workbench.

"The main reason for my stopping by was to invite you to a feast tonight, a celebration of my discipleship. Jesus will be there. You and Elizabeth are invited. Will you come?"

Orion's eyes grew wide. "Yes! Of course we will come."

"Put on your best clothes. Give Elizabeth my regards." Matthew's eyes sparkled. "I must be going. I have a lot to do before this evening."

"Matthew, you are blessed to be chosen by the Master."

"So are we all," shouted Matthew as he breezed out of the shop. Orion stood there letting the impact of Matthew's invitation hit him. He was excited, happy, yes, but also shy, alarmed, perhaps even a bit frightened. His arms and legs trembled with the force of his feelings, as though his body sensed that lightning was about to strike. He walked slowly, as though floating, over to where Elizabeth was hanging clothes to dry. While her hands clasped the line, he put his arms around her waist, holding her from behind, her sweet fragrance filling his head.

He said with enthusiasm, "Tonight we are invited to a feast at Matthew's house. There is a special guest." Then he whispered in her ear, "The Master."

She spun around with joy, jumping up and down like a happy child.

The tax-collector's house was one of Capernaum's largest. Orion had been inside only once before, on a point of business, but he still remembered admiring the quality of the furnishings—the handsomely tiled floors, finely worked tapestries, the abundance of silver and brass. Nothing was ostentatious, but everything showed the power of Matthew's income and good taste. As they walked to the feast, Orion and Elizabeth talked about Matthew's choice—his renunciation of all that in order to wander the countryside in willful poverty.

"I hope I fit in," said Orion.

"What do you mean?"

"Rich people. And I'm...."

"Extremely handsome," Elizabeth cut in.

"So says the most beautiful woman in Capernaum."

Matthew himself greeted them at the door. "Welcome, you two! Thank you for sharing this night of rejoicing with me." Behind him, a roar of voices billowed through the open door.

Orion said, "It sounds as though you're sharing this night with quite a crowd."

"Lots of people. People from all walks of life. Diversity—that's how the Master likes it."

"Is he here?"

"Not in the main room. He will be out shortly. Come in. The wine is excellent. Will you have some?"

They stepped into the torch-lit room and the hubbub of conversations. Matthew had not exaggerated his claim of diversity. It was a huge room that opened to an expansive courtyard, but Matthew had managed to fill it with guests. All of Capernaum was represented, Jews and Gentiles, merchants, tax-collectors, shopkeepers, and people of various trades. Religious authority was well represented—Pharisees, Zealots, Sadducees—though Orion noticed that these tended to segregate themselves in small groups from which they looked around rather solemnly at the general party.

People began moving to their assigned places at long tables lined with cushions. The roar of voices increased, mixed with laughter and the clashing of plates and cups.

Then Jesus entered, and the room fell silent.

He wore simple white robes. Somehow the light in the room seemed to concentrate on him and flicker in his eyes. As the silence became complete, he raised both arms and acknowledged everyone present with a warm, quick, glance. He said, "The Father's blessing on this house and all in it. A blessing on our generous host and the new life on which he is about to embark."

The silence continued. People seemed to be waiting for more. So Jesus addressed the room generally:

"You have heard that it was said, 'Love your neighbor and hate your enemy.' But I tell you: Love your enemies and pray for those who persecute you, that you may be children of your Father in heaven. He makes his sun to rise on the evil and the good, and sends rain on the righteous and the unrighteous."

Jesus paused scanning the crowd. Everyone was staring at him. When the moment was pregnant he said, "If you love those who love you, what reward will you get? Are not even the tax collectors doing that?" A wave of laughter ran through the room. " And if you greet only your brothers, what are you doing more than others? Do not even Gentiles do that?" More laughter followed. "Be perfect, therefore, as your heavenly Father is perfect.[6]"

Then he took in the variety of people present. "Love your brothers and sisters beyond your differences."

With that invocation, servants came forth bearing large platters vegetables, fish, and steaming spiced lamb, more wine, and shining bunches of grapes.

---

[6] Matthew 5: 43-48

Throughout the meal Orion was distracted. He wanted further contact with Jesus, who was seated, talking with a large group for what seemed like most of the evening, at the far end of the large room. Orion was careful to observe what he could. When Jesus spoke he used his whole body, his hands danced to the rhythm of his words, and his facial expression changed to act out his message. It was the same when he spoke on the shore; he made stories come alive.

As he looked upon Jesus, Orion began to feel that same force that had struck him at the lakeside sermon. With that came a jolt of fear. What if this force overtakes him again, here at the party? He would lose control. And then Jesus turned his head and looked directly at Orion.

Their eyes met for just a moment, but to Orion it was an eternity. He stared into the Master's eyes as if he were gazing into the depths of the night sky. Those eyes seemed to take him far beyond anywhere he had ever known or even imagined. He felt as though he was falling into a cavernous pit. His stomach churned; he felt his balance going. He felt his identity—his name, his assumptions, his sense of self—began to dissolve into the vastness contained in that gaze. Everything he had known was like a drop in of water in the Sea of Galilee. Then fear gripped him, and he averted his gaze.

When he looked up again, Jesus had resumed conversation.

Orion closed his eyes. Elizabeth, who had been talking with other guests, noticed his stillness. She reached out and placed her hand on his. Then his awareness came back to the banquet with the sounds of harsh words. A Pharisee sitting at a nearby table was criticizing Jesus' choice of dinner companions. "If this man is so godly, why doesn't he sit at this table, here, with those who share his privilege?"

Just then Jesus rose from his seat, the folds of his robe opened with his fluid movement. The room was becoming silent as they noticed Jesus. The move was perfectly timed so that most of the guests could catch the Pharisee's ensuing comment: "Why is he eating and drinking with these tax collectors and sinners?"

Jesus heard this, and he turned to them slowly, looking at them with a steady gaze he said, "It is not those who are healthy who need a physician, but the sick; I desire mercy not sacrifice. I did not come to call the righteous, but sinners."[7]

And the Pharisees looked at each other and down at their plates, and fell silent, but they were not appeased. After Jesus had resumed his seat and the voices rose again in a general roar, Orion could hear the Jewish leaders return to their criticisms. From bizarre religious reasoning, they saw themselves superior to Gentiles, Romans, and other sinners who were in their midst.

Indeed, Jesus was different from these Pharisees and the other teachers who discriminated. He ministered to Samaritans, to women, to all who asked. He did not judge. He primarily forgave others. He saw harlots as God's children. Nor did he ban from his talks those who wished him ill. His love was a bright light that shone on everyone within sight. To him, the differences

---

[7] Matthew 9:11-13

of earthly existence were thin facades, easily penetrated.

Orion looked at Matthew and the other men and women who were close followers—at Simon, Andrew, James, and John, the other men from Capernaum whom Jesus had chosen to be his close disciples. No two of them were alike. There was Simon Zealot, a leader within that strict order. Standing next to him was Matthew, a publican and tax collector whose lifestyle and work Simon regarded as sinful. The close women followers were also different. Jesus saw something deeper within each of them that made them all equal in God's Light.

At the close of the evening, after the plates had been taken away, Jesus rose, and called out a prayer. "Blessings in the name of the Father and of the Son and of the Holy Spirit. May God's peace be in your heart."

It was to Orion as if a great source of light was moving through the room. And he felt that light shining in him as well. He seemed to see that light shining back at him when Matthew bade them goodnight.

As they walked home, Orion told Elizabeth about meeting Jesus' eyes. Then he thought out loud. "Jesus spoke of the trinity with his final blessing, and he also spoke of embracing the great diversity around us. It's amazing that such diversity comes from this Source."

Elizabeth looked at him. He did not see her looking; he was absorbed by this thought. But when she finally caught his eye, a smile lit up his face.

That night, Orion again prayed for a symbol, something to represent this aspect of the Master's teaching. He remembered Aristotle. He contemplated the vast, diverse universe. He reflected on the trinity as part of the Godhead—the source of Light that makes the great variety of this land. Then the second symbol came to him. The Trinity is entwined with its differences as one. From the trinity evolves the great diversity of the universe which is also entwined on some level.

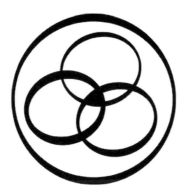

The following evening Philip, Marcus, and Jude met by the fire in Orion's courtyard. The men sat with wine and some fish stew, which Elizabeth had prepared. Orion felt comforted and even strengthened by this group of men who all shared his admiration and concern for Jesus.

He told them, "The Master starts his gatherings with a prayer to God. I found a powerful connection with my family when we pray together. Shall we do the same?" They all nodded their heads in agreement. "Let's take a moment of prayer to invoke God's presence." They all focused in silence. Thus they set the pattern for starting all their brothers' meetings.

Then Orion talked about the banquet. He even tried to put into words his moment of contact with Jesus. Then he added, "I share concern for Jesus. I also want support in bringing his teachings into my life."

Marcus, the ironsmith, said, "There's many clashes happening in town. Many factions. I was in an argument the other day with a client who wouldn't pay me because I supported Jesus."

"Wouldn't pay you? What was his reason?"

"See if you can find reason of any kind in this: he said that Jesus is a devil, and seeing I am in league with the devil, he would not compensate me. Then he spit on me."

"Spit on you!"

"With all these wild projections going on about the Master, I feel I am in danger. But here in this forum, I feel safe and my connection to Jesus is strengthened."

Jude spoke next. "I have been disillusioned with the synagogue hierarchy." This was difficult for him to admit. He leaned forward as he spoke. "There is a plot to end Jesus' ministry. The majority of elders in the synagogue want to silence his teaching. There are even some who want to see him dead. This is in contrast to Aaron, the chief rabbi, and a few others like me. Despite my opposition, they have assigned three spies to follow Jesus and be at all of his public ministries. They elected Isaac to lead the investigation. The spies report to Isaac."

Orion growled, "That bloated fiend. Now there's a real devil for you."

"I have since heard that Isaac is having these spies

spread rumors around town. They are getting people riled up about Jesus. I'm not surprised to hear what happened to you, Marcus. Their deceptive tales are beginning to change the sentiment in Capernaum."

Marcus said, "I've seen men asking about Jesus, trying to get information. And now there's a new surge of wild talk about Jesus being the Messiah—that he will lead an uprising against the Roman oppressors."

"I'm not surprised," said Jude. "And that leads right into my most recent concern. Tomorrow, Isaac will set forth by boat to pay a call to Herod Antipas in Tiberias. The conspirators are hoping to convict Jesus on civil charges."

"He'll wind up just like John the Baptist!" said Marcus.

"Can we do anything?" Orion asked. "Can we send representatives to Herod?"

For a moment, no one spoke. Then Jude said, "Orion and I will get word to Jesus. One of the many who know the truth can then go to Herod, if necessary. But I don't think Herod will go for Isaac's claims. He has his own spies who are likely reporting facts, not distortions. I will let you know as soon as I find out."

"Religious delusion, fear of change," said Orion. "A few Pharisees threaten the most profound messenger of our time." The men were silent. Noise from the street mixed chaotically—camels, carts, horses, people.

Philip broke the silence. "The miracle Jesus bestowed upon me is reflected in every image that I see. He has the power to do whatever he wants—or whatever is God's Will. My worrying is not going to help the Master."

"I agree, Philip," said Marcus. "Jesus has taught me to let go of my worry and guilt. To trust in God's grace. You know, my boy Nicholas died two years ago. He was the same age as Orion's son Julian; they were friends. I grieved for two years. Every time I saw Julian, I felt a terrible emptiness. Jesus showed me how to become whole again. "

They talked until Elizabeth and the boys returned. As they said goodnight, Orion realized that they all felt buoyed by the energy they had jointly created.

Jesus was meeting with his disciples in a house on the edge of town, and there was a crowd all around the house. Orion and Elizabeth were among them. While they waited, bits of information leaked out from the house and were passed around the crowd like crumbs of bread.

"What's he doing now?"

"He's eating."

"What is he eating?"

It wasn't much to go on, but it helped them feel connected to the Teacher.

Then Orion noticed a small group of individuals working their way through the crowd toward the main entrance of the house. The central figure of the group seemed to be an older woman. "Who are these people?" asked Orion, and someone said, "It's Jesus' mother, and his brothers and sisters."

A little while later, this story came out to the crowd:

"Someone went to Jesus and said, 'Your mother and your brothers and sisters are outside, asking for you.' And Jesus replied, 'Who is my mother? Who are my brothers?' Then he looked around him and said 'These are my mother and brothers. Anyone who does God's will is my brother and sister and mother.'"

The people around Orion and Elizabeth were surprised to hear this. It seemed disrespectful. Aren't we supposed to honor our parents? "Why would he say such a thing?" asked a voice nearby.

"It's simple," said Orion to all who would hear. "He is saying that we are all part of God's family, all moving towards God, all children of the Father, brothers and sisters, that we are all related and part of that whole."

People looked at him. Some nodded in agreement.

"You can read it in Heraclites, too, if you have a mind. 'Listening to the Word, it is wise to agree that all things are one. We are not separate.' That's Heraclites."

"Oh. Heraclites," echoed back.

"Who's Heraclites?" said someone.

Then the door opened. A wave of excitement went through the crowd. Jesus stood in the doorway and greeted his mother and then embraced each of his siblings, speaking softly to them. Then he turned and addressed the crowd: "Love your neighbor as yourself. So in everything, do to others what you would have them do to you, for this sums up the Law and the Prophets."

A voice in the crowd shouted, "And who is my neighbor?"

In reply, Jesus said: "A man was going down from Jerusalem to Jericho when he fell into the hands of robbers. They stripped him of his clothes, beat him and went away, leaving him half dead. A priest happened to be going down the same road, and when he saw the man, passed by on the other side. So too, a Levite, when he came to the place and saw him, passed by on the other side. But a Samaritan, as he traveled, came to where the man was, and when he saw him, he took pity on him. He went and bandaged his wounds, pouring on oil and wine. Then he put the man on his own donkey, took him to an inn, and took care of him. The next day he took out two silver coins and gave them to the innkeeper. 'Look after him,' he said, 'and when I return, I will reimburse you for any extra expense you may have.' Which of these three do you think was a neighbor to the man who fell into the hands of robbers?"

A voice from the crowd called out: "The one who had mercy on him."

Jesus looked in the direction of the voice and said, "Go and do likewise.[8]"

On the way home Orion asked Elizabeth, "Do I help others in need?" He knew he would get an honest response.

She said, "You don't hesitate to help others. You give to the beggars. You help out your neighbors. You are like the Good Samaritan."

---

[8] Luke 10:30-37

She reminded him of the injured caravaner he once brought home and nursed for a week until the man was able to resume his travels.

Orion then looked at his wife, "The neighborhood loves you. You are caring. You often help the neighbors when they are sick. Jesus was saying we are not separate. I cannot love God without loving humanity. Perhaps we were closer to God than we thought."

After the family said its prayers and the boys fell asleep, Orion sat by the fire with Elizabeth, who spoke, "Some of my close friends who are followers of the Master will be starting a group. We will share a meal together and support each other in our growth. Your group of brothers is an inspiration for all of us."

Orion responded, "We are acting closer to our deeper nature when we connect in these ways."

In silence he thought about what Jesus had taught that day. We are all connected, part of the same web, sharing the same thread with the Source. In the stillness of the night he looked at the ball of wool Elizabeth had spun lying in her basket. An image came to him that represented this interconnected web.

He thought of his family, and then he thought about his brothers. Within those groups he felt uplifted and strengthened. He felt larger groups had the same potential—the town of Capernaum, for example. Instead, a handful of individuals were creating havoc within this group. He thought how wonderful it would be to have a large community that was like his two smaller groups.

The following morning Jesus left Capernaum before sunrise. The men and women who were close followers, including Matthew, went with him to teach at other cities in Galilee. In the void of his absence, rumors flew. Gossip and projections distorted one position and undermined another. Jesus' acts took on different meanings, depending upon what was being projected.

Isaac returned from his meeting with Herod and gave his account to the elders of the synagogue. Jude was in attendance.

When the meeting ended, Jude got Philip, Marcus, and Orion together. The men sat overlooking the courtyard on the shaded porch that extended from Jude's bedroom. Alexander was in the shop attending sales.

"There is good news," said Jude. "Isaac did not get his way with Herod Antipas. He pleaded his case. 'Arrest Jesus for conspiring a revolt against Rome,' he said. 'He is planning rebellion.'

"Herod settled it quickly, 'I have had spies following Jesus since that wine trick he performed in Cana.

I know that the crowds have urged him to be their leader in armed rebellion, to be their king. But his response has been consistent. He always tells them that he is not here to rule an earthly kingdom. He is only for a heavenly kingdom, whatever that may be. For now, I can't see that he poses a threat to our rule.'"

"That is good news," said Marcus with a sigh of relief.

"Yes, it is. Herod is not pressing charges. But we must watch for Isaac's next move. He has begun to single out our senior rabbi. He yelled at Aaron in the meeting for still allowing Jesus to teach in the synagogue. I am worried about Aaron."

The four men talked about how to prevent further efforts by the enemies of Jesus.

Orion realized that these men had become part of his extended family. They began meeting at least once a week, sometimes more often depending on what they heard from Jesus—news, rumors. Mostly they discussed his sayings and talked about how to integrate them in their daily lives.

CHAPTER 4

The four men sat in Orion's courtyard in the early evening. "Tell us, Jude," said Orion, "how are things at the synagogue? I hope you don't have more bad news for us."

"In fact, I do," said the cantor, looking into the fire as he stroked his long beard. "We met today. These meetings are called every few days, it seems. Every time Isaac hears a report from one of his spies, he calls everyone to the synagogue to hear his filthy lies and distortions about Jesus."

Marcus the ironsmith shook his head, "Rotten!"

"It certainly is rotten," said Jude. "And it's effective. The opposition to Jesus among the Pharisees and Sadducees is growing. When they hear what Jesus is saying about them, their faces turn black with rage. They get so angry that they can barely speak. They stutter and spit!"

Philip let his head roll back and laughed, "Hee hee

hee." For an instant, Orion remembered how the man looked before the Master cured his blindness.

Orion turned to Jude, "What is Jesus saying?"

Jude said, "Here are some things I heard. Knowing you would ask, I tried to memorize the words exactly. Of course, these words are being reported by spies, but...."

Orion finished Jude's sentence: "But, knowing the Master, the spies are probably being accurate!"

"Yes," Jude said. "Except for the fact that they take his comments out of their proper context. And yet—it's true. He's calling them hypocrites."

"Hypocrites, is it?"

"Yes. Apparently the Master said to some Pharisees: 'You nullify the word of God for the sake of your tradition. You hypocrites!' And then he quoted Isaiah as evidence against them."

Philip laughed with glee. "Oh, he knows how to poke at them!"

"He said, 'Isaiah was right when he prophesied about you: These people honor me with their lips, but their hearts are far from me. They worship me in vain; their teachings are but rules taught by men.' And then he told them this: 'Listen and understand. What goes into a man's mouth does not make him unclean. But what comes out of his mouth, that is what makes him unclean.⁹'"

"Unclean!" said Marcus softly. "Like lepers."

Jude continued, "Jesus also suggested a response to the Pharisees, "Leave them; they are blind guides. If a blind man leads a blind man, both will fall into a pit.'"

---

⁹ Matthew 15:7-14

"Blind, are they?" said Philip. "Hee hee hee! I fell in a few myself."

"He certainly speaks his truth," said Marcus.

Orion said, "Jesus threatens the framework of the Jewish religion—the members of the hierarchy, their roles and claims. He's saying that our salvation is not to be found in any religious organization. It is our individual connection to God."

Jude answered, "It's a message that many do not want to hear. The opposition is gaining ground."

"Despite the miracles," said Philip, closing his eyes and nodding his head. "Despite his messages from the heavenly Father."

"Pressure is building to ban Jesus from the synagogue. Aaron defends Jesus. Aaron sees him as a great teacher, as do many in the congregation. But...."

"But the politics," said Orion. "And the manipulation of many by a few."

"Tell us more about this meeting today," said Marcus.

"Near the end, Isaac made his boldest accusation. He accused Aaron of stealing from the synagogue."

"What!"

"That's ridiculous."

"Isaac announced that some money was missing from the synagogue treasury. He blamed Aaron, of course, because Aaron is the only one with unauthorized access."

Philip mused, "And Isaac discovered this before anyone else...."

"Not only that," said Jude. "Isaac knew right

where to look for the missing coins when they searched Aaron's residence."

"They searched his house?" said Orion.

"Yes, of course. Aaron denied the accusation and welcomed the opportunity to prove his innocence. 'I have nothing to hide,' he said."

Setting two more pieces of split firewood on the red coals, Orion said, "And Isaac, that fat old goat, knew right where to look for the stolen goods." He pushed one of the logs.

Philip, imitating Orion's serious voice and facial expression, looked at the others and said, "You won't find Greeks doing that sort of thing." Everyone laughed.

"Don't forget," said Orion. "We invented the Trojan horse."

Again, a burst of laughter. But Jude's laughter was small and brief. He said, "The elders have asked the Jerusalem Sanhedrin to settle the case of Aaron's guilt."

"Well, that's good," said Orion. "The leaders in Jerusalem will put an end to this small-town farce."

"No they won't," muttered Marcus.

"If the synagogue of Capernaum succeeds in banning Jesus from the home base of his ministry, other synagogues will feel free to do the same. The goal is to stop his teaching throughout the land."

All were silent for a moment in contemplation of this absurdity.

Then Philip chimed: "Who cares?"

"What do you mean?"

"If the Master stayed only in the synagogues, he would have missed out on the chance to meet our friend here, Orion. The synagogues are too small for Jesus."

After they left, Orion stayed by the fire thinking about life's uncertainty. This amazing resistance to Jesus by his own people. How could anyone criticize such an inspired teacher? Even though a fire blazes in the night, darkness surrounds it, pushing to return. Jesus had opened an entirely new awareness of life's possibility.

The next day, word again spread through Capernaum that Jesus had returned, that he would be speaking once again at the lakeshore. Orion dropped his work, gathered the boys and Elizabeth, and made haste to find him. After they passed the agora, they could see a small crowd, perhaps two dozen people, filling the street ahead.

"That's him!" cried Alexander. "He's probably walking down to the beach."

"Let's catch up," said Julian.

"Careful, boys," said Orion. "Not so speedy. Look again." The large white horse and the flash of red fabric told them that Publius, the centurion, was also approaching the Master. The Roman soldier was straight ahead of them, approaching the crowd, tall in the saddle, letting his steed shuffle forward at an easy walk. "We might have trouble."

"Should we hide?" said Julian.

"No, it's all right. I just don't want you rushing in there."

They kept walking as they studied the scene ahead. The centurion moved closer to the crowd, and as he neared, everyone in the group turned to look at him.

Then people stepped back, opening a corridor between the slow-moving horse and the robed figure who was, no doubt, the reason for the soldier's approach. Orion and his family reached the scene just at the moment when Publius pulled back on the reins. It was a curious sight—Jesus, standing in the middle of the street, calmly regarded the centurion, who towered above them all, fierce-looking in his armor and helmet and red cape. For a moment, no one spoke.

Then Publius dismounted. He removed his helmet. "My Lord..." he began, then hesitated. To Orion's amazement, the centurion actually went down on one knee. Then he called out, "Lord, my servant lies at home paralyzed and in terrible suffering."

Jesus said to him, "I will go and heal him."

The centurion replied, "Lord, I do not deserve to have you come under my roof. But just say the word, and my servant will be healed. For myself, I am a man under authority, with soldiers under me. I tell this one, 'Go,' and he goes; and that one, 'Come,' and he comes. I say to my servant, 'Do this,' and he does it."

A look of astonishment came over Jesus' face. He brought his hands together near his lips, and for a moment he studied the soldier. Then, turning to the people nearest him, he said, "I tell you the truth, I have not found anyone in Israel with such great faith."

Then Jesus said to the centurion, "Go! It will be done just as you believed it would.[10]"

Publius bowed his head. Without another word he returned the helmet to his head, remounted his horse,

---

[10] Matthew 8:6-10

and had the animal turn about. For a few moments, the only sound at all on this Capernaum street was the clopping of hooves receding in the direction of the Roman garrison.

Orion stood transfixed. His own feelings about the centurion—a hostility bordering on violent hatred—had just been completely overturned. In a moment, he ceased viewing Publius through the filters of his own prejudice and began seeing him through the eyes of Jesus.

Not so for others in the crowd, evidently. He heard someone close by ask, "Why is he helping a Roman soldier? He even praised him! How can this man lead the rebellion against our oppressors?"

Jesus didn't hear, or chose to ignore, these comments. Instead he turned and began walking once again to the lake, moving at a robust pace. Orion stared at him. The words used by Jesus kept revolving in his mind: "It will be done just as you believe." He asked himself, "What is it that I believe?"

The crowd followed Jesus. Others were arriving. People were trying to press against the Master, touch him, question him. The disciples pushed back against the crowd, gently but vigorously making room for their beloved teacher.

Seeing all this congestion, Orion steered his family to take a side street to the lake. There it was quiet enough to talk while they walked. He said, "I will never look at a Roman uniform with those old feelings of anger."

Elizabeth touched his arm and repeated Jesus' words: "It will be done just as you believe."

"Yes. That was the amazing statement. Before he heals someone, he always asks if they believe in their own healing. Once he knows that they believe, he floods that belief with the power of God. The miracle begins with our own belief in our cure or creation."

"What we believe in our deepest hearts we make true."

Alexander said, "When I'm selling pots, if I really believe that I'll have a good day of sales, I do."

Orion placed his hand on his son's shoulder and said, "So it's crucial to hold uplifting and encouraging thoughts that support the best in each other." After a moment he added, "This makes me think of Tiberius."

Julian piped up. "You mean your leather teacher, Dad?"

"He was that, and much more. After your grandfather died, he took me in. He was kind to me and supportive. He held firmly to the belief that I would become a highly skilled and successful craftsman. What he believed came to be."

Elizabeth smiled. "You had a few beliefs of your own about that."

"That's true, but why? Where did my beliefs come from, if not from him? Especially because my father was gone at such an early age." Orion put a hand on the head of each of his two sons. "I believe in the two of you. I believe in just that same way."

After a moment of silence, Julian spoke up. "How did your Dad die?"

When Orion replied, his voice was low and hard-edged. "He was killed. He was killed by Herod Antipas."

"Orion…."

"No, it's the truth, and I'll speak it. He was killed by Herod Antipas."

They paused to look at the people thronging on the

shoreline. Alexander said thoughtfully: "That must make it hard to feel happy when you look at a Roman uniform."

Orion responded,"Jesus just showed me to look beyond the uniform."

As soon as they entered the crowd, they picked up the news. The servant of Publius had returned to health, suddenly and completely.

The shoreline was already tightly packed with people. The pressure on Jesus was palpable, physical, perhaps even ominous. Several close disciples worked their way toward one of Peter's boats and launched it for Jesus to board through the mobs of people. Then they positioned the boat offshore and anchored it.

He stood up, looking majestic as a light breeze lifted his words and carried his full, rich voice so that everyone could hear. "I tell you the truth, if anyone says to this mountain, 'Go, throw yourself into the sea,' and does not doubt in his heart but believes that what he says will happen, it will be done for him. Therefore I tell you, whatever you ask for in prayer, believe that you have received it, and it will be yours.[11]"

He gestured the words, giving them expression and energy that extended to the crowd.

Orion said the words over and again to himself: "Do not doubt in my heart." He had never doubted his skill as a craftsman in leather. Jesus was urging them to possess that same sense of confidence. The same, and yet

---

[11] Mark 11:22-24

much larger. Actually, Jesus was showing the highest possibility we all are capable of achieving—our connection to God.

While he sat on the beach thinking of these things, Orion remembered the teachings of the Greek philosopher Heraclites. Heraclites liked to point out that nature works by way of opposites, or complements. When Jesus says that all things are possible, then nature responds that all things are uncertain. Possibility and uncertainty are joined twins. So if we embrace great possibilities, then we must also embrace great uncertainty. Life is uncertain. We must face the fear of uncertainty.

As if Jesus were reading Orion's thoughts, he then spoke about confronting that fear. "Is not life more important than food, and the body more important than clothes? Look at the birds of the air; they do not sow or reap or store away in barns, and yet your heavenly Father feeds them. Are you not much more valuable than they? Who of you by worrying can add a single hour to his life?[12]"

Leaving that thought to resonate in his minds of his audience, Jesus then sat in the boat and motioned to one of the disciples. One man lifted the anchor, another raised an oar. They rowed away, followed by the other disciples in two boats. Orion silently watched them grow smaller as they gained distance.

Orion turned to Elizabeth, "I have never seen such a man." Orion paused, "Worrying doesn't change the uncertainty that is part of life. Fear can stop one from leaving the safety of the shore. Trust in God will appease the fear."

---

[12] Matthew 6:25- 27

Elizabeth spoke up, "We had some of that connection, even when we came here twelve years ago."

"How so?"

"We had each other. We had faith in each other. The fact that we trusted each other gave us strength to start a new life here."

"And now we have God."

"That brings us all closer together."

Orion took her hand and squeezed it tenderly. She called the boys, and they turned for home feeling contented and grateful.

Now, sitting alone in the night, Orion felt inspired to make a symbol for this idea about the interplay between possibility and uncertainty. The evening had turned cold. Orion set several large sticks onto the fire pit, then he picked up a chisel and began cleaning it with a dry brush. Each time he stroked with the brush, he noticed sparks flying in patterns through the dark. Each stroke revealed a new possibility. Nothing was certain about the outcome of the sparks. It occurred to him that this was the image.

Several days later the four friends gathered once again around the golden flames of Orion's hearth.

"They have ousted Aaron," said Jude as he stroked his long beard. "Aaron is such a good man. Generous. The congregation loves him. It is inconceivable that he would steal. And yet the Sanhedrin found him guilty."

"Will he be arrested?" said the ironsmith, Marcus.

"No. Out of respect to his years of service, they will not press charges. They have simply moved him out of their way."

"What will happen next?" said Orion.

"Now we are to be led by Erez."

Philip could not contain his laughter. "Erez! Hee hee hee!"

"Who is this Erez?"

"He's long and skinny like a willow stick," said Philip. "His right eye twitches like this, and he talks with a lisp." The old man gave a grotesque imitation that made the other three laugh out loud.

Then Jude spoke again. "Erez has been another loud voice against Jesus. He is not well liked by the congregation, and I don't trust him. But, like sheep, they follow the recommendations of the elders."

"The synagogue will suffer because of this," said Philip, shaking his head.

"They vote tomorrow to ban Jesus."

"Bastards," said Marcus. "Fools."

"I don't know how much longer I will be able to attend those meetings," said Jude, "now that Aaron is no longer in power."

Jude shook his head. "How will this end?" he wondered aloud.

Two weeks later Matthew the tax collector—now apostle—returned to Capernaum. As he made the rounds, greeting his numerous friends, he made it clear to all why he had returned. Everyone brings some kind of skill to the ministry of Jesus, and his skill happened to run along the lines of financial management. Everywhere the Master went, a group of at least fifty, often more, both men and women, went with him. This couldn't be helped. Jesus was a magnet. He never wanted anything for himself. He ate when something was provided and slept anywhere, even on the ground in his robes. But those who followed him had needs.

The fact that Jesus had picked a number of brawny fishermen certainly helped to deal with the crowds and the risks of living in the open countryside. Certainly Simon "The Rock" and the sons of Zebedee played important roles every day in the ministry of Jesus. The apostles had families and responsibility to those families. The poor people who gathered at every stop were ministered to. So Matthew had returned to Capernaum for the explicit purpose of fund-raising. Being well liked and highly skilled in the business culture, he was the most likely candidate for the task.

There was a fund-raising dinner at Matthew's house, and many of his wealthy friends and business associates came, as well as a few friends who were not wealthy—Orion and Elizabeth, for example. It was a lively affair, with much talk and laughter and very good food. Matthew sat at the head table with his wife and daughter at his side. The volume of the conversation increased in steady proportion to the volume of wine consumed. Finally, though, Matthew stood up. Holding his goblet upside-down, he struck it with a fork repeatedly until the gathering turned its attention his way.

"This is a festive occasion, for it is a celebration of the one who shines God's Light upon us."

Someone called out, "Tell us how Jesus has recently shown the power of God!"

"Yes! Tell us, Matthew."

Matthew took a deep breath, "We had just crossed over the lake to Gerasa. Remind me to tell you later about what happened there, how he drove the devils out of a madman and forced them to inhabit a herd of swine. But that's another story altogether.

"When Jesus had again crossed over by boat to the other side of the lake, a large crowd gathered around him while he was by the lake. Then one of the synagogue rulers, named Jairus, came there. Seeing Jesus, he fell at his feet and pleaded earnestly with him, 'My little daughter is dying. Please come and put your hands on her so that she will be healed and live.' So Jesus went with him. A large crowd followed and pressed around him. And a woman was there who had been subject to bleeding for twelve years. She had suffered a great deal under the care of many doctors and had spent all she had, yet instead of getting better she grew worse. When she heard about Jesus, she came up behind him in the crowd and touched his cloak, because she thought, 'If I just touch his clothes, I will be healed.' Immediately her bleeding stopped, and she felt in her body that she was freed from her suffering.

"At once Jesus realized that power had gone out from him. He turned around in the crowd and asked, 'Who touched my clothes?'

"'You see the people crowding against you,' his disciples answered, 'and yet you can ask, 'Who touched me?'

"But Jesus kept looking around to see who had done it. Then the woman, knowing what had happened to her, came and fell at his feet and, trembling with fear, told him the whole truth. He said to her, 'Daughter, your faith has healed you. Go in peace and be freed from your suffering.'

"While Jesus was still speaking, some men came from the house of Jairus, the synagogue ruler. 'Your daughter is dead,' they said. 'Why bother the teacher any more?'

"Ignoring what they said, Jesus told the synagogue ruler, 'Don't be afraid; just believe.' He did not let anyone follow him except Peter, James, and John the brother of James. When they came to the home of the synagogue ruler, Jesus saw a commotion, with people crying and wailing loudly.

"He went in and said to them, 'Why all this commotion and wailing? The child is not dead but asleep.' But they laughed at him. After he put them all out, he took the child's father and mother and the disciples who were with him, and they went in where the child was.

He took her by the hand and said to her, 'Talitha koum!' ('Little girl, I say to you, get up!'). Immediately the girl stood up and walked around.[13]

"Listen!" Matthew said. "This power comes from the Father. It is Jesus' ministry to shed light on our connection with God. His miracles make us take notice. His actions show us the compassion of God. We help those in need, we feed the hungry, and we assist the elderly. We are bringing hope and joy into people's lives."

Then Matthew spread his arms wide to encompass all his guests. "You all can become part of this ministry by giving to it. There is no better way to do good with your abundance. Through giving you receive, and this begins a powerful cycle of exchange. What a blessed way to use your resources. My friends—give what you can.

"Even though Jesus is doing wondrous things, we no longer have the support of the Capernaum synagogue. Therefore, your help now is timely."

Matthew passed the plate, and it came back with very generous donations. Orion and Elizabeth put something into the plate. It felt good to contribute.

This time the four men gathered in the courtyard of Marcus's ironworks. It was early afternoon. The metallic smell of the craftsman's forge gave the air a rough incense even where they sat under the shade of an ancient olive tree. Marcus began, "I have never heard so much gossip, so many harsh words. There are so many

---

13 Mark 5:21-42

factions now. Each one has its own idea about Jesus. I try to keep my mouth shut and just listen. The disparity of views I have heard about Jesus is amazing.

"Many still think Jesus will lead a revolt against the Romans to regain the land. Some believe the distorted messages of the synagogue elders, the idea that Jesus is misguided, that he is the devil. Others think Jesus is crazy, claiming senseless connections with God. There are those who think he is too radical with his teachings of love and forgiveness. There is fear as well, from those who feel that Jesus opposes traditions and the sacred religious rules handed down through generations."

Orion added, "And there is a reminder every day from our brother Philip when he walks down the streets, looks people in the eyes and greets them with a smile. He reminds them of the power and possibilities Jesus brings."

Then Jude spoke. "Publius has been the next target of Isaac's strategy. Isaac has succeeded in removing him from his post in Capernaum."

"What?" said Marcus. "How could he do that?"

"He went back to see Herod Antipas, claiming Publius is corrupt and untrustworthy because he sides with Jesus who healed his servant. This time Erez was with him, making some comment about instability in the region if Publius is not removed. Herod agreed to replace him."

Orion said, "It's a sad day for this town when Publius leaves." The other men smiled, knowing his past reactions.

A week later, Jesus was once again at the lake. The crowd that gathered was bigger than ever. There were at least two thousand people packed together on the shoreline. Somehow the disciples had managed to keep some open space around Jesus, and Jesus had beckoned the youngest in the crowd to come close to him. One little child toddled up and grabbed the Master's robe with both of his hands, leaned against his legs, and looked up into his face. One of the women disciples moved to take the child away, but Jesus looked up and said, "Let the little children come to me, and do not stop them; for the kingdom of heaven belongs to such as these.[14]"

After he had his moment of contact, the child went off, and Jesus opened the gathering to questions. At that time the disciples came to Jesus and asked, "Who is the greatest in the kingdom of heaven?"

He called another little child and had him stand among them. And he said: "I tell you the truth, unless you change and become like little children, you will never enter the kingdom of heaven. Therefore, whoever humbles himself like this child is the greatest in the kingdom of heaven. And whoever welcomes a little child like this in my name welcomes me.[15]"

Memories of Orion's children when they were younger captivated him, the simple beauty of their innocence, curiosity, and wonder. He too had once been alive like that, open to life. Then all so suddenly his life had shifted. These memories came back with charged turbulence. He felt the anger, the injustice over his father's

---

[14] Matthew 19:14
[15] Matthew 18:1-5

death, feelings deeply embedded.

Orion startled, hearing the voice of Jesus as if addressing him, saying,"For if you forgive men when they sin against you, your heavenly Father will also forgive you. But if you do not forgive men their sins, your Father will not forgive your sins."

Blood rushed in Orion's head, bringing with it a deluge of feelings.

He stared out onto the platform where Jesus spoke and saw a large, burly man with bushy hair and coarse beard approach Jesus. Orion recognized him as the disciple Peter, and Orion heard him say: "Lord, how many times shall I forgive my brother when he sins against me? Up to seven times?"

Jesus answered, "I tell you, not seven times, but seventy-seven times.[16]"

In that instant Orion saw what he needed to do… face the rage from his youth.

Jesus ended with a blessing, "Be open to the grace of God and it will flow into you."

As the crowd was breaking up Orion turned to Elizabeth. "I have some thinking to do. Please take the boys back home. I will be along in a while." He quickly made off before the crowd engulfed him.

Elizabeth gathered up the boys, and he watched them disappear into the crowd. Orion could feel rawness in him. He had to go away, to some place where he could not be seen. Then he remembered the cove where they had picnicked. He could go there and be safe.

---

[16] Matthew 5:14-22

Quickly he strode along the shore. He leaped across the stones and crevices with a precision and a balance he didn't know he was capable of. By the time he got to the cove he was covered in sweat, and he could feel the blood rushing in his veins. He spun and grabbed a large rock, then hurled it from him with a force so great that it split apart when it hit the ground with a loud percussion. He was determined to tame this wild internal beast, this rage so like the son of fire that was his namesake.

His body tightened and vibrated like metal. He wanted to attack, strike out. Everything had changed in his young life—quitting school and learning a craft to help support the family of two younger brothers and sister. What flamed his anger was the fact that, after his father's death, Herod Antipas refused to pay the back wages due his family. He claimed that the person the wages belonged to was no longer alive, and so the debt was canceled. Orion picked up a log and bashed it against the rocks. The splinters of wood flew with a loud *whack*. He realized what that feeling was doing within him, consuming, constricting, and draining.

Then Orion prayed, "Heal the wounds that still fester with hatred and the desire for revenge."

His sudden stillness and prayer jarred his memories even further. He now recalled the incident in Caesarea Philippi, after his father's death, when he was working in Tiberius's shop and a tax collector and his enforcer were attempting to extort money from Tiberius. Orion was only fifteen at the time. The Roman soldier beat Orion close to death.

Orion tried to take a breath, but what felt like a heavy band tightened around his chest. He knew that this band was formed by his own thoughts, his hatred and blame, as confining as chains. He hurled another rock, and it also split, and a chip of it flew up and bit into his cheek, burning him. It suddenly became clear to him that these feelings were hurtful, consuming, and draining. He became aware of the energy he was holding, like poison in his body. He did not want to hold that which kept him from his connection with God. He fell to his knees, and his heart flooded with prayer:

"O God, heal this wound that has festered for twenty years." Then he affirmed, "I release this anger and constriction in my heart. I accept and forgive all that has happened. I am no longer a victim of the past."

A still silence followed, and then Orion heard the gentle sound of small waves lapping the cove. A light breeze caressed him, and the heaviness that confined him gave way to a long deep breath that rose to his heart. And from within his heart he saw his father again, the smile and the soft touch of his gray-blue eyes as he explained philosophy and science and how to hold an oar and hook a fish. The memories conjured up feelings deep inside Orion. The energy had gathered in a concentrated ball in his pelvis. With outward eyes closed, he noticed the energy begin to move up his belly. He took a long deep breath, and the energy rose to his heart.

A wave of grief like storm winds off the water swept over him as he felt the loss of his father. Great sobs shook him, and his heart heaved as if it were going to leap out of his chest. The thick black cord attached to Herod was cut, and his next breath opened into stillness and a peace such as he had not known since he was a small child.

Orion looked up and saw a thin crescent of moon rising, and the few clouds beamed with a gentle pink from beneath.

His heart was open, his spirit light. As he walked home he breathed with a freedom that he had not felt in two decades. Without thinking he began humming a tune his grandmother would sing when he was a child. A joyous feeling was glowing in his heart. He was not the victim of his past, at least as far as he could see in the moment.

In that lightness Orion felt open and flowing. That blockage within him had been breached and the water of life was now flowing more freely through him. Forgive others and be open to the flow of life. Be open like the child Jesus had pointed to. Be open and listen to the messages from God. As he walked home, the fading light of day made the Sea of Galilee appear to have shadows of waves flowing across its surface as far as the eye could see. That is when the image came to him.

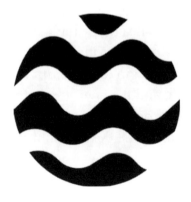

CHAPTER

Orion stood at the entrance to his shop leaning on the wooden doorframe, his eyes closed. He just stood in silence and put his focus on listening, the way Philip once showed him. The streets were filled with talk of Jesus.

The tailor next door was seething. "I tell you, this man is a crazy. He compares heaven to yeast in bread? He speaks gibberish."

"You think he is crazy because you cannot comprehend," said a voice in reply. "Those miracles are proof! What kind of skeptic are you?"

From the other direction, probably the carpenter's shop, another argument was raging. "Jesus is the devil."

"This is a holy man!"

"What do you know?"

"I talk to my goats. And when I tell them what

Jesus said, they stand still and listen. Goats standing at attention! Imagine! You should be grateful for such a prophet."

"When Jesus is in town, we are overrun with people. And now we have warring factions. It is because of Jesus that Publius was removed." Yes, that was the carpenter's voice. Orion could discern it plainly as it grew louder and louder. "His presence does us no good!"

From another direction, this exchange: "He has the power to run the Romans out. God bless him. He will show that he is the Messiah."

"Messiah? Ha! When will he show us this wonder?"

"Soon."

"That's rubbish."

Then behind these voices Orion heard hoof beats that grew steadily louder, then the snorting of a horse. He opened his eyes and lifted his head. Quickly he stepped back into the shadow within the door. Pangs of fear leapt from his gut and chest. His heart pounded hard and fast.

The rider was dressed in the uniform of a centurion. Could he be Publius's replacement?

"Oh God, please not him."

Orion stared from the shadows as the soldier passed. There was no mistaking this man, even though nearly twenty years had passed since Orion last beheld his vicious countenance. That long scar across the man's right cheek, and the misshapen nose—as though he'd once taken a blow that split his face open—this sign alone distinguished the man. Plus, he was larger than life, almost a giant, muscular and powerful. A haughty scowl was chiseled on his face.

As the centurion continued down the street, Orion took a deep breath. Memories of his beating came rushing back.

Later that same day, the four brothers met in Orion's courtyard. Philip began: "The new centurion has just arrived. His name is Baraccus."

"The man is a devil," said Orion. "Never forget. He would take pleasure out of killing any one of us."

The others were quiet for a moment. Then Philip said, "Orion, you seem to have some personal history with our new centurion."

"That history is written on my body." He opened his mouth and pointed to several broken teeth. Then he showed them scars on his legs and on his back. "These are the marks of Baraccus."

The others murmured sympathetically. Jude asked, "How did you manage to attract this kind of attention?"

"Trying to protect an innocent man from brute injustice. The man was my teacher, my mentor, practically a father to me. I was the apprentice in his leather shop. I was just a lad, had barely begun to trim the hairs on my chin. One day a tax collector came into the shop, a crooked tax collector."

"A crooked tax collector," said Marcus wryly. "How unusual."

"Now, Marcus," said Philip. "Out of courtesy to our friend Matthew, we'll have no tax collector jokes."

"But this one really was a crook," said Orion. "He had come to extort money from my teacher, a huge sum, on the spot, with no justification. No, I take that back. He had just one justification—his escort, a soldier who was built like Ajax."

"Baraccus, no doubt," said Jude.

"The very same. When the old man refused to let them steal from him, Baraccus went to work."

Marcus inserted a comment: "I caught a glimpse of this Ajax fellow today. He does look like someone who enjoys his work."

Philip said to Orion, "How did it go?"

"Baraccus stepped up to my teacher—he was a gray-haired old man—and gave him a brutal blow to the side of the face. Knocked the man to the floor. I thought perhaps he'd killed the man in one blow. And I...."

"Yes?" said Philip.

Marcus stepped in again. "You were Orion."

"What do you mean?"

"You exploded like Vesuvius."

"Me?"

Orion's friends all laughed.

"Well, perhaps I *have* done that once or twice." They laughed again. "In the old days. Before I started listening to Jesus. But that's the odd thing. That's why I hesitated just now. This thought came to me."

"What is that, Orion?" said Philip.

"I told you about my inward change after Jesus' last talk, about forgiving Herod Antipas in my heart, about shedding the poison of my anger."

"Yes."

"I realize that my anger is, or was, also directed to this man, Baraccus. To this incident."

"Well," said Philip. "Now you have the good fortune to forgive Baraccus, too. You can even forgive him to his face."

Orion felt his own face and ran his tongue along the sharp edges of his broken teeth. "I'm wondering why God would choose this moment to send Baraccus back into my life. Is God testing my resolve to forgive and let go?"

The men were silent for a moment. Marcus said, "So how does your story turn out?"

"You mean the attack in the leather shop?"

"Yes."

"Fortunately, my teacher was not dead. By the time he got back onto his feet, Baraccus had already inflicted a lot of damage to my youthful frame. He gave them the money."

"Oh."

"But even after the tax collector had taken his bribe, Baraccus continued to beat me. He beat me until he was satisfied. I couldn't get out of bed for two months."

He paused, and then added, "Be careful. This new centurion is no Publius. God, what trials have befallen us?"

It was late afternoon, a month after Matthew's fundraising dinner. Orion missed Matthew. He missed the man's light-hearted vitality. While Orion stitched at his work bench, he mused about that quality of light-heartedness. To laugh, to be of good cheer, to elevate the spirits of those about you—the ability to do that takes a high being, a high energy. Brilliant linear beams of sunlight poured through the half-closed shutters, turning dust motes into points of fire. At that moment, as if he'd been summoned, Matthew himself poked his head into the shop, smiling broadly.

"Orion!"

Orion looked up. "I was just thinking about you." He leaped up and grabbed Matthew in embrace. They circled and held each other at arm's length and laughed to see each other.

Orion called, "Elizabeth!" Then to Matthew: "Can you sit with us in the courtyard?"

"Yes, for a short time. How has it been for you and your family?"

"We have been very well. However, things are tense in town. Controversy over Jesus has been spinning around. Isaac's spies are stoking the fires within different factions, making Capernaum like an angry beehive. We are keeping to ourselves—except for a small group of brothers: Jude the potter, formerly blind Philip, and Marcus the ironsmith. We have been exploring Jesus' teaching. And you! You are in the midst of it all! How very fortunate you are, Matthew."

Elizabeth and Alexander peered into the shop. "Matthew!" She greeted him warmly. Alexander stood tall while the apostle praised him. "You're growing by the day, aren't you? And getting some muscles. Pretty soon you'll be carrying your father around, won't you?"

"Where's Julian?" said Orion. Elizabeth went off calling for him.

Soon they were all settled in the shade of the porch. Orion said, "Tell us what it is like to be with the Master."

"I have never met anyone like Jesus. His connection with God is strong; that power comes right through him. He is unpredictable. And yet he is extremely patient with all of us and our shortcomings, which are plentiful, let me tell you, and glaringly obvious in the light that he radiates. His insights go straight to God. I do not understand all he says, but I trust that the understanding will come some day. At times when I am with the Master a kind of bliss fills me, even when I'm busy attending the large crowds that that come for Jesus. I am blessed to be so close to the Master." Matthew's hands extended to the heavens. "I am very blessed." Then he beamed a smile that came from a genuine inner joy.

"Matthew, tell us something that Jesus taught," Alexander implored.

Matthew reached into the satchel hanging over his shoulder and pulled out a scroll.

"Let me see. These are notes I have been taking of the Master's teachings. Every phrase leaves much to ponder." He began reading in a clear, deep voice.

"If you are offering your gift at the altar and there remember that your brother has something against you, leave your gift there in front of the altar. First go and be reconciled to your brother; then come and offer your gift.[17]"

While Matthew rolled up the scroll. Orion asked, "He often speaks about reconciliation, doesn't he?"

"Every day. It's a simple message, and very practical. When we do something to other people, we are doing it to God. There is no separation. We are all family, and we are all connected to God. That's why it's important to reconcile with your neighbor whenever possible. When you reconcile with him, you are reconciling with God."

With those words, Matthew stood up. He said, "Jesus will be on the shore in two days in the late afternoon."

"We'll be there, of course," said Orion. Everyone rose, and Orion walked Matthew to the door.

Orion returned in a thoughtful mood. He said privately to Elizabeth, "You know, this morning one of my leather suppliers came to the shop and delivered the wrong hide."

"You can't use it?"

"I could use it, yes, but I don't want to. It's inferior stuff, with thin patches that will start to tear within a month of use. Maybe someone like Bishmehoth would

---

[17] Matthew 19:14

94

use it, but not me. And it certainly isn't worth what I paid. And just as I was examining the hide, the fellow scooted out of the shop."

"That's disappointing."

"I am going over there now to talk to him, see if we can come to an understanding."

"I'm sure he has his own story. You might ask him. I'm sure you'll rectify it and get what you paid for and keep him as a good neighbor."

Orion smiled. "That's a good thought." He hoisted the bad hide, folded into a bundle and tied with thin strands of leather, up onto his right shoulder and strode out into the late-day sunshine.

Sunset found him stepping forth from the supplier's warehouse with a beautiful, smooth hide on his left shoulder. He felt he had handled it well. The supplier was cordial. He hummed the song from his childhood, the same one he sang after his experience at the cove. He was thinking about how good it feels to rectify things.

The following morning Philip came into Orion's shop, a concerned look on his face. "Shortly after sunset I noticed Isaac limping his way out of town, moving at a hard pace. I knew he was up to no good, so I followed him. He never noticed me. And when he got to the edge of town, guess who was there waiting—Baraccus!"

"Where?"

"The olive grove by the caravan gates. I hid myself in the grove. The sky was still light enough for me to see them. Baraccus has the eyes of a lion, doesn't he? And

Isaac was bent over, gasping for breath and sweating like a fountain."

"Could you hear their conversation?"

"Hear them? Me? I can hear the fart of a flea."

Orion smiled and clapped his hands once.

"So this was Isaac." Philip began mimicking him, gulping for air. "We must... put an end... to the ministry... of Jesus in Galilee.... He must be stopped.... We are willing to pay, of course."

"Pay."

"Then Isaac reached in his pouch and pulled out a piece of papyrus and a small leather bag. He jingled the bag. Baraccus took the bag. Then Isaac thrust the papyrus at him. 'Here is a list of Jesus' supporters in Capernaum,' he said. 'There are twenty-one names here. Some are wealthy merchants.'

"'Wealthy merchants? hmm...'—Baraccus seemed to take more interest in the papyrus. 'All these people pose a danger to Galilee,' said Isaac. Then he talked about the names on the list. He talked about Jude— Jude, who dared to oppose him in the synagogue."

"Opposed him? Jude must have asked an intelligent question once in a while."

"And you, Orion."

"Me?"

"For luring the chosen people onto the path of rebellion."

"Why would I do that? I am a better craftsman than his cousin. That's more like it."

"Baraccus opened the pouch in his hand. I saw the

silver flash in the dusk. He put the coins back in the pouch and said, 'This will do for the first payment.' Then he took the papyrus and looked at it. He smiled. Orion, I tell you that the sight of his smile made me wish for a moment that I could once again be blind."

"Well said."

"Oh, and this is interesting. As they were parting, Isaac said, 'There will be disturbances when Jesus speaks. Don't break them up.' Baraccus gave a grunt, like an agreement. He seemed quite pleased."

"I will talk with Matthew. You warn the other brothers of this alliance."

Later that week Orion was carrying a load of wood along the main street. His head was down. Suddenly he felt tension in his stomach. When he looked up, there was Baraccus, sitting on his horse, staring at him as he approached. When Orion was about ten feet away, Baraccus dismounted. Still bent under his load of wood, Orion looked up at the scarred face. Baraccus said, "You look familiar. Do I know you?"

Orion shook his head, shifted the load on his back, and kept walking.

Baraccus grabbed Orion's shoulder. "You're a follower of Jesus." Orion nodded his head. Baraccus grunted, then said, "Don't follow too close."

When Orion kept walking, Baraccus thrust his foot between Orion's legs and pushed with his left hand. Orion spun and fell. Firewood went flying. Orion threw out his hands to catch himself as he hit the street. As his head came down, it collided with a rough log, tearing the skin on his forehead. Baraccus laughed. He walked to his horse and mounted. As he rode off, he guided his horse toward Orion, who had an eye on him and jumped back. Baraccus passed, then stopped his horse and turned it about. For a moment he just looked at Orion, who stood there and returned the gaze.

"I know you," said Baraccus. "I've seen you before." After a moment he wheeled the horse around. "I'll think of it," he said.

Orion stood there in the street, his forehead throbbing. He felt fear and anger that embraced his past. He prayed. The more he was able to feel the trust of God, the more the fear subsided. But the danger remained.

That evening, Orion talked with his brothers about what had happened. Jude had had a similar experience. "I was walking toward the lake when he confronted me. But I didn't get laid out on the ground."

Marcus grunted. "We're all in danger now. To think otherwise would be foolish."

At least now I can see them," said Philip. "Before, people would hit me whenever they wanted. I was 'unclean.' When you're blind, you don't know what is out there."

After a pause Orion said, "What's your advice, old man?"

Philip laughed at that question. "I don't know if anyone has ever asked for my advice before. Here it is. You always have a choice—fear or trust. These are the two nets that you have to cast into the sea. When you throw the fear net, every sound brings tension. Anticipating something bad. When you throw the trust net, you know that you will be taken care of. You feel more Light within your sightless eyes."

After a moment of silence, Orion said, "Either way, you could get beaten."

Philip agreed. "Either way, you could get beaten."

The next day Orion's family went about its chores until mid-afternoon, and then they all prepared to go to the lake to hear Jesus' sermon. The four of them walked in silence until they approached the shore. The beach was filled with people.

"We won't be able to hear," said Elizabeth.

Orion studied the situation and said, "Stay close to me." He began shouldering his way into the throng. "We can always make a place for ourselves," he said to them. "Come, Julian, come up here with me. We will find our place." And of course when they got close to the lake there were many open spots. "All we have to do is believe," said Orion.

And then they watched, along with so many others—young, old, Gentile, Jew, native, and foreign—as three boats glided to shore. Jesus stepped out of the first one and onto the platform.

He scanned the crowd. He took a long time. He looked at every individual person. And then he spoke.

"There was a man who had two sons," he said. "The younger one said to his father, 'Father, give me my share of the estate.' So he divided his property between them."

As Jesus waited, a ripple of conversation went through the crowd, then ceased.

"Not long after that the younger son got together all he had, set off for a distant country, and there squandered his wealth in wild living."

Once again Jesus looked at individuals in the gathering, looked at so many, thought Orion, that the looking itself became his message.

"When he came to his senses, he said: 'How many of my father's hired men have food to spare? And here I am starving to death! I will set out and go back to my father and say to him: 'Father, I have sinned against heaven and against you. I am no longer worthy to be called your son. Make me like one of your hired men.' So he got up and went to his father."

A man somewhere near Orion said, "Take you back. Is this a joke? You spent all his money!" People laughed a little, then hushed.

"But while he was still a long way off, his father saw him and was filled with compassion for him. He ran to his son, threw his arms around him, and kissed him. The son said to him, 'Father, I have sinned against heaven and against you. I am no longer worthy to be called your son.' But the father said to his servants,

'Quick! Bring the best robe and put it on him. Put a ring on his finger and sandals on his feet. Bring the fattened calf and kill it. Let's have a feast and celebrate. For this son of mine was dead and is alive again; he was lost and is found.' So they began to celebrate.[18]"

Celebrate? Orion wondered how he would react if one of his own boys did that—wasted the value of the family, earned through his years of work. Then he thought of the love and compassion of a father. He celebrated the return of his son. That is how God is with us when we return to Him … and come back to the Light. He looked at his own two sons, then back at Jesus.

The Master continued, "Love your enemies, do good to them, and lend to them without expecting to get anything back. If anyone strikes you on the cheek, offer the other also; and from anyone who takes away your cloak do not withhold even your shirt. Then your reward will be great, and you will be sons of the Most High, because he is kind to the ungrateful and wicked. Be merciful, just as your Father is merciful.[19]"

Just then Orion spotted Isaac in the crowd. The words came flooding back to him like a torrent: "Love your enemies." Orion flinched deep inside because he knew he was not living up to that vision. Love God; love your neighbor—yes. But love your enemy, this was an entirely difference stance. Orion had no love for Herod Antipas. He did forgive Herod. But love him? He had no love for the Pharisees who belittled him and were trying to end the ministry of Jesus. And most diffi-

[18] Luke 15:11-24
[19] Luke 6:32-36

cult, most perplexing of all was to love Baraccus.

Orion considered how Jesus handled the Pharisees and scribes who tried to trick him. They greatly profited from the status quo that Jesus was challenging. Yet Jesus kept a balance and did not ruffle or react. In fact he loved. He embodied the two most important commandments: *Love God* and *Love your neighbor*. Both were prefaced by love. Orion could feel Jesus' love when he was in his presence; there was no contraction.

Jesus concluded his sermon quietly by blessing the crowd. He turned and seemed to float to the water's edge, climbing back into his boat and gliding away.

The following afternoon, Orion took these feelings and confusions to Marcus, Philip, and Jude. Sitting in the shade of Marcus's courtyard, he brought up his contrasting feelings and struggle.

"I was very enraged by my father's death. I was angry at the foreman who didn't support him, and angry at Herod for forcing him to work in unsafe conditions and refusing to pay death benefits. And when I saw Herod's men, I wanted to attack them. I wanted to hurt somebody."

"Those emotions can eat at you, I'm sure," said Jude.

"And I was able to release that poison. And that was freeing. But love my enemies? Love Isaac, and Herod—and Baraccus? Why love snakes when they can poison you?"

"The important thing is to try," said Philip. "All

that time that I was blind people condemned me for my deformity. I could feel it and read it in their voices. And I couldn't see any of them. Imagine if I had set about resenting certain voices! I would have been so caught up in aiming hostilities that devils would have taken my mind. That emotion of hate would have consumed and poisoned me. Forgiveness was the one most important thing. Every day I had to forgive all of that." He held his arms up, palms to the sky. "It's freeing." His eyes sparkled with joy.

Marcus laughed. "It's easy to feel good when you're in the circle, when you're safe. This group here, we share many values. The primary one, of course, is being disciples of Jesus. But the elders in the synagogue have a different set of values. Jesus is asking us to love them anyway."

"As hateful as they are," said Orion.

Philip calmly responded. "To see beyond their actions—even when those actions are trying to harm us. To see beyond the evil games of others, to the love that permeates all, that would lift the real blindness."

Jude let out his frustration, "I have become estranged from the hierarchy of the synagogue. I am no longer the lead cantor. Why? Because I stood up. Because I expressed my support for Jesus. Then I became the target of their ridicule. They have lied to discredit me. When I'm at Jesus' sermons, I see representatives from the Jerusalem Sanhedrin, from the Capernaum synagogue. I see Herod Antipas's men. They are all plotting his downfall. I consider them enemies. And Jesus is asking me to love them? That is not what I feel in my heart. I know it in my head. But I have to say I'm with Orion."

Orion continued, "When I am in Jesus' presence, I feel uplifted. I am in the presence of love. I know he is asking us to walk on the path of love, the path of God, above the traps that bind us. To remove ourselves from the battle even though we are in it. But I do not yet love these people. I will acknowledge my connection to God even under the most trying times. But to love Baraccus? That is purely conceptual."

After the men went their ways, Orion decided to go to the lake to consider everything that had been discussed. He headed to the shore and leaped onto the rocks, jumping from one to another. It was a little game that helped him focus and keep his balance. Then he heard someone calling his name. He looked up and saw Matthew smiling at him, and behind him stood Peter, James, and Jesus!

Orion nearly lost his balance. Jesus was smiling at him. They were all smiling.

"Come on up here, Orion," Matthew shouted. "There is someone I want you to meet." Again Orion almost lost his balance as he twisted around to face the men on the path above him. He felt like a little boy. When he got to the top of the slope, he was out of breath—not from exertion but from joy.

"Jesus, this is Orion. He is an excellent leathersmith. We've been friends for twelve years."

Jesus looked at Orion, smiling gently and lovingly. "I remember you from Matthew's celebration feast. I remember your eyes."

Orion looked into Jesus' eyes and again felt the ocean of vastness and stillness. He said, "Master, you have changed my life—my family's life. And I am challenged to hold the love you speak of in my heart."

Jesus responded, "This love is not tarnished by others."

Orion fell to his knees. Something inside was awakened deep in his heart. Jesus placed both hands on Orion's head. Orion closed his eyes, his eyelids fluttering as currents of light flooded him. Orion felt a surge of energy go through him. When Jesus removed his hands, he could still feel the imprint. He calmed his restless doubting. His breathing was deep and quiet. He bowed his head and got to his feet, feeling raw inside. He glanced at Jesus, and they both smiled.

Jesus turned to Matthew, motioning to go. He looked back to Orion and said, smiling: "Go with God." Then he gathered his robe and headed up the path to Capernaum. Matthew looked back at Orion and gave him a wink.

Jesus had gone. Orion stepped slowly and carefully down the slope, feeling dazed and filled with energy. He found a shady spot along the lake and lowered himself softly. He closed his eyes. His whole chest cavity was filled with energy ready to spill out. He couldn't hold back what was to be released. Leaning forward, he put his head to the ground. His heart was being stretched open, and the ball of energy rose to his throat. His body convulsed. Great torrents of tears streamed from him, and he sobbed until the sobs became sighs. Then stillness and a peace much bigger than himself swept over him. It was a peace beyond understanding. He understood that the vibration of the heart is a timeless, formless connection. It cannot be tarnished by the actions of others. Love is the light that embraces darkness. Love is being in harmony with the emotion of God.

Then another symbol came to him, flashed in his mind. It was so simple—the interfacing of love.

To be in the energy of God is to feel the love that falls on everything, the great love that somehow includes Isaac and Baraccus.

CHAPTER 6

Orion was busy in his shop sitting by his anvil, cutting leather and stitching. It was late, well after sunset. The flicker from oil lamps illumined the room as he worked with precision and speed. Although he'd shuttered up the shop, the muffled roar from the street kept pouring in, exciting him. It sounded like a hive of bees out there, with an occasional harsh cry near his door, or the bawling of a camel nearby. He knew why the town was so busy at this late hour—Jesus had just returned. People were gathering again, like a wild swarm determined to find its new place to make honey.

Then a sharp knock from the street side struck his door. Orion walked across the room, sensing that something important was on the other side. He threw back the deadbolt and pulled the heavy door inward.

There was Matthew in the dim light. "I have a new customer for you."

Behind him stood Jesus. The Master's face was deeply hooded in white, no doubt to prevent being recognized as he moved through Capernaum's streets. But Orion saw him immediately—the shining eyes, the slight but merry smile, and something else less easily named, the presence of the God-spirit that is submerged in each person was here in this man, shining right on the surface. Orion knew that he would never forget this single glimpse of Jesus' face as it came toward him from the dark street, hooded in white. He felt as though his heart would burst. He was speechless for a moment, then he uttered, "Welcome, welcome."

Jesus strode in with a fluid gait. His eyes sparkled in the dim light.

Matthew waited outside. "I'll leave you alone and make sure no one disturbs you." He closed the door.

"How may I serve you, Master?"

Jesus looked at Orion and smiled, pausing for a moment before saying, "To start, a pair of sandals. I have put many miles on these." He pointed to his feet. "I would like a similar pair."

Orion escorted Jesus to a stool, where he examined the simple, sturdy design of the Teacher's footwear. Orion smiled to see them. This country-style design was the first type of sandal he had ever learned. They were easy to make but uncomfortable to wear. Very few customers asked for them anymore. He said, "The good thing about this type of sandal is that it lasts forever."

"Not quite forever," said Jesus. "As you can see."

The soles were cracked a thousand times; the heels thin as fabric. In several places the leather was holding together by mere fibers. "I can honestly say that I have never seen sandals as worn-out as these," said Orion. The next phrase that occurred to him was this: "It's a miracle that you got so far." But of course he didn't say it. He glanced quickly at Jesus. Jesus was looking right at him. Both men laughed out loud, and they kept laughing. Orion wasn't sure what was so funny—talking about shoes with the Messiah!—but he couldn't stop. And Jesus laughed the way a thirsty man drinks water.

"I can make you a much finer sandal than this one."

"Oh, please don't do that, please don't." Jesus kept laughing. "You don't want your excellent work to come to such a bad end."

Again they joked. "All right, it's country sandals for you!"

Orion grabbed some calipers and then reached for the large, callous left foot of Jesus. As he touched Jesus' feet, waves of energy and peace passed over him. He was lifted up by the powerful force that Jesus channeled. He made his measurements in a surreal state.

Then Orion spoke like an excited child. "Master, your teachings and presence are seeds of truth planted in my heart. I have used my craft to give a visual to these seeds."

"Let me see what you have done," said Jesus, wide-eyed and earnest.

Orion untied his bundle of leather and then briefly described each of his symbols. Jesus listened carefully and silently while Orion explained, and then he held the symbols in his hands and spoke: "These are the seeds of truth that harvest the Light. When I saw you at Matthew's and again on the hillside by the lake, I could see that you are a bearer of Light."

Orion was astonished to hear these words.

Jesus continued. "These seeds—which I have described and you have depicted—will one day come to full fruition. But that day has not come. Be patient and courageous, for this is not an easy journey."

Orion asked, "What shall I do Master? I am not worthy; I am an ordinary man." He paused, looking at Jesus' unbending stare. Then, in that moment, he surrendered to his fate. "How shall I prepare?"

"Integrate these seeds of truth within you, and listen when you are called by God to serve."

Orion looked in Jesus' sparkling eyes. In a glance he was swallowed into the abyss that was more infinite than the universe. It was a glance with no mind, no thought, a witness of deep peace, a blessing, a knowing, and a conviction.

'Yes, yes, Master, I will."

Jesus then said, "Tell no one of this. When the time is right, who you are will tell them."

Orion's response came from deep within him. He bowed his head. "I will tell no one." Then Jesus tenderly placed his hand on Orion's shoulder.

When Jesus removed his touch, Orion felt as if he

was coming back to the surface reality. He asked, "Before you go, Master, please bless my family."

Jesus reached out his arm as he stood and placed a hand on Orion's shoulder, saying, "Gather them together."

Orion quickly stood and pulled back the curtain to the courtyard. He called Elizabeth and the boys, "Come! The Master is blessing our family. He is here, he is here. Be swift."

They all came running to the porch and bowed to Jesus. In reply, the Master bowed to them playfully. Then Jesus stood straight, took a deep breath and on the exhale he closed his eyes, slowly raising his right hand to heart level, with thumb and forefinger joined, "May God's blessing be with you on your journey to realize the Light within. Amen." He then touched the heads of each.

Jesus turned to leave, and Orion rose to escort him to the door. "I will have your sandals soon."

Jesus turned at the open door and said, "Good! I have quite a journey ahead of me."

The following day the main street of Capernaum was crowded with people of every description—they came from as far away as Samaria, Judah, Phoenicia, and Decapolis—plus their baggage, their camels and donkeys. Orion had never seen anything like it. The street in front of his shop was packed to a standstill with a constant uproar of shouting and the crying of animals.

Feet and hooves stirred up the dust of the street, mixing it with dung and urine and spittle, changing the very smell of the town. Strangers blocked the entrance to his shop simply because they were pushed by traffic to take any refuge they could find. At the same time, new customers kept elbowing their way into the shop, demanding in strange accents that he repair these sandals, this harness, this saddlebag, and right away. Orion had to send Alexander across town to purchase two more hides. The poor boy was gone for hours and returned with tears of frustration in his eyes. Orion worked carefully with great focus. He put extra time on the sandals that would be caressing the Master's feet. His thoughts were also focused on the idea that Jesus would be teaching this afternoon.

When the time came, Elizabeth got the boys ready and they left together. Julian was speechless at the drama in the street. He walked with eyes wide and his mouth open, until a cranky camel kicked a cloud of filth into the air, whereupon Julian clapped his hand to his face. Next a gust of wind sent more dust swirling. Elizabeth walked with a handkerchief pressed to her nose. She held onto Orion's shirt with her free hand. So did Alexander, who had Julian's hand clasped in his other. "Hold tight," said Orion. "We don't want to lose anybody!"

"We'll never find a place close enough to hear him," cried Elizabeth.

"Philip and Jude went down earlier. They're saving a spot for us. They knew how busy I was today."

At the shoreline the crowd was packed so tight that the family hesitated. The wind was blowing in gusts against the sea, and the sky was troubled by heavy clouds that seemed to be scraping against each other.

"There's Jude," said Orion." They could see an arm waving in the distance. "Let's go. Just stay with me." They worked their way through the throng, stepping painfully, apologizing, ignoring the looks of resentment.

The friends had managed, somehow, to retain a small clearing in the crowd. Philip was there, and Jude with his wife and three daughters, as well as Marcus with his petite wife and husky-looking boys. Everyone was bundled tight in the powerful breezes that blew sand in their faces. There was just barely enough room for Orion and family to press in. When they sat, everyone's knees were touching.

"This crowd is bad," said Orion.

Philip laughed. "This is so bad that it's wonderful. Word of Jesus and his miracles has spread up and down the caravan line from Egypt to Mesopotamia. These people have come to see what we have seen."

"Looks as though a storm is coming."

"He is the master of blindness, the master of death. I think we will probably be all right."

"Look," said Marcus. "He comes."

He pointed to a boat that was being rowed along the shoreline. The boat kept some distance off shore. Gusts and waves rocked the boat erratically. The crowd had become so tightly packed that it formed a solid wall against the water. Some people had even waded into the sea, and waves splashed against them. Orion saw one man clinging to others on solid land just to avoid getting knocked into the deeper water.

About ten boat-lengths offshore, Jesus motioned his apostles to stop rowing. He then stood up in the boat; he was calm and radiant even in this turbulent atmosphere. He faced the open water and raised his arms. At once, the winds ceased. The clouds seemed to pull apart, and sunlight poured down, suddenly warm and bright on the shoreline. The waves went still, and for a few minutes all Orion could hear was a small lapping of water on shore and a murmur in the crowd that grew louder and louder. Jesus stood in the boat praying. The apostles lowered anchors, one from the bow and another from the stern. When they had the boat secure, Jesus turned to face the multitude.

As always, he waited, silently taking in the crowd with a long, sweeping gaze. When he spoke his voice came to Orion clear and close, as though he were standing just a few feet away. Orion wondered if the voice sounded this intimate to every one of the thousands assembled there on the shore.

The Master began as if in mid-thought. "Therefore, everyone who hears these words of mine and puts them into practice is like a wise man who built his house on the rock. The rain came down, the streams rose, and the winds blew and beat against that house; yet it did not fall, because it had its foundation on the rock. But everyone who hears these words of mine and does not put them into practice is like a foolish man who built his house on sand. The rain came down, the streams rose, and the winds blew and beat against that house, and it fell with a great crash.[20]"

"Foundations," Orion thought. "What is my foundation? What is my house?" He looked around him and felt the solidity of his family, and not only his family—also the three men whom he now considered to be brothers and their families as well. He looked around at the thousands of others, and he wondered about them. Then he spotted Barak, Isaac's son, sitting in the sand, staring with a look of shock. His mouth was open as he stared in wonder at the Master. Smiling to himself Orion turned to Jesus whose voice was slow and powerful.

"Listen! A farmer went out to sow his seed. As he was scattering the seed, some fell along the path, and the birds came and ate it up. Some fell on rocky places, where it did not have much soil. It sprang up quickly, because the soil was shallow. But when the sun came up, the plants were scorched, and they withered because they had no root. Other seed fell among thorns, which grew up and choked the plants so that they did not bear grain. Still other seed fell on good soil. It came up, grew, and produced a crop, multiplying thirty, sixty, or even a hundred times."

Then Jesus said, "He who has ears to hear, let him hear.[21]"

Philip added: "And he with eyes should see."

---

[20] Matthew 7:24-27
[21] Mark 4:3-9

"Seeds of truth, planted in me by Jesus. " Orion mused. "But what are these seed-killers he talks about?" He wasn't sure that he understood the analogy. As Jesus continued to speak at length about the work required to produce a bountiful spiritual crop, Orion wondered what threats could be looming, why on earth anyone would stand in the way of the relationship with the Father. When Jesus finished speaking, his boat-handlers pulled up anchor, and the crowd began slowly to disperse. Orion's group stood and stretched, waiting for the opportunity to move. That is when he spotted Barak moving quickly through the crowd; he had a shawl draped over his head, as if to conceal his presence. Orion shrugged his shoulders thinking it was odd, then turned to Elizabeth and Philip and asked, "What does Jesus mean by the rocky places? And what are the thorns?"

"Exactly the right questions," said Philip. "Also, what makes the soil fertile? What are the right conditions to harvest the abundance from our heavenly kingdom?"

"And the answers?"

"I don't know."

Elizabeth offered, "These are good questions to ask our friend Matthew."

Orion looked back at the Master's boat when again he saw Barak gazing out toward Jesus. His curiosity grabbed him and he turned to Elizabeth, "I will be home later." Then began walking toward Barak, knowing the boy had been deeply touched by Jesus.

Before Orion could reach him he began walking briskly along the shore with glances at Jesus' boat that was now barely visible.

Orion followed the boy in the waning light to his home. It was a large somewhat ornate structure with several large windows that were open, for the night was hot. Then in plain view Isaac met his son with a fury, "Where have you been?"

The oversized boy stammered, "Playing by the lake, sir."

Isaac grabbed his son's hair and pulled his head back. "Don't lie to me boy. My spies saw you in the crowd and your strange behavior."

Then he tightened the pull on Barak's hair, "Ah, ah!" In his fear Barak said the first thing on his mind, "I saw Jesus, he calmed the waters. I felt something in my heart."

Then Isaac erupted into a rage driven by the fear that Jesus was destroying his religion. It was the only place he felt important. A self-ordained enforcer, he had chosen his role to maintain the traditions of his forefathers and hand them to the next generation. Now his only son was falling under Jesus' spell? As he had been taught by his father, Isaac let his terror out as rage—a sharp reaction learned in early childhood and honed during his entire life.

Isaac yelled, "Jesus is a destroyer of our sacred religion." His fist came down hard on Barak's face. The boy staggered back, blood flowing from his nose, crying.

"You will not see him again! He is the devil." Another fist caught him on the chest.

Isaac took a few more steps to his son cowering in the corner. "He is a criminal, a false prophet." He pushed Barak with his heavy weight against the wall. "Any follower of that man is going to hell."

Barak slid to the ground crying. Then Isaac kicked his back. "No son of mine will follow that evil one." Then he left the room.

Barak lay there crying, bloody and torn. At the beach he had begun to understand why people followed Jesus. Yet his father was the center of the world he knew. He gave him the only love he had known since his mother's death. He desperately wanted his approval. He should stand by his father and defend the Jewish religion.

Shortly after, Isaac again appeared in front of his son. Sniffling with clotted blood in his nostrils, Barak asked, "Please forgive me father?" Isaac held Barak as he pushed away the day's memories of Jesus.

Orion walked home, shaken by the violence he had witnessed. That is when he realized that this clash had many faces.

The following morning as Orion was walking through the crowded town; he saw Matthew ahead of him and quickly caught up. "Matthew!" he cried. "I am glad to see you. Can I talk with you as you walk?"

Matthew nodded, "I would enjoy your company. I am on my way to the lake."

"I have the Master's sandals."

"Let me see what you have done." They made their way to a quieter side street and along a wall they squatted as Orion presented a package made of a hide that was soft as silk and the color of the sun. Matthew placed it on his cloak and untied the leather bonds. Matthew smiled, "He likes this simple style." It was the finest leather he had ever seen. The sandals were soft and sturdy, the stitching was beautiful, and the smell was like perfume. "The Master will be pleased," as he carefully tied the yellow package.

Orion then asked, "There were things that Jesus said in his sermon. I've been wondering about them. Can you answer some questions?"

Matthew laughed. "Actually, I don't know if I can. Every time he speaks, I come away with a new set of my own questions. But I keep asking him for explanations, so I might be able to help. What do you want to know?"

Orion then asked him the same questions that he'd asked Elizabeth and Philip. Matthew looked at his friend and smiled, then put his hand on Orion's back. They moved out of traffic and Matthew paused to consider his answer.

"I had the same questions; many of us did. Last night Simon Peter asked Jesus to explain the seed parable. Jesus said: 'The farmer sows the word. Some people are like seed along the path, where the word is sown. As soon as they hear it, Satan comes and takes away the word that was sown in them. Others, like seed sown on rocky places, hear the word and at once receive it with joy. But since they have no root, they last only a short time. When trouble or persecution comes because of the word, they quickly fall away. Still others, like seed sown among thorns, hear the word; but the worries of this life, the deceitfulness of wealth and the desires for other things come in and choke the word, making it unfruitful. Others, like seed sown on good soil, hear the word, accept it, and produce a crop—thirty, sixty or even a hundred times what was sown.[22]'"

"I want to cultivate good soil," said Orion. "Good soil has depth; it is not superficial. My family and community of brothers are such environments. We are creating the environment to grow into the Light."

Matthew looked at his friend. "Your family and your community of brothers is fertile soil. Perhaps this is the beginning of a community of Jesus followers in Capernaum?"

"The controversy is very strong in town. It's important to have a place of support, like the quality of support that I get from the community traveling with Jesus. My fellow travelers provide a foundation for me because we all practice his teachings as a community."

Orion nodded. "My family and brothers make travel on the path to God much easier."

The men gathered the next day at Orion's courtyard. He told them about his conversation with Matthew, then he offered the following opinion: "We have a solid foundation right here. We have fertile soil for growth right here in this gathering. Why? Because we practice the teachings of Jesus in the way we interact."

---

[22] Mark 4: 16-20

"That's right," said Marcus.

"We do this in simple but important ways. For one thing, we maintain our focus on our connection to God—we pray together. Also, we have a good relationship of support—we meet regularly. Also, we are openhearted with each other, like children."

"Children with beards," said Jude with a laugh.

"It is a funny image, but you know what I mean. We listen to each other with our minds open."

"Well said."

"We believe that life is full of possibility. Philip reminds us of that every time we look at him."

"And every time I look at you," said Philip.

"Two other points," said Orion. "We are diverse. In other words, each of us has a very different history, but our attraction to Jesus has brought us into a relationship that makes our differences insignificant. Best of all, there is harmony among us. I feel a genuine love for all of you."

"I feel it too," said Marcus in a whisper.

"It's just a fact. What I'm saying is that we have our fertile soil right here. We have the power of a supportive group. Right here, this is a haven from the hostility and fear and deceit going throughout the town."

Jude said, "Perhaps we should try to expand our little community of four, include more of the faithful in Capernaum."

"Perhaps we should," said Orion. "One thing is certain. We should pray to be instruments of God. The Father will guide us. All we have to do is listen, be open. Then the right thing will appear at the right time.

121

Besides, there is a lot happening now in town. I think our immediate work should be to continue to assist the apostles."

"There are so many people in town I can barely breathe," said Marcus. "This morning I got up on my roof to get some idea how many people have come here. There must be five thousand people out on the streets and in the marketplace. That is more than Capernaum can sustain. And there are more still coming."

"Where are they all lodging, I wonder?" said Jude

Philip found the whole situation quite amusing. "Hee hee!" he cackled. "Our friend Jesus is as famous as Elijah around here. Word of his miracles has spread up and down the caravan line from Egypt to Mesopotamia. Who would have guessed how many blind people there are in this region."

"Is that why they come, so that they can truly see?" said Orion. "Or do they come just to stare?"

"We should always think the best of them," Philip replied. "You said it yourself. We must be open-minded."

Jude said, "I'm afraid that the people of Capernaum are not so open-minded about all the chaos. Many are angry. They say that the town is being overrun. Supplies are running thin. Jesus is losing support at home while his reputation grows elsewhere."

Marcus said, "I'm sure Isaac is pleased about that."

"Oh, yes," said Philip. "He is out there every day, fanning the flames of discontent."

The next day, the streets were filled with pilgrims. Camels were tied to every available post and tree, blocking traffic. Vendors lined every avenue, squatting on rugs spread out where they didn't belong. Many of them were cooking food. The fragrance of roasting meat mingled freely with the odor of excrement. Where there were no vendors, piles of litter complicated the walkway. Orion found himself elbowing through the crowds and sliding between donkey carts to do errands.

Once again he ran into Matthew on the street. The apostle looked exhausted.

"Matthew, how are you doing with all this?"

"There are so many people coming and going that we haven't had time to eat. The audience is too large to fit in our usual spot by the lake. The town is... well, as you experience it. So we've decided to move on, get out in the open—and see if we can get some rest. Jesus has already gone ahead with most of the others."

"That should clear the streets."

"It should, but look around. Most people don't know that he's gone. And the crowd keeps growing. As Jesus travels, people recognize him, and they go running ahead trying to guess where Jesus will stop. Every time we reach a resting place, we find a crowd already gathered."

"What direction are you going?"

"South along the west side of the lake. You might want to come a little of the way. You know the first small hill after you leave the lake on the west road? Jesus is sure to stop there and address the crowd."

"No rest for him."

"No. He doesn't seem to need it. He never tires. And he can't deny the desires of the people when they assemble for him. He says they are like sheep without a shepherd."

"I will tell the others, and we will come to the hill."

Orion passed the word to Jude. Then he gathered the boys with Elizabeth and headed out along the lake with a string of others. When they arrived at the site, Jesus and several of his apostles were seated on a slope overlooking the large flat field where the crowd had gathered. Orion and the others took a place in the field. In time, Jesus stood up and walked to a high point along the slope. For a moment he put his foot on a rock and Orion could see his handiwork on the Master's feet. His chest expanded as he turned to Elizabeth, "The Master is wearing the new sandals."

A light breeze stirred up behind Jesus and carried his voice forth from the earthen pulpit. "Do not think that I have come to abolish the Law or the Prophets," he began. "I have not come to abolish them but to fulfill them. I tell you the truth, until heaven and earth pass away, not one letter, not one stroke of a letter, will pass from the law until all is accomplished. Anyone who breaks one of the least of these commandments and teaches others to do the same will be called least in the kingdom of heaven. But whoever practices and teaches these commands will be called great in the kingdom of heaven. Unless your righteousness surpasses that of the

Pharisees and the teachers of the law, you will certainly not enter the kingdom of heaven.[23]"

Orion pointed. "Look over there to our right. Two of Isaac's spies seem offended. It must be discouraging for them to see such a large following, and to be rightly chastised."

"It must be infuriating to hear that they don't belong in the kingdom of heaven," she replied.

By this time it was late in the day, so his disciples came to him. "This is a remote place," they said, "and it's already very late. Send the people away so they can go to the surrounding countryside and villages and buy themselves something to eat."

But he answered, "You give them something to eat."

They said to him, "That would take eight months of a man's wages! Are we to go and spend that much on bread and give it to them to eat?"

"How many loaves do you have?" he asked. "Go and see."

When they found out, they said, "Five—and two fish."

Then Jesus directed them to have all the people sit down in groups on the grass. So they sat down in groups of hundreds and fifties. Taking the five loaves and the two fish and looking up to heaven, he gave thanks and broke the loaves. Then he gave them to his disciples to set before the people. He also divided the two fish among them all.[24]

---

[23] Matthew 5:17
[24] Mark 6:35-41

Orion looked around the crowd, counting. He estimated that the assembly included more than five thousand men and at least four thousand women and children. He and his family were a small speck in this vast crowd. He realized how graced he was to have been blessed by Jesus' own hands.

Then he and Elizabeth saw the food being passed around. It was a mystery how so much food could have appeared, out here in the open countryside. They were given fresh bread and salted fish from baskets that seemed bottomless. Orion said, "This is a feast! How can this be?"

A voice nearby said, "Take all you want. There's plenty."

At that comment, the group around them seemed to explode into joyful conversation, shouts, and laughter. Orion felt light-headed. It was as if they'd all been drinking wine. Elizabeth couldn't stop expressing her wonderment. "All of this came from the hands of Jesus after he blessed five loaves of bread and just two fish. How can it be?"

"I wish I knew," said Orion. "If I could, imagine what this would do for my sandal business."

"It's no joke," she said. "I am seriously amazed."

"Oh yes. We are all seriously amazed. That explains why so many people are laughing like drunkards." He thought for a moment and said, "Congratulations, my wife. We are in the midst of a miracle. I had never seen miracles before Jesus."

"I don't know why you say that."

"Oh? Name another."

"When Alexander was born. That was the first miracle."

"What about meeting me?"

"The day I met you? What about the day *I* was born?"

They laughed.

Orion glanced up to the hillside. "Look," he said to Elizabeth. "Our host."

The white-clad figure of Jesus sat alone, not eating, still as the stones about him.

After all nine thousand people had eaten their fill, twelve baskets of broken pieces remained. While word of this was passing through the crowd, Jesus left the hillside and, flanked by his chief followers, began walking back the way they had come, back to the lake. They walked briskly, outpacing most of those who pursued. At the lake, Jesus boarded a boat and left.

Later that month, the same boat approached Capernaum over the still waters of Galilee. Jesus was returning, unannounced. He had slipped away from the throngs and came back to the base of his ministry. Of course, it was impossible for him to arrive undetected. Fishermen on the shore recognized the boat and began spreading the rumor that Jesus would be teaching that afternoon.

Orion and his family went to the shore, eager for another experience of the power of Jesus. But the shore-side scene was not at all what they expected. The gathering was small, only about two hundred people. One of the first people Orion saw was Isaac himself. The hunched graybeard was huddled with a group of men. They were goons, the meanest sort of men that you could find in Capernaum. With them was Isaac's son. The hulking boy regarded them with an expression that was both a grin and a scowl at the same time. Orion felt sure that he saw the shadowy gesture of money passing hands, coins slipping into pouches. Worse yet, he could see Baraccus, mounted and waiting, in the distance under the fish-market roof. Foot soldiers, at least ten of them, stood alertly at his side.

Orion leaned over to Elizabeth saying, "This doesn't feel good."

"We are not going to abandon our teacher," she said. "No matter what!" Orion was startled by her sudden ferocity of tone.

Orion spotted Philip and Jude. The families greeted. Philip held onto Orion's hand and looked him in the face earnestly. "And so it begins," said Philip.

"I don't know what you mean," said Orion. "These fools with their bad intentions…."

"No." Philip kept clasping Orion's hand and looking into his eyes. Orion squinted as though he was looking at the sun. "We have been preparing. Now we must be ready."

"I don't understand…."

"We shall see this play out."

Julian, putting his small soft hand into Orion's,

said, "Where are all the people, Dad?"

"They are afraid to be here."

After a moment, Alexander said, "Are you afraid, Dad?"

"Of course not."

"Me neither," said Alexander.

"Me too," said Julian, looking around with wide eyes.

Jesus and his small entourage arrived as people stood up and moved closer. His eyes looked around him as if sensing the uneasiness. Jesus walked to the platform—a sturdy construction that the fishermen had erected during the first months of his ministry, before the crowd pressure had driven him to teach from an off-shore fishing boat.

He stepped onto the platform, the water behind him, and stood still, his posture unchanged. He bowed his head in prayer and then he slowly lifted his it and scanned the audience. He looked at Isaac and his goons, grouped at the edge of the gathering. He looked up at the Roman soldiers. He looked back at the people who had come to hear his words.

He turned to Peter and John, saying something to them. The two apostles went off in a hurry.

Then he spoke.

"There was a landowner who planted a vineyard. He put a wall around it, dug a winepress in it, and built a watchtower. Then he rented the vineyard to some farmers and went away on a journey. When the harvest time approached, he sent his servants to the tenants to collect his fruit.

"The tenants seized his servants; they beat one, killed another, and stoned a third. Then he sent other servants to them, more than the first time, and the tenants treated them the same way. Last of all, he sent his son to them. 'They will respect my son,' he said.

"But when the tenants saw the son, they said to each other, 'This is the heir. Come, let's kill him and take his inheritance.' So they took him and threw him out of the vineyard and killed him.

"Therefore, when the owner of the vineyard comes, what will he do to those tenants?"

To Orion's surprise, a voice from behind answered this question. It was Isaac, booming forth with a practiced eloquence.

"He will bring those wretches to a wretched end!" said Isaac. "And he will rent the vineyard to other tenants, who will give him his share of the crop at harvest time!" The men around him laughed

Jesus said, "Have you never read in the Scriptures: 'The stone the builders rejected has become the capstone; the Lord has done this, and it is marvelous in our eyes'?[25]"

Isaac made no reply.

"Therefore I tell you that the kingdom of God will be taken away from you and given to a people who will produce its fruit."

Then Jesus looked up at the Roman soldiers, who waited for their turn. One of Isaac's henchmen yelled, "You can't take away God from us. You're a madman!"

---

[25] Matthew 21:33-45

Then another cried, "You are the devil. Get out of here!"

Orion jumped to his feet. He looked toward Isaac and shouted, "Have some respect! Listen to his words!" Jude and Marcus stood up. So did many in the crowd. But other people sitting in the audience started yelling at Jesus, "Go away. You're a devil. Be gone."

Orion was stunned. People right next to him were shouting these ridiculous words.

Then Isaac's bully gang started slinging stones. The first stone hit the front of the platform, chipping away a thumb-sized splinter. Orion instinctively ran toward the sling-wielding thug, who was grabbing another rock from his pouch.

Jesus turned away from the crowd. As it so happened, Peter and John had brought up two boats and come close to shore, and Jesus began walking toward them.

Then two more stones shot past, each one burying itself in the sand at Jesus' feet. Orion shouted: "Let him talk! Let him talk to those who know him! You devils!" Jude and Marcus both tried to clutch Orion's shirt, saying, "Stop it now. Hold on, Jesus is leaving." But Orion tore past them and started running at the Pharisee attackers. He couldn't stop. He had thrown himself on a collision course beyond thought or control.

But as he drew near Isaac's group, another stone flashed past his head. He could hear it whistling meanly in the air. Then, behind him, came a terrible cry of pain. Immediately after came several shouts of dismay. He heard Elizabeth call out: "Jude!" In an instant he recognized the source of that first pained cry. Just as impulsively as he had begun the attack, he stopped and whirled around. There was his friend, Jude, down on his knees, his hands clutched to his head. Blood flowed freely from between his fingers. Marcus had his arms out to steady Jude. Philip and Elizabeth came to his side. Obviously they had all come in pursuit of Orion, and Jude had taken the punishment that was meant for him.

Noticing Jesus was in his boat Orion ran back and threw his arms around Jude.

Seeing that they'd actually hit someone, the stone slingers paused in their attack, unsure what to do next. At that point, Baraccus and his soldiers came forth. Baraccus, who was mounted on a black charger, rode quickly into the space between the warring parties. He put up his hand and held his palm toward Isaac and his group—signaling stop, as though he was their commander, as though he had orchestrated the whole thing. Orion found that very strange. Then as his troops ran up to take guard positions by the stone-slingers and around the fallen Jude, Baraccus rode down to the lake shore, trotting back and forth by the water. By now Jesus was in the boat with Peter and John. "Jesus of Nazareth," shouted Baraccus. "You are not welcome in Capernaum! The residents don't want you here!"

A great cry of protest rose from the crowd. "No! No!" It was actually difficult to tell what this shouting meant—for Jesus or for Baraccus. Baraccus played it to his own advantage, knowing he had the full authority of the Roman Empire behind him. "Preacher, be gone.

Take your trouble-causing business to some other town. This has been your last visit to Capernaum."

Jesus motioned to his apostles to leave. Then he turned back to face the parties on shore and the profile of the town behind them.

"And you, Capernaum, will you be lifted up to the skies? No, you will go down to the depths. If the miracles that were performed in you had been performed in Sodom, it would have remained to this day. But I tell you that on the day of judgment it will be more bearable for the land of Sodom than for you.[26]"

Orion and the others did not wait to watch the boat shrink toward the horizon. Jude needed their help. He was conscious, though dazed, and he was able to walk. But the bleeding and the pain needed attention. Slowly they helped him stagger back home, ignoring everyone else and the shoreline. Orion felt hollow and sick at heart.

The success of Isaac's strategy was repeated in other regions of the Master's ministry. By the end of July 29AD, the temperature of the air was not the only hot occurrence. Yet despite their efforts to warp the truth and discredit Jesus, his enemies could not distort the honest power of his person. His message, his energy, the light of his presence could not be denied.

With the Master ousted from town, Orion felt more dependent on the environment that nurtured his spiritual connection. His family continued to strengthen

---

[26] Matthew 11:23-24

his foundation by practicing Jesus' teachings. The routine of family prayer took on deeper significance. They redesigned their rooms to remind them of their connection to God, using sayings from Jesus, flowers, and simple things. The values they enacted created a group behavior that aligned with the words Jesus taught.

Situations that were normally upsetting, like Alexander ruining a hide by leaving it next to the fire, rolled off him like water off a gull's back. He saw light in people and greeted that light. As Jude healed, even the sight of Isaac and Baraccus was generating less constriction in his heart. Orion's smile and energy proved to be magnetic as more people frequented his shop for conversation. His daily prayers turned into a more continuous dialogue with God.

The meetings with his brothers twice a week supported his connection to God. It was a time they all valued. They discussed the conspiracies to end Jesus' ministry, the latest of his teachings, the miracles, and their personal challenges and realizations. Most important, they were real and honest with each other. There was safety based on respect and openness. But could he sustain that happiness when he would get tested? And we all get tested; he knew he would be tested.

From the caravan travelers Orion heard stories about Jesus. There was one common theme—the opposition to Jesus by the established Jewish elite.

During the Jewish holiday season a customer came into Orion's shop. His skin was like dark, aged leather damaged by the sun, and he carried two bags in need of repair. After they agreed on the mending, the traveler started talking with excitement.

"I have seen a great prophet in Jerusalem. When he approached the city, people lined the streets on the way to the gate. They were rejoicing and with a loud voice singing, 'Blessed be the King that comes in the name of the Lord.' They laid palms at the hooves of the colt he rode. When Jesus entered Jerusalem, many praised him as the Messiah. The next time I saw Jesus was in the Temple courtyard, where I was delivering some rare birds for offerings at the altar. Then on the opposite side of the courtyard Jesus began teaching a large group. I started walking toward him, but before I could reach him, he moved to merchant stands. Then I saw him turn over the tables of money-changers, and he began letting animals loose saying, 'This was a house of prayer, but you have made it into a den of thieves.' I can tell you from experience that a few are getting very rich from courtyard business. But this was the first time someone had the guts to tell the truth in the open. Then I heard Jesus again. This time I was in a crowded street, and he spoke of God, like a poet."

Early that Friday Orion stirred restlessly before the cock crowed. He felt anxious and rose out of bed while the rest of the family slept. While stretching his body he walked into the courtyard. It was very dark; clouds took away the celestial light. As he busied himself feeling for kindling and his flint, he thought of Philip and the world of blindness. The glow of his fire took away the damp chill as he sat and stared at the embers.... And he couldn't stop thinking of Jesus. The dawn seem to make a slow entrance, starting with a faint light that eventually made shapes visible, shapes that seemed to have a sinister look.

During the day his restlessness would not leave him. He tried to work, but he ruined a good hide with blunders, something he hadn't done since his apprentice days. He didn't know what was stirring, but by mid-afternoon he had to leave.

He closed his shop door and made his way to the lake. As Orion approached the shore, he spotted his boat and decided to go on the water. Orion pushed the boat out and jumped in. He let out a grunt, "Arrgghh!," as he pulled hard on the oars. He kept on pulling hard with each stroke, his back and legs strained, but it felt good. The physical effort was helping to relieve the gnawing uneasiness he felt.

When he was out over a mile, he stopped. His breathing was heavy and his skin sweaty. He lay on his back looking at the sky. He thought of Jesus again, and the anxiety returned. The boat rocked with waves that seemed to accentuate the turmoil he felt. He noticed the sky beginning to change colors as the sun set. The sky darkened to the east. Orion intuitively sat up fast and gazed at the last glimpses of the sun. And from the depths in the southwest came a shooting star that streaked across the sky. Orion followed the blazing light, and in that light he saw the image of Jesus. The light penetrated his eyes and seemed to enter the cells of his body. He sat still, taking in its movement into the distance.

Then he heard the dull roar of thunder, and he turned again to the southwest, where a big storm was brewing, coming from the direction of Jerusalem. He could see flashes of lightning in the dark, billowing clouds.

Orion rowed quickly, facing the storm as the bow moved at a good clip toward shore. The streaks of light that shot across the sky were like nothing he had ever seen. The wall of the storm cloud was enormous, pumping with an energy that seemed other-worldly. He was astonished not only by its size but also by the intensity of the almost constant flashes of lightning that glowed in the growing darkness. But what amazed Orion the most was the suddenness of its appearance … it had come from the direction of the star.

When Orion entered his shop, he began latching down windows. Elizabeth came in from the courtyard. "Orion," she called with enthusiasm, "did you see the star that blazed across the sky?"

He looked at her with a smile, "'Yes."

Elizabeth continued, "When I saw that star shooting across the sky, it was as if Jesus was visiting me. It was as real as the time he was actually here and blessed our home and family. There was a light that went in me."

Orion looked at Elizabeth and felt how their love had deepened through their common focus on God and Jesus' teachings. "I had a similar experience on the lake.

There is a big storm brewing, from the direction of Jerusalem and the star. I have had an uneasy feeling all day. Something is happening."

Elizabeth walked to Orion, reached out her arms, and placed them around his waist. Looking at him with her beautiful eyes, she lovingly said, "One thing that has happened is that we were visited and blessed by Jesus."

The following day Orion was working in his shop on his back porch when Jude came in. "Oh, my friend…" he began, then stopped as if frozen in place, his hands against his heart.

Orion stood up with a concerned expression, "What's wrong, Jude? Is it your head wound?"

"No," said Jude with a groan. "It's not me. I have to tell you something, and yet I cannot bring myself to say it."

And suddenly Orion knew. "The Master?"

"He's gone."

"Gone? Where did he…"

"He's dead. They killed him."

"What!" A pang of fear hit. The earth seemed to shake under him, and he had to lean on the doorway for support. "Jesus raised others from the dead, could he not save himself? This must be a lie. This must be one of Isaac's rumors."

"No. This is the truth. It is a terrible, terrible truth."

Then Orion believed. He could not deny the

storm, the shooting star. "What have you heard?"

"In Jerusalem. Jesus was taken and charged by the Sanhedrin. The following day, the Romans tried him. They tortured him. They mocked him. They called him the king of the Jews, and they found him guilty of that pretension."

"How did he die?" said Orion quietly.

Jude could barely speak the word. He had to spit it out. "Crucifixion."

Orion didn't say a word. He hung down his head. The world seemed to be spinning. It was a long, long time before he took in a deep breath and let it out slowly. "Did you tell the others?" he asked in a whisper.

"No, you were the first."

"Are you able to tell the others? I don't think I can function right now." He began to sob, and Jude held him to his chest. The men wept together.

Orion closed his shop and went to his back room, where he and Elizabeth collapsed on their bed and sobbed as they held each other. He remembered the deaths he had witnessed one time back in Caesarea Philippi, when a man convicted of murder and theft received the same horrifying execution. It was a painful, slow, and humiliating demise.

Orion gathered his spiritual brothers. Philip spoke up. "I met a follower of Jesus on the caravan route today. He saw how Jesus faced his death. He was calm. He bore incredible pain without a scream, without anger, without fear. He even forgave his persecutors while going through his torture on the cross."

Orion said, "It's hard to accept that our teacher is

dead. I feel terrible anger. Hatred. But then I recall Jesus' message of loving your enemies and the importance of forgiveness, what he actually did while on the cross. This is difficult to swallow. There was no one I admired more; I have never seen such a light of consciousness."

Jude, Philip, Marcus, and Orion consoled each other after Jesus' death. They met frequently and exchanged whatever they could learn about the horrifying events in Jerusalem. Jude was especially keen on gathering information from the synagogue. By the fire Jude sat with his brothers and presented the picture that had emerged.

"Thousands lined the streets to greet Jesus' arrival. There were so many people, swarming and adoring him, that the Sanhedrin was frightened. They became even more concerned when he chased the money-changers and merchants from the temple courtyard. That's when they began plotting his death with fierce resolve. They called in Isaac, who was in Jerusalem for the Passover—after all, he had gained quite a reputation for the little stunt he pulled to get Jesus out of Capernaum. They all agreed that the Romans should execute him. They had two concerns— one, if they killed Jesus, they risked a popular uprising. And two, they had no legal authority anyway."

Then Jude bowed his head and said with a sigh, "Judas Iscariot betrayed him for thirty pieces of silver."

"Judas Iscariot?" cried Marcus. "One of the Master's own apostles?"

"When the Sanhedrin got Iscariot's information,

they acted quickly and arrested him. Everything moved quickly after that."

"Not quickly enough, I'm sure," said Orion. "Crucifixion is a terrible thing. What became of the betrayer?"

"The villain hanged himself after he realized what he'd done."

"Fair enough."

Jude said, "You should know that Isaac played a key role in all of this. After the arrest, Isaac personally paid and orchestrated a crowd to be at the governor's courtyard. He offered them all a bonus if they would influence the judgment to crucify Jesus. He had them yelling to free a murderer and thief, to kill Jesus instead. They yelled, 'Free Barabbas. Crucify ... crucify Jesus.'"

Orion blurted out, "That scheming, manipulative snake. He will burn in hell for this." His brothers around him nodded their heads in agreement.

Marcus said, "I'm sure you have thought of this, but it must be said. We have to be on guard against Isaac ourselves. We are pegged as followers of Jesus. With Baraccus in his pocket, he is a real threat to us and to our families. We could be next."

Realizing this sent them even deeper into despair. They were not sure what to expect, but they all agreed to keep a low profile.

Marcus said, "Here is the most important question. What now? Is this the end of his ministry?"

Philip answered, "All things are possible through God. This could be a new beginning."

The family's evening prayers fervently asked for guidance and understanding. The boys had many questions that Orion had difficulty answering. They simply could not grasp how or why Jesus would be killed. Orion had to admit that he shared their astonishment.

When the boys were asleep, Orion turned to Elizabeth and asked, "Is this it? The Master is gone, and we have in his place a snake and a beast in Capernaum. Is this God's justice? Is this the world's response to one who holds the Light?"

Elizabeth said, "We have been taught by the Master to trust in God. That will dampen our fear."

In the distance a rooster crowed. They clasped each other's hands. They sat huddled and frightened, trusting and grieving, unsure of what would happen next.

"I don't know what I would do if they did harm to our family." A silent, deep uneasiness went through them like a chill as they sat together in the darkness beneath a moonless sky.

PART TWO

Communities of Light

CHAPTER 7

"He's alive! He's alive!"

Orion could hear Philip's voice out in the street, growing louder with each shout. "He's alive!" Then suddenly Philip was there in the doorway of the shop, leaning with one hand on the doorframe, the other hand against his heart, and he panted. "Orion...."

Orion stood up from his work, tools fell from his hands. A strange sense of unreality seemed to be whirling in his head like a blasting of trumpets too loud to be heard. "Jesus is alive?"

"Yes!"

"Three days ago he was crucified and now he lives?"

"Yes. Yes!" Philip panted. "Mary Magdala... the apostles... others... have seen him. In the flesh!"

"I don't understand."

"Yes you do, by all that is holy. The Master lives!"

Now Elizabeth was standing in the back door to the shop, wiping her hands on a towel.

Orion shook his head, looked at Elizabeth, and then with a baffled slowness said: "So he never died?"

"Of course he died. That's the whole point! All of Jerusalem watched it happen. It went for hours. Of course he died." Philip looked fiercely at him, and then at her. "And now he lives. He bears the wounds of the crucifixion on his hands."

Elizabeth gave a loud, undulating cry like the call of a wild beast in the mountains. Orion felt dizzy and disoriented. He stared at Philip, who leaned, victorious and elated, in the doorway.

"It's true, Orion." By now Philip had regained his breath. He seemed to be savoring the rich flavor of the news he'd brought. "The other miracles—they were all a prelude to this. He has transcended the physical world. He has vanquished death itself." The two men looked at each other, nearly in tears. Then they embraced. They embraced Elizabeth, who shook with spasms of emotion, perhaps sobs.

Orion looked up to the sky and said, "Praise to you, God! Praise to you, Jesus!" Then he asked Philip, "Did you tell the other brothers?"

"No, I came here first. I'm going to tell them now."

Orion said, "Let's all meet here. Let's celebrate." To Elizabeth he said, "Put the kettle on for tea. And get out that good wine. We have some nice cheese, too. I'll call the boys!"

Within an hour the courtyard of Orion and Elizabeth was filled with joyous laughter. Orion, Philip, Jude, and Marcus had gathered with their families. "Tell us what you heard, my brother," called Orion to Philip, who was standing by the oven in the center of the court.

"I met two travelers, who got the news directly from James."

"James?"

"Zebedee's son."

"You know James," said Marcus to Orion. "The skinny fellow with the narrow beard, the one who always had the last word about dealing with the fishing nets."

"Right, James. Well, if he said it, it's sure to be true."

"These travelers told me that Mary Magdala and Mary, the mother of James, went to Jesus' resting place to prepare his body for entombment. You have heard about that resting place."

"Tell us again."

"As soon as the Roman soldiers would let them, the disciples took the Master's body down from the cross. They wrapped it, just as it was, in cloth. Then they carried it to a cave and laid him there, then left.

Marcus interrupted. "Didn't they at least wash and anoint the Master's body?"

"Philip continued, "The Sabbath had arrived preventing them from preparing the body. In a sealed tomb Jesus' body would be safe until they returned for proper entombment. But just as soon it was lawful to do so, the women returned with the necessary cloth and ointments to…"

"Don't forget the stone," said Jude.

"Of course. The Sanhedrin was afraid there would be a popular response to their murder. They are still very afraid of that. They wanted that body out of sight—cut off all contact with his followers. So they pushed a huge stone against the mouth of the cave, sealing it off and then placed Roman guards at the blocked entrance. No one could get in there."

How did the women think that they could get to the body for burial preparations?"

"They didn't know, of course. Nobody knew what would happen. They just knew their duties at the time of death, so they prepared and they went to the site."

"And what did they find?"

"This is where the amazing stories begin. When they arrived at the tomb, they were shocked to find that the giant stone had been rolled away. A gleaming figure, someone unknown to them who seemed to be shining with light, was in the tomb and said to them, 'He has risen from the dead: behold the place they laid him.' To their astonishment, all that remained on the slab was his stained burial shroud.

"Then Jesus began appearing to people. He first appeared to Mary Magdala. He then met two travelers on the road to Emmaus and broke bread with them. He then went to his apostles. They kissed his hands and his feet, they cried and prayed and ate with him."

"We are witnessing the fulfillment of the scriptures in our day and age. He is Elijah come again," said Jude.

Orion had been deeply troubled by the sudden and sordid death of the Master. But maybe it was a way to show the world that there is a force beyond the body. His heavy heart was now soaring. No one could deny the Master's torturous public death. Now he lived!

During the weeks that followed, they were all eager for news about Jesus. They heard a wide range of stories, everything from accounts that he had materialized in front of large groups to flat-out denials that anything had occurred. Isaac and other Jewish leaders at Capernaum believed that the body had been stolen from the cave. The Roman guards stationed at the cave that night had said as much. While they were sleeping, they said, the dead man's bereaved followers rolled back the rock and snatched the body in order to perpetrate a hoax. This resurrection idea was the fantasy of gullible fools.

But when Orion went to the marketplace, he heard other versions of the story. One caravan driver told it this way: "While the women were on their way, some of the guards went into the city and reported to the chief priests everything that had happened. When the chief priests had met with the elders and devised a plan, they gave the soldiers a large sum of money, telling them, 'You are to say that his disciples came during the night and stole him away while we were asleep. If this report gets to the governor, we will satisfy him and keep you out of trouble.' So the soldiers took the money and did as they were instructed. And this story has been widely circulated among the Jews.[27]"

Orion had learned to trust the stories of the men who traveled the merchant road. Such men were tough and blunt, and they had no loyalty to the lands they traversed.

The day after that, Marcus stopped by Orion's shop and said, "That story you picked up, about the bribing of the Roman guards...."

"Yes?"

"I just had it confirmed by someone who ought to know—our good friend the centurion."

"You were with Barracus? How did that come about?"

"I was shoeing his horse. While I worked, I overheard him talking to some of his cronies."

"Eavesdropping can be a dangerous hobby in those situations."

"I know. I made myself as inconspicuous as possible. Whenever he spoke to me, I just grunted. Nngh. Nngh. He must have thought I was feeble-minded. I hope so."

"And what did you hear?"

"Barracus was talking about an old friend of his, a hardened soldier. The two of them had served in several campaigns together. As it turns out, this friend was one of the guards at the tomb of Jesus. He told Barracus what really happened that night at the cave. He told him, 'No mortal came to that tomb.'"

---

[27] Matthew 28:11-15

"No mortal? Is that so?"

"That's what the old soldier reported. He told Barracus this: 'There was a violent earthquake, and we all fell flat on our faces. And then an angel came down and rolled back the stone and sat on it.'"

"An angel!"

"That's what I heard. 'His appearance was like lightning, and his clothes were white as snow.' Barracus described this soldier as having the courage of a lion. They had fought side by side in many fierce battles. But the old friend told him: 'I never felt fear like that. I shook and became like a dead man.' Then he told Barracus that he had been given a large sum of money to say that the body had been stolen by the followers of Jesus."

"There you go. The same story. I wonder what Barracus thought of all that."

"It is Barracus's considered opinion that this old friend has finally 'gone round the bend and lost his mind.' For him, any talk of angels or God is pure pagan rubbish. He said, 'In this world, only the strong and cunning thrive,' and he went on like that for a while. But he did seem a bit rattled by the sudden craziness of his friend."

"Why else would he be talking about it like that?"

"Exactly. For him, these wild ideas are dangerous, contagious, like some sort of plague that's threatening his territory. I heard him tell his men to be prepared for quick and brutal action. He predicts a backlash to the crucifixion, perhaps an uprising by the followers of Jesus. He is readying his troops for a swift and merciless crackdown."

"We're in a dangerous situation."

"What do you think we should do?" said Marcus.

"Keep quiet. Wait. But that's not enough. We are strongest when we are together. Without a sense of community, we'll be scattered like seeds in a whirlwind."

One week later a man named Simeon, a mason, came to Orion's shop. Orion knew the man slightly—his wife Martha was a close friend of Elizabeth—but they had never had much of a conversation before. Orion was surprised that the man would be seeking him out.

Simeon got right to the point. "I know about the group of men you meet with, the group that focuses on Jesus. My wife has told me a little about what you are doing. I would like to join your circle."

Orion regarded the man carefully. He was short and solidly built. From what little could be seen—forearms, neck, calves—his musculature was impressive. The expression on his face was somber, even gloomy, but Orion decided that this expression was most likely the man's natural temperament, not a sign of some inner hostility or malice.

"Elizabeth has spoken of your wife Martha many times."

"Good things, I hope."

"Oh, yes. She thinks very highly of her. She says that Martha is very wise, despite her youthful appearance."

"Then your wife is a good judge of character."

"Also that Martha is a true devotee to the Master."

"That she is."

"But I have never heard the same spoken about you."

Simeon thought for a moment. "I was a follower of him. But when Jesus refused to lead a revolt, I withdrew. What hope was there in merely talking about change but never taking action?"

"That's right. We had you placed in the 'disappointed Messiah' camp."

"Yes. But now I know better."

"Oh? What has changed?"

Simeon looked him steadily in the eyes and said, "Everything has changed. The whole world has changed."

Orion considered that comment for a moment. "Come tomorrow at noon to Marcus's house, and you can ask the group."

The next day they gathered under Marcus's olive tree. All had wine and were in good spirits, eating grapes, dates, and bread. There was much talk about Jesus' next move. Orion said, "Perhaps he would even return to Capernaum someday—wouldn't that give Barracus the scare of his life?"

Simeon appeared just after everyone arrived. Orion rose and greeted him. "Simeon, glad you could come." The other brothers were just as warm in their welcome. Jude offered a cup of wine, but Simeon held up both his hands.

"First, there is something I want to say to all of you."

"All right."

"Let's hear it."

The men put down their cups and sat, giving their full attention to the newcomer. Simeon gathered his thoughts and began. "My wife, Martha, will tell you that I am a stubborn man, set in my ways."

"Just wait till you hear what our wives have to say about us!" said Marcus, and everyone laughed. Everyone but Simeon.

"But I have learned a few things," he said. "For example, I know one of those travelers from Emmaus who encountered Jesus after his resurrection. I once did some stonework for his father. He is a trustworthy source. So I went to him and questioned him at length. I am convinced that Jesus has conquered death."

Now the room was silent.

"I understand now. I understand that Jesus was talking about a heavenly kingdom, not this earthly realm. I mean, I still believe that he is king of this earthly realm. But now I realize why. He conquered the earth by transcending it. He has been leading a revolution, but one that was too subtle for me to grasp at first—a revolution of the spirit. This is the revolution I want to participate in, participate wholeheartedly—not a futile revolt against the Romans." Simeon hesitated for a moment, then got to the point: "I would like to have the support of this circle in becoming a follower of Jesus."

The four men listening looked at each other. Philip said slowly, "Well, in that case, Simeon, there's something you really ought to do."

"What is that?"

"Accept that glass of wine we offered you."

"With pleasure," said Simeon.

It was late in the afternoon, and Orion was putting the final clasp on a new sandal design when he heard a familiar voice at the door.

"Busy as usual, aren't you?"

Orion glanced up to see Matthew's grinning face. He sprang to his feet and gave his visitor a warm embrace. "Matthew, what a joy to see you!"

Matthew looked like a different person. There was an inner light that emanated from him, like the light of Jesus in many ways. He glowed like the Master, and his eyes sparkled as he spoke.

"So much has happened since I last saw you. I can't begin to tell you now. I am inviting close followers of Jesus to my house tomorrow night. But I must be cautious. After all, Jesus was strongly opposed in Capernaum, and the Romans are searching for any sign of trouble that might come from Jesus' death. I need to be discreet."

"Of course," said Orion. "We all understand the need for discretion. And yet we also have a need for community. After you left, a small group of us began to meet regularly to talk. We pray together and share the news and talk about how best to welcome the light of God into our homes. At first it was four of us. Philip you know, and Jude, who was cantor. Also, Marcus the ironsmith has been with us from the beginning. Now a mason named Simeon has joined. Is it all right if they come, also?"

"Yes, of course. I know all these men. In fact, I

planned to invite them, but you can save me the trouble. What you and your brothers have been doing is exactly what this gathering is about. We must limit this to men and women. Not children yet. Later we can involve them."

Orion nodded. "I will tell the others. Plan on having nine participants from our little community." Orion clasped Matthew's hand. "I know you have to go. You have a lot to take care of. I just want to say that it is good to see you. We have been eagerly awaiting your return and more news of recent events. You are shining like the Master."

Matthew grabbed Orion's hand in both of his and said, "Praise Jesus! I will see you tomorrow." And he walked out the door.

Orion felt intuitively that something significant was about to happen, but he had no idea what it was. As the time approached, he and Elizabeth put on their best clothes, feeling eager anticipation, and made their way to Matthew's house.

Matthew welcomed them at his entranceway. They sat on cushions arranged on the open floor. There were twenty-four people gathered, both men and women. Nearly everyone Orion saw was familiar. He and Elizabeth greeted each of them with a smile and a nod as they found their way to cushions.

When all had arrived, Matthew disengaged from various conversations and took a stance at the far end of the room. He spoke in a clear, uplifting tone, with power and assertion and a sense of knowing, like the Master. "It is good to see you all, my fellow disciples of Jesus," he said. "I have many wonders to share with all of you."

The room was starkly silent.

"In Jerusalem, on the day following our terrible ordeal, all of us who traveled with the Master were in the deepest despair. The eleven us huddled in a room. We were frightened. We hid there for three days. Then Mary Magdala came to us and delivered the shocking news—that he had appeared to her. Of course we were skeptical. Who could believe such a story, relayed by one grieving woman? And yet...."

"And yet it was Jesus," said someone in the room.

"Precisely," said Matthew. "After all that we had seen, what were we to think? Why would he appear to Mary Magdala first? So we talked about the situation. "And while we were still talking about this, Jesus himself stood among us and said to us, 'Peace be with you.'"

A murmur went through the room.

"We were startled and frightened, thinking we saw a ghost. He said to us, 'Why are you troubled? Why do doubts rise in your minds? Look at my hands and my feet. It is I myself! Touch me and see. A ghost does not have flesh and bones, as you see I have.'

"When he had said this, he showed us his hands and feet. And while we still did not believe it because of joy and amazement, he asked us, 'Do you have anything here to eat?' We gave him a piece of broiled fish. He took it and ate it in our presence. While he ate, he said to us, 'This is what I told you while I was still with you:

Everything must be fulfilled that is written about me in the Law of Moses, the Prophets, and the Psalms.'"

Again quiet comments erupted in the room. Matthew said, "I know what you are thinking. I felt it, too. My mind opened to a whole new understanding of his words. He said to us, 'Thus it is written, that the Christ would suffer and rise again from the dead the third day, and that repentance for forgiveness of sins would be proclaimed in His name to all the nations, beginning from Jerusalem.[28]' Then he looked at each of us in turn."

Someone in the room sobbed.

"He told us, 'I am going to send you what my Father has promised.' Then he thought for a moment and added, "But you are to stay in the city until you are clothed with power from on high.[29]' Then he led us out as far as Bethany. He lifted up his hands and blessed us. While he was blessing us, he parted from us; a cloud received him out of sight, and he was carried up into heaven."

"Carried into heaven!" Orion marveled out loud. Elizabeth had her hands to her mouth and was staring transfixed at the floor.

Matthew's voice was choked with emotion. "And, after worshiping Him, we returned to Jerusalem with great joy, and were continually in the temple praising God. We waited in the city as instructed by Jesus—until, as he had promised, we would receive the Power from on High.

"When that day came, Pentecost, we were all

---

[28] Luke 24:36-47
[29] Luke 24:49

together in one place. And suddenly there came from heaven a noise like a violent rushing wind, and it filled the whole house where we were sitting. And there appeared to us tongues as of fire distributing themselves, and they rested on each one of us. And we were all filled with the Holy Spirit and began to speak with other tongues, as the Spirit was giving us utterance. When this sound occurred, a large crowd gathered. There are many Jews living in Jerusalem, devout men from every nation under heaven. These men were bewildered because each one of them was hearing us speak in their own language. They were amazed and astonished. They said, 'Why—are not all these who are speaking Galileans? So how is it that we each hear them in our own language to which we were born?[30]'

"I felt an energy beyond my earthly existence. When that energy took over my awareness, it drove my actions. I found myself doing things that I had never done before. I felt like an empty flute, and God was playing his tune through me. I still feel that way. I always will. And I am amazed at what gets played.

"This Holy Spirit brings a different perspective to all that you do. It is our connection with God more fully realized. It is real, something that we all can experience. It is our deeper reality.

"Close your eyes. Pray. Open your hearts and minds to the presence of the Divine Light, the light that is always present within us."

Orion closed his eyes to the external world. The

---

[30] Acts 2:1-8

inner one was able to see.

Matthew's voice flashed through the room like a stroke of lightning. "Oh Lord, grace us with your Light."

Orion felt himself being emptied. "Like a flute," he thought. Suddenly the crown of his head, then his whole body, was flooded with light. Suddenly he was carrying within him a presence that had no form. A power and Light from within and from beyond. Although his eyes were closed, at one point he could see from a position above. He saw himself. He saw Orion lying on the stone floor, flat on his back with his arms outstretched, trembling with all that was flowing through him. His body contorted sporadically and he made sounds. Time had no meaning in the vast space of overflowing energy and Light.

Orion let the waves of energy flow over him. He could hear people moving and groaning. Some were babbling gibberish. Some were weeping with joy. All of it was muffled background noise to the divine presence that was blessing them all.

Then Matthew's voice sounded as if coming from deep within a tunnel: "Bring the awareness of this inner light throughout your day and among your relationships. Praise the Holy Spirit. We are all brothers and sisters baptized in the Light. We are all beings of Light at our essence."

Slowly Orion became aware again of his hands and his breath. He felt buoyant, alive, renewed. He sat up quickly and looked around the room. He saw everyone disheveled, fumbling, and glowing. Elizabeth looked up and smiled in a way he had never seen before.

Matthew said, "This is the spirit of Jesus, the same spirit within each of us. It is a miracle. I know that as much as anyone. I was a tax collector. I used to study lists of numbers that represented reality. Now I see our deeper reality. When you consciously and energetically enter that doorway, you know what Jesus was talking about. The heavenly realm is here, now."

Orion looked around at those present, his heart open. "This is heaven," he said quietly to himself.

On the way home Orion said to Elizabeth, "Remember the day Jesus arrived, over two years ago, and we were having a picnic on the shore?"

Elizabeth nodded.

"I asked a question. 'Is this the peak of our existence?' You responded, 'Only the gods know.' Tonight I had a glimpse into this knowing of the gods. God is always streaming his radiance upon us."

The following day the same small group of twenty-four gathered once more at Matthew's house. Everyone was still feeling the elation, openness, and connection from the night before. Matthew told them, "We are not separate. There is great strength when we unite our efforts into a collective force. That is why we have come together as community, to nurture this blessing we received yesterday evening.

"While we were traveling on the road, my brothers and sisters and I formed a community that reinforced and nurtured the Master's teachings." He looked at

Orion. "Some have already begun this form of community in Capernaum—for example, Orion and his brothers and also Elizabeth and her sisters. We can build on that. Jesus showed me the strength of relationships. A community such as this one gathered today is a powerful way of reinforcing the Holy Spirit that graced us last night. With your brothers and sisters, the journey to God can be straighter, lighter, more joyous and enlivened."

Matthew picked up a scroll from the table next to him and held it lightly in his hands. "Jesus taught us how to function as a community. A spiritual community will continue to act as he acted and speak as he spoke. When we meet like this, we are basically integrating the Word into action, taking Jesus' teachings into our groups. Everything is possible when you come into community in this way. Listen. This is what Jesus said."

Matthew opened the scroll and read. "'Again, I tell you that if two of you on earth agree about anything you ask for, it will be done for you by my Father in heaven. For where two or three come together in my name, there am I with them.[31]'"

He walked over to his wife Leah, reached down, and took her hand in his. "There is a presence we invoke, a spiritual force that becomes part of our family or community. The group becomes more than the sum of its individual parts. Just as Leah and I generate a force through our union. We can all be uplifted, healed, and renewed by it. That force is magnified when that union

---

[31] Matthew 18:19-20

includes God." Matthew looked lovingly into Leah's eyes, and then returned to the head of the table. "It is necessary in a spiritual community to be open-minded. To get to know each other. To share, to ask questions, to offer insights. Community requires engagement."

Matthew waited for a moment, as if to let the thoughts of the others rise to the surface. He said, "Whenever you feel moved, speak up. Now is a good time to discuss this undertaking."

Orion stood up. His heart was pounding, his breath shortened. He took a deep breath and let go of the fear. "I want to say how grateful I am to my family and to my brothers. They all have enriched me. This group of neighbors came together because of our love for Jesus, and we have that—but we have more than that. Like my family, my brothers are there when I need help. I can talk to them about things of the heart. I could not have imagined how meaningful it would be to have this community, where the joy is more joyous and the pain more bearable. Together we are the fertile ground where the good seed of truth grows."

Others in the room expressed their desire for this kind of uplifting relationship. The decision to move forward with a spiritual community was unanimous.

Matthew was pleased with the decision. "I am convinced that this is the right course of action. In order to help establish this community, I would like to offer a gift. My wife, Leah, our daughter, Inna, and I have agreed to provide this house as the community center. You see, Leah's widowed mother has become frail in her old age and needs companionship. So my wife and daughter will go to live with her in her house near the sea. This building will become our community home."

People in the room applauded and shouted their gratitude. Matthew added, "My first request is that we serve the needy. This was my first duty during the time I traveled with Jesus, and I would like this to continue to be our purpose. Why? Because I have learned that when we extend kindness, concern, and love, we align with the nature of God."

Everyone in the room pledged to give a portion of income, both to serve the needy and to help fund Matthew's travels. Some suggested that they appoint an organizer for the community's work of service. Jude spoke up. "We all know who that person should be. Who better than my friend Philip? He knows better than any of us what it means to blind, poor, rejected, mistreated."

Then Philip spoke. "Well, I would take the job, gladly, if you ask. But I would add something more important to my qualifications as Jude stated them. Not only do I know what it means to be needy. I also know what it is like to be treated with kindness and respect, the way that Orion and his family always treated me, even back before Jesus came into our lives. It is another miracle that I now have the ability to extend that kindness to others."

The shared intention of twenty-four people became its fertile ground, where the seeds of truth planted by Jesus grew in their hearts and minds.

On the walk home, Orion and Elizabeth were both excited to tell the boys about these developments. But the shock of what they found temporarily distracted them. When they pulled back the curtain to their court-

166

yard, they saw Julian lying on a blanket, bloody, cut, and bruised. He was whimpering. Alexander was next to him, washing his wounds with a small cloth.

When Julian saw his mother, his whimpering broke into a sob. Elizabeth cried out and ran to him. Orion and Alexander looked at each other, and the boy responded to his father's silent question. "It was Barak."

"Barak, Isaac's son." Orion's jaw clenched and his fists tightened.

"Remember that time at the lake when Uncle Jude got hit with the slingstone? Barak was in the fight. He's a bully. I get taunted by him, too."

Orion moved to Julian's side. "What happened, son?"

Julian looked at him through his swollen left eye as Elizabeth continued to clean the cuts on his arm and legs. "I was playing along the shore by myself, skipping rocks and humming a song. Then Barak sneaked up on me. He was like a mad dog. I didn't do anything to him." Then Julian started crying, and he wailed and sobbed for a while, the whole time looking straight into his father's eyes. Orion could read the little boy's question there: "Why would someone do that? Why, Dad, why?" Orion felt his heart break, and anger spilled out like molten metal.

"What did Barak do, son?"

"He said… He said, 'Hey aren't you one of those Jesus followers?' I tried to run away, but I tripped. Then he stood over me and yelled, 'People who follow Jesus will go to hell!' I said, 'What do you know? You don't know anything.' But then I tried to get up and he…." Julian gave another long wail. "He punched me."

Alexander asked, "Where did he punch you?"

"In the face!" cried Julian, and then he let go and sobbed again.

"Looks like he did more than just hit your face," said Orion quietly. "You have blood all over the place."

"He pushed me down. I fell down a hill. He kept kicking me. He kept calling Jesus a criminal and that evil one. Then he said I was no better than an animal."

"He is an animal," said Alexander.

Elizabeth held her baby as he cried in her arms. They washed and dressed his wounds. Orion's anger was boiling. After they put Julian in his bed, Orion went to fetch a satchel and a heavy cloak. "Where are you going?" said Elizabeth.

"I'm going to have a talk with Barak and Isaac."

She grabbed his arm. "No!" Her grip on the fabric of his sleeve was relentless, and Orion knew he would not be able to break it. "You understand what's going on here. They want to provoke you. They want you to come out and fight. They know they have Romans on their side. No more blood. Let it end."

"I wasn't going to fight them."

"Orion!"

He knew she was right. Together they prayed to release his anger.

The next meeting took place on the Sabbath. The Jewish members of the new community had suggested that day in particular, happy to realize that they all lived within the walking distance allowed by religious law.

As Orion and Elizabeth neared the community center—that fine home of Matthew with its magnificent date palms, which now in some way was also theirs—they began to walk more slowly.

"I feel as though I'm stepping into the void I saw in Jesus' eyes," said Orion.

"You are," she said.

Orion responded, "We are stepping into the unknown, together."

In that mood, hand in hand they crossed the threshold into the new community center and began to meet the people, many of them strangers, who would share the adventure of forming this new community. Whatever trepidation they might have felt at the threshold vanished almost immediately. Strangers greeted each other with open arms. Lively voices and laughter filled the hall. "Have you met my cousin Jaspher...? Ah, yes, I knew your father. He was a good man.... Why, we buy oranges from your shop every week. Where do you get such excellent fruit...? Four sons and two daughters? Well, the Lord has certainly blessed you. I look forward to meeting them...."

Orion realized that everyone was a little nervous. No one knew exactly what kind of a community they had formed, how it would function. And yet no one held back, no one seemed wary or doubtful.

Eventually Matthew convened the meeting and focused the attention on the one important question: what kind of unprecedented community had they come together to create?

"Within our spiritual community we should seek

to integrate Jesus' teachings. His wisdom should determine our structure, values, practices, and culture. If we align with the One who shines the Light, then our community bathes in that Light." Matthew paused thoughtfully then said, "If the Master were here, he would ask for the participation and involvement of everyone. So I would like to hear from you. Speak about the values that Jesus instilled within you."

Orion stood. Ever since his experience of the Holy Spirit, Orion had felt empowered in his speech, as if something was moving through him. He spoke, with a deep conviction that was echoed in the power of his voice. "The Master planted his Word in my heart. Even though I had days of darkness and doubt, I feel renewed in the Holy Spirit. I have been practicing six of the Master's teachings that, to me, are key values. I would like to share these six with you.

"Part of my craft is to make etchings and designs on leather. I prayed for symbols that would represent the spirit of the Father. That way, my craft would proclaim my beliefs. My work would be more prayerful."

Matthew said, "And your sandals would be walking all over town proclaiming the Word of God. That's very clever of you, Orion!"

"Yes. My sandals would show the Light even if the man who wore them was blind. Here are the six symbols, if you don't mind."

Voices in the group said, "Excellent.... Please show us.... Yes, take them out of your bag!" Orion opened his satchel and withdrew a roll of leather pieces. He untied the strip that bound the bundle and held up the pieces one at a time.

"I call this one 'Intention.' First and foremost, we put our intention on the connection with God. My family and brothers align our focus together in prayer. Our spiritual focus binds us together in common unity. We acknowledge this Light in each of us. This is the prized pearl of our existence. We are all on the same path to the Cosmic Source of radiance and Light. When we worship together, we combine our praise and raise it to our Source."

"This one symbolizes 'Relationship.' We are all interconnected with each other through the Light and its radiance. God is not separate from us. God's radiance is a part of us all. And we are part of it. What we do to others, we do to God."

"Exactly!" said Matthew. "Like the Good

Samaritan, we have compassion for others as God has for us."

Orion smiled, "So when we acknowledge that we are not separate from others, we are expressing our deeper nature. When we are part of a larger community, we are expressing God's nature."

"That's the essence, right there," said a voice. "Could there be anything more?"

"Oh, yes," said Orion. "Look at this one. I call this one 'Diversity.'"

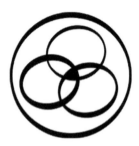

"Because we are interconnected, we must embrace the diversity of the universe. This diversity is born from the mystery of the Trinity, and it is our deeper nature. When we embrace differences, we are seeing the many faces of God. That's why we accept and love all our brothers and sisters regardless of their origin or their faith."

"Jesus did that," said a voice. "He honored the Light in every person and ignored their differences, rich or poor."

"Jew or Gentile," said someone else.

"Man or woman." That was Elizabeth's voice. A murmur of approval went through the room.

Orion held up the fourth piece of leather. "Now,

this design was inspired by the Master's miracles. I call it 'Possibility.'"

"We all possess a creative spark. Because of that spark—as Jesus demonstrated time and again—all things are possible. Before he healed someone, Jesus would always ask, 'Do you believe in the possibility of your healing?'"

"This is true," said Philip. "He asked me that question."

"Yes. Philip is a constant reminder of possibility. Of course, you see how powerful this force is. It flashes with energy. It's moving powerfully. Anything can happen. The outcome is always uncertain."

"That's right," said someone. "Who could have imagined those events in Jerusalem?"

"So we must accept that uncertainty," said Orion. "Otherwise we dampen the power of possibility. That is why trust in God is so important. For in God lies our ultimate possibility."

The room was silent, thoughtful. Then Matthew said, "Believe in the possibility of others. Affirm the greatest potential in each person. Jesus did that for me."

"He did that for all of us," said Philip.

Voices in the room said, "That's right.... He did that for everyone.... This is a new way of seeing...."

Orion unfurled the fifth design. "This one— 'Openness.'"

"Do you remember how Jesus was with children?" An approving hubbub stirred the room.

"If we want to enter the kingdom of the Father, we have to be like children. But what did he mean by that? This symbol represents my belief about that—be open. Be like a child, spontaneous. Don't judge, don't scorn. Forgive. Of course we have to realize that other people can do us harm. We need to be aware of the risks and the realities. And yet we need to take an open stance in all our dealings. Keep that energy of our God-connection flowing in all our interactions. This is why forgiveness, with awareness, is vital to our community."

Another voice: "Stay open to the Father, no matter what."

"That's the idea," said Orion. "Now, here is the last one. We might as well call this one 'Love.'"

"Yes!"

"The emotion that aligns with the Father is love. Love brings us closer to God because with love we radiate the energy of God. Love is emotional harmony with God, and that harmony enlarges our individual power. If we fall out of harmony with God, our power diminishes."

Matthew said, "This love is our greatest mystery. It goes beyond the dynamics of earthly life… an unconditional love."

"Yes," said Orion. "This love is our alignment with God. It transcends earthly relationships and activities, yet it is not separate from them. That deeper vibration of love shines on all, even those who shun the Light… it embraces the darkness."

Everyone was silent. Orion replaced the leather pieces in his satchel and looked around the room. Everyone was looking at him. There was admiration in their eyes, even a bit of surprise at what they had heard. Clearly his symbols and his interpretations had resonated with each of them.

Then Matthew spoke. "The close disciples I traveled with would discuss the Master's teachings in terms of his quotes. But I have heard no one assimilate the teachings like this. The symbols are the Word of Jesus illustrated. These are, indeed, the values that we practiced within our traveling community. You have captured the law of Light."

A general discussion broke out. Then Eva, Marcus's wife, spoke with clarity and strength, "Clans roam the desert. Their greatest strength is their community. The women in those clans share the same red tent when the moon is full and become sisters in their intimate sharing. That is how my community of sisters are to me." She looked at Elizabeth, Leah, and the others. "We share the intimacy of our thoughts and feelings, and we share the teachings of Jesus. It took work to keep our women's circle uplifting. It required awareness and sensitivity to handle upsets. But we all grew through the exchange. In that way we all grew closer to the Light. I can see great possibilities by making the circle larger. My hope is that we will use our relations to grow in Light."

Philip and Jude spoke; so did Simeon's wife, Martha. No one suggested changes to the six symbols, only reinforcing what Orion had shared. The conversation focused entirely on ways to integrate these values in the life of the community.

Then Matthew said, "I will be traveling soon, spreading the gospel to other towns. I will leave in two weeks. There should be three of you who will oversee the community in my absence. I would like you to choose these three. Think about who you want to select."

The congregation nominated men and woman; there was no discrimination. Orion's name came up several times, with praise that made him blush. In his mind he felt excited about the prospects.

In the end, three leaders were selected. Orion came first. Marcus's wife Eva was also chosen; she was articulate and had an uplifting wit. The group also chose Cornelius, a wealthy merchant in his thirties who was respected for his generosity and fairness as well as his good business sense.

After the meeting Matthew spoke to the three of them and Philip. "You are about to undertake a big task in this endeavor. I want you all to question if you can take on the responsibility of this ministry. It means commitment. Can you give the time to minister to others? Think about it. Talk with your families. Your work will be critical to demands of this community. Also, you are aware that Capernaum is a hostile environment for Jesus and his followers. Let me know tomorrow."

On the way home, Orion reflected on the importance of relationships that supported his spiritual growth. He said to Elizabeth, "When we made our commitment to God, that day on the shores of the Sea of Galilee, we did it as a family. Our pattern of praying every day, the reminders and images we keep in the house, your fresh flowers—in these small ways, our family life has helped us keep our spiritual focus without resistance."

"All these things together changed our home and our lives," said Elizabeth.

"The same thing can happen with this new community."

"We know it works."

Orion spent most of the evening talking with Elizabeth and the boys. Should he accept this leadership role? They went over many scenarios, trying to imagine how this decision would change their lifestyle. "I will still be working my craft to support this family. But my days would also involve meetings, teaching, and various demands of the community. Not only that, let's not be naive and think that Capernaum will embrace this community. The opposition that Jesus faced is still here."

Elizabeth and Alexander wanted Orion to follow his guidance and be a leader in the new community. Julian, on the other hand, was uneasy about the whole thing. "Why can't we just be the way we were?" he asked. "I don't feel good about this. It's that gut feeling you talk about dad."

Alexander said, "Your instinct is mixed with your beating. You have a black eye."

"What's your point?"

"The point is, things are different now. We can't go back to the way we were even if we wanted to."

Julian thought about that for a moment. Then he said, "Dad, if you become a leader of the new community, will Barak stop beating me?"

"I would like to think so," said Orion.

"But I doubt it."

"Look, Julian," said Alexander. "What did we decide to do about Barak from now on?"

"Always go in a group with older boys. Don't go out playing by myself."

"There's safety in numbers. Isn't that what the

grown-ups are doing by forming the community?"

Orion said, "Well, nobody has put it that way. But I think you're right."

"See, Julian? It's important. So say yes."

"Yes."

The following day, all four of the Matthew Community leaders agreed to their new duties and vowed to work together. Matthew instructed them to work as a team, using each other's strengths. He made Orion responsible for classes on the teachings of Jesus. Philip would see to the community's work to help the needy. Eva would lead the day-to-day operations and meetings of the congregation. Cornelius was to govern the finances.

Then Matthew presented Orion with a satchel that contained a large scroll. "This is my record of the teachings and deeds of Jesus. I wrote his words as accurately as I could remember them. This is one of only three copies. I want you to use these teachings in our ministry here. But don't let them leave the premises. Protect the purity of these words."

Before Matthew departed, the community came together to say farewell. This time, the children attended. Eva had arranged for a group of volunteers, mostly adolescents and elders, to watch over the children who were twelve or younger. So Alexander sat in the main hall with the adults, and Julian found himself one of the oldest in the children's group. Immediately, he became an outspoken leader of the young ones, almost assuming his father's position among them.

In the main hall, Matthew spread a table with loaves of bread and jugs of wine. He said, "The very last time we ate with Jesus—before his resurrection, that is—the Master performed a kind of ritual using bread and wine. We all found it quite beautiful and a little shocking, as you will see. I memorized his actions and the words he spoke, especially his statement, 'Do this in memory of me.' Now I am going to show you what he did and ask you to participate in this last supper. Please watch carefully. I suggest that this ritual be used by the community to bring everyone together and to remember why we are here."

At the end of this service, Matthew said, "I will be receiving weekly communications by letter from your leaders here in this community. I will write to you as often as I can. There will be other apostles coming through Capernaum. Please welcome them as you would me."

When Matthew left, the life of the community began in earnest. Orion began leading an evening group that prayed and discussed various ways to put Jesus' teachings into action. Meanwhile Philip went right to work to help the disadvantaged of Capernaum. He collected money with which he bought food, clothing, and medicines, and he gave these things to the needy. He brought together work parties to repair broken roofs and to dig sanitation pits. He arranged volunteer teams to visit the sick, the elderly, and those in prison. This work was widely observed throughout Capernaum. People found it most interesting that a blind beggar had become the unofficial minister of charitable works in their town.

At first Philip would joke that he couldn't find enough people to serve. Ever since Jesus had come to town, you just couldn't find many needy people in Capernaum. But the town's position on the trading route soon gave Philip plenty to tend to. Misery of all sorts came to town with the caravans and from the surrounding villages. Many of these downtrodden and rejected individuals asked to join the Matthew Community. Of course the community accepted them all, regardless of gender, race, social standing, or religion. They embraced the diversity of these first converts, not putting one above the other. Women were equal to the men. All were brothers and sisters in the eyes of God. They kept their business to themselves, and they said nothing publicly about their meetings and beliefs.

Rumors began circulating in Capernaum that the followers of Jesus had formed a community.

CHAPTER

The courtyard of the Matthew Community was filled with activity. The entire community was working together, even the children. In the far corner of the courtyard, a new building was taking shape—a room for the young children to use during services and a shelter for those in need. Community members who worked in construction trades headed up the crews. Orion knew a little about roofing, so he volunteered for that group. Once the men got on the roof, Orion realized why he had always felt a sense of recognition about the fellow named Shem, their crew leader. Shem was the one who had once cut a hole through a different roof in order to lower the paralytic to the Master. Later in the day, Orion recognized the paralytic himself, a slender fellow who never tired of carrying hods of clay up the ladder.

Orion spent most of the day on the ground,

planing timbers and preparing clay for the men who were coating the roof. He felt like one of the children, shoveling dirt and shaving the great sticks with a two-handled knife. Shem was a good leader, and they all worked with a smile.

The sun was intense. Orion saw his younger boy hurrying past with a pitcher. "Hey, how about some water here?" Julian came over, spilling water as he ran.

"Dad, it's a real building, isn't it? I've never seen anybody build a building before. I think it's a good one."

Orion looked into his son's beautiful round eyes and said, "It is a good one. You're right. These people in our new community have great skill. I think some of them are the best in Capernaum. I suggest you watch our lead carpenter, the bald man over there."

"Uncle Ezra?"

"Yes. Look how he handles his tools and works with his joinings. This kind of skill is rare. Learn what you can from him before it's gone forever."

After Orion quenched his thirst, Julian asked, "Dad, is this place going to be our home?"

"We have our own home. That will not change. But this is another home, shared with a larger family. We have a lot to gain from the big family."

They were both surprised to suddenly hear a heated argument where they were watching Ezra. Bahn, a fine stone mason was arguing that the floor should be made of cut and polished stone. Ezra wanted wood, and Jude clay. Each believed his solution was the best, and they began raising their voices louder so that everyone in the courtyard turned to the commotion.

Orion instinctively stood on a pile of wood and announced, "Everyone come gather. Take a rest from your tasks. We have a decision to make." After the community gathered, each craftsman presented his arguments to the group. After a short discussion, they decided on the clay tiles for the children's space; it was easier on the knees and no splinters. The community thus started to learn its collective power in resolving arguments.

Work continued. By dusk they were rolling the roof, smoothing the clay surface.

Several days later, Jude came to Orion while he sat with Eva, Philip, and Cornelius on the back porch overlooking the community courtyard. They were discussing plans for the growing community. Jude stood in front of them pensive. "Isaac headed up a group who had an audience with Herod Antipas," then he took a long breath. "The meeting was about our community. They tried to portray us as subversive to the Roman rule. He said that we should all be prosecuted, starting with the community leaders. But Herod saw through it. He told Isaac, 'Jesus was asked to lead a revolt and refused; now you tell me his followers are leading one? I cannot imagine any validity to your accusations. These are families, parents, and children.' Then he dismissed them with annoyance."

Orion said, "Isaac is like a wild dog that won't let go of a bone."

"There is more. He is trying to stir things up in the synagogue again. But most people do not see the threat that Isaac is trying to conjure. The general feeling is that they have struck off the head of our movement, so we no longer pose a threat. Some have distaste for any more violence—particularly those who saw Jesus' torturous death. They want to leave us alone, and they think our movement will quickly die away."

"Let them think it," said Orion. "I'm glad they don't know the truth. We are certainly not dying away. How many members do we have now?"

"Eighty," said Eva.

Jude shook his head. Then he smiled. "You should have seen Isaac seethe when someone asked, 'Why can't our synagogue help those in need, like the Matthew Community does?'"

Orion, laughing, asked, "How did he respond to that question?"

"He said, 'Their charity is attracting beggars from other towns because of the free meals and shelter.' Some people actually rolled their eyes at that—the insensitivity of these synagogue leaders toward their fellow man."

"When he starts seeing members of his own synagogue join our community, that's really going to rile him up."

"He will be scheming to destroy us," said Cornelius. "In his twisted heart, we are nothing but a bunch of dangerous pagans and Jewish subversives who worship an executed criminal. According to him, we are taking people from the 'true' path, a truth he defines. He is a deluded fanatic."

186

Orion said, "He concerns me, all right. But so does his son, Barak. Isaac has schooled him in this disease of the heart. He encourages his son to pick on the kids of this community. He takes pleasure in making them hurt and cry."

Eva asked, "Does this Barak have a mother?"

"Isaac's wife left him several years ago," said Jude. "Shortly thereafter, they found her dead body on the road to Bethany."

"Some mystery about that," said Philip.

"Rumors, that's all," said Jude. "Wicked rumors."

"Well, she was killed," said Philip. "Stabbed by robbers, they say. But the assassins didn't bother to take her jewelry. Could be they had another source of income in mind."

"A hired job?" said Orion,

"Wicked rumors," Jude said again.

"You know, it's not just that father-son team," said Philip. "Let's not forget our dear centurion, Barracus. I keep seeing Isaac and Barracus in out-of-the-way places. They always seem to be shaking hands and nodding."

"How is it, Philip, that you keep seeing this?" said Orion. "Do you follow Isaac around?"

"Every chance I get," said the old man, and gave one of his trademark laughs. "Hee hee!"

"Either way," said Eva, "all we can do is try to grow."

Philip said, "And it's good to remember that we are not the only ones planted with the seeds of truth." The others murmured their agreement. "When the

Master left, he was like a big breeze hitting a ripe dandelion head. Those seeds have scattered all over the country."

"Then we have hope," said Jude.

"Oh, yes," said Orion. "There is always hope."

With Capernaum on the caravan routes and Philip checking on the needs of travelers, it was easy to get information on the spread of Jesus' message. Communities had sprouted in villages, towns, and cities everywhere Jesus' ministers went. There were not only the twelve apostles but also seventy-two ministers who had been ordained by Jesus. Each one of these twelve and seventy-two had a valid claim to authority as a conveyor of the Master's teachings. These ministers, like Matthew, were traveling on routes that took them along the Mediterranean basin, into Africa, and throughout Asia Minor. Wherever they stopped, spiritual communities sprouted and became repositories of Jesus' teachings. In this way, the word sowed by Jesus grew in the hearts and minds of those who were open.

Close disciples were always welcome guests in these newborn communities. One of the most memorable visits to Capernaum came from the apostle Thomas.

Thomas had sent word along the caravan route that he and six companions would be arriving. On the appointed day Orion and Philip waited at the community house. In mid-afternoon the guests arrived on foot, leading two heavily laden donkeys. There were three women in the group. The fact that men and women were traveling as equals was something new. The women didn't bow their heads when they talked to men; they voiced their opinions clearly. How different it was from the Jewish and Greek traditions. Was a new kind of social order implicit in the communities inspired by Jesus? He knew the answer was yes—but to what extent?

Thomas was clearly the center of the group, the one who led from behind. A slender man with black hair down to his shoulders, he looked taller than his six-foot frame. Orion recognized him from the first time he had seen him in Capernaum, during Matthew's memorable celebration. He liked Thomas's piercing brown eyes, his prominent nose and chin, the fluidity of his movements. His entrance seemed to light up the space.

Orion and Philip gave their guests a quick tour of the community center. Thomas was quite impressed with the new construction, the reconfiguration of Matthew's splendid house for putting the Master's principles into action. Then they left their guests to wash and rest before the afternoon sermon.

That afternoon, a large crowd gathered, the largest the community center had ever seen—over three hundred people, some having traveled from surrounding towns.

Thomas began his sermon in this way: "There is a deeper essence within each of us. It is the same essence that comes from God, the source of all there is around us. When you experience that Source, then you know the deeper truth of what Jesus was telling us. When that Light shines through you, you experience heaven on earth."

Like Matthew always did, Thomas carried a satchel containing scrolls. These scrolls bore his hand-written record of the sayings and works of the Master. Now he withdrew a scroll from the satchel and unrolled it.[32]

This is what Thomas read: "Jesus said, 'If they say to you, Where did you come from?, say to them, 'We came from the light—the place where the light came into being on its own accord and established itself and became manifest through our image.' If they say to you, Is it you?, say, 'We are its children. We are the elect of the living father. [33]'"

Thomas set down the scroll and looked at the assembled group. There was a great seriousness to his presence, a natural gravity that contrasted in a fresh way with Matthew's innate levity. Orion was fascinated to see that the same light shone through both apostles. Thomas said, "Everything comes from light. Everything comes from the living Father. When Jesus spoke of his Father, he often used this expression in Aramaic: 'the cosmic birth-place of all radiance and vibration.'" Thomas's intense eyes swept the room as he repeated the phrase. "The cosmic birth-place of all radiance and vibration. This radiance and vibration appears as Light. We are born from this Light. We are inherently connected to this Light. We are children of the Living Light."

---

[32] The Gospel of Thomas, Appendix A
[33] Thomas 50

Then Thomas picked up a Hebrew text from the table at his side. "My Jewish ancestors profess the same understanding. Let me read to you a familiar passage. 'The earth was without form and void, and darkness was upon the face of the deep; and the Spirit of God was moving over the face of the waters. And God said, Let there be light. And there was light.'[34] Thomas set down the Hebrew text and looked again at his audience. "This light precedes matter. It's not part of this physical realm. It is not the light from the sun or other stars, not the light from fire. It is the power of God's first creation. Jesus says that this first Light not only brought forth the Universe but also pulses through all physical forms. It is here and now. It is the essence you see and touch. We are all part of the Light.

"The illusion of separation keeps us attached to the delusion of this world. To break through this illusion at first requires faith that there is a God. Also, we need to hold a conscious intention to realize this connection. We must sincerely seek our connection to the Father. We need to intend it."

Then he read from the scroll again. "'He who seeks will find, and he who knocks will be let in.[35]'" He set down the scroll. "When we are let in, we are made whole. This door is our birthright. We are already connected. It is not that we have to do anything. We simply open a door already present within us. But we must use our will to seek and to knock. God's grace opens it when we are ready."

---

[34] Genesis:1
[35] Thomas (94)

Then he instructed the congregation: "Close your eyes and pray to receive the Light of God. Knock with your intention."

There was a moment of stillness. Thomas said, "Let us all open our hearts and minds to receive the Light of the Holy Spirit."

It happened again. The same overpowering force he had felt in the group with Matthew overcame Orion's body. A powerful energy rose from the base of his spine and shot up to the crown of his head. Separation, time, even the physical realm vanished in God's Light. As a wave crashing on the shore, spilling out white foam and aqua blue, this wave of energy drenched all who were in the room. He heard others letting out sounds of ecstasy and wonderment. There was no time, just the moment. Then the wave receded, and they were all left in the wake—stillness, no mind, no thoughts, but a cellular knowing remained. People slowly sat up straight again and opened their eyes.

Thomas then read another scroll. "Jesus said, 'I shall give you what no eye has seen and what no ear has heard and what no hand has touched and what has never occurred to the human mind.[36]'"

The service ended after a final prayer and blessing. Orion and Elizabeth stayed at the community while the boys went home. Thomas invited Orion to sit with him the following day.

---

[36] Thomas 17

Orion arrived with his satchel holding the six symbols. After they greeted each other, Thomas wanted to know what Orion was carrying. Orion said, "Images. Symbols cut into leather. For me, they represent the essence of our Master's teachings. This community uses them to guide its decisions and culture. I would like to know your thoughts about them. "The two men sat on cushions facing each other, and Orion arranged the symbols.

Thomas smiled. "I've heard rumors about these symbols."

Thomas pointed to the first symbol and smiled. "A spiritual community focuses on the Light," he said. "Excellent. I give you this interpretation of your symbol, in the words of the Master. He said, 'The kingdom of the father is like a merchant who had a consignment of merchandise and who discovered a pearl. That merchant was shrewd. He sold the merchandise and bought the pearl alone for himself. You too, seek his unfailing and enduring treasure where no moth comes near to devour and no worm destroys.[37]"

"That pearl. That's what I see at the tip of your image. That pearl is the grand prize of our existence. The pearl isn't physical, and yet there is no treasure more valuable, and you have drawn a path to it. To merge with the Light of God is the ultimate goal."

Thomas next pointed to the symbol underneath the first, diversity/balance, and he placed his finger on the center where the three rings meet. "There is a balance of the trinity we call God. I remember once Jesus saw some infants being suckled, and he said to us, 'These infants being suckled are like those who enter the kingdom.' We said, 'Shall we then, as children, enter the kingdom?' And he replied 'When you make the two one, and when you make the inside like the outside and the outside like the inside, and the above like the below, and when you make the male and the female one and the same, so that the male not be male nor the female female; and when you fashion eyes in the place of an eye, and a hand in place of a hand, and a foot in place of a foot, and a likeness in place of a likeness; then will you enter the kingdom.[38]"

"What a thing to say!" Thomas placed his finger in the center of the three rings again, "But you can understand it better when you realize that God resides in that deeper core balance."

---

[37] Thomas 76
[38] Thomas 22

Then Thomas pointed to the last figure, "The love that embraces all, good and evil. God's radiance shines on all of us. If we are to be in the Light, we must do the same."

Orion said, "The enemies we have in Capernaum are devious, as you know. I struggle to keep my heart open."

"Some of us are harshly tested. Our great challenge is to love, to love without conditions, to love regardless of the abuse."

Orion said, "I want to confess something to you. If it wasn't for the example and teachings of Jesus, I would have killed Isaac months ago. Forgiveness is terribly difficult."

Thomas then said, "The Master forgave and prayed for his persecutors, even when they killed his body. If we can stay that rooted in love, we transcend to the love beyond the physical."

"There is a question that comes up in my study groups around Jesus' death. Was Jesus a victim of the Jewish leaders, the Romans, or a heavenly plan?"

Thomas was silent for a long time. Orion felt that the apostle's eyes were nailing him into place. Then he said, "If you will be speaking for this community, then you must understand this one fundamental truth. Jesus chose to die; it was the will of the Father. And he chose to die precisely in this way. The reason he did that is not to encourage us to suffer. No. We must not emulate this choice. We must, like children, receive the benefits of his gift. He suffered; therefore, we suffer less." He paused again, then said, "He made a public display of his physical destruction to show us the Light beyond the physical."

Thomas looked at Orion with great compassion. "Orion, you must stay conscious of what the Jewish elders and Romans are plotting in Capernaum. Avoid traps. You have taken on the force that managed to expel even the Master. If they abuse you; don't shut down in anger. Forgive. Keep your eye on the pearl."

Months later, consternation struck the Matthew community. At first Orion had no idea exactly what or why was causing the stir. He arrived at the community center in the late afternoon, having finished his duties in the leather shop, and immediately felt a palpable tension, edginess, among the community members. He seemed to catch the tail end of sharp retorts passing between husbands and wives. Women were clustered together, talking heatedly and then looking around the room, flashing defiant glances. Some of these women had been as meek as lambs heretofore; now their expressions were fixed and fierce, like the lioness protecting her cubs. No one spoke to Orion. "They don't want me to know," he thought. "I'm the parent. The children have been quarreling."

Philip came up to Orion and grabbed his elbow. "We have a new teacher coming to visit! One of the Master's closest friends!"

"Philip, what is going on here?"

Philip leaned his long gray beard toward Orion and quietly said, "Don't worry," he said. "Let things run their course."

"I will, Philip. Thank you for your advice. But I would like to know what these 'things' are."

Philip stepped closer so that his nose was almost touching Orion's nose. "It's all about the new teacher."

"Who is he?"

"You mean who is *she*."

Orion's breath caught in his throat.

"Mary Magdala will be here tomorrow mid-day."

Orion thought about that for a long time as he listened to the voices in the room. The men were talking with the men; the women with the women. Something was brewing.

Mary of Magdala came to the community in the late afternoon. Over fifty people had gathered to greet her, most of them women. Her beautiful features were magnified by the glow she radiated. Tresses of her long red hair draped her flowing white garments and the loose veil that framed the deep, dark pools of her eyes. She could have been in her late twenties, but she had an ageless beauty. Her stride was effortless, like that of the Master.

Her traveling companions included both men and women, and they attended her with the same respect that others had shown to Matthew and Thomas. Without question, she was their spiritual leader. Her gender was irrelevant.

As he watched the visitors interact, Orion remembered something that Thomas shared from his scroll: "When you make the male and the female one and the same, so that the male not be male nor the female female; then will you enter the kingdom.[39]" Jesus had ordained

---

[39] Thomas 22

her, and Orion knew—without knowing exactly how he knew—that the power of the Holy Spirit ran through her.

When the time came for Mary to address the group, she looked at each of them. "What a marvelous community this is," she said. "So many dedicated women and men. Word of what you are doing gives other fledgling communities hope."

A voice from the group, a woman's voice, said, "We are simply living as he told us to live." Another woman said, "The Master taught we are equal, yet the culture says, 'men rule.'"

Feminine laughter erupted in the room.

"Tomorrow I will speak to all of you. But this evening I want to meet with my sisters, and only my sisters. At sunset, here in this room. Does my wish agree with the practices of this community?"

The room was silent for a long time, then Orion said: "You are the teacher; we will follow your wish." He heard some male voices murmuring assent, but not many.

They showed her to her room, where she rested from her travels.

As the group dispersed, Orion found Elizabeth and touched her elbow. "What do you think?"

She looked at him and said, "About what?"

"What are the women saying about all this?"

She smiled. "The women are happy to know that they will meet together as a congregation. There is something sacred that can come from a women's circle. It will feed my spirit."

"I understand what you're saying. Feed the spirit. It's just the same when I gather with my brothers."

"Just the same?" she said. "I don't think so."

"What?"

"It's not the same."

Just then Jude came up to say hello. He offered them figs out of a sack he had brought from home. The two men talked about planting more fruit trees around the community center. Orion remembered the parable of the seeds and producing an abundant crop. "We may as well let every aspect of our community bear fruit."

Jude responded, "I'll get some healthy stocks tomorrow," then left.

Orion turned back to Elizabeth. "What do you mean, it's not the same? How is it different?"

She sighed. "It's just... like that." She gestured with her hand toward the spot where Jude had just stood.

"Like what?"

"Men think about Jesus. They talk about what it all means and make it into something. But women understand Jesus. Our feelings bring a different perspective."

Orion opened his mouth to say something but then he didn't know what to say.

While Elizabeth was away at her women's gathering, Orion sat by the fire with the two boys; it was odd not having her there during this time of the evening. To pass the time, Orion asked, "Do you want to hear a story?"

The boys responded with an enthusiastic "Yes!" They looked forward to these times and would get so caught up in his stories that they would be in a trance.

Orion put another log on the fire as sparks flew. "These sparks honor the Great Hunter I am about to speak of." Julian got closer to the fire.

Using a deep, slow storytelling voice, Orion began, "The Great Hunter was on a quest to meet the Beast of Night in mortal combat. In one hand he held aloft his blazing torch. In the other, his flashing sword."

"Was he afraid?" asked Julian.

"Oh, yes, he was afraid. The howling of the Beast would make anyone's hair stand on end."

"Even yours, Dad?"

"Even mine."

Alexander looked at his father's tightly curled black hair and said, "You would look funny with your hair sticking straight out." Julian giggled.

"But the Great Hunter had no time for fear, and he certainly had no time to care about how funny he looked. Fear or no fear, a hero must do what must be done. He found the hideous beast on a dark moonless battlefield. They fought hard and long. He charged at the Beast of Night and slew it.

"Victorious, he walked away. However, victory was short lived. After he traveled a short distance, he heard the snorting of the beast he had slain. Again he faced the beast, and they fought long and hard."

"Was he tired, Dad?" said Julian.

Alexander said, "Of course he was tired. He already killed the beast and it came back."

"Why does it keep coming back, Dad?"

Orion said, "That's what you're supposed to learn at the end of the story." Orion resumed his storytelling voice. "The Great Hunter rushed at the beast. He knew from experience that the beast's hide was as hard as bronze. So he charged with no hesitation he went right against the breast of the monster, and he plunged his sword right into its rotten heart."

"Ooh."

"How rotten was it?"

"The dark fluid that gushed forth smelled like…" Orion struggled for the appropriate metaphor, "like the open latrine of a caravan."

"Ooh."

"And the beast died. And the Great Hunter left that scene, and he traveled a good distance, but in the night he could hear the beast again. It returned."

"Oh, Dad."

"However, this time the Hunter joined forces with others, for he had made it back to his home. He called together his community; his group was like our community, they practiced the teachings of Jesus. Their community gathered in a large field, they all began to pray, and the Light surrounded them. When the beast entered the space he could barely breathe. The air was too pure. Being surrounded by goodness was too much to bear, for the contrast showed the beast who he truly was. Then he saw the anguished faces of hundreds of people he had killed. The beast felt grief for the first time. The grief weighed so heavy that it went to the center of the field where a spear was stuck in the earth. He grabbed the spear and flipped it, pushing the handle down in the earth with the spear pointing to the sky. The beast extended his arms to the sky asking for forgiveness and to be taken by the Light, and then with a mighty roar he fell on the shaft. The spear went through the beast. As he was dying, the purity that surrounded him consumed him. The Great Hunter slew him in a totally different way, and the beast did not return."

Orion finished his story by placing more wood on the fire. Sparks rose up as if to honor the Hunter again.

"Why did he kill the beast three times, Dad?" said Alexander.

"What happened next?" said Julian.

Now Elizabeth's voice came by surprise from behind them. "What happened next is that the Great Hunter went home and took care of his wife and his children."

"Mom!"

They welcomed her back from the meeting of women with Mary Magdala.

"How did it go?" said Orion. "Can you talk about it?"

"Of course. Orion, I have never met a woman of such understanding. She touched many issues of my sisters."

Elizabeth sat by the fire and enjoyed the warmth in the night air. Then she looked at Orion with a slow, loving gaze. "One of the many things I love about you is the way you treat me as a partner. Even though we have different roles in our household and our community, you treat me with love and respect.

"Mary described the ideal marriage, and I kept

thinking—that's my life. Some women, however, have been treated like slaves. The abuse saddens me. One woman had many bruises." Elizabeth turned to her boys, "When it's your time to marry, don't ever abuse your wife."

At sunset the next evening, the entire community gathered. Orion had no expectations, only curiosity. He had never seen Mary of Magdala as a teacher, only as one who ministered to the many who came to see Jesus. But when he entered the community home, he was barraged with animated expressions of enthusiasm. Everyone had come, and the mood was eager.

Orion worked his way to the cushion provided. The house was packed; so was the courtyard. Then the roar of conversations fell as she arrived. Again she was dressed in white. Her veil was tied tightly around her face. She stood in front of the group with confidence, the expression in her eyes commanding respect. In the silence of their attention, she unbound a scroll and unrolled it for them to see.[40] "This is true," she said. "These are sayings of the Master, his words. While he ministered over the years, I wrote them onto this scroll." Then she began reading.

"Peter said to him, 'Since you have explained everything to us, tell us this also: What is the sin of the world?'

---

[40] Gospel of Mary, Appendix B page xiv

"The Savior said, 'There is no sin. It is you who make sin when you do things that are like adultery, which is called sin.'"

The room was silent as Mary closed her eyes and bowed her head in prayer. There seemed to be a glow around the edge of her garments. Mary's voice again was both calm and strong as she continued to read. "'That is why the Good came into your midst, into the essence of every nature—in order to restore it to its root.'"

Then Mary of Magdala lifted her veiled face and sang in a penetrating, high-pitched chant: "Those who have a mind to understand, let them understand!"

Orion looked around the room. Women were whispering to each other. Men were staring.

The room was silent as she gestured now with the scroll. "These are the Master's words. 'Beware that no one leads you astray saying lo here or lo there! For the Son of Man is within you. Follow after Him! Those who seek Him will find Him.'"

The room swelled with voices as Mary lightly turned the scroll. But when she again spoke with her bell-clear voice, all listened.

"Jesus said this: 'Do not lay down any rules beyond what I appointed you. And do not give a law like the lawgiver—lest you be constrained by it.[41]'"

Mary lifted her head and looked over the group. "Be careful to keep the purity of the Master's teachings."

Suddenly she pulled the white veil away from her face. For a moment her face was naked and shocking,

---

[41] Gospel of Mary, 4:25-39

lean and tight-mouthed but beautiful in a way that disturbed everyone in the room. She said, "They could veil the truth just as the Pharisees have cloaked the Light. Stay with the words of Jesus. His words will lead you to what is within—to the hearth, where the flame can burn at any moment if you ask. It is the essence of nature and the root where all are restored."

Orion reached out and held Elizabeth's hand. Mary of Magdala began to pray by singing wildly in Aramaic. A great rush of energy washed over everyone. There was no denying—Orion had experienced this before with the other apostles. Similar and yet very different. The elation and bliss that followed in the wake was personalized. She was like a beam of sunlight pouring out to all who were open.

CHAPTER

It was a sunny afternoon, aside from an occasional cloud. A light sea-breeze sent freshness into the courtyard of the Matthew Community. In the new shelter, Julian played with friends, kicking a ball between them. Elizabeth and Eva tended the cooking fire. Orion was talking with Philip and two travelers.

"Have you heard news of Matthew or Thomas?" Orion asked.

"I met Matthew in Antioch about a month ago," said one of the travelers. "He has founded another community, like this in many ways. That is where I first heard of the Master and our God-Connection. During Matthew's sermon, I received the Holy Spirit. Now I see the Light. I am traveling to places like this, communities that reinforce the Light in me and in others."

The second traveler spoke. "I have come from the

opposite direction, Africa. On my way through Egypt, I met Thomas, who was traveling on a caravan going to Tripolitania. More than a hundred travelers were camping at the oasis. Many delayed their departure to hear more from this inspired minister of God. He talked of God with such clarity and knowing. One evening by torch-light I prayed with Thomas and his followers. I had an experience that I cannot put in words. But I believe it was a glimpse of God. The experience has changed my life and what I value.

"On my route, I have visited many communities that were born from Jesus' ordained ministers. These communities have been like an oasis in this world. The communities I visited are smaller than yours. They are run out of peoples' homes. They are not as able as you to serve the needy. Each of them uses the resources it has."

The traveler paused and looked around. "To think that the Master was in this room. To think that he started his ministry in this town. Praise God! You are blessed to have actually met him."

Philip and Orion smiled at each other. Orion said, "Yes, I have been blessed by Jesus, by his apostles, and by this community, which is an oasis for me and my family."

Philip added, "Jesus gave me sight of this physical world. He also gave me spiritual sight. He gave that sight to the many people he touched. Through that sight you can encounter the Master's presence no matter where you are."

"Amen," said Orion. The others nodded.

The sun was getting low as their conversation ended and the travelers prepared themselves for a meal. Orion called Julian as he came running from across the courtyard.

"Let's go home, son."

As he walked home with Elizabeth and Julian, Orion said, "It's amazing what happens when you expand your world. Before Jesus, my duty was to our family. But now my family has extended throughout our community and to all who are followers of the Light."

Nine months had passed since Jesus' resurrection. The apparent tension between the synagogue and the followers of Jesus had subsided. Orion and Elizabeth worked at the community center almost daily, cooking, teaching, or ministering to those present. The center had become a second home for them and the boys.

Alexander was less involved in the community because of his business activities. He was very observant young man with a keen mind. A natural merchant, he related well with people, and he was a better salesman than Jude. He took the initiative to carry their wares out of the shop to sell them directly on the caravan route. His passion for the work expressed itself in longer and longer days.

Julian, on the other hand, immersed himself in the community. He became a leader among the children. His excited innocence sparked fun in the activities of all the kids. Being ten years old, he was one of the oldest children of the group that would gather during Sabbath services. He became less timid. An inner strength blossomed as he learned self-confidence and leadership.

A similar inner strength seemed to bloom within all the participants in the community. The more people gave, the more they received from spirit. Eva had the power of the Holy Spirit running through her. She spent more time at the center than anyone. Marcus earned the family income, so Eva was able to concentrate full-time on the community center. She orchestrated the Sabbath services, arranged schedules, and took care of guests who would also talk at services. She enjoyed serving, and she worked with a smile and love. Beyond that, though, she showed a previously untapped ability as an impassioned speaker.

Orion blossomed as a teacher. He developed a unique approach to bringing Jesus' message into daily life. When he facilitated weekly study groups, a large portion of the congregation attended. At these meetings, he developed a natural ability to stimulate introspection and awareness and often brought in science and nature to illustrate the Master's teachings.

Philip was an avid talker and promoter of the faith. His miraculous healing was living proof of Jesus' power, and his enthusiasm and humor were contagious. He would meet every passing caravan and talk about the good news to anyone who would listen. He would extend help to those in need. He often brought sick people back to the community and personally cared for them with the support of other community members. Those who were in need of food or shelter were also invited to the community.

Cornelius managed the rational, business aspect of the community. He oversaw the tithing and the accounting. Through his leadership, the community was generating substantial funds, which went to helping the needy and funding Matthew's ministry abroad. Some of the funds also supported the Jerusalem center, which was headed by Peter. But there were insufficient funds to support the three leaders of the Matthew Community, so Orion continued his work in the leather shop. This was a good balance for him.

Julian began helping Orion in the shop. The boy even began creating designs on leather—not because Orion encouraged him to do so, but because Julian had a genuine interest in craft and artistic expression. Some days father and son would spend hours working together and talking lofty thoughts of spirit. Julian was inquisitive about life, philosophy, and the teachings of Jesus. In this way he was similar to Orion, who loved discussing the teachings of the Master and their significance in his life. They had frequent discussions about Jesus, during which Orion reflected on other religions, each of which had its nuggets of truth. These nuggets reinforced Jesus' teachings. Orion would often dwell on his youthful training in Greek philosophy, the way his own father had done with him. The feeling of continuity and shared passion drew him closer to Julian.

One day Julian was at his own bench not far from Orion when he asked, "Dad, why do people do hurtful things to others?"

"What do you mean?"

"Barak pushed and kicked James until he cried."

"Son, that is a deep question. To answer it, I'm

thinking of two insights—one from the greatest of all Greek teachers, Plato, and the other from the Master himself. Plato said, 'There are two patterns in the unchanging nature of things. One is divine happiness; the other, godless misery. When they do acts of injustice, unhappy people grow less like the first pattern and more like the second.'"

Orion thought about what he'd just said, then added: "Our actions do one of two things. They either bring us closer to the Light, or else they remove us farther away. The actions of Barak bring godless misery on himself."

He finished driving a nail into sandal heel, then continued. "Here is something that Jesus said about the source of hurtful acts. 'The good man out of the good treasure of his heart brings forth what is good; and the evil man out of the evil treasure brings forth what is evil; for his mouth speaks from that which fills his heart.[42]'

"Son, it is important to remember that what we hold in our hearts is not hidden or secret. It can be taught. It can be fed by others. Barak's teacher is his own father. Be careful. Keep a good distance, and don't engage him."

Julian nodded.

Later that day, Philip walked into Orion's shop. Orion stood up from his work and stretched his back.

"The hard-working tradesman!" said Philip.

"Yes, I need to work. It's good for me, and it gives

---

[42] Luke 6:45

me valuable time with my son. What can I do for you, my friend? Not seeing enough of me at the community center?"

"I'm always glad to see you, no matter where." Philip smiled with a shrewd look in his eye.

"What is it?"

"I met a very interesting traveler. An unusual man from India. He is on his way to Egypt. He speaks Greek. You should meet him."

"Oh? Where can I find this traveler?"

"He is resting at the community center."

"I'll be there soon."

When Orion arrived, Philip introduced him to a dark-skinned man who wore nothing but a white cloth wrapped around him in a strange way. His head was entirely shaved except for the white stubble that was starting to surface. He was short with a thin, supple body, wiry and strong from living outdoors. His bare feet looked like leathery paws.

"Here is our newest guest," said Philip.

Orion said, "Welcome as family, for we are all brothers and sisters in the Light."

The dark man's eyes gleamed. "Thank you for your hospitality. Philip has been most gracious. My name is Pradeep."

"Your Greek is excellent. I am surprised. 'Pradeep' is not a Greek name. What does it mean?"

"My name was given to me by my teacher, a master in Sankhya philosophy. 'Pra' refers to prakriti, the ultimate energy that makes our entire physical realm. It is the undividable, which you Greeks call the 'atom.' But prakriti is not a thing, not an object. It is actually energy. At the origin of this primordial energy is the Light. We all come from this Light, which emanates from the one God. So Pradeep means that light-energy. We share this source with all our brothers and sisters."

"The Master said a similar thing." Orion quoted from the record of Thomas "'If they say to you, 'Where did you come from?', say to them, 'We came from the light, the place where the light came into being on its own accord and established itself and became manifest through their image.[43]'"

"Quite so," said the stranger with a satisfied smile. "Shall we sit and talk for a while?"

The three men sat cross-legged on cushions. Pradeep waited, politely allowing his hosts to begin.

"Tell me about this energy," said Orion, "this prakriti. I would like to undertand how it relates to the teachings of my Master."

The dark man from India lowered his eyes and began speaking in quiet but clear tones. "Everything you see is made of energy. Everything physical is actually made of prakriti. This indivisible essence of energy can be shaped by consciousness. This power of consciousness, we call parusha. Parusha, yes. What we intend—the way we think—this is the originator of everything that manifests in our lives. Merging with God, that is our highest possible intention."

"Then we agree," said Orion. "Jesus taught us to love God with all our heart and mind. The love of God is the most important commandment. Jesus used Aramaic

---

[43] Thomas:50

214

to name God 'the cosmic birthplace of radiance and vibration.' Is this radiance and vibration the same as prakriti?"

Pradeep nodded.

"Does prakriti have a behavior?"

"Yes."

"If prakriti is shaped by consciousness, is its behavior, then, a reflection of the consciousness of God?"

Pradeep smiled. "An excellent question! Yes. There is an imprint on prakriti that is the consciousness of God, and this imprint produces the nature of this primordial energy."

Orion stood up. "I will return in a moment. I want to show you something."

In a minute, Orion came back carrying the six symbols he had cut into leather. Each one now bore a Greek word inked underneath. He pulled out the first one. "This image symbolizes our community's intention. It depicts a harmonious focus on our God-connection."

"Yes," said Pradeep, smiling. "It also depicts the manner in which things take form in this world. The subtle energy of prakriti collapses and combines to form an atom. Such a particle, in combination with many,

many others, makes up our world of substance. When we align our focus to the place we have come from"—Pradeep pointed a strong, black finger at the top of the image—"which is also the place we are going, we find a higher energy. We find a place beyond physical form."

"Yes!" said Orion. "Here again I quote the Master, from the writings of his apostle Thomas. One time the disciples asked Jesus, 'Tell us how our end will be.' He said to them, 'Have you discovered, then, the beginning, that you look for the end? For where the beginning is, there will the end be. Blessed is he who will take his place in the beginning; he will know the end and will not experience death.'"

"Quite true."

"When I experienced Jesus in Capernaum, I saw a man who 'took his place in the beginning.' He was immersed in his connection to God, so much so that he seemed to glow. He was conscious of the higher energy of existence."

"And he still is," said Pradeep with a smile.

Orion pulled out the next symbol. "We are all related. Everything is woven together in a complex web of interactions and relations."

"Oh, yes," said Pradeep. "We all are part of this common source. The correct word for this in Sankhya is 'samanvayat.' When we engage in relationships with others, we are touching something sacred and inherent to all life. When we are with others, we are creating an interconnected field that mimics the way every particle comes into existence. We are all a part of a universal brotherhood, which Sankhya identifies as 'eka-vidha.'"

"Like our community."

"Yes. Your community represents eka-vidha."

"When we are in our God-connection, we become inherently more connected with all that is around us."

"The illusion of separation vanishes."

Orion pulled out the third symbol, diversity. He briefly explained the idea of the trinity.

Pradeep smiled, "Nature thrives in its diversity. Prakriti is the seed of the diversity of our physical universe. Within this seed lies the expression of the vast material realm—trees, rocks, oceans, our bodies, and everything we encounter."

He paused for a moment, and Orion began to reach for the next symbol. But Pradeep had more to say.

"Diversity is nature's way. When we embrace the

diverse expressions of humanity, we are embracing the nature of energy."

"The nature of God."

"Yes. That is why prejudice and intolerance oppose the very energy that makes us live. Intolerance weakens any group field. In my homeland, for example, we have a disease that is known as the caste system. Perhaps one day the country will change." Then Pradeep added, "By the way, we also believe in the trinity. The expression of the trinity comes through the three forces we call 'gunas.' Thousands of years ago, Sankhya philosophy used the term 'mulaprakriti' for this energy in its purest essence, in its state outside of our dimension, the three gunas or forces are all held together in a state of balance called 'samyasvastha.' In this state, energy maintains a dynamic balance without undergoing change. But when it enters our dimension, the energy gets expressed as diverse forms."

"What do you mean by dimension?"

"There is a subtler realm that we cannot see, smell, or taste. It is the dimension that Jesus called 'heaven.' We are connected to this realm. But to see and experience it requires a shift in energy, a shift in consciousness, which Jesus mastered. He showed the way to heaven."

Orion then pulled out the next one, labeled 'possibility.' He said, "Like a spark from a flint, life's form and potency are filled with possibility and uncertainty."

Pradeep said, "The spark of Light makes all things possible, even heaven on earth. When we see a possibility, we are seeing the nature of prakriti. When we act with possibility in mind, we are aligning with a primordial force. Energy exists outside of our dimensions of space and time. The vibration and radiance from God is filled with numerous unrealized possibilities for actions. In other words, prakriti is pure possibility. We are literally surrounded by it."

"All things are possible through God. The Cosmic Birther provides a constant flow of radiance and vibration that is possibility."

Pradeep added, "You are wise to say that the twin of possibility is uncertainty. Prakriti has no certainty, 'ekantatah-abhava.' This is nature's way. Each interaction is the unfolding of uncertain possibilities."

"I have a tool that helps me deal with uncertainty. It helps me manifest possibility."

"And what is that?"

"It is my faith in God."

"As I said, you are wise."

Then Orion unfolded the next symbol. "The nature of God is open, flowing. Heraclitus addressed the fluid nature of existence two thousand six hundred years ago when he said, 'You cannot step twice into the same river, for fresh waters are ever flowing in upon you.[44]'"

Pradeep studied the symbol. Quietly he said, "Within groups, as within life, there is a constant process of emergence. An everlasting becoming. The fresh waters of energy are ever flowing in upon every group. This quality of energy puts our world in constant flux. This condition is known in Sankhya to be 'saliavat parinamatah.'" For anything to emerge, it must have openness to its surroundings. It must be able to open to what nurtures it. It must discriminate what does not nurture it. Being fluid and open to change, requires not being stuck in old ways. The rigid framework must collapse."

Orion then showed him the sixth symbol. "This is unconditional love. Our energy can vibrate together with all that is around us. This energy-together embraces everything, even the shadow. I find this quality the most difficult one to hold."

[44] Heraclitus, translated by John Burnet (1892)

Pradeep responded, "The energy that emanates from the Source is always in motion. The motion of this pure energy, the undistorted energy signature, is love. It is a love beyond all conditions. It comes from the Source, before conditions exist. It embraces all, even the shadow. Each person at his essence is the Light of God, always essentially the Light of God, even if they later become lost and fall into the dark side. From what I have heard of Jesus, he even extended love to those who crucified him. He was one with God. He was living God. Therefore, his physical destruction did not sever his connection with God, who is always emanating love."

Pradeep spread all the symbols on the floor in front of him, and he smiled. "The nature of God can be displayed. This is brilliant."

Orion said, "This is my way of understanding what Jesus taught us. He taught us to align with the energy that emanates from God. He said, in other words, here is the way to experience heaven on earth—by aligning with our deeper nature. It shifts our energy. I have experienced this shift within our community. When these six words become values in the group, the group has more uplifting energy. It makes sense. If we align with the nature of God, our energy shifts closer to the Source."

Pradeep and Orion looked at each other knowingly. Then Pradeep stared at Orion, as if seeing through him. His expression changed. The smile left his face. Something else crossed his face, a look of alarm, almost of horror. For a moment, he seemed to cringe. The change shocked Orion. Then, just as quickly, Pradeep resumed a look of equanimity and calm, though now he did not smile. He said, "We all get to discover whether or not we can maintain the vibration of our God-Connection. Some situations require great faith."

He was silent as he looked at Orion.

"What is it, my friend?"

"Some challenges are too big even for the bravest souls." Pradeep looked around him, at the building that now sheltered them from the heat of the sun. "I feel some foreboding."

"About what?"

"About this center. About you."

That evening Orion conducted his weekly class. Pradeep attended. The Indian offered to teach them a powerful practice that would enhance their God-Connection. He taught them about meditation and stilling the mind. He also taught them a practice:

With everyone comfortably seated he called out, "Breath deep, stretch your stomachs. Then he pointed to a place on his lower brow in between his eyes. "This is where I want you to focus. When you close your eyes, draw them to that spot. I will lead you through the next steps.

"Take long, deep breaths; close your eyes. When you are on the right spot you can feel a pressure, a force. Now welcome the Light into your third eye. If thoughts come up, let them go and bring the focus back to that spot."

Orion immediately felt the force and became bathed in the radiance from the source.

"At that place of focus, our major energy channels merge," Pradeep explained. They begin at that point, or else they end at that point—depending on your perspective. At that point, unity and duality meet. If we visualize a thought form while holding that attention, we empower that intention. We feed the form with subtle energy because it's where unity meets duality, where the subtle energy shifts to the physical realm. Now if we hold an intention for the highest, our God intention, it becomes empowered."

Afterwards people lingered, asking many questions. It was late when Pradeep finally went to bed. He did not sleep well that night, feeling restless; he sensed something sinister was brewing. He felt his own safety was in peril if he stayed much longer.

The following morning Pradeep came to Orion's shop. Orion said, "Did you sleep well, my friend?"

"I did not. I was restless. I cannot stay any longer."

Orion frowned, but he would not contest Pradeep's mysterious ways. He took the man's hand and said, "I wish you good fortune on your spiritual journey, brother."

Pradeep clasped Orion's hand with both of his own. Very intently, he said, "I have an uneasy feeling about your future. Be careful. Be aware of those who wish you ill. Stay strong in your God-Connection."

Pradeep left Capernaum with the very next caravan to Egypt later that day.

Matthew returned four days later. He had been away for nearly five months. The community celebrated the return of his presence, which was somehow more radiant and magnetic than ever. He was able to impart the blessing of the Holy Spirit, and the words he spoke were filled with conviction. Although his stay was brief before departing for Jerusalem, he baptized many new converts. Twelve families from the synagogue were among those who joined.

Aaron, the former head of the synagogue at Capernaum, was one of the reasons for this growth. His shocking defection stirred up the dying embers of opposition in the synagogue. Aaron was considered by many to be a saintly man; everyone knew that the bogus charges about stolen money had been a set-up. Erez, who had taken Aaron's job, was a poor replacement, incapable of providing Aaron's insight and presence.

The faithful who attended the synagogue realized that the scheming of Isaac had deprived them of what nurtured their spirit. Although they did not speak openly about this to the synagogue hierarchy, they did talk among themselves. The situation was comparable to what had happened with the leather shops. Isaac had convinced them to leave Orion, who was a high-quality craftsman, to patronize the shop of his cousin, Bishmehoth, who was incompetent. Once again, they were getting a bad deal. People spoke openly about following Aaron's example. There was mutiny simmering at the synagogue.

Erez and a group of synagogue leaders felt they must end this drain of members by stamping out the Matthew Community. In their delusion they felt it was their calling to protect their religion. It was their holy war to stop this threat. They all agreed to pitch in some money to pay Baraccus. Then Isaac selected four men and one teenager—his son Barak. The plan was simple: burn down the buildings of the Matthew Community. They had two who were assigned as lookouts, two who would spread oil, and the last to set it ablaze. They even worked out a strategy and practiced it in the dark.

On a moonless evening, a rare night with no guests sleeping at the center, Philip awoke to strange noises in the courtyard. He got up. When he looked out from the darkness he could see three men. Two were carrying large jars, splashing the contents on the walls of the children's building. Then he recognized the one with the torch as the light illumined his face—Barak. The flames danced on the torch he carried. As he lit the fires, he paused to enjoy the sight of the flames as they engulfed the structure. Philip slipped out the back window and hid outside behind some construction material. Within minutes all the buildings were ablaze.

There was nothing that could be done except to assure that the flames spread no further. Philip got behind the courtyard wall, alarmed the neighbors, and stood in a gathering crowd as he watched the fire. The only water Philip was able to muster came from the upwelling in his eyes as he watched his beloved community collapse in the brightly glowing flames.

That night Orion and his family were awakened by Jude, yelling, "The community houses are on fire!"

Everyone dressed and ran toward the structures, their second home. As they ran, they could see the glow of the fire and smell the smoke rising. Orion thought of Philip. He knew that the old man had stayed the night at the center. So when Orion arrived at the scene, he was relieved to see Philip standing in the road. Everyone gathered around Philip, and they gripped each other and cried loudly as they watched the fire take its course. When Julian saw the children's house cave in, with sparks flying high into the air, he broke into inconsolable wails.

"What happened?" Orion shouted over the din.

Philip said, "There were three in the courtyard who started the blaze. I recognized only one, Barak."

Julian overheard. He looked up at his father with tear-filled eyes. "Why would they do this? We have done them no harm!"

Orion grabbed his hand. "People do terrible things in the name of religion."

When dawn light brought its first gray recognition to the ugly black smoking heaps that had once been their home, the community gathered in a great huddle to pray. They prayed for the community and for the rebuilding of the space. Elizabeth, Orion, and Alexander joined the others in sifting through the charred remains. Julian couldn't bear the thought of touching the ashes of loss. Too distraught to remember his promise to his family, he felt compelled to leave this area. So he headed off toward the shore with his friend Timothy, who was a little younger than Julian.

The two friends walked about a half a mile from town along a high ridge, where they could see the entire town. The boys stared at the smoke rising from the pile of ash that had once been their community dwellings. They were in a focused stare, unaware of what was lurking near them.

The boys were startled when they heard someone in back of them. They spun around, and there was Barak. A pang of fear shot through Julian. Feeling cocky from his success the night before, Barak was ready to inflict more misery on others. He knew that these boys were in his clutches. Like a beast after his prey, he could see and smell the fear that came over them when they saw him.

Barak called out: "The followers of a devil, a dead criminal. Why don't you go play in your playground, in the ashes?" Then he let out a laugh.

Julian's defiance came up. "You were one of them who lit the fire! Someone saw you. You will get your due for your deeds. Evil is in your heart."

Barak sprung out at Julian. In a quick motion, the bully was within arm's length of Julian. "You can't prove a thing," he said. The prospect of prison brought up fear. He had heard stories of Herod's dungeons. As it was with his father, Barak's fear turned into rage.

He pushed Julian as the boy staggered backwards. Julian pleaded, "Leave me alone." But Barak advanced and hit him in the chest. Timothy was also yelling at him, but Barak ignored—no, enjoyed—the pleas of both boys.

Barak's anger shot through his chest, pooling in his fist. With the rage of a pent-up bull, he let go a blow that caught Julian on his cheekbone. The blow lifted Julian off his feet, and he flew backwards—backwards in the air over a steep ledge. Down, down he fell to a loud thud. He laid still on the rough rock surface thirty feet below.

Timothy was frozen with terror. Then he ran to the edge, only to see Julian still in a pool of blood. When he turned toward Barak, he saw that brutish figure charging toward him, black against the morning sky. Timothy ran like a deer. He stumbled twice. Both times, Barak came within gripping distance, but Timothy yelped and wriggled out of reach and ran again. Quickly he gained distance on his pursuer, and then Barak gave up the chase.

Barak walked back to look over Julian's body, which he kicked out of the frustration that his misdeeds would now be revealed to others. Without the least bit of remorse for his actions, he ran to his father. His only concern was his next move. At home, Barak told Isaac what had happened. Isaac gave his son some money and told him to travel to Bethany, where he had relatives. Isaac would send for him later, after things settled down.

Near the center, Timothy found his mother, Rachel, who was on her way home to fetch some tools that would help with the clean-up of the ruins. He sobbed his story to Rachel, and the stout woman ran to the center, shouting for Elizabeth and Orion. Timothy ran alongside. She shouted to him: "Get Jude and others to come." Timothy darted away, not sure where to go.

Rachel ran up to Orion and Elizabeth and blurted out, panting, "Something happened to your little one! It's very bad! Barak hurt him. He attacked my Timothy, too. Come!"

A flash of fear shot through Orion. "My son! Take us there, hurry!"

Timothy came running, with Jude and Marcus and several others pursuing him. "Where is he?" shouted Orion. "Take me to him."

Outside of town, Timothy pointed toward the ridge. Orion pushed Timothy out of the way and ran faster than anyone, all the while praying to God, "Let him be flooded with your Light. Protect him with your heavenly hosts." He got to the ridge well ahead of anyone else and blundered around, looking desperately everywhere. Then he looked over the ridge-edge and saw his doom in a glance—the pathetically broken body of his son, lying inert on the stones, blood spread like a pillow beneath his head. Roaring like a wild beast, he dashed down the slope and picked up Julian's lifeless body. He wailed terribly. Then he was frozen, his mouth agape in a silent howl that would not come forth. And then he wept, rocking back and forth with Julian clutched to his breast.

Elizabeth's screams were heart-breaking. She seized her son's body out of Orion's arms, and she bent over the still flesh of her son, screaming like a mad woman, kissing his face and his shoulders and his chest and his hands. She then threw her head back and screamed at the sky. Then she worried over the boy's body again, frantically muttering, "My baby, my baby, come back, come back. Oh, he's still alive!" She put her ear to his chest and heard nothing, nothing at all. and she buried her face in his chest and screamed the most pitiful sounds anyone had ever heard. By now Orion had turned to the side, his back bent like a slave, his head buried in his arms as he emitted the most agonized sounds that a man can make. Others gathered around and knelt by them, encircling them with useless arms as both parents let the blood of their dear son flow over their arms.

After a time, Orion raised his head and saw Alexander standing there, numb and shocked. "Come, my son," he called. Alexander dived into his father's arms, and the two wailed together.

Finally, when he was able, Orion came fiercely alive to the reality of the moment. He realized in a flash that Julian had left, that he was now on a journey from the body into the Light. He looked up at those gathered about—Jude, Rachel, Marcus, others who were running to the scene. Orion became focused on his son's transition and not his loss, "Let us pray for Julian on his journey from his body. See the Master greeting him and leading him to the Light." The community prayed out loud for Julian, for the bright spirit who had blessed them all with his presence. Orion realized that there was nothing more he needed to say, that the community would say it for him. And so he just sobbed as though he was vomiting out all the pain it was capable for a single person to feel.

That night Elizabeth and Orion held each other, crying and praying. He said, "I want to lash out at Barak. At Isaac. I want to crush those bastards with my hands."

"No!" Elizabeth shrieked. "I have lost my son. I will not lose my husband, too. Baraccus and his garrison will crush you."

"They have crushed me already."

"They haven't crushed you. They haven't crushed me. Only you can crush me."

Their words were wild, lunatic. There were no words for this. Eventually Orion settled into the silence of a mortally wounded beast who waits attentively for the next necessity. He knew that he had not reached the end of it.

The Matthew Community had its own responses. Everyone stopped by the house to say kind but futile things. Julian had been dearly loved by all of them. Many spoke about taking the law into their own hands. They knew that Baraccus was on the take from Isaac; therefore, justice would not be carried out. When he heard them speak of these things, Orion said nothing. He could feel the poison of hate come into his body. His body constricted as waves of this anger consumed him.

He tried with all his might to remember Jesus' teachings. He seemed to babble to himself, "Love my enemies. Not the destructive emotion. Let the love from God consume me. The love from God. Take the appropriate action." But he couldn't remember exactly how the principles of love applied in this situation. All day, the struggle of love and hate pulled at him.

By the end of the day, Orion felt as empty and numb as though he himself was a corpse. He didn't know why exactly, but he knew he needed to walk. He needed to be by himself, to let his mind look in quick, flinching glimpses at the new reality—that he no longer had a son named Julian. The reality of that fact was more than he could bear except in small, shocking sips. Elizabeth was lost in her own grief. When others attempted to follow him, to be his companion, he told them he needed time alone. Not seeing or feeling anything in particular, he walked to the shore and began to head west. He picked his way along the shoreline, noticing how flat and dead the sea looked. "Is this the same sea where the Master quelled the storms and shined the light? It is empty now. The Master is gone. So is my son. Emptiness rules the water."

He walked well beyond the town activities. Now there was no one between him and his pain, nothing but the rawness that seemed to be screaming from every cell of his body.

So the sounds of two men's voices ahead, just the other side of a spit of land, made him slow down and consider going back. The thought of going back hurt terribly.

"I tell you, I have paid you good money. And for what? For this!"

"I have provided the services you purchased."

"This is not about buying certain services. This is about doing a job. Getting it done, fast."

In a flash that sent blood rushing to his head, Orion recognized the voices. He was listening to Isaac, who was working his influence on the Roman centurion.

"Any means to that end!" he heard Isaac say. Orion flattened himself against the head-high projection of rock that separated him from those two. Emotions, like a great wave, smashed against him.

"What do you expect me to do?"

"Finish this once and for all. You don't want a civil war on your hands. You don't want to have to explain why—even though you had clear, early information about an uprising within your jurisdiction—you did not crush it out immediately."

"These people have not broken a single law. They are not fighting."

"They will be fighting! The people of Capernaum are rising up against them. You saw what happened today. The people torched their headquarters. More rioting is bound to come."

"Who set the fires? How many people?"

"Nobody knows."

Orion shifted around stealthily until he could actually see the two of them. Isaac had a heavy pouch in his hand, and he pushed it into the centurion's chest. Baraccus took the pouch in both hands and opened it, ogling the coins. Isaac threw up his hands and turned to the side. Baraccus turned, spear in hand, and walked briskly away, taking the footpath away from the shore where no doubt he had tied his horse.

Isaac took the shoreline path with his slow, hobbled gait, going west, toward Orion, not far ahead. His head was down. His bulky frame stumbled on the rocky path. Here was the man who had conspired to kill Jesus, who had somehow killed Julian. Rage flashed through Orion. He scrambled uphill and made a detour around Isaac's position on the path. He took a position leaning against a boulder. He watched the old man shuffle toward him, head down, no doubt calculating the cost of his latest maneuver. At the point of contact, Orion stepped into the path.

Isaac saw instantly that he was trapped. So he stiffened his body and moved forward. With each step that Isaac took, Orion felt his anger pulsing higher. The old Pharisee's attention was necessarily on the ground, but then he glanced up to see the intense stare on Orion's face. Instantly, Isaac left the path and started shuffling through the bushes as though he wanted to reach a nearby knoll.

Orion yelled out, "Where is Barak? What is your hand in the death of my son?"

"Get out of my way. I'm not answering your questions."

Orion advanced, and Isaac climbed higher.

"What is your hand in the destruction of my community?"

Isaac then produced a small whistle made from

bird bone, and he blew a shrill high note that penetrated the entire landscape. He scrambled a few steps higher and began waving and beckoning in the direction just taken by Baraccus. He blew the whistle again, then made emphatic "come back" gestures.

Orion just stared, perhaps apathetic about what would happen next.

Isaac hobbled back down the hill and took a stand well beyond the reach of Orion.

"Blame your Jesus for not raising your son from the dead. As for my son, Baraccus is not going to prosecute." He let out a deep laugh. "The world is better off without another pagan."

Something snapped inside Orion. The floodgates of emotion burst open. There was no rational mind, no other inner voice, except the wish to kill this monster and scourge of humankind. There in front of him was a rock the size of a closed fist and round.

When he held the rock in his hand he had a moment of hesitation. Then a wave came over him. His rage and intention flamed down his arm and into his hand, and the rock he held became infused with his rage. He planted a back foot and cocked back his right arm. Then he shifted his weight into a forward lunge— accompanied by a mounting yell from deep inside the navel—and he willed this stone to make contact with the skull that was housing such evil. Even before the stone left his hand, Orion knew it would hit the mark some thirty feet away.

The projectile sped through the air with no arc. Like a lightning bolt from his hand, the stone made a direct hit on Isaac's temple. There was the sound of hard nut cracking, of a clay bowl falling onto the earth. A spurt of blood confirmed the hit. He was already unconscious on his downward descent, a descent that would go beyond the physical. His stretched-out body fell back. The first body part to meet the earth was his head, and this was greeted by a pointed rock. The back of Isaac's head split open, and he lay still except for the stream of blood meandering with a hissing sound on the sun-hot rocks.

After an almost inconsequential moment of enjoyment, Orion said out loud, "Oh! My God, what have I done?" He ran to Isaac. There was the old man, broken in much the same way as Julian had been broken. The sense of retribution turned to vomit in his mouth. Then he saw Baraccus running toward him at aggressive speed, with spear lifted over his shoulder. "Halt!" yelled the centurion. "I saw you strike him down."

The instinct of self-preservation took total control of Orion's body. He turned and ran like the wind. Even though Baraccus was running hard, he still managed to smile. It had been years since he had killed anyone, and now the hunt was on. This was what his years of training had honed and acknowledged—a killing machine. He enjoyed this.

As Orion ran, he prayed. "O Lord, forgive me. Give me another chance to serve you on this earth." He ran like a rock skimming over a flat pond.

Baraccus was considered to be the best spear-thrower in Galilee and Judea. Some of the local Greeks had nicknamed him "Apollo"—curiously enough, after the god who was nemesis in the mythic tale of Orion. Now Baraccus had the living Orion within his accurate range, a hundred feet, and he knew he would get no closer at the pace Orion was running. So he cocked back his spear arm, taking long sideways strides, as his left hand pointed toward his target. Then he twisted his body, flinging his right hand forward and launching the spear. The momentum of his run and the thrusting of his legs and torso gave extra power to the spear. He released—"wooosh!"—then ran a few more steps to absorb his forward movement. Then he stopped to watch his projectile heading toward his prey.

Orion knew he was in grave danger. He thought of Elizabeth and her warnings. "Please forgive me." Then a burning sensation penetrated his back, and he heard the sound of cracking ribs. He couldn't breathe. As he fell forward, he saw the spearhead jutting from his blood-drenched garment. There was no pain, just paralysis, just the inability to move and breathe. Just the gurgling sounds of blood flooding his lung. He prayed, "O, Father, forgive me. Protect my family, my spiritual community. Jesus, Father, give me another chance to prove my worthiness."

Then the life left his body.

CHAPTER

What was not extinguished was the light of Orion's soul. Orion, like his mythic namesake, had been struck down in his prime, yet he had earned his first star. Of course, he did not meet the requirements for the second star—to love and forgive his enemies just as Jesus had. Such brilliance is difficult to achieve, though the number of stars scattered throughout the night sky suggests that many have done so.

While Orion's soul was in that timeless space, he saw that he would return to earth. His prayer for another chance would be answered in a universal heartbeat—some twelve hundred years in Earth time.

On the physical plane—in Capernaum and the regions being settled by Christianity—cause and effect continued to operate with the energy of a spinning planet, where time was absolutely determined by the regular pattern of turning toward sunlight.

31 AD Capernaum shifted the day Orion died. No one was really sure what had happened that afternoon, but they were sure about their profound loss. The grief that hit the Matthew Community only brought them closer. The following day, a stream of well-wishers stopped by to see Elizabeth and Alexander. Later that evening Jude, Marcus, Philip, and Eva sat with Elizabeth in her courtyard. Elizabeth felt raw, violated, raped of her former life. But in its place, beyond the framework of her shattered family, she found love, support, and empathy.

She told them: "The grief I felt for the loss of Jesus was changed by his resurrection. We were all changed. So I know where they are. They are with the Master in the Light. And I feel certain that Orion will come back to fulfill his goal of God realization." Then her mouth contorted into an open cry, but no sound emerged. Terrible sobs began to clutch her throat. "But I am so sad. I have been stabbed with a dagger in my breast." As she finished this comment, her voice rose at first into a spasm of crying and then into a loud, full-throated wailing that rang in her courtyard.

Within a week Baraccus was moved out of Capernaum. Herod Antipas wanted to cut down on the bribes and corruption that were lowering his tax revenues. This business in Capernaum clearly showed that Baraccus was playing one faction against another, no doubt for his own personal reasons. Baraccus admitted that the northern borders were better suited for him— plenty of barbarians to pursue and little need for diplomacy. He enjoyed the new assignment for a brief period.

Then he was captured by an army of hairy German savages and treated to the same slow, agonizing death that he had inflicted upon hundreds of others.

Over the months Elizabeth got more involved in the community, and Jude became a mentor and supporter for Alexander. As the injustice of what had happened came to light, the community grew stronger. Quickly they constructed a new community facility. Engraved on the facing of the cornerstone and on a marble slab that was part of the archway for the main door were the six symbols from Orion. These symbols served as the cornerstone of values that united this diverse group. They became fundamentals of the first Matthew Community.

The strain between the Jewish and Christian communities continued. When Aaron replaced Orion as the community spokesman, many synagogue members left to join the Matthew Community. Rivalry, judgments, and mistrust were the currency of exchange between the Jewish and Christian Communities. For thirty years the division quietly grew, never escalating again to the point of arson and murder. But when these two tense religious communities erupted again, the explosion topped anything seen before.

Capernaum was not an isolated case. Communities had formed in towns and cities throughout Roman rule, each one founded by an apostle or by one of Christ's closest disciples. The Master had ordained twelve apostles and seventy-two disciples. Together these men and women were the repository and messenger of Christ's teachings. Nearly all of Jesus' teaching had been delivered verbally. The only media he used for writing during his active ministry was the sand. The apostles and Mary Magdala were clearly the most authentic word about those marvelous things the Master once said and did.

50 AD Spiritual communities were founded throughout the Mediterranean Basin and as far away as India by Jesus' close disciples, including Peter, Matthew, Mark, John, Mary Magdala, and Thomas. Converts who had never met Jesus also built communities. The most successful of these, of course, was Paul. Each community had a founder who embedded a philosophy and creed based on his personal experience with Jesus and his interpretation of the Master's teachings. These communities often began with just a handful of people and sprang up in the homes and courtyards of ordinary people, determined believers in Jesus and the power of a spiritual community. They would invite a teacher and set up services for visiting apostles or disciples. They would hold weekly services and help the needy in their area.

The majority of the teachers traveled from community to community. Some stayed in one location and ministered to those about them—Peter, for example, resided in Jerusalem. His community became the primary center for this growing Christian ministry. Each community evolved differently. For example, the Thomas and Matthew communities had much in common; however, they were very different in philosophy and culture from the Paul and John communities. The Mary Magdala community was very different from the more traditionally Jewish community led by Peter. Thomas communities predominated in Syria, Mesopotamia, and Egypt, while the Paul communities gained strength in Italy and Greece.

There was no dominant strain of Christianity. Some followed the Torah; others did not. They still considered themselves either Jew or Gentile. They embraced a wide range of customs and cultures. And yet they all had basic elements in common. They were community hubs often run in private homes, where the needy could come for assistance and where members of the community would congregate. They followed the teachings of Jesus and demonstrated spirit through their daily acts. Many were willing to pay the price of persecution. Each had a cultural cornerstone written in the gospel, or many gospels, which it revered. The community in Capernaum adopted the gospels of Matthew, Thomas, and Mary Magdala. The gospels shaped the cultures of these growing communities.

60 AD As these communities grew and spread, so did their clashes with other religious groups. The authorities demonized this new religion. Roman emperor Nero in 64 AD played his fiddle while Rome burned, and he blamed the blaze on the Christians. Afterwards he cleared the burnt-out slum and built himself the new palace he had long wanted. Forces of the empire hunted the Christians and put them to death in barbaric ways for the entertainment of its citizens.

Shortly after in 66 AD, the Great Revolt erupted in Palestine. Violence caught up the Jewish population throughout the region. In Capernaum many Christians refused to take part, calling it a Jewish war. The friction between Christian and Jew intensified until finally the two groups turned against each other. During the 66-70 AD conflict, Capernaum was largely destroyed—not by the Romans but by the residents.

The Romans punished the Jews throughout the land for this rebellion. They destroyed the temple in Jerusalem, killed over one million people, and sold nearly that many as slaves and gladiators.

100 AD Christian groups declared their allegiance to specific apostles or disciples, claiming him or her as their spiritual founder. The gospels chosen by the community became their link to the Master. Some claimed to have secret knowledge from Jesus.

With the founders no longer alive to rebuke claims, who really knew what was truth or distortion? The Christians of the Thomas gospel claimed that their patron apostle understood more than Peter. The John Christians called their apostle "the beloved disciple of Jesus." John challenged the claims of the Peter Christians, and he confronted the Thomas Christians. The entire movement became contentious.

The Thomas and Matthew communities were put under the heading of "Gnostic," which basically meant "wanting to know." The Gnostics tolerated different religious beliefs and did not discriminate against women. They believed that God was within each of us and that their community was dedicated to supporting their God-Connection. They revered their gospels and simply adhered to Jesus' teachings. In some regions, the Gnostic movement was the primary form of Christianity. But it did not predominate. Paul communities took the lead, flourishing in many urban areas.

Although Christianity considered itself a single religion, it can best be described as a complex network of individual parties, groups, sects, and communities. Some of these communities clashed.

120 AD The battle was most contentious between the John and Thomas communities. In fact, the John community adopted one of old Isaac's favorite weapons—lying in order to discredit the other view. By 120 AD the John community had produced its own gospel, one that deliberately attacked and discredited the teachings of Thomas and his followers.

The gospel of John is the only gospel that portrays Thomas in a negative light. It casts Thomas as the only apostle not empowered to forgive sins. It portrays him as the "doubter" who was chastised by Jesus for his lack of faith. The following is from the gospel of John, chapter 20:

24Now Thomas (called Didymus), one of the Twelve, was not with the disciples when Jesus came. (When Jesus anointed them to forgive sins) 25So the other disciples told him, "We have seen the Lord!" But he said to them, "Unless I see the nail marks in his hands and put my finger where the nails were, and put my hand into his side, I will not believe it." 26A week later his disciples were in the house again and Thomas was with them. Though the doors were locked, Jesus came and stood among them and said, "Peace be with you!" 27Then he said to Thomas, "Put your finger here; see my hands. Reach out your hand and put it into my side. Stop doubting and believe." 28Thomas said to him, "My Lord and my God!" 29Then Jesus told him, "Because you have seen me, you have believed; blessed are those who have not seen and yet have believed."

Another passage portrays Thomas as being lost, or at least unsure of the way:

John chapter 14: 5Thomas said to him, "Lord, we don't know where you are going, so how can we know the way?" 6Jesus answered, "I am the way and the truth and the life. No one comes to the Father except through me. 7If you really knew me, you would know my Father as well. From now on, you do know him and have seen him."

In the gospel of John, Jesus makes an incredible proclamation: "No one comes to the Father except through me." The implications of this statement are profound. In John's approach to Christianity, the only way to reach God is through Jesus, and the only way to reach Jesus is through the lineage of his ordained ministers. Philosophically, this stance allowed the John community to position itself as the anointed descendant, the only one that could forgive sins, the single authority over salvation, and the gatekeeper of the kingdom of God.

This attack on the Thomas communities found strong supporters in the church hierarchy, which was determined to consolidate the young religion. John's approach was useful to church leaders because it empowered them through these claims in the gospel. But the sharp contrast of John's gospel from the gospels of Matthew, Mark, and Luke deserves scrutiny. John's is the only gospel that discredits the Apostle Thomas and elevates Jesus to the role of necessary intermediary between people and God.

In Matthew, Mark, and Luke, Jesus talks frequently about the kingdom of God and hardly at all about himself. In John, by contrast, Jesus talks a lot about himself and hardly at all about the kingdom of God. For instance, Jesus uses the word "kingdom" eighteen times in Mark, forty-seven times in Matthew, and thirty-seven times in Luke, but in John the word comes up only five times. He uses the word "I" nine times in Mark, seventeen times in Matthew, and ten times in Luke; in John "I" appears one hundred and eighteen times. And the differences are not just statistical. When Jesus uses the word "I" in Matthew, Mark, and Luke, almost all of his self-references are of a conventional kind. In John, by contrast, Jesus regularly makes staggering proclamations about his own importance: "I am the bread of life," (6.35) "I am the light of the world," (8.12) "I am the way, and the truth and the life," (14.6) and "Before Abraham was, I am." (8.58).

Thus, the gospels of Thomas and John are poles apart, philosophically. John empowers Jesus and his heirs as the only way to salvation. Such a religion, therefore, requires a hierarchical organization that claims to be the intermediary of all people's God-Connection. Thomas focuses instead on each person's connection to the Light.

180 AD Irenaeus, the bishop of Lyons, played an important role in consolidating the Christian movement. He strongly opposed any philosophy that empowered individuals over the authority of the church. Therefore, he rejected the gospel of Thomas, in which Jesus suggests that we have spiritual resources within us, that we are made "in the image of God." Irenaeus warned his flock to despise "heretics" who spoke like this, those who "call humankind the God of all things, also calling him light, and blessed, and eternal." He argued for the acceptance of just four gospels, including of course the gospel that most closely aligned with his philosophy— the gospel of John.[45]

With John's gospel as its central doctrine, the young church sanctified an authoritarian approach. Priests and bishops could claim to be the living repre-

---

[45] Beyond Belief, Elaine Pagel pp.87

sentatives of Jesus. The only way to enter heaven was through the church. Religion took ownership of each person's heavenly connection. Certain men elevated themselves to the powerful status of God's chosen representatives.

The community at Rome exerted broad influence in the ancient church. Irenaeus himself looked to the bishops of Rome as guardians of true Christian doctrine against the heretics. For him, the living tradition of a Christian community founded by an apostle was even more important than the written scriptures, and Rome was the primary example of such an apostolically founded community. The bishops of Rome embodied the continuity of faith from the apostles.

The Thomas communities felt that religion should not be centralized and dogmatized. Thus, the divide between certain Christian communities continued to widen.

300 AD At this time there were more than five hundred and fifty Christian communities in the Roman Empire.[46] The landscape of the Christian movement at this time was still diverse; it still reflected the diverse ministry of Jesus himself, who made no discrimination among those who were truly seeking. His true legacy was about seeing beyond differences, about seeking the very thing that transcends all forms—our God-Connection.

But now certain political developments worked against this legacy. Constantine had taken over Roman

---

[46] Sittengeschichte Roms II, pp. 540-43

rule from his father. He had to struggle to maintain control of the far-reaching empire. He never swerved from his ambition to eliminate all rivals and to become the sole ruler of the Roman world. He saw that the Christians would be good allies, as their community locations coincided with the empire borders. *(See map.)*

In 313 AD Constantine passed the Edict of Milan, establishing toleration of Christianity. Ten years later Constantine—who until then had granted the Christians parity with all other pagans—now came out openly in their favor.

In 325 Constantine decided to demonstrate his authority by convening an Ecumenical Council at Nicaea. The purpose of the council was to settle doctrine debates that were separating many of the Christian communities. The council formulated the Nicene Creed, which was accepted by all but two of the delegates. The Nicene Creed defined Christ as sharing the same substance with the Father.

Meanwhile, a cleric named Eusebius undertook the task of uniting the Old and New Testaments into a single document that could be approved for all Christian communities. His selection criteria for the gospels were historical: Had the gospels been used by previous generations? Did they show a consistency of style? Did they agree with established church views? Adherence to that last question guaranteed the selection of the gospel of John and the rejection of the gospel of Thomas. The New Testament took its present form—four canonized gospels and twenty-one epistles that were sanctioned by

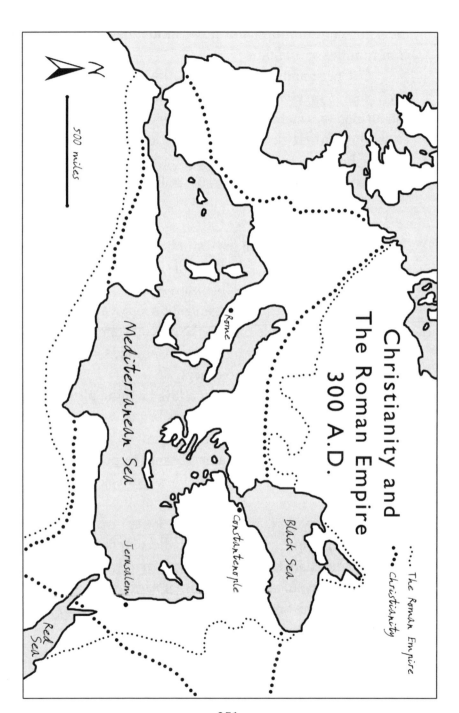

Christianity and
The Roman Empire
300 A.D.

500 miles

Mediterranean Sea

Rome

Jerusalem

Constantinople

Black Sea

Red Sea

····· The Roman Empire

••••• Christianity

the Paul communities, the most influential of all the communities at that time.

In Christianity's early years, the main issue had been mere survival. But when Christianity became established as a state religion, its main concern changed. Now the church needed to defend orthodox dogma against heresies that kept springing up like so many mushrooms in the more favorable political climate.

360 AD The Roman Catholic Church became empowered through the backing of the Roman Empire. Claiming to represent all Christians—"catholic" means universal or whole. This organization enjoyed certain tax incentives available only to the official state religion. This status empowered the Roman Catholic Church to impose its own dogma onto others.

Later the church enforced a law banning all Jesus texts that it had not approved. Thus began a campaign of mass destruction against the unapproved writings of Jesus' close disciples. It became a crime to possess any text deemed heretical. Offenders were punished by the government. In this way, all copies of the gospel of Thomas were eventually destroyed—except two.

Monks in Egypt treasured the diversity of the original Christian texts and housed them all in their libraries. But in 367 AD the bishop of Alexandria issued an order for the monks to destroy all such writings, sparing only those of our present New Testament. However, monks at the monastery of St. Pachomius gathered dozens of the texts to be destroyed and hid them in a heavy six-foot jar. This jar was buried in a cave on a nearby hillside. They also took a smaller jar, hid three texts within it, and dug it down along the outside foundation of the monastery.

380 AD At the First Council of Constantinople, 381 AD, the bishops of the church concurred that the bishop of Rome should have the "first place of honor" (or "primacy of honor") among them. This act formalized the hierarchical structure and one central bureaucracy.

Now began a long period of Ecumenical Councils, at which Orthodox Church leaders established the framework for their united religion. They virtually eliminated groups who opposed their philosophy and beliefs. The Thomas and Matthew communities, for example, empowered women. They did not genderfy the God-Head. They encouraged the Light to shine within each individual. Worst of all, they did not want to empower a hierarchy. So of course they were branded as heretics, and their leaders were excluded from the ruling council of bishops.

The Ecumenical Councils dogmatized certain questionable beliefs: that Jesus is God; that there are only four canonized gospels, that Mary the mother was a virgin at Jesus' birth, that the Bible is irrefutable. Other doctrines followed: the Holy Lands should be wrested from the infidels, the Pope is infallible…. This dogma has served to obscure the Light. The church that emerged from these councils bears little resemblance to the primitive Christian communities formed by Jesus' closest disciples. The new dogma distorted the simple truth of his gospels.

460 AD The fall of Rome ushered in centuries of chaos—invasions of the empire and the establishment of independent principalities in Western Europe and Africa. The Roman Catholic Church became more and more the cultural center of the Latin-speaking world. At some points, in fact, the bishop of Rome found himself to be the only civil authority in the city of Rome. In this historical climate, the church began to acquire extensive properties and civil authority.

The papacy was established in Rome. The Pope acquired absolute authority on matters not only of theology but also of civil rights. Church and state, Empire and Papacy, became indistinguishable. This joint power led to great abuses of political as well as theological importance.

The seductive appeal of such an authoritarian religion is that it makes us want to believe the doctrine we are being fed. For example, we find comfort in the belief that heaven waits in the afterlife and that our religion provides a guaranteed entry ticket. Do this, obey that commandment, get this reward—in this way, religion potentially lulls the individual into delusion. Unquestioned, such a religion becomes a cruel prison of rote, ceremony, and images that form a lifeless shell.

This is not to suggest that the early church had no enlightened beings, no saints. There were many. However, history shows that the purer, simpler truths of Jesus were hazed over by the imposition of hierarchy, dogmas, and riches.

1200 AD Great saints like Francis of Assisi transcended the church's enforced limitations. Francis broke church mold by directly integrating the teachings of the gospels in his order's culture and practices.

And yet, just as there were sparks of Light, there were also dark shadows cast. The Inquisition, charged with the task of eradicating heresies, became a permanent institution in the Catholic Church. Beginning in the twelfth century, Church councils required secular rulers to prosecute heretics. In 1231, Pope Gregory IX published a decree calling for life imprisonment—along with salutary penance—for any heretic who confessed and repented. Those heretics who refused to repent faced capital punishment. By the end of the decade the Inquisition had become a general institution in all lands under the purview of the Pope.

The judge, or Inquisitor, could bring suit against anyone. The accused had to testify against himself; he had no right to face and question his accuser. The Inquisitor accepted testimony from criminals, persons of bad reputation, excommunicated people, and heretics. The accused did not have the right of counsel. Blood relationship did not exempt one from the duty to testify against the accused. Sentences could not be appealed. Various means, primarily ingenious forms of torture, were used to get the cooperation of the accused. Death was administered by burning at the stake, and the execution was carried out by secular authorities. Regardless of the outcome, whether death or prison, the church confiscated the defendant's entire property. Abuses occurred, all under the guise of religion.

1300 AD The Franciscan Order gained in popularity. Its fundamental purpose was simplicity —to live according to the teachings of Jesus as recorded in the gospels of Matthew, Mark, and Luke.

In this context, Orion was given another chance to earn his second star, to be a bearer of Light.

PART THREE

The Franciscan Monk

The bearer of Light has come back to a distant place and time...
1300 AD; Toulouse, France. With twenty million inhabitants,
France is the most powerful nation in Europe. The French
pope Clement V has changed the location of the papacy to
Avignon in southern France. Some two hundred miles to the
west is Toulouse, a thriving city, where the bearer faces his
next test.

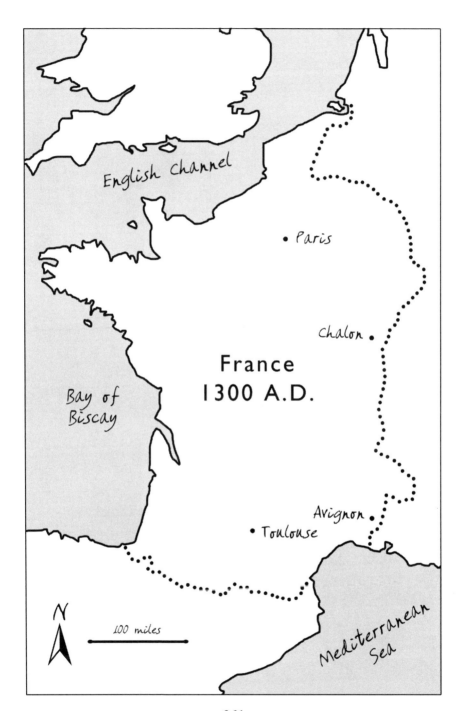

English Channel

• Paris

Chalon •

France
1300 A.D.

Bay of
Biscay

Avignon •
• Toulouse

N

100 miles

Mediterranean
Sea

CHAPTER

Jacob lay in deep sleep, dreaming about a distant land along the shore of a large body of water. It was a happy dream. In it, he lived in a simple house with his wife and two boys. Then the clanking of a bell began to pull him from this distant life, this illusion. The high ringing of the bell pulled him back into his body. Now, once again, he could feel the boards under his back and legs, the warmth of a worn blanket draped over his body. The echo of the bell bounced off stone walls, lingered for a while, then grew fainter as its source moved along to other corridors.

He pulled off the blanket and swung his legs over, noticing the stiffness in his lower back. After a year in the monastery, his body still missed the feather mattresses of his youth. But when his bare feet hit the cold stone floor, the sudden shock felt almost pleasant. He rubbed and stretched his back.

The stimulation of cold water on his face brought him back fully into his body. Last remnants of his dream vanished. Every morning since he had joined the Franciscan order, his first prayer had always been the one given by Francis himself. Jacob said the prayer aloud as he stood at the basin splashing himself with cold water:

Lord, make us instruments
of your peace.
Where there is hatred,
let us sow love;
Where there is injury, pardon;

Grant that we may not
so much seek
To be consoled as to console;
To be understood
as to understand;
To be loved as to love.

Where there is discord, union;
Where there is doubt, faith;
Where there is despair, hope;
Where there is darkness, light;
Where there is sadness, joy.

For it is in giving
that we receive;
It is in pardoning
that we are pardoned;
And it is in dying that we are
born to eternal life.

Amen

The life of the Franciscans was simple and dutiful. Every day began with vespers. Jacob slipped on his robe. The roughness of its coarse fiber always reminded him to search deeper than his skin for the source of true peace and solace. As he walked down the passageways to the chapel, the other novitiates greeted him with their eyes. They knew this was an important day for him. And yet they walked in silence.

Jacob stopped in the courtyard and took a moment to gaze up at the stars, something he had always loved doing since his early childhood. He located the constellation Orion. The three stars on Orion's belt brought a deep familiarity that he could not describe. The sparkling and cool, crisp air on his skin woke him to the liveliness of the moment. But he couldn't tarry. The bell to start vespers was about to ring.

He made his way into the chapel, a simple stone structure whose walls seemed to vibrate with God-connection. Moving into his pew, he knelt in prayer. He felt an excitement inside when he thought about tomorrow, the day of his ordination.

Then vespers began. The sound of the men's voices filled the chapel. The deep cadence of their Latin verses echoed off the chapel walls and reverberated hypnotically. "Dominus excelsus… " He was lifted by the vibrations of the chanting. Everything else melted away. He felt at one with all about him and perfectly focused on God. In that state, he reaffirmed his choice made just over a year before, to renounce the privileged life of his youth.

In his previous years, Jacob had been well known around Toulouse. For him and his band of friends, life had been a series of merry gatherings. His joy for life had been contagious. The others admired him for his insights. A Greek scholar, he enjoyed quoting philosophers in his discussions. He loved to dance and flirt, and he had cultivated a reputation as a "lover of life." A handsome fellow with curly brown hair, he was considered one of the top eligible bachelors in the region. Everyone recognized his pedigree—his father's wines were considered the best in the region.

Jacob was the only son of the wealthy Laurier family, which owned a large vineyard and winery on the outskirts of Toulouse. His father had always assumed that his heir would eventually take over the property and business. And yet the parents were kind-hearted people who always supported their son's personal desires, even when these desires conflicted with their own. This tolerance, however, had been severely tested when Jacob announced that he was renouncing their way of life—a life that most people in Toulouse envied.

The decision to give himself to God had struck him in a single day, as if without cause. That moment, over a year before, arrived when Jacob climbed to his favorite place on his father's land—a high rock outcrop with an old shade tree. He had brought with him a book of Plato. It was a cool autumn day. Mist lay heavy in the vineyards, and the crystal clear sky promised that tonight would bring the first frost of the season. He knew that this weather shift would usher in change, the death of the old and rebirth of the new.

While he leaned against that tree, a surge of energy shot up his spine to the very top of his head. He saw an inward Light that somehow connected him to a vastness that he had not realized, yet seemed familiar. He became aware of a presence that emanated from that Light. The energy took over his body and he became a witness to what was happening to him: crying, animal sounds and movements. After a while he became still; he could not move. Then this thought struck him like a clap of thunder: "God is nothing like what I thought. God is an experience that is always there to embrace—an energetic experience, an awareness." He felt as though something from the past had surfaced. A truth was reawakened. He knew that his feelings were irrational—they had nothing to do with his comforts and his inheritance—but he could not doubt them. He wanted to shout from the rooftops: "God is real!" Instead, he chose to stay in prayer, keeping his focus internal. In that stillness a deep connection opened again. He vowed to follow the guidance of the Light from that day forward.

Heretofore, his primary focus had been the winery, women, and Greek philosophy. Jacob had great appreciation for life's variety and an exuberance for living. He enjoyed the finer things; he admired beauty. Yet when the Source of that exuberance and beauty was revealed, it shifted his focus, without effort, without regret. Actually, the way Jacob saw it was that he had no choice.

Now his primary focus was his God-connection. As he looked for an environment that would support his new intention, the Christian monastic orders stood out—specifically the Franciscan order. There was something very familiar about the Franciscan community, which followed the teachings of the gospels with simple devotion. The words of Jesus were the way of the order, nothing more.

After prayer and reflection, he decided to enter the Franciscan order and leave the life that now seemed shallow and unreal.

Let go of his wealth and embrace the life of a monk? Many of his friends thought he had gone mad. After all, he had what most of them could only dream of possessing—and he was renouncing it? This made no sense. His parents pleaded and the neighbors made comments, but Jacob saw that he had no choice. He had to follow this inner calling.

At first his father questioned this "awakening" and debated his decision. But when he finally saw Jacob's resolve, and saw how greatly the boy had changed since his awakening, the old man blessed the journey with tears in his eyes—tears, for he knew he was letting go of his own dream to see his legacy continue beyond his own life.

Now, as a novitiate, Jacob was being groomed to teach. This path was inevitable. Even the Rector, who heard him debate other monks on philosophy, thought he was brilliant. This was an era when great universities were beginning to blossom in France, stirring up an appetite for Greek thought. So there was a need for such teachers. Jacob was a natural to fill the bill.

Next to Jacob knelt Bertrand, the chief librarian. Bertrand was his mentor, assigned to Jacob because Bertrand himself was a brilliant teacher.

Monasteries such as this one in Toulouse were stockpiling all the literature that had survived the Dark Ages. Bertrand knew that his job as librarian had historical importance. His monastery had been actively building its library for the past seventy years.

Fully aware of Jacob's skills, Bertrand had assigned the young man to the duties of organizing and translating their Greek literature. The task brought Jacob excitement and wonderment as he read and analyzed the texts. In doing this work, he was exposed to innumerable ideas that lay outside the Christian framework. The treasure of Greek books included works by Plato, Aristotle, Homer, Heraclites, and Pythagoras. There were books on sacred geometry, the alchemy of metals, and the mystery of self. But the new information did not trouble Jacob's Christian faith. Far from it. The study of other philosophers simply deepened his appreciation for the truths of Jesus. He and Bertrand spoke often of these new insights.

Privately, Jacob realized what he was searching for—the truth about the Light he had experienced. To him, it had been a tangible experience, a blessing from the Holy Spirit. The gospels of Jesus shed the most understanding about his experience. But these ancient Greek texts elaborated portions of Jesus' teachings and regard them from different angles—just as the large quartz crystal at the university, with its six sides, provided six different perspectives of the same crystal. For this past year Jacob had been consumed with exploring Jesus' teachings from different perspectives. He found that the simple, focused life of the monastery made it much easier for him to live the gospels and teachings of the Master.

Jacob's enthusiasm and sincerity endeared him to the other monks. When his time had come to be assessed for initiation, he was voted into the order unanimously. Now he stood at the doorway of his ordination.

Jacob knelt, responding with the other brothers "et cum spiritu tuo" as the final blessing of the service. The brothers proceeded to breakfast. Jacob stayed kneeling in his pew, hands folded, eyes closed. He could hear the shuffling of feet as they left this place of worship. Today he would be given a day off from his normal duties, a day to reflect and pray about the vows he would take. While deep in prayer, he connected with the experience that had changed his life forever. One year and a few months… a lifetime ago.

Jacob felt deeply in his stillness. His long, deep breaths grew still and quiet. He felt the Light within and without. He knelt for hours in this unmoving posture.

Then he picked up his worn bible and read carefully each of the three gospel passages that had guided Francis in developing the guidelines of the order. First of all, his choice was to be a commitment for life. He read, "What therefore God has joined together, let no man separate.[47]" He had joined with God at the moment of his awakening. The second joining would be his ordination. "…let no man separate."

Next he considered the second guideline, the commitment of celibacy. Again he read from Matthew: "For there are eunuchs who were born that way from their mother's womb; and there are eunuchs who were made eunuchs by men; and there are also eunuchs who made

---

[47] Matthew 19:6

themselves eunuchs for the sake of the kingdom of heaven. He who is able to accept this, let him accept it.[48]" If celibacy would support his focus on the Light, Jacob knew he could accept it. His sexuality was strong, but he chose not to feed that energy. He chose not to form competing connections to anything physical. Let his God-connection be his lover!

But he did think about what he was leaving. He thought about Catherine, a joyous figure, a wonderful dancer, beautiful with black hair and big brown eyes. Once they had talked about spending their lives together. He loved kissing her, and he enjoyed her wit; she would be a great mother and wife. But all of that had changed in a flash of Light.

Then the third guideline, the task. The journey. This time he read from Luke: "And He sent them out to proclaim the kingdom of God and to perform healing. And He said to them, 'Take nothing for your journey, neither a staff, nor a bag, nor bread, nor money; and do not even have two tunics apiece.[49]'"

Since his awakening, he had ceased caring about the physical world. But he did dare to consider the abundant life handed to him by his father. For a long time, Jacob wrestled with the realization that he was rejecting his father for a new relationship with the Father. He understood that the Father would bring even greater abundance than anyone could amass on the earthly plane. And yet his sense of duty plagued him for several hours until he finally placed that too in perspective.

[48] Matthew 19:12
[49] Luke 9:2-3

He turned again to Matthew: "Simon Peter answered, 'You are the Christ, the Son of the living God.[50]'"

The son is like the father. Jesus expressed the nature of his Father. Jacob would do likewise, no matter what. The gospels of Matthew, Mark, and Luke would be his guide, as they had guided Francis of Assisi. Ultimately, he would be guided by his God-connection, the Light that had brought him to this new form of life.

Jacob's day of silence and reflection ended with him going to bed. In sleep, he experienced standing along the shore of a large body of water, walking through a large crowd of people who wore the garb of an earlier era. He sat in the warm sand, and there on a makeshift platform appeared Jesus. The Master's gaze slowly swept the crowd. He seemed to give a glow. Then a bell began to toll, and Jacob awoke slightly, struggling not to lose every tang of his dream images.

That day, the day of initiation, Jacob made his way to the chapel with five other novitiates. The chapel was packed with people; many stood in the aisles and stood outside the door and windows. The presiding head of the diocese of Toulouse, Cardinal Chapelle Taillefer, was there to preside over the ritual. His gem-like vestments glittered in astonishing contrast to the simple robes of the monks.

---

[50] Matthew 16:16

These shining, costly garments gave Jacob a profound hesitation about the vow he had come to make. Other commitments implied by his vow, even celibacy, had not seriously shaken his resolve. But here at the last possible moment, he realized that he had not given adequate reflection to a matter of serious consequence—the contract he was about to make with the Holy Catholic Church.

He saw in a flash what his own beliefs were—that the hierarchy of the church had drifted away from the Light, that the simple truths of Jesus had been manipulated and ignored, and that politics, abuse, and twisting of the truth were all part of the church hierarchy. After a hard battle, Pope Clement had managed to move the papacy from the Vatican in Rome to Avignon. The shifting of the enormous bureaucracy has been a huge expense. Money and power governed the Roman Catholic Church.

During the past year, whenever Jacob had been serving the needy, he couldn't help but notice where the financial support had come from—most of it from private donors such as his father. Hardly anything came from the deep treasuries of the church itself. The richly clad prelates offered little more than their blessing. Suddenly Jacob realized that he was surrendering his life to a system that thrived on exactly what he was rejecting—wealth, comfort, and the exercise of worldly power.

"And yet I have no choice," he thought. "This is what God has given."

In the crowd he glimpsed many of his old friends, young men with whom he had spent many idle hours in the taverns of Toulouse. They stared, whether in admiration or disbelief he could not tell. They regarded his handsome features. They saw him kneel before the Rector and the cardinal with an intensity of focus. They now witnessed the finality of his choice.

Jacob knelt, head bowed, while the Rector clipped his curly hair, preparing it for the shaving of his crown. The voices of the monks and the feeling from the chants praising God gave an emotional completion to the finality and rightness of this lifetime commitment.

Jacob had joined a monastic order not bound to a cloistered life within the confines of the monastery. The Franciscans and the Dominicans constituted mobile striking forces that the church could utilize wherever necessary. The cardinal would orchestrate movement throughout his entire diocese. For this reason, Jacob's first assignment as a monk was to preach on the street corners of Toulouse.

One spring day shortly after his ordination, Jacob walked with Bertrand up the main road into Toulouse. The early morning warmth radiated from a bright sun that was just now clearing the tall stone buildings of the town. Horses, carts, and foot traffic all pressed around them as they approached the city gates. This activity heightened to a roar once they entered the city's confines.

Jacob felt nervous. In his youth he had often passed by preachers babbling on street corners. They were an annoyance. But he remembered a few great preachers—Brother Alfonse, for example, who spoke of truths that resonated with the Greek philosophers he studied and admired.

Bertrand pointed to a corner and nodded. "This is a good place for you to start." As people raced irritably past the corner, a horse paused to relieve itself with great abandon. An old woman, shrieking obscenely, was flinging rotten cabbage at a younger woman who shouted back at her. Bertrand sighed. Then with great sobriety he said, "We all have to start somewhere."

"Of course," said Jacob meekly.

"Let's stop at this vegetable stand." Bertrand addressed the attendant of the vegetable stand, a gnarled old man with a habit of spitting vigorously. "My good man, can we borrow a crate until this afternoon?"

The withered fellow pointed angrily to one at the edge of his stand. "You bring it back when you're done. And no preaching in front of my stand! You'll drive away my customers."

"Then we will preach across the street," said Bertrand cheerily. "In that way, we will drive people toward you!"

Jacob grabbed the box. "God bless you," he said.

"Hasn't happened yet," cracked the old man, and he continued to stare with hostility at the two well-shaven monks.

They walked across the street and placed Jacob's lecture platform along the side of a building. Bertrand said, "Let it come from within. I will be back to see how you are doing."

As Bertrand disappeared into the crowd, Jacob stood up on the box. How to begin? Weakly he said, "Brothers and sisters, I have come to tell you some good news." No one stopped. Jacob realized that his voice was soft, that he was extending his own fear and discomfort. "I have come to tell you of a better life." People walked by as if being annoyed by his presence, as he himself had done in the past. One person smirked, "Do your preaching in your church!"

For the next two hours, the only satisfaction he felt was the sight of people, avoiding him, crossing over to look at the produce at the vegetable stand. "Well, at least I'm paying for the loan of this crate," he thought to himself.

When Bertrand came by to check on him, Jacob said, "I have experienced fear, frustration, and humility—no, humiliation. Bertrand, you are such a great preacher. How do you do it?"

"Actually, I don't do a thing," said Bertrand. "I let my passionate connection with God be my focus. Then it just comes through. Let go. Let God be your focus—not the reactions or thoughts of others."

They prayed together. For an instant, Jacob felt the faith and conviction that had led him to this place. Something moved through him and uplifted him. He shifted from fear to an almost reckless overflowing with the message of Jesus. When Bertrand left, he once again climbed onto his puny platform.

"I have come to tell you about the Light," he shouted. "First I will read to you from the gospel of

Matthew. 5:16 'Let your Light shine before men in such a way that they may see your good works, and glorify your Father who is in heaven.' These are the very words of our Master. Let your Light shine. This Light shines in each of us and comes forth in our good deeds."

Then he saw someone walk past carrying a crate of wine from his own father's winery. He pointed and shouted to the milling crowd, "Even a winery, such as the one that made that fine vintage, is nothing compared to the wealth that the Light brings to us all. I have come to beg you. Ask God to reveal his Light to you. If you sincerely ask, it will be granted. We are God's children, and He will answer your calls. If you seek the Kingdom of God on Earth, it will be revealed—in its own time."

Then he lost himself. He simply poured himself into expressing his passionate feelings about certain texts and their meaning. A few people began to gather, then more. People who recognized him from before stopped to listen, at first feeling pity for Jacob. Then they noticed a light shining through him.

Bertrand stopped by later and grinned. There was no way he was going to approach Jacob or interrupt his experience. The young man held a small crowd spellbound, fielding their outcries and complaints, and firing challenges back at them. Even Bertrand had rarely seen such an inspired and passionate performance. He knew in a glance that his student would soon outdo him.

In time, Bertrand chose his moment and elbowed his way through the crowd. He walked directly to the crate, put one arm around Jacob's waist, and said,

"Come, brother. Enough for today." Jacob came off the cart holding Bertrand's arms and stood there for a long time, trembling with a powerful energy.

Over the weeks Jacob's talks became widely noticed. Crowds jammed his corner, attracted by the drama of this fiery young fellow's performance. Soon he was being asked to give sermons in rural churches.

At this time, universities were growing throughout Europe. Moreover, the translation of Aristotle and other philosophers into Latin was challenging the narrow ideas of many Christian scholars. Any scholar who could see ways to integrate these foreign ideas with the core beliefs of Christianity was welcome to get involved in the risky business of university teaching.

The universities of France were founded and supported by the papacy in Avignon. Naturally, therefore, the teachers at these universities came primarily from the seminaries and monasteries. These clergy helped assure that the dogma of the church would be followed and taught. So clergy scholars with Jacob's potential were quickly receiving university posts.

The university at Toulouse was impressive for its time, with sprawling buildings connected by garden pathways and courtyards. Rose brick buildings presented impressive arched doorways and windows. There was a buzz of young students in dialogue heading to classes. The large stone structures and groomed grounds distinguished it from the rest of the city—here was an intellectual environment, a stark contrast to the uninterrupted squalor of the Dark Ages. Here Jacob felt at home. He began teaching Greek philosophy, and his research involved correlating Christian scriptures with older texts from the pre-Christian enlightenment.

His quarters at the university were modeled after the simplicity of the Franciscans. He spent at least three nights a week at the monastery, preferring the communal support of his brothers. He continued working with Bertrand, who supplied him with ancient Greek texts. He had his assistants and students to work on translations. With the routines of prayer and religious services, his life was very busy.

During his classes he would often refer to the gospels of Matthew, Mark, and Luke. But he never referred to the gospel of John. Even though the church still relied on John to form and reinforce its dogma, Jacob's intuitive sense told him not to build assumptions on this manuscript.

In his lectures Jacob spoke clearly, logically, and with passion about his topics. Lay people came to his classes, of course, but also clergy, who were hungry for his insights on the gospels.

Jacob's classes grew in popularity. After the first year, a waiting list formed as his rooms bulged to capacity. By his second year as a professor, he was given the largest rooms in which to conduct his classes.

Although he was very busy, he always took time to visit his parents. His father had become very proud of his son's accomplishments, particularly at such an early age. But the old man still hoped that Jacob would take over the business he had worked so hard to build. "Son, please reconsider," he said on one visit. "You could become a lay professor and still teach at the university while you oversee the winery. Besides, the staff is very competent. The winery actually runs by itself under their care, and...."

Jacob stopped him in mid-sentence. "I cannot do this, father. My fate is cast as a monk. Be at peace with my decision. Did you remove me from the will as I asked?"

Sheepishly his father responded, "No, I did not."

Jacob handed him some sheets of parchment and an ink brush. "I have renounced worldly possessions. Please remove me from your will."

As he watched and gave orders, his father transferred all assets to his wife, then after her to the foreman and to his remaining brother. Then they all signed it. Only then did Jacob feel that the matter was done.

During one visit he found his father very ill. As the old man's health deteriorated, he gave one last plea for Jacob to leave the order and take control of his business. Jacob lovingly refused.

Not long after, Jacob gave the eulogy for his father.

Later, he visited his grieving mother as often as he could, given his monastic and scholarly duties. Jacob's mother was proud of her son, the man of God and professor. At the same time, she was torn with grief. She wanted him at the vineyard, she wanted grandchildren, and she longed for his company now that the death of her husband had left her alone.

During this period, the Toulouse monastery sent monks to foreign lands as missionaries. One of the mandates for brothers from the Toulouse Diocese was to locate literature that would build the repository of knowledge they were housing in their monastery. While in Egypt, two monks came across three ancient texts.

One day, Bertrand issued an urgent summons to Jacob. When Jacob hurried from his duties at the university, he found two unknown monks in the library with Bertrand, standing tall and smiling proudly as they spoke of their find. "We got to know a Bedouin clan," they explained. "There are great similarities in the teachings from their master, Muhammad, and Our Lord Jesus. Their customs and interpretations may differ, but the deeper message is the same. While we camped with them, another clan joined us for several days. At their time of departure, the leaders of this clan came to us saying, 'You are supposed to have this.'"

"What?" said Jacob. "What did they give you?"

"These three scrolls," said the monks, setting the brittle artifacts carefully on a small table inlaid with mother-of-pearl. Jacob could see at a glance that these scrolls were authentic discoveries. The woodwork, varnish, and manner of securing the roll all looked familiar to him—quite like the antique Matthew scroll that Bertrand kept in an iron vault hidden within the stone walls of the library's cave.

One of the monks said, "They found a sealed jar. It had been buried along the foundation of an old Christian monastery. In the jar were these three books."

Jacob made room on the stone floor and knelt with the three scrolls before him. Tenderly, he opened them one at a time. The first two were written in ancient Greek. One was Aristotle, the other Plato. He realized instantly that these manuscripts would correct many defects in the present Latin and French translations. He knelt over these scrolls for a long time, touching them gingerly, unwilling to open them very much so soon. "These two texts go far back in history, farther perhaps than anything I have seen. These are close to the original source. This is a remarkable discovery."

When Jacob opened the third text, his heart began to race. This was not ancient Greek. This was a strange language, one that combined Greek lettering with hieroglyphics. The Greek passages that Jacob could read clearly fit the linguistic style of the time of Jesus. But he would have to decipher this. As he held the text, his hands began to tremble. "This appears to be in Coptic. The translation will take some time. I will take this to my room. All of these. Thank you, brothers. You have advanced the cause of knowledge and provided a great service to all people. May Jesus be with you at all times."

Then in his cell on his little writing stand he carefully unrolled the brittle papyrus of the Coptic text. He heard the crackling sound of unbending centuries. He felt light-headed and dizzy. Something was happening to him, but he couldn't tell what. He ran his finger along the first words: "The Gospel of Thomas."

"A lost gospel?" he wondered. And then he wondered if this document before him could tell him something new about the Light that had changed his life.

Something struck him like lightning. He seemed to remember this text. He closed his eyes and received a vision of the apostle Thomas, the most philosophical of the apostles. Now he was in Capernaum. The Master, Jesus, appeared. He walked to Jacob as if floating, with great compassion in his eyes. Then Jesus handed him the scroll and said, "These are my words. Stand for the truth." Then he placed his hands on Jacob and blessed him.

Jacob knew that this experience of Jesus was all in his mind. But he actually felt the physical impression of hands on his head. Warmth and energy flowed through his body. A sense of oneness and knowing came to him.

After this experience, the translation proceeded quite swiftly.

His translation read, "These are the secret sayings which the living Jesus spoke and which Didymos Judas Thomas wrote down."

And he said, "Whoever finds the interpretation of these sayings will not experience death."

Jesus said, "Let him who seeks continue seeking until he finds. When he finds, he will become troubled. When he becomes troubled, he will be astonished, and he will rule over the All."

Jesus said, "If those who lead you say to you, 'See, the kingdom is in the sky,' then the birds of the sky will precede you. If they say to you, 'It is in the sea,' then the fish will precede you. Rather, the kingdom is inside of you, and it is outside of you. When you come to know yourselves, then you will become known, and you will realize that it is you who are the sons of the living Father. But if you will not know yourselves, you dwell in poverty, and it is you who are that poverty.[51]"

Jacob set down the parchment and closed his eyes, praying, for he realized the blessing this discovery would bring to humankind. It wasn't long before the translation was drafted. He then realized he needed to go slowly and pray on how to disclose this treasure. So he began introducing parts of the text into his classes, without divulging the source.

Jacob kept teaching this way for several weeks. His words took on an even greater conviction when he saw his students embrace these new teachings. That conviction—and the message he had received (he believed) directly from Jesus—brought him to a crossroads.

He met in private with Bertrand. "I have translated the third text, the one in Coptic. It is disturbing. It has stirred something ancient within me that I cannot explain. I have reflected on the words and their meaning. I have begun to share them with my students. The results have been profound.

"We are harboring an ancient text that I believe is from Jesus. We do not know of any other in existence. This text sheds more light on the message that the Master brought to humanity. I believe these writings come from the apostle Thomas."

"Thomas?"

"So it says." Jacob looked at his mentor, wondering

---

[51] Thomas 1-3

how quickly the implications would sink in. "Bertrand, did it ever occur to you that there were many more gospels than the four that we have been allowed to read?"

"Of course," said Bertrand. "I am a librarian. I care for all books, living and dead."

"Or resurrected," said Jacob.

Bertrand looked worried. "This could be an incredible discovery," he said, "an illumination for mankind. Can you give me a translation?"

Jacob handed him a bundled manuscript. "I have it in French for you right here. I also conducted some research and found that the church's hierarchy banned this gospel, along with many others, about one thousand years ago. What we have are teachings of Jesus that the church did not want to give to Christians."

"I knew about the lost gospels, of course. But I never hoped to read one."

Jacob tapped the manuscript. "You can read one now. I have a busy week at the university. When I return on Friday, let's talk."

Bertrand read the translation and was shaken by its contents and its implications. Some of the teachings seemed strange, different from other gospels.

Bertrand felt he should go to the Rector to discuss this profound discovery. The Rector was alarmed. "Can you possibly imagine the torment we will get—not just me but all of us—if we're found to be hiding this banned material? I want to see Jacob and this antique scroll here in my office now. See to it immediately, brother Bertrand."

Bertrand found Jacob at the university and waited till he had finished a lecture, then cornered him and apologetically gave him the order to respond quickly to the Rector's summons.

When Jacob arrived, scroll cradled in his arms, the Rector boomed out: "This text was condemned for a reason one thousand years ago. The pope and cardinals have screened out the four gospels of the New Testament based on strict criteria. It is the vow of our order to obey the mandates of the papacy without question. This text must meet the same fate as its fellows did a thousand years ago. Burn it!"

Bertrand gathered up the translation. Jacob tightened his grip on the original scroll.

"May I say something?" he said.

The Rector had taken his position next to a blazing fireplace. "No you may not." He ceremoniously sprinkled holy water on the two documents, as if he was handling something from the devil. The texts met the blaze as Jacob and Bertrand looked on in silence. Bertrand mourned the loss, and Jacob prayed about what he should do with the two copies he had hidden.

That night Jacob had a dream that felt more real than his daily life. He wore a hood in this dream, and walked in a dim light, walked in a line with a group of initiates. They were all following Jesus. Jesus turned toward them, and they all sat in a semicircle. The Master spoke. "Do not waver in times of trial. Hold fast to the highest truth that lies beyond the earthly realm. Take a stand for Truth." Then Jesus walked to Jacob and handed him the leather-covered document that the Rector had burned.

After this, Jacob decided to focus more on the university than on the Church. He realized that he had to stop speaking so openly and boldly about new ways. But he liked the fact that his students wanted to broaden their minds and were eager to ask questions. He watched for students who were most inquiring and most responsive to the gospel message.

After all, they were interested in broadening their minds; his class was about bringing other philosophies and understandings to these inquisitive minds. He noticed which students responded the best to the gospels. Of these, he chose twelve along with a few colleagues he felt he could bring into confidence.

As Jacob organized this group into a weekly discussion session, he knew that he was disobeying his Rector—and the papacy—for teaching this material. He was well aware of the fate of the Knights Templar. Through the collaboration of Pope Clement and King Phillip of France, these emissaries of good had been imprisoned and tortured. All of their considerable wealth had been confiscated.

But he was compelled by his dream. And he was inspired to know that this gospel conveyed previously undisclosed teachings of Jesus.

In his first private gathering with the selected cohorts, Jacob said this: "My commitment is to the truth…. a truth that follows the path of my Lord Jesus. This is why I am compelled to speak to you."

"There were more than four canonized gospels that recorded Jesus' teachings. There were many more, and nearly all were destroyed. I came in possession of a copy of a gospel that was found in a monastery ruins in Egypt. I cannot prove the authenticity of this document, so you are welcome to doubt my conviction. You have been hearing me quote from the text over the past month.

"I have no doubt that these are teachings from Jesus. My research concludes that this text is ancient, dating back to at least 300 AD. I have also learned that this gospel, handed down by one of Jesus' closest apostles, was condemned by the young church. The church wanted to present a united front against terrible opposition. I have no judgment against the early church fathers, who were striving valiantly to consolidate various Christian sects. However, after studying this text and absorbing its truth, I feel compelled to share with you some of its content."

Cries of approval and hand-clapping erupted in the room.

"All right. Listen to this from the Master. 'If they say to you, "Where did you come from?" say to them, "We came from the light, the place where the light came into being on its own accord and established itself and became manifest through their image." If they say to you, "Is it you?" say, "We are its children, we are the elect of the living father." If they ask you, "What is the sign of your father in you?" say to them, "It is movement and repose. [52]""

Jacob looked up from his documents and surveyed the faces in the room.

"Movement and repose," he said.

He tapped the parchment with his fingernails. "Is it possible that this document holds the secret of our existence? Could it be the Light we are returning to is the secret revealed? Movement and repose—how can that be? Expand beyond your normal framework of looking at things. God within us is beyond our activities and rest, for God is our very essence and is embodied by both.

"We are all children of God. We are all connected by the Light of the living Father. And we have free will. Every one of us chooses the Light or the darkness. That Light is truly lit when we dwell in the Kingdom of God. And we can dwell in the Kingdom of God right now, if only we can perceive."

An excited murmur ran through the hall.

"You must understand." Jacob's volume hushed the room. "These words I have spoken, these were not my words, not my understanding, oh no. I am simply delivering the forgotten gospel of the apostle Thomas."

Someone in the hall called out a question: "What exactly is the Kingdom of God?"

Jacob closed his eyes. The room was quiet for a strangely long time. Then Jacob said, "Here is my answer to that question.

"Plato says that there are two patterns in the

---

[52] Thomas 50

unchanging nature of things. One is divine happiness, the other godless misery. When we merge with the patterns of the divine, we truly enter the Kingdom of God. The patterns that align with the divine are all laid out in the gospels. When we align with this divine pattern, we become one with the Light, our source… and we enter the Kingdom of God.

"What the Church disparagingly calls "gnostic" turns out to be perfectly Christian—but Christian in a way unfamiliar to us. For example, says Thomas, when the disciples asked Jesus, 'When will the kingdom of God arrive?' Jesus answered, 'It will not come by watching for it. It will not be said, look, here! Or Look there! Rather, the kingdom of God is spread out upon the earth, and people don't see it.'

"Paradise is not restricted to the hereafter. Thomas writes that our direct connection to God is all around us and it is in us. The Light of God can be seen and felt. We are the Light. This has nothing to do with the hierarchical forms that sanction their claim to the Light. We do not have intermediaries between us and God, but we can offer each other support on our journeys. This shakes the foundation of the church.

"The gospel of Thomas is as old as the earliest New Testament gospel—presumably Mark. Thomas contains one hundred and fourteen sayings and parables that are ascribed to Jesus, sixty-five of which are unique to it. Thomas's Jesus speaks of illusion and enlightenment. Instead of coming to save us from sin, he comes to guide and open up spiritual understanding."

So began the downfall or upliftment of Jacob, depending on one's perspective. He felt he must keep a low profile about this discovery. He would do anything to prevent its destruction. Such a treasure should not be lost to all mankind.

Despite Jacob's precautions, Nirart de Sanz, a young Dominican, overheard two of Jacob's students discussing the banned gospel and its origin. His ears perked up as he heard Jacob's name. This was the reason de Sanz wandered Toulouse University—to find suspect heretics and inform his superior, the Inquisitor. The Inquisitor in this region had been the chief prosecutor of the Knights Templar, and was rightly feared.

CHAPTER

On a brisk morning in April, 1310, Nirart de Sanz, spy for the Inquisitor, slunk quickly through the narrow streets of Toulouse heading for the Dominican monastery. He had to hurry. His lord, the great Inquisitor of Toulouse Sivis de Tremblay, had little patience for the stone cells and austere life of the monastery. Sivis greatly preferred any one of his several small palaces located in the hills and countryside surrounding the city—emblems of the wealth and luxury granted him by special dispensation of a grateful Pope Clement V. Nirart de Sanz knew that his lord would not be inconveniencing himself for very long among the other Dominican monks.

And he hurried because, frankly, Sivis de Tremblay terrified him. Sivis was personally responsible for a high percentage of deaths by the stake in France. He was an expert and emotionless torturer. The only thing he loved in life was the wealth to be had by confiscating the property of heretics. They said that Sivis had added more to the coffers of Holy Mother the Church than any other inquisitor.

Nirart de Sanz pulled his cloak tighter to his chest and shivered. How long would he go on like this, errand-boy for the increasingly dangerous Sivis de Tremblay? He had begun as a clerk for Sivis back when Sivis was merely a lawyer in the court of King Phillip. But Phillip's systematic campaign to destroy the Knights Templar in order to seize their wealth and assets, a cold-blooded injustice largely engineered by Sivis, had propelled the crafty old lawyer into a position of eminence and made him a favorite with Pope Clement V.

The Knights Templar! The wiry little spy hated thinking about them. For when he did think about them, he found himself touching an unappeasable wound in his heart, the pain of guilt for the small role he had played in their destruction. But this morning he couldn't keep them out of his mind because his mission today—to make an announcement that would destroy the life of a harmless Franciscan friar named Jacob—stunk with the same foulness of wrongdoing. But what could he do? If the Franciscan's flagrant heresy ever came to light without his assistance—as surely it would!—no doubt he himself, Nirart de Sanz, would be accused of conspiracy with the heretics. He did not desire to burn at the stake along with Jacob and God knows who else.

Besides, who was he to question the will of God as expressed through the pronouncements of the Supreme

Pontiff? He was no one. All he knew was what he observed.

For example, he knew that the Knights Templar were fine people, the best in the land. Warrior monks who had fought alongside Richard the Lion-Hearted in the Holy Land, they had sworn themselves to poverty and to a life of service. Respected for their valor, they excelled in fund-raising and managed tremendous wealth that they held in trust for the good of the common people. They grew their funds well. When the Vatican, alarmed by their monetary skills, had threatened them with the old laws against usury, The Knights Templar invented new a system of money-handling— banking, they called it—which allowed their treasuries to increase without risk of sinful self-gain. The Knights Templar was the single most important source of public assistance in Toulouse, and their activities put the Church itself to shame.

He also knew that King Phillip had been desperate for money to finance his war against England's Edward I. The Knights Templar became his quarry, but how? There was only one legal way to seize their assets—by having them arrested on grounds of heresy. It didn't matter under heresy laws whether they confessed or refused to confess—the confessed went to life imprisonment; the unconfessed went to hell at the burning stake. Either way, their money went to the King. And to the Pope. So the Knights Templar were tortured into confessing ridiculous crimes: spitting on the cross, sodomy, worship of the Baphomet. And the man behind this clean sweep of wrongdoing was the Inquisitor of Toulouse, Sivis de Tremblay.

Nirart de Sanz rang the bell at the gate to the monastery and was admitted. He walked into the foyer and went to the room at the far left, whose door was open. There was Sivis, propped up in a throne-like chair, impatiently eating dried figs and candied meats from a silver bowl. He was a fat man with pasty skin who walked with a pronounced limp—gout, Nirart de Sanz assumed, for gout was an ailment that Sivis could amply afford. An ugly man, Sivis had been born with the gift of a golden voice and was considered one of the best debaters in the kingdom. He certainly knew how to sway opinions. His rhetoric had caused the expulsion of all Jews from France in 1306. Nirart de Sanz couldn't help but feel some awe around this hideous figure.

"My boy!" said Sivis with delight in his voice but a steely coldness in his eyes. "How pleasant to see you. Have you brought me a bone to gnaw on?"

Nirart bowed. "I have, Inquisitor. I have found someone teaching heresy at the university. He also is in possession of a banned text, which he calls the gospel of Thomas. He claims these are the words from Jesus. His name is Jacob, a Franciscan who teaches Greek philosophy at the University of Toulouse. He is the son of the winemaker, Jacques Laurier."

"Jacques Laurier!" said Sivis, suddenly smiling from ear to ear. "What excellent wine!" Then his comment broadened into a question, as though he was opening a gift. "Didn't Laurier pass away just a few months ago? And isn't the son the only heir?"

"That is not for me to know," said the spy.

"But you do know, Nirart. Out with it."

"Yes, your Excellency. Only the widowed mother and some workers live on the estate."

"Well done. This case will be given the highest priority. You may go, Nirart. Oh, and you can be sure that some of the value of this terrible matter will go to the improvement of your circumstances. Well deserved."

After the spy left, Sivis opened a closet and withdrew his finest cask of Laurier wine. He pulled the cork. After savoring the bouquet of the wine and studying its ruby color, he drank a toast to the old man who had created such a masterpiece.

Then he thought about Jacob. With a laugh he raised his glass again. "To the destruction of heretics."

In the middle of the night at the Franciscan monastery, the brothers were startled awake by a vicious banging of doors, shouting, the tramping of boots. Guards marched through the contemplative corridors. They stopped in front of Jacob's cell and burst in.

He was dressed and ready. He knew as soon as he heard the footsteps that these men were after him. Of course they charged him with heresy. Jacob was not surprised by the charge, only by the speed and violence of its delivery. He had barely begun to talk about the new gospel. The guards entered his cell; he yielded completely. They took great delight in tying his bonds too tight and pushing and kicking him on the way to the wagon that carted him off to the dingy cold prison on the outskirts of the city.

Jacob couldn't stop shivering from the cold and fear that swept his body. He prayed, "Lord, is this my fate? Do you want me to end my life in this way? What shall I do? Please guide me."

The guards led him along black stone walkways illuminated only by the torches they carried. Down the stairs Jacob's steps clanked with the chains that bound him. The stairs ended in a large chamber filled with all sorts of mechanisms for torture.

They pushed him into a cell bigger than his cell at the monastery. But the creaking and slamming of the door of bars, the key locking, the musty smell mixed with the strong scent of feces and urine—this was nothing like home. The energy of fear and domination echoed off the walls through the darkness that surrounded him.

He struggled the entire night. Hearing the echoes of other prisoners' suffering made him cringe. The cold dampness in the air could not be stopped by the lice-ridden sacks he found in the corner.

He lay huddled, his mind racing. He thought about the abuse being levied on society under the banner of religion. Waves of righteous anger flooded his nerves. When he felt that anger, he realized that he was straying into darkness. So he fervently prayed to Jesus, to the Light, for the strength to uphold God's energy. The anger passed.

He trusted that he had been led to this situation for a reason. He did not doubt his right—indeed, his duty—

to examine this antique text with a select group of fellow scholars. He also believed that the gospel of Thomas was an important aspect of Jesus' teaching, a revelation for humanity. Then he thought of the lost treasure, these authentic teachings of the Christ. "They call themselves Christians, and yet they silence his message?" The anger arose again. His body began to tighten, constrict. So he directed the intensity of that energy into a prayer. "Why, Lord, would You allow Your message to be destroyed? Through You, all things are possible. Must I die declaring Your truth? Why? Help me see Your grace in my torment. Fill me with Your Holy Spirit."

Then it dawned on him: the truth Jesus declared cannot be destroyed. This message will come back to humanity—when people are worthy to receive it. Jacob's body relaxed, then a wave of acceptance and peace came.

Later, he heard someone yell in pain. Fear flowed through him as he thought of torture, life in prison, burning at the stake. His entire chest collapsed and his heart raced as the very anticipation of these fates shocked his thoughts into horrifying images. A bolt of fear came from his gut through his nerves. Then he prayed as though he was clinging to the only thing that would appease the consuming fear. When he was able to shift his thoughts to his connection beyond this physical realm, a deep sense of peace came—only to be disturbed again by the echo of someone's groans.

The push and pull of his emotions battled on through the night. Finally light could be seen from a window near the top of the twelve-foot ceiling.

He scrambled up the wall to the window, from which he could survey the prison courtyard. It was a flat mud expanse offering nothing to consider except five tall stakes, all in a row, with firewood stacked under each. Jacob remembered something he had learned about this place. Sixty years previous, the Count of Toulouse had burned eighty heretics here while he watched. He refused to let them recant. "Eighty stakings!" Jacob thought. "What a difficult thing to do. Did they burn them in batches of twenty, or did they pack the place and create a bonfire?" In this bitterly cold dawn, contemplating the journeyman-quality work of these instruments of torment, Jacob felt weary to his soul.

As he scrambled down the wall, he heard a voice from the door of his cell. "Hey, what's your name?"

He crossed to the barred door and listened for a moment. "My name?"

"That's right. Who are you?"

The voice was coming from the next cell over. Jacob realized that he and this other fellow were leaning against the same wall.

"Brother Jacob Laurier. I am a Franciscan monk."

"Is your father Jacques, who owns the winery?"

"Yes."

"I know your father. How is he?"

"He died six months ago."

"I'm sorry to hear that. I have been down here for two years."

"What happened to you?"

"I am a Knight Templar, Arot Syton. I had a prospering bank. I lived a simple life of service. My fellow knights and I had been to the Crusades and faced perilous encounters. Facing death together countless times brought us close. We were truly brothers. We would hold private meetings and discuss how we could serve and protect those in need. Yet we could not protect ourselves from the atrocities of those holding state and church power."

Jacob said, "I know who you are. Although we have not met, you have inspired me. Your bank sponsored most of the charities that served the needy in the diocese of Toulouse. When it went, everyone suffered. I know my father gave more after they shut your bank down."

"The King and the Pope seized all of my properties," said Arot. "They have drained the bank. Most disturbing is that we can no longer fund these needed services. Why? Because of the greed and manipulation of a few. Whenever the gap widens between the rich and poor, we move farther away from the Light."

The voice from the next cell pressed on, eager to be heard.

"Now look where this money is going—to fund an unjust war, one being fought against another nation that has not attacked us. The Pope and his cronies have also lined their pockets with booty taken unjustly. We live in an era where a few hoard wealth, and they manipulate and lie to get more.

"Whenever a people such as ourselves has leaders who claim direction and power from God above, that people is in danger. Leaders who are inspired by God always feel that they have license to be unjust, to cause suffering. How can war, theft, nepotism, and deceit be guided by God? Yet many of us are actually gullible enough to believe that the actions of the Pope and King are God-inspired."

Jacob told his story.

"Allow me to give you some advice," said Arot. "There is little left of my physical existence. They have tortured and mangled this body to point at which pain is ever present. I have let go of this physical existence. My connection to the Light has grown in proportion.

"They wanted me to lie about my brothers. They tortured me, trying to make me agree that my brothers had said one ridiculous thing after another. I never knew the body could hold so much pain. But now I have let loose my grip on earthly life. It will be a blessing when they take me to the Light. I am at peace with my fate; I'm to be staked in ten days."

Jacob blurted, "How can you be at peace? You are the victim of terrible injustice!"

Arot's voice was calm. "I know that. And when I think of that, I call on Jesus. He forgave his persecutors. He did not waver from his connection with God. If I'm to be in the Light, I too must forgive. There is no room for hate, no room for anger or revenge, not there in the Light. In this life, I choose the Light. Soon I will be free. And once I am free, I know what I will want—that the

Light shall encase this Earth and even fill the hearts of my oppressors.

"One of these days societies will wake up and proclaim the obvious, that we are all God's children. We will not always be lulled into the trance of religious authority. I feel very close to God, and yet I am branded a heretic. I am excommunicated, sentenced to burn in hell. I am condemned by a Pope who is consumed in politics, manipulation, and nepotism. The King's greed knows no bounds. They want more, while humanity suffers. At some point it will end, but I'm not going to see it this lifetime.

"The most important thing I can do with the remainder of my life is focus on the Light. The world does not need more hate."

Jacob said, "I was struggling throughout the night. I went back and forth with fits of anger that took me away from the Light, and then I fell back into peace, only to be thrown into turmoil again."

"I have had two years to think about this," said Arot. "When I first arrived, I was much worse than you. Let us support each other. Let us meditate and pray that the world, someday, will not be subject to this type of abuse. Let us send God's Light to those in power, that they be touched by the Light of peace. "

Jacob passed that day in prayer with Arot. They sat with their backs together against the same wall. They sat for long periods in stillness as Jacob meditated on his God-connection.

Then a voice came from the depth of stillness: "The truth will set you free."

He knew then what he had to do. There was no choice. He thanked God for the guidance and example of Arot. "Lord, give me strength not to sway from the Love and the Light. He kept repeating the prayer from Francis: "Where there is hatred let us sow love; where there is injury, pardon; where there is discord, union."

Sivis sat in an open carriage by himself. His two assistants were sitting up front on the little driver's bench. The countryside was magnificent, and the prospects of the day invigorating. His first project was this surprise visit to the Laurier estate.

The sudden arrival of his carriage in the winery's lofty porte-cochere triggered a rush of activity with the staff. The widow herself, Helen, came forth quickly. Sivis saw that her face was lined with grief. Certainly she was accustomed to receiving visitors at the winery. And yet she seemed to be nervous to have such a high-ranking official of the church entering her home.

To put her at ease, Sivis said, "I admire the fine wines you produce, the best in the region. While I was traveling on your road, I did want to visit this fine winery."

Helen smiled and ordered one of the hands to put two stone casks of their best in his carriage. She led the three men to her porch, where they sat. They all sipped tea in the shade. He offered his condolences for her husband's death and asked how she was coping. She was grateful for his sensitivity to her feelings.

"I am an admirer of your son, Jacob," he said. "He is considered one of the best professors at the university, quite an accomplishment for such a young age."

Helen spoke with pride. "He always had an interest in Greek philosophy. He was a good student. And his choice to enter the Franciscan order was quite heroic."

"That's right. Your son has renounced worldly possessions. Now that you've caught my attention, do you mind if I ask—who, then, is the heir to the estate?"

She said, "Jacob is the legal heir. My husband wanted this for his son. Although Jacob asked several times to be removed from the will, and we actually signed a document that removed him, I still have the original will. In case he changed his mind."

At that, the mood of their little gathering altered abruptly. Sivis set down his teacup and rose to his feet. "Thank you, Madame Laurier, for your easy candor. Because of it, our work as ministers of God can proceed without delay."

"Why, what do you mean, your Holiness?"

He loomed over Helen. "Your son has been charged with heresy. You must cooperate with me, or you will also be charged. If that happens, your son will certainly be found guilty. That would mean the stake. Will you cooperate?"

Helen looked as though she might vomit. Then she forced a deep breath. "Yes, I will cooperate."

"Where is the will and deed for this property?"

Helen was in shock. She slowly stood up and went to the fireplace, where she removed a stone and slid out a metal box. She opened it and handed over the documents, including the original and amended wills.

Sivis grabbed the sheets, scanning them quickly with a big smile.

Then Sivis looked at Helen. She was obviously in poor health. He felt an urge to shock her even more, perhaps thereby hastening her early demise. So he let out a tirade.

"Your son is a heretic, guilty of possessing banned material, disobeying direct orders from his Rector, plotting against the papal throne, and teaching heresy to his students. Pray that he recants so that his life will be spared to spend his remaining years decaying in prison."

Helen collapsed on the couch. Had she fainted? The two companions rose from their seats. Then Helen began to sob. A smile came to Sivis's face. They slammed the door as they left the house.

Sivis had the driver tour them around the barns and wine cellar. The two companions started cataloging what they saw. Sivis kept thinking, "The best wines in the region will be mine." Then he said aloud, "Make sure you take a thorough inventory. Any sale or removal of these assets will be considered theft from the Church, and the thieves will be prosecuted."

After the inventory was done, he summoned his assistants. They opened a cask that evening, toasting to their fortune.

The next task was to summon the Franciscan monastery's Rector and its librarian, Bertrand. The two monks walked to the city center, where the Inquisitor held court in his ornate chamber. Sivis liked to sit on an elevated podium with a large desk separating him from those he was questioning. His two assistants, Nirat and Pariset, flanked his sides.

He began by making the Rector aware of the consequences of not telling the truth. The Rector then told the truth—that he had burned the texts and sent a report to his superior. Sivis then turned his attention to the librarian. Bertrand began pleading with him. "Examine this document, please. Reconsider whether this is from the devil or from Jesus. I was deeply touched by most of this gospel, although I did not understand it all. We have taken a vow to harbor knowledge in our libraries. This could be from Jesus. We owe it to humanity."

Sivis snapped, "Silence! You are not to lecture the Inquisitor, nor question me. You are only to answer my question. You will suffer the same fate as Jacob if you do not stop this impudence." Bertrand remained silent as he was dismissed by the Dominican.

These two interviews had been enough to condemn Jacob. But Sivis wanted to find out what Jacob had told his students.

It was easy to get testimonies from the remaining twelve students. The mere threat of pain was enough to get them babbling like rivers. After six of these interviews, Sivis felt that the repetitive stories provided enough evidence.

He then wrote his report to the Pope and requested a personal appearance for the purpose of discussing the documents and the condition of the confiscated assets. At the meeting in Avignon he proposed to Pope Clement that he, Sivis, would manage the Laurier estate and that the profits from all sales of wines would go to papal accounts. This was acceptable.

Then the Pope glanced through the gospel of Thomas and laughed. "No wonder they condemned this text. Let this friar burn with his book if he won't recant." The deal was done, and Jacob's sentence was final.

Arot's time had come. That morning they both prayed that he would remain in the Light, that he would not waver in the love and forgiveness that Jesus taught. The guards came down, clanking the chains they carried. They opened his cell door. They shackled him and led him out of his cell.

Jacob stood by his barred door. Arot turned toward him. Their eyes met for the first and only time. A light shone from his eyes, and Jacob saw love, acceptance, and peace. Arot smiled faintly. His face looked familiar even though Jacob was sure he had never met the man before. Arot said, "Remember the stance of Jesus. Love your enemies. Stay in God's Light of love." There was no tension in his voice.

A guard yanked his chains. "Get a move on! I got a bunch of potatoes to bake in your ashes. Ha Ha." They slowly walked up the steps, no more words spoken, just the rattle of chains.

Jacob heard them outside in the courtyard. The chains being wrapped around the stake could not contain the spirit that was about to soar when released from the confines of the physical realm. He then climbed to the window to see the bishop's representative blessing this unrepentant sinner. How ironic that the condemned heretic was actually forgiving and blessing them. They came with torches lit. Arot closed his eyes as Jacob prayed with him. Arot did not yell or call out, he did not speak. He surrendered to the flames.

Jacob could not watch any longer. He slid down the wall and he began to weep—in part for his loss, and in part because he had just witnessed his own future.

All of a sudden, a chilling breeze swept through his cell. It was Arot by his left shoulder, saying, "It's not that bad. Just focus on the Light."

The day of Jacob's trial arrived. The stage was set in a large hall of ornate wood panels and high ceilings. In the front on an elevated platform sat a solemn group of invited prelates, civil officials, municipal magistrates, and nobles. Those closest to the Inquisitor arranged themselves according to their status, with the Bishop of Toulouse at his right. The side pews formed ten rows on either side and ran the length of the hall, some five hundred feet. The place was packed with a variety of people and motivations for attending. Some looked at this as sport, not unlike the spectacles of Nero. There were also many clerics who had great respect for Jacob both as a teacher and as a monk who had led an exemplary life. His students attended. They too had been inspired in their God-connection through Jacob's example and teachings. Others had known Jacques, Helen, and their son for many years. Many felt inspired that Jacob had abandoned all earthly possessions for heavenly ones. Nearly everyone felt the absurdity, that such a pious man would be subjected to this.

Two guards escorted Jacob along the center walkway. They walked slowly. Jacob looked at as many people he could. He looked in their eyes, beaming the love of his God-connection. He had not prepared to speak. But he knew what he must do.

Sivis began by listing the summary of charges against him. The Inquisitor's voice had a tone of emotional conviction that was harsh and final.

"This court has found the accused guilty of the following crimes. First, you have in your possession blasphemous material condemned by the Holy Catholic Church. Second, you have disobeyed a direct order from your Franciscan superior by not burning all copies of this material. Third, you have promoted heresy at the University, heresy that proclaims the words of the devil. Fourth and most heinous of all, you have denounced the Holy See, the hierarchy of the church, and the canonized truths of the gospels. How plead you, Jacob Laurier?"

This was Jacob's first opportunity to address his accuser. He spoke in a deep baritone voice that seemed to shake the windows:

"Our Franciscan brothers were given the gospel of Thomas by Bedouins in Egypt. They found it along the foundation of an abandoned Christian monastery. When I translated the Coptic text, I was struck by the profound message it holds. Imagine if another gospel surfaced; a new document full of the lost teachings of Jesus. Imagine if this gospel proclaimed a message that can set us all free, a message that can help realize heaven on earth.

"The message from the gospel of Thomas does not contradict the canonized gospels; it reinforces them. Those gospels directed Francis of Assisi. They direct my order; they inspire me daily. Wouldn't it be a travesty if the church destroyed the fifth gospel of Jesus, which has finally surfaced again?

"I realize that this text was banned nearly one thousand years ago. At that time, however, there was a great effort to consolidate a diverse and dispersed religion. There was political pressure also, from Constantine. This gospel empowers individuals versus an institution. Thus it did not serve the philosophy of consolidation.

"The decision to ban the text was not based on its authenticity but on the implications of its content. Let a group of scholars and clerics re-examine and reconsider this gospel, which I believe was written by the apostle Thomas. What a great loss to humanity if we were to destroy what Jesus brought to us through his immense sacrifice!

"My plea is that the church re-examine this text. Explore its authenticity. At the very least, keep it as a philosophical treatise. Regardless of the author, it is a treasure in furthering our understanding of metaphysics. It can be treated the way we treat the works of Aristotle or Plato."

Sivis was simply irritated by this long speech. "We cannot treat this text like other literature because its author claims to be quoting Jesus. The decision to ban this text was made when a great deal more facts were at hand one thousand years ago. Your conjecture and speculation have no substance. His Excellency Pope Clement V has already ruled that this text is to remain banned and that its possession alone is grounds for heresy. The decision is binding."

Sivis looked sharply at Jacob and said, "Do you confess to the charges?"

Jacob stood still, his head bowed. He silently prayed, "Father I am your servant. Thy will be done." Then he turned slowly to face the nearly five hundred people who had gathered. He looked at his fellow monks and said, "I was drawn to the Franciscan order because of its simple adherence to the gospels. Imagine discovering more teaching from the Master, lost for one thousand years. I do not deny that I disobeyed my Rector by not burning every copy of this text. I do not deny that I disclosed this gospel to twelve students, nor that I quoted bits and pieces to my classes."

Jacob turned back to Sivis.

"There is only one point on which we disagree—the question of the authority of this text. As a scholar of such antiquities, I have come to believe that this author is the apostle Thomas. Why was this gospel suppressed? Because its message is not friendly to the Church. This gospel was banned when the Church first consolidated its existing structure. Now, so many centuries later, we can certainly examine this manuscript without danger to the Eternal Mother Church."

"Silence," Sivis yelled. "Enough of this. You have pleaded guilty to the charges. You have no right to canonize what is heresy, nor to accuse the Church of some self-serving motive to banish the teachings of Jesus."

Then Jacob walked down the center aisle. He looked at family, friends, brothers, students, and neighbors, all sitting in pews on either side of him. "Many of you have known me at different stages of my life. Some of you do not know me. I awoke to a deeper reality, a Light beyond the physical realm. What supports and strengthens this Light are the teachings from Jesus. That is why I was guided to join the Franciscans, who simply adhere to Matthew, Mark, and Luke.

"What a glorious blessing to have these teachings from the Master. And now—to think that we might have another gospel! It could bring us understanding. It could free us to see Jesus from a new perspective."

The Light seemed to radiate from Jacob as he spoke in a deep, full voice, clearly heard by all.

"I will not denounce the gospel of Thomas. May its pages be revealed at a time when mankind is ready to receive them."

"Bam! Bam!" went Sivis's gavel, then he spoke: "I am invoking the Decree of Mercy. This court finds you guilty of all charges. You are hereby excommunicated. You will forfeit all possessions, including the Laurier estate, to this court."

At this, a mumbling moved through the room.

Jacob's heart sank. He looked at his mother, who was weeping for the loss of her son.

He said, "Your Holiness, I do not own the Laurier estate. I have taken a vow of poverty. My father changed the…."

"Bam!" Sivis slammed down his gavel, drowning out any further words. "I will continue with the judgment. For your crimes, you are given one chance to spare your life from the stake. You may denounce this alleged 'gospel of Thomas' and recant the blasphemy that you have fed your students; however, you will spend your remaining days in prison."

Jacob said, "You cannot confiscate from me what is not mine."

"Bam, bam!" went Sivis's gavel. "If you refuse to recant, you will be burned at the stake, and the fires of damnation will continue to consume you throughout eternity."

"My father changed the …

"Bam, Bam!" with an even louder stroke charged with anger.

Then Jacob changed his tone. "These sacred teachings will bring us closer to the Light. Please, at least have some other scholars examine this artifact."

"Enough! You will not waste any more time with these pleas. The Pope has spoken on this. There will be no further consideration. This is your last chance to spare your life. Will you recant?"

Jacob was silent. He closed his eyes. After a moment he slowly turned and began looking at every witness in the room. He consciously wished the blessing of the Lord on every one of them. He looked at those dignitaries on the front podium and forgave any injustices.

Then Jacob turned to face the dignitaries on the front podium. "I petition the court. The Laurier estate is owned by my mother. I was removed from the...."

"Bang! Bang!" The mallet crushed any further statements.

Sivis responded. "Without abjuration the church has no choice but to pronounce upon Jacob Laurier the sentence of death at the stake. He will now be handed over to civil authorities, who will carry out the execution at ten a.m. tomorrow outside of this courthouse."

Sivis dismissed the assembly amid mumbling, heated conversations, and some muffled shouting. These people had witnessed injustice but feared to say so. Sivis had no problem with that.

That night, Jacob reflected on Jesus in the garden of Gethsemane. He thought quite a bit about brother Arot. He prayed for strength. He prayed for the forgiveness of his prosecutors, for the Catholic Church, Clement V, and Sivis. He truly wanted the vibration of love, not hate. Hope, not despair.

Then, as if to test his capacity to love, Sivis came walking down the torch-lit chambers. Jacob could hear him talking to the guards. The rattle of keys stopped at his door as the bolt slid from the frame.

The guard yelled, "Get over here."

They took him to the torture devices. They pushed him flat onto a wooden table, then they clasped shackles around his ankles. They raised his arms above his head and shackled his wrists. Sivis looked at him. "I want you to admit that you are the legal heir to the estate. Sign, and the tension stops."

He then nodded to one of the guards, who began cranking a wheel that made the shackles move in opposite directions. They worked very slowly and delicately. One by one, every joint in Jacob's body began to scream with pain. Then something snapped. A jolt of pain like lightning flashed through his body. Then the tension slacked, and Sivis again commanded: "Sign this document and this will end."

Jacob looked at him. "Don't take away my mother's home."

Sivis smiled. He enjoyed torturing heretics. They were so noble. He vividly remembered the pleasure of torturing the Knights Templar hour after hour, their courage and faith only deepening them farther into pain he inflicted. It filled him with hope, to think that such valiant souls still walked the earth. And this boy Jacob, he admired this one very much. Couldn't wait to see the execution. Let's see if he squeals like a live pig being roasted.

The tension came on again. Jacob focused on that place beyond the physical. He did not feel anger toward Sivis. All his focus was on the Light.

By the third round, the pain was so great he fainted.

The guards came for him the following morning in his prison cell. His body pained. His left leg and right arm were swollen. He could barely walk. They chained him. Then they carried him up the stairs. They put him in a caged transport that brought him to the courthouse. A large crowd had gathered.

He walked slowly to the stake. Oil-soaked wood was stacked with thick precision all around the base. Jacob was happy to see that. He imagined that the executioners, out of love for him, had built an exceptionally beautiful and fast device for sending him into the light. For that, he thanked them in his heart. He limped up the steps and platform of the pyre; then they chained him to the stake.

Jacob cried out: "Please, someone, place a crucifix at eye level."

For a while now, Bertrand had been noticing the elaborate staff in the hand of the cleric standing next to him. The head of the staff bore the full crucifix, including the figure of Christ's body nailed to the wood. Bertrand grabbed the staff. "You'll get it back," he said. Then he pushed his way through the crowd and stood in front of Jacob.

Jacob looked at Bertrand and managed a slight smile, to assure him. He knew this would not last long. Soon he would be free of this physical shell.

Sivis came with the two copies of the gospel of Thomas. "May you burn in hell for your heresy with these false texts." He then placed them at Jacob's feet.

Jacob, shackled to his death position, replied, "I wish you the love of Jesus in its purest sense. For if that love resided in you, you would not engage in these activities."

Then he raised his voice so that all who were present could hear. "May this gospel surface again when humanity is ready to receive it. Please pray with me and help send my spirit into the Light of God." He then raised his head. "Into your hands, Father, I commend my spirit."

He had succeeded in signaling the moment of his death. As if on cue, two men stepped forth with flaming torches. They lit the wood. Jacob's heart raced. Within moments, thick black smoke stung his eyes and choked his lungs. He gasped, but there was nothing more to breathe than smoke. He felt the heat, heard the crackling of the wood. He couldn't breathe. Then he surrendered, letting go of the tension. His eyes focused up in the place between his eyebrows, pulled like a magnet. The light grew more intense, and then his spirit exited through the crown of his head. Jacob looked down on the burning shell that had once been his body. He saw his own ashes mixing with the lost gospel of Jesus.

In this timeless place, he could see his past. In a moment he re-experienced his previous life as Orion. He saw that Isaac had come back as Sivis, back to give him another chance to love perfectly despite abuse. Julian had returned as Arot. Philip had returned as Bertrand.

He saw the future. He saw Sivis taking over his father's estate. From then on the wine turned to vinegar and the vines were ruined by blight. His mother was well cared for by their wealthy neighbors. King Phillip succeeded in ridding the Templars of their power and wealth. In 1314 the last Grand Master of the Knights Templar, Jacques de Molay, was burned at the stake. As he burned, De Molay cursed King Phillip and Pope Clement, inviting both men to join him within a year. Clement died only one month later, and Phillip IV seven months after that.

Then Jacob came back to the moment, where he saw his body in flames, then ashes. He had risen from the ashes into the Light, ready to serve God again.

The second star is the brightest of the three on Orion's belt. Jacob had faced the biggest challenge—to love one's enemies. But there is a third star.

There would come a time when the world was ready to embrace the Light, when it was able to hear the gospel of Thomas and to end abuse and manipulation by those in power. A new dawn would come, and this bearer of Light would be a part that dawn.

PART FOUR

The New Age Comes

The bearer returns when the Gospel of Thomas resurfaces. A large portion of his adventure takes place on the East Coast of the United States, from Central Falls to Washington DC.

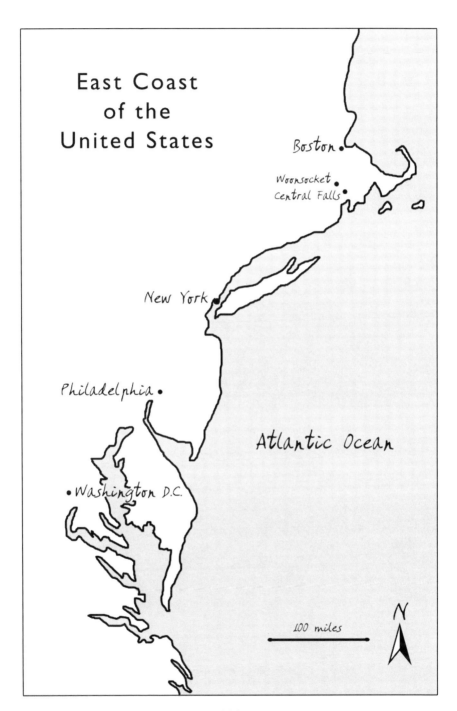

East Coast
of the
United States

Boston

Woonsocket
Central Falls

New York

Philadelphia

Washington D.C.

Atlantic Ocean

100 miles

N

CHAPTER 13

The gospel of Thomas resurfaced on a December day in the year 1945, near the town of Nag Hammadi in Upper Egypt. Mohammed Ali Samman had gone off in search of some sabakh, a natural fertilizer, in the mountains close to his village. The Arab peasant was digging around a boulder when he happened upon an old, rather large red earthenware jar approximately one meter high. At first Mohammed hesitated opening the jar, fearing that the jinn—the genie or spirit who might be enclosed—would do him harm. But his desire to discover hidden treasure provoked him to smash the jar with his pick. Inside he discovered no treasure and no genie, but books—more than a dozen old papyrus books bound in golden brown leather. Little did he realize that he had found an extraordinary collection of ancient texts, manuscripts that had been hidden for some fifteen hundred years.

At the same time in a different part of the earth, a child was born in Central Falls, Rhode Island, on the northeast coastline of the United States. The healthy boy was named Christopher Conrad. His reintroduction to the light of day would prove to be far more complex than the reintroduction of the ancient text.

In Egypt, unaware that his discovery was priceless, Mohammed tossed the books onto the pile of straw that his mother, Umm-Ahmad, used to start fires in the oven. She began tearing scraps from the old books to make kindling. Later, when a neighbor filled his head with the crazy notion that these old books might actually be worth something. Mohammed plucked them out of the scrap pile and set them on a shelf. Soon after that, he gave them all to Al-Qummus Basiliyus Abd el Masih. His reason was this: around the same time that he discovered the books, Mohammed got involved in a vendetta killing. Because a culprit named Ahmed Ismail had killed their father, Mohammed and his brothers tracked the man down and slit his throat. Fearing reprisals by the police, Mohammed passed the books to the priest for safekeeping.

Al-Qummus Basiliyus Abd el Masih was struck by the originality of the collection. He sent a sample of the manuscripts to the Egyptian historian Raghib. Recognizing their worth, Raghib had them forwarded to Cairo. There, the books sold quickly on the black market and caught the attention of the Egyptian government.

Authorities moved swiftly to confiscate all the old texts, thereby preventing their dispersal outside the country. The texts were taken to the Coptic Museum in Cairo.

Scientists who studied the artifacts deduced that they had been hidden around 390 AD by monks from the nearby monastery of St. Pachomius—hidden to escape destruction by the emerging Orthodox Christian Church in its violent efforts to expunge all heterodoxy and heresy. St. Pachomius, of course, was the same old monastery whose crumbling wall had disgorged the Bedouin-discovered texts that had found their way to Brother Jacob in 1305.

These new Nag Hammadi manuscripts included the gospel of Thomas, a copy of Plato's Republic— fifty-three works in all. Among the codices were apocalypses, gospels, a collection of sayings by the resurrected Jesus to his disciples, homilies, prayers, and theological treatises.

The same year the gospel of Thomas was rediscovered, a healthy boy was born to Jacques and Gabriel Conrad on the East Coast of the United States. The young couple had arrived in Central Falls, Rhode Island, two months previous. They had come from Montreal in search of mill work, as did many Canadians during that period. In fact, so many French Canadians immigrated to Central Falls that they made an enclave, formed by tightly packed, three-story buildings centered around Notre Dame, the French Canadian Catholic Church. The Conrad's rented a modest apartment not far from the church.

When they arrived, Gabriel was too pregnant to venture out much, and Jacques was working overtime to begin their savings. The only time they went out together was for an event or service at the church. They developed a very friendly relationship with the pastor, Father Le Pier, and asked if he would be the child's godfather. Without much thought he accepted.

Christopher was a happy baby, an enthusiastic maker of gurgling sounds and singing squeals. He was a beautiful expression of the love Gabriel and Jacques shared. The family was prospering. Jacques was promoted and received a raise, and he was even able to put a deposit on a new Ford.

When Christopher was six months old, the young family got in the front seat of their new car. Christopher was strapped in his own little seat placed between them. They drove off on a cold rainy afternoon to do some Christmas shopping. While they were on the road, the temperature dropped even further. A truck carrying lumber hit a patch of black ice, and the trailer of logs swung into their lane. Instinctively both parents reached over to protect their son, but their move did not protect themselves. They both died holding their son's chair.

The French community grieved their tragedy. Father Le Pier, being the legal guardian, pondered what to do with this child, who had no relatives in the area. Whenever he prayed, he kept getting the same instruction: "Leave Christopher at the St. Francis Orphanage." This orphanage, the largest in Rhode Island, was located about forty miles away in Woonsocket, another French

Canadian enclave. The French Canadian Catholic Parishes in Rhode Island were well connected and supported their parishioners in need, including this orphanage. The Franciscan order staffed the facility, which housed both girls and boys.

So Father Le Pier drove to Woonsocket with Christopher's basin strapped to the front seat. When he approached the orphanage, it stood out—a four-story granite edifice on the top of a high hill. It had an almost medieval façade, but the surrounding woods were lovely and the shrubbery was neatly trimmed. The place was beautiful in its context.

When Father Le Pier walked up the large stone steps, Christopher started laughing and waving his hands. There seemed to be a higher force directing the fate of this amazing child. Of course, he couldn't prove this, but he felt it deeply. How else could you explain his survival of that terrible crash without a scratch?

Sister Agnes and Brother Charles both came out to greet them at the high double-doors of the main entrance. They were co-directors of the facility, which housed a hundred and fifteen children. The great majority of these children—eighty-two, in fact—were boys, so Brother Charles had his hands full overseeing most of the wings. They had been expecting the new arrival. Sister Agnes showed Father Le Pier the wing dedicated to infants and toddlers up to age five. Thirty-two children resided here, with ten nuns serving their needs twenty-four hours a day. Father Le Pier met Sister Mary Oliver, who was responsible for this wing; she took one look at Christopher and scooped the baby into her arms. She wrapped him in her long black garb as Christopher smiled with eyes wide open. Their eyes met and Christopher held a steady gaze; in that moment a deep bond formed. She said, "We are in the presence of a very old and wise soul." She rocked him, within minutes Christopher was sleeping peacefully in Sister Mary Oliver's arms. She was beaming. The glow from her face was framed by a white ruffled bonnet. Father Le Pier said goodbye as Christopher slept. The boy already seemed so comfortable in his new home.

The orphanage became Christopher's family, his fate. Most outside observers would describe his path as a difficult one, but for Christopher it was the only world he knew. He accepted his environment and learned from it; his brothers and sisters taught him valuable lessons about the virtue of belonging to an extended family, a community.

Christopher never questioned the existence of another place, a Higher Power. In fact, as a child he would sometimes fall into raptures in which he seemed to travel to this place, a place not dreamed yet not physical, a place of light, of great vastness without form. These were times of bliss. During nap times, he often shut his eyes and drifted into the Light. When awake, he experienced the Light as energetic enthusiasm, joy that reflected from those about him. He did not think of these experiences as moments of "knowing" in an old soul. For him, it was just the way it was.

Sister Mary Oliver had no favorites, and she often announced that fact to all who would hear. And yet she gave Christopher extra attention. He was a ball of energy, excited and sometimes too loud. He also was a prankster. He liked putting dead bugs in the girls' books and short-sheeting beds. He was a winner of all games. He became a natural leader in his age group. Sister Mary Oliver grew so found of this lively child that she even took him with her to daily mass. During mass Christopher always became quiet and introspective. He learned to kneel and fold his hands, just the way Jesus did in the holy pictures. He always began his prayers the same way: "In the name of the Father, Son, and Holy Ghost." Then he would recite requests to God, as though God was standing by ready to take his orders. He learned his doctrines. He learned about sins and the power priests had to forgive sins. He was an obedient learner of the Catholic way.

At the same time, he was a tireless question-asker, and every so often he would make comments that astonished the adults. For example, one afternoon when he was four he came to Sister Mary Oliver and said, "I know why I don't have a mom and dad." She looked at him with a question. He said, "I have a different family, a big one. There is even a bigger one, the whole earth. The bigger my family, the closer I come to God."

Not everyone saw Christopher for who he was. Sister Rachel, for example, was the strictest nun at the orphanage. She took pleasure in administering her own brand of punishment. Christopher instinctively avoided her even at age five. But one rainy day he was running and yelling in the corridor. Sister Rachel rounded the corner briskly and caught him in a corner. "Christopher! You are noisy and rambunctious."

Christopher looked at her and saw an old, wrinkled face etched with a scowl and creased with deep lines around her mouth. She spoke through clenched teeth. Her eyes were squinting beads. Obviously she was not at all from the place of Light and fun. The contrast struck him as funny, and he laughed out loud. Then he blurted, "But it's play time!"

She grabbed him by the ear. He yelled, "Ahh! Ahh!" as she painfully raced him along the corridor, down the stairwell, all the way down to the musty basement. "You have sinned for showing disrespect to an ordained nun. Do you know where sinners go? Do you know? Hell is where sinners go. Hell is a place of fire and eternal pain. Rats come and eat you there. They chew out your eyes." She pulled him past the big boiler. He had never seen this underground place before. There was recess in the stone and a solid wood door with massive hinges. Sister Agnes threw back the deadbolt and pulled open the door, revealing complete darkness. "The rats of Hell are like the rats behind this door." She pushed Christopher into the darkness and slammed the door, sliding the bolt.

He screamed and cried. He pounded on the door. But nothing happened. He moved his hands along the wall on either side of the door, searching for a light switch. Nothing. So he put his back to the wall next to the door and slid down to the floor, huddling in the dark. After a few minutes, he heard some scurrying and the fear got worse. He was shivering. He clasped his hands to his face. Then the boiler went on and the flames roared. He thought of Hell and Damnation. "All I said was, 'This is playtime.' I am not wrong. Sister Rachel is wrong. There is no reason for this." He huddled shaking for several hours, listening to rats, the boiler, and the imagined cries from Hell.

Later Sister Rachel unlocked the door and asked, "Did you learn your lesson?"

Sniffling, he looked up. "Yes, I learned your lesson," he said.

The following day he was alone with Sister Mary Oliver, and he told her what had happened. A week later Sister Rachel left the orphanage and Christopher never saw her again. But he remembered the experience of Hell.

As he grew older, he noticed that his connection to the Light was weaker, that it happened much less often. He accepted this in good spirits. Of course, he didn't understand why this change was happening—that his experience of the Light was being overshadowed by the images of religion, images of God as a powerful man with a flowing white beard, images of Jesus, Heaven, Hell. He accepted these things as a matter of faith. "God is an all-powerful man we can only know through the Holy Catholic Church. If I lead a good life according to the Church, I will go to Heaven when I die." So his mind was imprinted.

Christopher, in turn, made lasting impressions on the others. Sister Mary Oliver had run this ward for fifteen years, and she never had experienced such a joyous time. When he turned six years old, it was time to separate him from the girls and the care of the sisters. They all missed his presence.

Four other boys made the transition with him. They were all the same age, and they formed a bond that got stronger over the years, especially when they earned their place among the big boys. These five became inseparable in their playtime, and Christopher learned how important his relations with his brothers could be.

One of his buddies, Billy, climbed up the old maple tree in back of the orphanage. "Hey, Christopher. I can see a bird's nest up here."

Sensing danger, Christopher said, "Don't climb any higher, Billy."

Ignoring this advice, Billy kept scaling upwards toward the nest. Just then two blue jays swooped down. The first one flashed, squawking, near his face and Billy swung his arm to scare it away. Just as he was most off-balance, the second bird struck, driving fearlessly right at Billy's eyes. Frightened, the boy swung with both arms, then lost his balance and fell like a stone. Halfway down, he struck a branch. This blow stopped the speed of his descent but knocked the wind out of him. He fell, helpless and inert, all the way to the ground, which he struck with a thud and a moan. Then Billy lay on the ground without moving.

Christopher ran to Sister Mary Oliver for help.

They brought Billy in to a sick room. He was alive but unconscious. After a careful examination, the doctor announced that he couldn't find any broken bones or evidence of internal bleeding. "There's just the worry about his head injury. We won't know anything for sure until he wakes up. We'll keep him under observation all night."

They told Christopher that he could go, but the boy refused. He insisted on staying by Billy's side till he woke. So they brought a big stuffed chair into the sick room, and Christopher stayed there through the night, praying and waiting and sleeping in short naps. By dawn, the two boys were talking together and giggling. When the doctor came in that morning, he examined Billy again and gave him a thumb's up. Winking to Christopher, he said, "Well, son, looks like you have a thick head and a good friend."

Then he spoke to Christopher, "How old are you, my boy? Six? I'll tell you, even at age six you show the love and compassion of a wise man."

Once he moved up with the older boys, Christopher no longer saw Sister Mary Oliver every day. But she remained his confidant and advisor throughout his youth. She was his model of unconditional love. On the boys' wing, though, he found a new mentor, Brother Lucian—a quick-witted, athletic young man who saw in Christopher the same spark and light that had always charmed Sister Mary Oliver.

335

For the next five years, life was dominated by routine. He woke every day at five-thirty. The pattern of the day: breakfast and mass, school, lunch, school, play, supper, study, prayer, and off to bed. The only interruption of the pattern came in the form of an occasional after-supper movie, which Christopher loved. They lived like a family struggling with hard economic times. They were cautioned to use only "three squares of toilet paper," and these only when solids were passed. The fear of God sometimes overrode the love of God, but generally the warmth of the friendships and nuns and brothers sustained a feeling of family. Prayer started each day and permeated their existence. Everywhere were holy pictures of Jesus, Francis, Mary, and a whole panoply of saints. The spirit of forgiveness was enforced; fighting and indeed any type of violence was forbidden.

Throughout his childhood, Christopher got into only one fight. This happened when he was twelve. A new boy named Glenn, one year older than Christopher, came to live at the orphanage. For some reason, Glenn felt the need to challenge the established boys. He picked Christopher as his chief target, thinking that he could take advantage of Christopher's light-hearted disposition. For two weeks Glenn taunted Christopher every day, creating insulting nicknames for him and daring him to physical action. Christopher ignored him as long as he could. In time, though, it was clear that his patience was only aggravating the problem.

Christopher went to Sister Mary Oliver for advice. He explained the dilemma. She looked at him affectionately and with a bit of humor in her eyes. "Christopher, what do you want to do about it?"

"I don't know. I talked to Brother Lucian about it."

"What did Brother Lucian say?"

"He said to keep ignoring Glenn and he would stop. But he won't stop. Now he's pushing me. Yesterday he grabbed my hair and shoved my head against the ground.

"That's not okay, is it?"

"But it's against the rules to fight. Jesus said that we should love our enemies."

"Does love mean that we should let our enemies do wrong? That we should let our enemies hurt us?"

"I don't know."

"Yes, you do. Tell me, did Jesus ever strike out against his enemies."

"He drove the money-lenders from the temple. He must have been mad to do that."

"Perhaps he wasn't angry at all. Perhaps he simply knew that sometimes a strong man has to stand up for what is right."

The next day on the playground, Glenn began taunting Christopher. Word had got around that Christopher had gone to talk with Sister Mary Oliver. Now Glenn had a new name for his rival: "Sister's sissy." Glenn started pushing Christopher in the chest, trying to knock him down. Christopher said, "Glenn, if you do this, I will have to fight you."

"Oooh!" said Glenn. "Sissy's going to fight me." He grabbed Christopher's shirt in both his hands and

337

acted as though he would tear the shirt right off his chest. Glenn was easily six inches taller. Christopher punched him in the stomach as hard as he could. Glenn said, "Oof!" and doubled over.

Christopher stepped back to watch what would happen next. He wasn't angry, just curious. He was surprised to realize that he did know how to fight. Where that knowledge came from, he couldn't say. Glenn caught his breath, and then a fascinating show of pure rage came over him. He pounced on Christopher, but Christopher met his sloppy attack with perfectly timed punches hard to his mid-section that made him fall back until he landed on his back.

This time Glenn attacked with crazy, all-out fury. Christopher let him come running, then slipped to the side, grabbed Glenn's arm, and flung him forward the direction he was going. Glenn lurched forward and hit the ground, rolling a couple of times. The moment he stopped, flat on his back, Christopher was on top of him with his knees pinning the boy's shoulder to the ground. Glenn kicked his legs and twisted his torso, but he was pinned.

"Now are you going to stop?"

"Aargh!"

"Tell me you're going to stop!"

Suddenly a pair of big hands grabbed Christopher from behind and pulled him up off the ground. "That's enough!" shouted Brother Lucian. Then Christopher heard Brother Charles calling from his second-floor office window. Brother Charles was the fearsome disciplinarian of the orphanage. He had once been a boxer in the Navy. Brother Charles commanded: "Christopher! Glenn! Get to my office. Now!"

As they stood before the disciplinarian's massive desk, Brother Charles studied them both in silence for a long time. Then he said, "Christopher, I'm surprised at you. I've never known you to be a bully. What do you think you were doing beating up Glenn?"

Christopher began to speak, but Glenn cut in first. "It's my fault, Brother Charles. I started it. I've been bugging him for weeks. I didn't think he would fight me."

Brother Charles thought about that for a moment then said, "I see. Well, Glenn, I hope you learned something today. This boy just about kicked your butt."

"Yes, sir."

"You're lucky I stopped it. Now shake hands and be brothers."

The two boys became good friends after that. The adversary became the admirer.

All the boys knew that Christopher was different. He was a leader who didn't want to be a leader. Where he put his real focus was religion, as Sister Mary Oliver had taught him. All of his teachers reinforced images of God as a powerful heavenly Father, and he accepted these images with complete faith. The Roman Catholic Church taught him about sin, penance, forgiveness, the evils of sex, confession. These concepts became embedded in his subconscious, where they filtered his perceptions, decisions, and actions. They made an impression of the unimpressionable, gave form to what has no form. This conditioning turned into beliefs and took him farther away from the Light that he had experienced during his early childhood. By the time he reached puberty, he absolutely believed that the Catholic Church controlled his connection to God. So, of course he wanted to become a part of the organization that assured his salvation. He whole-heartedly chose to dedicate himself to religion by entering Our Lady of Providence Seminary.

The seminary was a converted mansion with newly built classrooms and dorms. Located on the shores of Narragansett Bay in Rhode Island, it was a beautiful spot with sweeping grass lawns and steep rolling hills—hills that he would later dread while he trained on the cross-country team.

All his classes were taught by priests. Both college and high school classes occupied the same buildings. Together, four hundred teenagers and young men all focused on the religious life of the priesthood. Everyone awoke at six AM daily. The entire campus attended morning mass together, followed by breakfast. Then there were classes, each with the same group of twenty four students. Lunch was followed by more classes, then sports, study, evening prayers, and lights out by ten PM. Christopher's days were packed with activity. He was a strong member of the track, cross-country, and debate teams; he was part of the choir and the student council. He had a knack for racquet sports, and he was acknowledged as the school's champion in both tennis and ping pong.

Certain aspects of seminary life appealed to him most of all. In chapel, all those male voices singing together—reverberating along stone walls—awoke in him a sense of deep familiarity, but he could not tell why. Also, the reading of scriptures fascinated him, especially passages from the synoptic gospels: Matthew, Mark, and Luke. He reflected on these passages every day. But he couldn't help noticing the contrast between the word of the gospels and the reality of life as a parish priest.

The latter he gradually began to piece together from his friendly associations with the priests who taught him. Father Gregory, the choir director, also taught math and worked as a parish priest for the diocese. Christopher often shared meals with Gregory and other parish priests, and Christopher would ask them about the lifestyle. One priest said, "You know, I rarely counsel anyone. My work is almost entirely occupied with the performing of rituals—mass, confession, baptism, funerals, and marriage." He heard another priest admit candidly, "I see the numbers in morning mass dwindling to a handful. Yesterday morning there were two elderly women who attended; this morning no one showed. Even at Sunday services we're seeing fewer numbers." Someone else said, "Fewer and fewer young men are choosing to join the seminary." In Christopher's mind, they were describing the decline of an institution.

Gradually the reality of this lifestyle sunk in. He wondered daily, "Is this the life and path I should choose?" When he was brutally honest, he admitted to himself that the Holy Spirit seemed to be absent from the day-to-day of these lives. Where was the Light of his early youth? At night he prayed to receive that connection, but he never really felt the Holy Spirit as Christ's apostles had described it. The images from childhood, catechism, the sisters and brothers, seemed less and less real as his awareness expanded.

By the end of his fourth year in the seminary, the church had been demystified for him. He had experienced the frailty of the priests as men. Though some stood out as models of compassion and service, most priests had personal issues and challenges, just like the rest of the world. The images and dreams from the religion were just that. Chris slowly realized that his childhood beliefs were crumbling. He knew he would finish out his senior year and then explore a new path.

But he still had a deep urge to explore the life of spirit. He needed some new framework, some way to make sense of the mystery that seemed to lie at the root of religion, but that was not religion.

His senior year school physics class gave him the first glimpse of his new path. Sitting at his desk the priest wrote on the blackboard in big letters: "Everything around us, including ourselves, is made of energy." He stared at those words, then something clicked.

"Everything?"

He looked around the classroom at the desks, the chalkboards, the priest, and his classmates—all made out of the same stuff. Made out of something invisible and yet real-beyond-real, something that seemed to have spiritual qualities and yet had never been mentioned in his catechism class. Something scientific that could be studied. He was seventeen at the time, and new ideas were dawning in his mind

He wondered how he would convey all this to Sister Mary Oliver, who was quite proud of his priestly prospects. He decided that he had to go to the orphanage and meet with her face-to-face. As he drove up to the familiar edifice, he saw that a nearby field had been recently plowed, the wide landscape turned up rich and brown. On the right side of the car, the sun was gleaming. On the left, dark clouds were churning up a storm. The sky was pumping with energy.

Chris asked to take a walk with Sister Mary Oliver. A few steps out of the building, he just blurted it out: "I've decided to leave the seminary. I don't think this lifestyle is for me."

As always, she was accepting and supportive. She listened attentively to his reasoning and nodded at Chris's conclusions. Then she asked, "What do you want to do?"

Before Chris could answer, a bolt of lightning shot across the sky. It struck a stand of trees at the edge of the plowed field. A deafening clap of thunder ripped through the air as a wave of energy shot through him.

It was as if nature itself was prompting his answer. Christopher pointed to the spot where the flash of lightning had hit the earth and said with a conviction that came from the core of his spine, "I want to understand that."

"What?" she asked.

"Energy. All aspects of energy."

He didn't know what else to say; he didn't know where this path would lead him. All he could do was stand there feeling the conviction—a knowing.

Sister Mary Oliver had a puzzled look on her face. His comment didn't really make sense in terms of choosing a profession. She glanced over to where the lightning hit, and then she turned to Chris with a smile. "You've got my support, whatever you decide," she said.

From the seminary he entered the University of Rhode Island, where he learned about energy in a practical, applicable way. He earned a bachelor's degree in electrical engineering, thereby discovering how energy gets transformed through the circuitry it passes. He became particularly fascinated with quantum mechanics. Sub-atomic particles seemed to dance along the boundary between the physical world and the mystery of spirit. He was delighted to discover that these particles acted according to principles of uncertainty and possibility. In other words, living matter is far less dogmatic than religion.

While still an undergraduate, he began doing research for the Graduate School of Oceanography. For this work, he traveled the length and breadth of the Atlantic Basin. After graduation he worked for the Massachusetts Institute of Technology and the Bermuda Biological Station. Stationed in Bermuda as a research associate, he began to see the correlation between nature and the behavior of energy.

He was part of a massive oceanography project involving fourteen countries. The assumption behind the project seemed obvious to everyone: if scientists understood the Earth's large ocean currents, they could predict global weather patterns. Christopher's job was to collect information from all the ships involved with the project, information about the changing locations of numerous markers that showed how currents were moving at various depths. He would plot the positions of all these markers at six-hour intervals, then fax this information back to all the vessels.

After Christopher had been reporting data for a period of time, he received a visit from the project supervisor, Dr. Rehnquist. Rehnquist said, "I wanted to come by to verify your methodology."

"Why? Is there something wrong with my data?"

"Well, I'd say there is either something wrong with your data or else there's something wrong with our assumption. I'm sure that you, too, have been surprised at the results."

"Yes, I have. The markers are traveling with no coherent patterns. The maps look as though a bunch of kids were drawing zigzag lines. And yet I'm sure I'm recording the data precisely."

"I'll check that, just to be certain. But knowing the usual quality of your work, Christopher, I feel sure that you're right."

"So, what does it mean, professor?"

"I'm afraid we are discovering that our large weather patterns are being driven by small eddy currents, numerous and unpredictable. And what influences these eddy currents is something even smaller. Look at how crazy these data are. These markers show currents in the Gulf Stream going in opposite directions, and yet they are only twenty meters apart in depth."

Christopher said, "It is as if God is saying that our future is uncertain, no matter how clever we may be in our pursuit of certainty."

Rehnquist smiled. "Well, that's not a very scientific explanation, but your point is well taken."

The following week, they recalled all the ships to port. The experiment was abandoned halfway through. They had discovered what they didn't want to discover: that weather is not a cause-and-effect phenomenon. Accurate long-range weather predictions were not possible, just short term probabilities.

Another project Christopher worked on involved researching the impact of lobster fishing along the Narragansett coast. In areas where the lobsters were over-fished, their main prey—crabs and sea urchins—flourished out of balance. When that happened, seaweed and kelp—the diet of these prey animals—were soon depleted. Then the sea urchins either moved on or starved to death, leaving the system devoid of the life that it once had. These observations gave Christopher a clear experience of life's interconnectedness. "It's the same with humans," he thought. "Whenever a member enters or leaves a group field, the change has a holistic impact. Life works this way on all levels." Now he felt he was getting a grip on something universal about energy, something that held true on the subatomic, the global, and the human scale simultaneously. His excitement over this led him to his next academic step. He entered Princeton University's graduate school, pursuing a master's degree in physics.

During his first months at Princeton, yet another thread wove itself into the fabric of Christopher's search. He became a practitioner of yoga. At first he couldn't see exactly how this interest fit into his other work, but he pursued it because it felt good to his body. Soon, though, he realized that yoga was the study of energy as it circulated within his own body. What excited him was the fact that yoga principles aligned with what he was learning in his graduate physics classes—that at our essence we are all one, all interconnected through a cohesive quantum field. He was fascinated to learn that the basic laws of energy and matter in yoga—comparable to those from physics—had been set down over four thousand years earlier by ancient yogis. Sankhya philosophy described the essential nature of energy and consciousness.

He began to notice this: when his own behavior mimicked the nature of energy—which was described in both quantum physics and Sankhya philosophy—he felt more uplifted, more accepting, and more productive. Also, when ecosystems aligned with energy's nature, they were healthier, more vibrant. The analogies were all around.

Christopher's first presentation to his professor, Dr. Michaels, set the tone for his studies. "Subatomic particles are in constant orbits around a moving nucleus, all moving in tremendous open space compared to their size. Therefore, openness, movement, and flow are part of nature's deeper nature. Highly productive ecosystems align with the nature of energy.

"For example, the most productive coastal ecosystems are physically open, allowing a high carrying capacity for nutrients. The most productive marine ecosystem in the United States is the Bering Sea, off the west coast of Alaska. It is a large open system where rich nutrients flow over a broad continental shelf. Currently this ecosystem provides over fifty-six percent of the nation's commercial catch of fish and shellfish.

"An even more impressive example is the open upwelling off the coast of Peru. Currents here bring a rich flow of nutrients to the surface, making this the most productive marine habitat in the world. During some years the entire fish harvest of the United States equals just twenty percent of the catch taken in this area, which is about half the size of Pennsylvania.

"Openness and flow provide a high carrying capacity for nutrients—this is an important feature of high-energy systems. Systems with a low carrying capacity tend to stagnate.

"Now this is why, by analogy, yoga postures and breathing exercises increase our own carrying capacity for nutrients as well as our ability to flush toxins. Openness to life, listening to others—all of these reflect the same unifying principle."

Dr. Michaels replied simply, "Chris, you've found your niche. Keep me informed as your work progresses."

He enjoyed the camaraderie at Princeton, the intellectual dialogues. One of his favorite conversation partners was a doctoral candidate in archeology, a Ugandan named Harold. They often sat together in the student lounge, shooting for connections between their two very different disciplines.

One day, Harold said to him, "You know, Chris, I see the passion you have for this study of energy, your fire, your drive to know. What's behind that? Why are you so compelled to find these answers? They seem very subtle, you know."

Christopher hesitated, then went ahead. "This is something I never speak of in academic environments. I'm afraid that my true interests would discredit me in the eyes of many scientists." He told Harold of his seminary background. He so much as confessed that his inner mission was spiritual, and that his research seemed to be heading toward an understanding of God. "Or at least of God's basic anatomy."

"So," said Harold without a touch of irony, "how is that going? Have you managed to get a glimpse of the old boy?"

"Yes," said Christopher. "And yet, truly, no, not at all. I see connections in my mind, but I don't experience them in my totality. It's like this. If I am made of energy, and this energy is moving freely from my dimension to another dimension, then I should be able to experience this connection. As I have read, the mystics experience this realm. So why haven't I experienced it?"

"Perhaps you have," mused Harold. "Perhaps you have, but you have forgotten."

The very thought jolted something awake in Christopher. After a long moment of quietness, he said, "When I was a child—before the age of seven, certainly not much after that—I had glimpses of this Light. But they were only that—moments of inspiration from a church service, moments in prayer, moments when I was utterly happy outdoors in the sunlight. But these moments were nothing like the connection I read about in the Bible. I know that there is something much more to life."

"Perhaps it is there," said Harold. "Tell me, do you pray any more?"

"No, not really. I lost interest."

"Perhaps you just needed a vacation from prayer. So that you could learn a new way to do it." Harold smiled kindly.

That night in his apartment, quite late, Christopher felt the urge to return to the old habit of prayer. He said aloud: "I am open to receive Your blessing, to follow Your guidance, to serve in any way You want to use me. I pray to experience Your Light. I humbly wish to return to that connection with You, that blissful experience that I tasted in my childhood."

Suddenly a sentence occurred to him. He seemed to hear it in the air, though where he had read it he could not recall. Certainly these were words of Jesus. "One who seeks will find, and for one who knocks it will be opened.[53]"

Several days later, Harold walked into Chris's cubicle at the university. He was very excited. "Chris, he

---

[53] Thomas 94

said. "I am remembering our last conversation. Something very exciting has come up. They have made an incredible find. In fact, the discovery was made almost exactly on the day we spoke. If you come to my office when you can, I will show you."

Christopher went immediately.

Harold produced an enormous sheet of printed paper. "You know I have been working at the dig in Capernaum, on the Sea of Galilee. I spend several months at the site every year. They keep me updated on their finds by sending information over the Internet. Look now at what they have found in Capernaum. It was part of an upper-class structure. It's a marble piece with six symbols etched in the stone. They haven't dated the marble yet, but they feel certain the work is about two thousand years old. I thought of you right away, for some reason." He unrolled a print-out of the symbols they found.

Christopher's head began to swim. It felt like the earth under him was shaking, his knees wobbled. He was touching something beyond this life. In a daze he asked, "Can I borrow this for a few days?"

"You can have this. I can always print out another. But promise you will share your thoughts about the meaning of these symbols."

"I will. Thank you," he almost stammered. "I will talk with you later."

Christopher rushed to his apartment to be alone. He was not sure what was stirring inside him, all he knew was that he needed to be quiet, pray, and listen.

CHAPTER

Christopher sequestered himself in his apartment, canceling all of his meetings for the week. He let go of his earthly obligations to remain focused on the revelation surfacing. He laid the symbols out on his dining room table with the gospel of Thomas, the gospel of Mary Magdalene, and the synoptic gospels.

He put out his yoga mat in the center of his small living room and began moving into postures. While in the spinal twist a burst of energy shot up his spine. When the sensation reached the crown of his head, he had an experience that changed his life forever. Imagine being in an airplane rising through dark clouds and suddenly, unexpectedly, you pop into the clear skies above the clouds. A veil is whisked away. Everything is vastness and light. Bliss permeated his body. He had reawakened that connection once more. It was real, and yet it was beyond physical reality. It was what he had been searching for without knowing it—not a person or a place, but connection, an innate connection with spirit. Surging through him was a blissful, rejuvenating, awesome energy.

Then it hit him—not consciously, but as though his cells woke up. Here it was, what he had prayed for, and not a glimpse but a full immersion into a dimension beyond this one. He awoke to another realm, a place in which linear time did not exist.

He recalled Jesus and his meeting in his leather shop, touching his feet, and hearing his words, "Integrate these seeds of truth within you and listen when you are called by God to serve." Jesus called him a bearer of Light.

In a flash he saw his life as Orion. He remembered etching these symbols in leather after hearing the Master speak. He recalled Matthew. He relived the support and joy of the Matthew community. Memories of the apostle Thomas, Mary Magdala, and of the Hindu traveler Pradeep came flooding in. Then he recalled Orion's final prayer. He had been given another chance to love unconditionally.

Then, in a second flash, he relived his experience as the Franciscan monk, the wealthy lad who chose the heavenly kingdom over his earthly inheritance. He remembered following the simplicity of the Franciscans in adhering to the gospels of Matthew, Mark, and Luke. He recalled how fulfilling it was to serve by teaching. And then he reflected on the gospel of Thomas. In an agonizing moment he re-experienced that terrible death and realized that he had indeed passed the test and loved in the face of abuse. He remembered his final prayer as Jacob—that the Gospel of Thomas would surface when humanity was ready to receive it.

In another flash his concepts of God, sin, religion, Heaven, and Hell had been shattered in the clarity of the Light—the Light that came from a formless God who dwelt within him. God is actually nothing like the images and concepts he'd been fed in his own religious past. God is not personified, not genderfied. Energy, Light, and a greater understanding came upon him.

He sat in stillness. The crickets of spring made their high-pitched pulsing sound. The night was calm. In the distance, dogs barked, and their echoes traveled through the darkness.

Now the words of the Master rang more clearly than they ever had. He read this passage from the book of Thomas:

"If they say to you, 'Where did you come from?' say to them, 'We came from the light, the place where the light came into being on its own accord and established itself and became manifest through their image.' If they say to you, 'Is it you?' say, 'We are its children, we are the elect of the living father.54'"

Christopher wrote, "Everything comes from Light and the One who gave it birth. We are inherently connected to that vibration and the Source of that Light."

---

54 Thomas 50

He then went to the gospel of Luke:

"What shall I compare the kingdom of God to? It is like yeast that a woman took and mixed into a large amount of flour until it worked all through the dough.[55]"

He wrote: "Primordial or Quantum energy is the 'yeast' that gives rise to our universe. Everything is given form through this fundamental energy. It is radiance from God, and when we attune to this energy, which is beyond the physical, we attune to the Holy Spirit and enter the Kingdom of God.

"Jesus showed that it is possible to attune to that Light while here on Earth. Jesus identified with the Light and with the One who radiates it. He was one with the vast ocean of energy that gives rise to the universe. There was no separation.

"Jesus said, 'It is I who am the light which is above them all. It is I who am the all. From me did the all come forth, and unto me did the all extend. Split a piece of wood, and I am there. Lift up the stone, and you will find me there.[56]'"

Christopher realized that he is, we all are, inherently connected to something much vaster than our physical universe. This connection is real and ongoing, even when it is completely absent from the radar screen of personal awareness.

He wrote, "The puzzle of our existence could be answered by understanding the energy that gives it form. Our energy vibrates at different levels, just like the electromagnetic spectrum. We are made of energy; we

---

[55] Luke 13:20
[56] Thomas 77

are always vibrating. Moods and emotions are simply ways that we sense this vibration. When our energy is vibrating at a high level, we feel uplifted, expansive. In that emotional state, our vibrations come closer to the vibrations of the so-called Divine Connection. The more sympathetically we vibrate, the closer we come to the threshold of the physical universe."

Christopher thought about the difficulty of holding the vibration of love when wronged and abused. He reflected on Isaac, the way that old Pharisee manipulated people with lies and gossip for selfish ends. He thought of Sivil, who abused religion and politics for personal gains. Both were under the delusion that their actions were justified for religious reasons. He thought of Jacob and his trial by fire. He reflected on Jacob's commitment to sustain this connection, in other lifetimes. He aspired to be a torchbearer holding the Light.

He turned to the gospel of Mary and read this:

"Beware that no one leads you astray saying, Lo here or lo there! For the Son of Man is within you.[57]"

The pure vibration of the Master is within us. Within every person exists the vibration of spirit to which we can connect at any time. We can obscure our radiance, we can place a veil over it—but at the core everyone is this inner Light.

Christopher wrote: "The Light is not something you get; it is something you are. It is a process of removing our forgetfulness, reawakening that vibration.

---

[57] Gospel of Mary: 34

However, just because you wake up for a moment does not mean you won't fall back asleep just as quickly. If you think you have it, you don't have it. This spiritual connection is now. It is a live energetic connection, unpredictable and moving. That is why it is critical that we understand the nature of this connection—what strengthens it and what dissipates it. Jesus described the nature of this connection as 'the Law.' When we align with this 'Law,' we consciously and energetically link up with the Light."

Now he returned to the gospel of Luke:

"It is easier for heaven and earth to disappear than for the least stroke of a pen to drop out of the Law.[58]"

Then he wrote: "This Law comes directly from the One—the Cosmic Birther of radiance and vibration—who extends this Law through the energy radiated. This law can be seen in the nature of the Quantum Field. The behavior of this primal energy is similar to what Jesus taught about the nature of God. His description was complete. That is why Jesus instructed us not to embellish these basic truths: 'Do not lay down any rules beyond what I appointed you, and do not give a law like the lawgiver lest you be constrained by it.[59]'"

But religions have embellished the Law. Christopher thought of religions that proclaimed the power of God and claimed to be God's ordained representatives. Often they constrain the believers with images, dogma, and beliefs that actually take beings further from the Light. And some enslave the masses into

---

[58] Luke 16:17
[59] Gospel of Mary:38

believing their empowerment and the righteousness of their unrighteous deeds. Christopher stared at the six symbols. These are not man-made rules, he thought; they are observations of our deeper nature.

Now, as a scientist but guided by understandings that most scientists would dismiss with a laugh, Christopher undertook a modern interpretation of each of the six symbols. He poured out his realizations onto paper. He thought of Harold and knew that he would show his archeologist friends a copy of what follows.

The Six Characteristics of Capernaum
and
The Nature of the Quantum Field

Nearly two thousand years ago Jesus taught in Capernaum. I believe these symbols represent Jesus' teachings on God's Nature as it is described in the gospels. From a modern perspective these symbols also depict the nature of quantum energy, the scientific essence of all matter. Jesus described the same deep truth about our existence, but modern scientists went about their description differently. Despite these differences of perspective and approach, they both describe the same essence. In summary, I believe that these symbols are the bridge between science and religion.

Let's start with a scientific view of that essence. David Bohm described our universe as an island on a vast ocean of quantum energy. The very underpinning of our universe is a field of energy. Scientists call this vast ocean the Zero Point Field, Dark Matter, or the Quantum Field. We realize now that matter is just a manifestation of that energy in physical form. Einstein's equation E=MC2 is simply a recipe for the amount of energy involved in creating the appearance of mass from this vast ocean. Matter is not separate from this infinite ocean of quantum energy. This infinite ocean of radiance and vibration is not separate from the One who gives it Birth.

Intention and Alignment

Scientists in the field of quantum mechanics discovered that the moment they inquire into the nature of sub-atomic particles, the phenomenon they are looking for happens. If they want to find an electron with no spin, they find it. If they think about an electron with no velocity or no momentum, then the electron they study will acquire those attributes.

John Wheeler, the theoretical scientist who is considered the Father of the Black Hole, concluded after his famous Delayed Choice Experiment that "Nature at the quantum level is not a machine that goes its inexorable way. Instead, what answer we get depends on the question we put, the experiment we arrange, the registering device we choose."[60] He wrote that "We are inescapably

---

[60] Helmuth, et al., In New Techniques and Ideas in Quantum Memory Theory ed. D. M. Greenberger (New York: New York Academy of Science, 1986)

involved in bringing about that which appears to be happening."[61] Our consciousness shapes subtle energy, just as ancient yogis taught.

Our thoughts and deeper beliefs hold vibrations. The vibrations we hold will attract an energy that compliments it. For example if we have a belief of low self worth, we will attract people and situations that reinforce our belief and the energy we hold.

Intention is extraordinarily powerful when it is focused. When our thoughts align with our deeds, our values with our actions, we access a power. We dissipate that power when we say one thing and do another. Integrity strengthens intention. Jesus showed us that the highest intention we can hold is our God-connection. It is the ultimate prize. "Seek his unfailing and enduring treasure where no moth comes near to devour and no worm destroys.[62]"

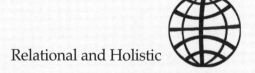

Relational and Holistic

Interconnection is the foundation of existence. Look at life itself. All living things exchange energy. If this exchange ceases, life itself ceases.

You need air, water, and food. The very composition of your body is constantly exchanged with energy from our surroundings. This exchange generates new

[61] J. A. Wheelers, "The Computer and the Universe," The International Journal of Theoretical Physics, (1982)
[62] Thomas 76

cells. Ninety-eight percent of the atoms in our body were not there a year ago. Our skeleton, which seems so solid, was essentially "not there" three months ago. The material world is fundamentally energy in constant relationship with itself.

Irish physicist Jon Stewart Bell demonstrated that all conceivable models of quantum reality must incorporate a relational connection. On a subatomic level, nature arranges instantaneous and ongoing connections between two photons. When subatomic particles contact, they create a link that physical distance doesn't break. Quantum energy creates relationships that occur faster than the speed of light across space and time. Scientists call such relationships "non-local." Einstein called them "spooky actions at a distance."

The nature of energy has forced scientists to pay attention to relationships. At the subatomic level, nothing exists unless it engages another energy source. This energy is part of a complex web of relations. Matter is the momentary manifestation of interconnected fields of quantum energy. These interactions appear as particles because the fields come together very abruptly in minute regions of space. We are made of these interacting particles. We are part of a relational field, all connected to each other and to the Source.

Jesus said, "Truly I say to you, to the extent that you did it to one of these brothers of Mine, even the least of them, you did it to Me.[63]"

When we engage in loving relationships with

---

[63] Matthew 25:40

others, we are touching something sacred and inherent to all life. When we network, we are creating an interconnected field that mimics the existence of every particle. When we live in, work, and participate in community, we align more closely with this characteristic of energy.

Diversity and Balance

Nature thrives in its diversity. Quantum energy is the seed of our diverse universe. It is the tiniest seed. Within this seed lies the manifestation of the vast material realm. Rocks, trees, oceans, and stars are all its expressions.

The disciples said to Jesus, "Tell us what the kingdom of heaven is like." He said to them, "It is like a mustard seed. It is the smallest of all seeds. But when it falls on tilled soil, it produces a great plant and becomes a shelter for birds of the sky.[64]"

Within the seed of quantum energy lies the expression of the vast material realm—including our bodies and everything we encounter.

This mustard seed gives birth to everything in the universe, including the broad spectrum of vibrations. For example, some electromagnetic waves are just one-billionth of a centimeter in size; some of them are over six miles. Energy's nature has a broad spectrum of vibrations.

When we accept the broad spectrum of expres-

---

64 Thomas 20

sions of humanity, we are embracing energy's nature. On the other hand, prejudice and intolerance dampen any group field. Energy's forces are also immensely varied. Intolerance of other religions, other paths, other cultures, other races takes you farther from the Light. For the same reason, the more we expand the range of acceptance of others—the more we tolerate differences and become less judgmental—the more we align ourselves with the nature of energy, and the closer we come to the Light.

If God is imprinted on the nature of energy, then we should be able to find the trinity in energy's behavior. Quantum energy is the source of three distinct forces: electromagnetic, gravitational, and nuclear (strong and weak). These forces differ profoundly in character. For instance, electromagnetic force includes both positive and negative expressions. Why then, as far as we know, is there no such thing as negative gravity? Nuclear force has a strong and a weak expression. But why does this force function only within the nucleus of the atom, while electromagnetism and gravity are infinite in range? These three forces are always actively present, setting the larger context for the evolution of our universe.

The trinity of forces is in dynamic balance while it is outside our dimension in the quantum field. The super string theory—now the most accepted quantum description—states that quantum energy in all its forms has symmetry and dynamic balance. Basically, opposing forces balance each other, just as the negatively charged electrons balance positrons. Physicists now realize that symmetry and balance are the keys to constructing accurate descriptions of nature.

To behave like the highest the aspect of energy means to embrace diversity and be in dynamic balance in your life. Diversity is nature's way; intolerance opposes God's nature. If we are to connect in that place beyond our dimension, we too must embrace that place of balance. Balance of work, play, family, community, and rest mimic the nature of this higher energy.

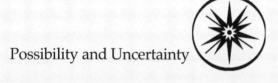

Possibility and Uncertainty

In the quantum realm, energy has yet to take on a particle form. Thus, quantum energy exists outside of our four dimensions of space and time. The quantum realm is not a world of actual physical events; instead, it is a world filled with numerous unrealized possibilities for actions. In other words, quantum energy is an omnipresent force that is pure possibility. We are literally surrounded by a vast ocean of possibilities.

When we act with possibility in mind, we see that we can be creative every moment. We believe in the fertile potential of others and ourselves. This is not blind optimism.

Where there is possibility, there is also uncertainty. This logical counter-balanced relationship was expressed by Werner Heisenberg, one of the leading scientists of the twentieth century, in his Uncertainty

Principle. Simply put: You cannot simultaneously know a particle's position and its linear momentum. In other words, you can never actually predict how a particle will manifest from quantum energy.

When physicists try to predict the behavior of quantum energy, they are forced to use a mathematical approach based on probability. Probability began as collaboration between mathematicians and gamblers to determine the odds in dice games. It is basically a systematic counting of the possibilities that a certain action can occur. Some events are more likely than others, and over an average of many events a given pattern of outcome is predictable. So Schrodinger's equation, which mathematically describes all the possibilities of a quantum wave, is basically the same as a bookmaker's odds—it's an educated guess in an uncertain situation.

While energy is in its potential state, it consists of probabilities, tendencies, and urges. Quantum physics undermines the whole idea of a mechanical universe in which cause leads predictably to effect. Uncertainty is the way of life. It is the deeper essence of our existence. Things that we take for granted as safe, secure, and permanent are illusions.

From the quantum perspective, *each interaction is the unfolding of uncertain possibilities.* The same holds true for any living system, for any group field.

Faith unlocks the door of possibility. God is the highest possibility. With faith we become less fearful of the unknown, less resistant to change. We become more flexible. Intuition guides our actions as we sail toward the shores of manifesting possibilities.

Open and Flowing

Quantum energy moves in and out of our dimension. When it's outside, energy moves faster than the speed of light. Einstein said that nothing in the material world can move faster than light—however, quantum energy does just that. Why? Because quantum energy is not a material thing. It is physically boundless. This energy originates outside our dimension, moves into our dimension, and then moves back out. When it's outside, energy moves faster than the speed of light; it has no form as we know it.

Werner Heisenberg, the German physicist who helped establish quantum mechanics and our ideas about elementary particles, called the nature of quantum energy 'the dissolution of the rigid frame.' At the core, there is no form—only an unseen quality moving in and out of the observable world. What has substance is actually insubstantial.

Energy is always associated with movement, activity—an ongoing flow in the moment of life. We do not exist in a static environment but in a dynamic, active world. We can counter this flow through physical and emotional barriers that separate us and dampen our energy. To achieve such openness and flow, we need to dissolve the rigid judgments and structures we build in our lives and in our relations.

Heraclitus addressed the fluid nature of existence two thousand six hundred years ago when he said, "You cannot step twice into the same river, for fresh waters are ever flowing in upon you." Within groups, as within life, there is a constant process of emergence—an everlasting becoming. The fresh waters of energy are ever flowing, making our world a constant flux.

For any system to emerge, it must have openness to its surroundings. It must be open to what nurtures it. The rigid framework collapses in a more spiritual group field, where listening, forgiveness, spontaneity are part of the group's culture.

Synergy and Love

Energy moves in waves. When two waves are in phase, the effect is greater than simply one-plus-one. With synergy, one and one make the power of four. Two energy units appear out of nowhere. The process of synergy leads to an energy manifestation. When a group produces more than the sum of its parts through the joint effort of its members, it is achieving synergy.

It is nature's way to be in synergy. Two cells out of sync will beat together when placed near each other. The power of synergy can be harnessed to create superconductivity and synchronous light emissions (lasers). A similar entrainment can occur for energy fields of individuals or groups. When any energy field aligns with its deeper nature a higher vibration exists, which makes all things possible.

"Jesus said, 'If two make peace with each other in this one house, they will say to the mountain, "Move Away," and it will move away.'"[65]

This higher energy field translates into exchanges that are uplifting, inspiring, and fulfilling. Love, respect, and a sense of brotherhood and sisterhood predominate. There is laughter and fun. There is forgiveness, because the Light embraces the dark.

In this higher vibration heaven opens its door. Jesus became fully conscious of his God-connection, and he taught that this heightened state of vibration is available to each of us. He described the characteristics of this place of being. He is a guide, showing the way to align with the God-Head. When we read his teachings, which were revolutionary at that time, and understand that Jesus was consciously connected to a realm beyond our reality, we have to marvel at the extent of his understanding of the quantum realm. Or was Jesus describing the nature of God, which scientist see reflected in the Quantum Field?

---

[65] Thomas 48

Then he turned again to his own notebook: "The consciousness of God is within each atom of the universe. Its nature is a roadmap on how to return to that higher frequency of our God-Connection.

"Like any reception device, our minds can resonate at the same level, the same frequency, as the Law. Radios receive their signal from the transmitting airwaves by aligning themselves to the signal being transmitted. When our behavior aligns with these energy characteristics, the body behaves like a tuning fork. It vibrates at a higher level and closer to God's Kingdom.

"Jesus taught us about the nature of his Kingdom. He revealed our inherent God-connection. Through his gospels Jesus exposed something governing every atom. He revealed the characteristics of God. He described the nature of the Light that precedes the light. It is the beginning of the physical universe. Why should it not, then, be the end-point to which we are evolving?"

Then Christopher sat still. He realized that he now had a new priority in his life, and that his life would never be the same. He had opened up his internal guidance.

He did not care for money, intimate relations, nor professional status. His primary focus was now his connection with God.

CHAPTER

At the end of the third day, Christopher was still sitting in his apartment not wanting to go anywhere. Everything else seemed so much less important. He felt no hunger after not eating for two days. All he wanted to do was to be still and focus on God's presence. Be still with the Light within his meditations. Be still with the breath within the breath.

But an inner voice, an intuitive pulse, started needling his awareness. He thought about the fact that he was alone, isolated in his apartment and separate from his associates at the university. Isolation—that's not the nature of spirit. To experience spirit is to experience interconnectedness.

He thought of the Matthew Community and the integration of the six characteristics. He thought of the Franciscan community in Toulouse and its pristine focus on the gospels. He recalled the gospel of Matthew: "Again, I tell you that if two of you on earth agree about anything you ask for, it will be done for you by my Father in heaven. For where two or three come together in my name, there am I with them.[66]"

Suddenly he realized what was being asked of him next. It came to him clearly: "Be in and support communities of Light."

Now he knew why his soul had chosen an orphanage upbringing and why he had chosen, for a time, the seminary. He could see what his third star would be about—supporting communities of Light. He did not know how or when it would happen. In a way, it didn't seem to matter because he had his connection with God and he trusted God's grace and unfoldment.

He began to imagine a fitting, spiritual community, an environment dedicated to supporting his God-connection. Just as a plant needs the right soil, water, sun, and temperature in order to flourish, we all flourish in the right environment. He wanted an environment where he could further integrate Jesus' teachings. He prayed for the right setting to grow into this understanding of his mission.

As Christopher prayed, images of white cloths, gardens, a large candle-lit room, doing yoga postures with many others. Kripalu Ashram came to his mind. He thought, "This can't be." How odd. "An ashram—a non-Christian community based on the Hindu traditions?" He laughed at his guidance. That night he dreamt he was with an old bald man with piercing eyes

---

[66] Matthew 18:18-20

and a gentle, loving manner. The old man wore a long orange robe that flowed around him as he sat on the floor. Christopher sat down in front of him, and the man began teaching him by writing on a slate. It was Swami Kripalu. In the morning he realized that his initial guidance was no joke. Perhaps it was just the thing that the rebellious Jesus would propose. Jesus had always been willing to challenge conventional thinking so that he could point to the deeper truths and get beyond the facade of religion.

His yoga teacher at Princeton had once recommended a retreat at the Kripalu Yoga Community, located in northeast Pennsylvania. During that visit, which had taken place seven months earlier, Christopher had been very impressed with the residents' focus on developing their inner light.

His attraction to yoga was that it had no dogma. It wasn't a religion. It was more like a science that focused on shifting one's energy vibration. The work involved practices— body postures, breathing exercises, meditation, selfless service, and detachment—that produced tangible results. You could tell when things worked right and when they didn't. When yoga occurred, your vibration matched the vibration of the Light. The experiential quality of yoga appealed to the scientist in him.

That day Christopher called the Kripalu community. The woman on the phone remembered him from his previous visit and made arrangements for his arrival. So he gave notice to his professors, and within a month he sold his sports car, bought a truck, and drove to Kripalu Ashram.

The autumn leaves had already turned and cold weather had come when Christopher arrived in Sumneytown, Pennsylvania. It was a town with little commerce, a remnant of eighteenth-century stagecoach days. He drove to the end of a quiet residential street and pulled into the gravel driveway edged by an old, two-story stone building. Following signs that pointed to the office, he passed the kitchen. The smell of fresh-baked bread poured through its windows. At the office he was greeted cheerfully by a woman dressed in a white sari.

"Come this way," she said.

She led him up a path still thick with marigolds, up stone steps to the men's dorm. When she approached the upper steps, she called out, "Sister on the floor."

One lone male voice called back, "All clear."

She swung open the door of the upper right wing—a large, open room rimmed with four bunks, dressers, and a makeshift closet. "They assigned you this bunk; there is a bedroll you can use in the corner." It was a top bunk, close to the ceiling. The narrow ladder served this bunk as well as the one next to it.

From a side room emerged a man in his mid-thirties. "Hi! My name is Parmananda. You can call me Parm." Everyone who lived here received a Sanskrit name—a reminder of the spiritual focus they have undertaken. Within each bunk were shelves and a cupboard. There was also some hanging space in the communal closet. Parm chatted away as he helped Christopher get settled. But Christopher hadn't brought much—some clothes and an old, worn woolen blanket that Sister Mary Oliver had given him long ago.

All the men were as friendly as Parm. Eight of them shared the bathroom. They were all amazingly courteous. The crowded conditions did not bother them at all. In fact, the group field sustained them.

At the time Christopher arrived, over two hundred residents were living at the two Pennsylvania properties. The ratio was about sixty percent women, ten percent children, and thirty percent men. He saw very quickly that the residents had adopted many of energy's characteristics into their culture.

The community practiced celibacy. Residents did not extend their sexual energy to others; instead, they harnessed that energy into their spiritual practices. There were no drugs, alcohol, television, or cigarettes. The aim was to co-create a vigorous, healthy lifestyle that would raise everyone's energy.

He quickly fell into the routine. At four-fifteen each morning, one of the brothers made his way through the four wings of the men's dorm playing a melodic tune on his flute. Everyone dressed, got out the door, and lined up for jogging on a stretch of road that was lit by candles. The brisk smells of the early morning enlivened the senses. Sixty-eight residents jogged in stride, all aglow in their white pants and colorful jackets. After twenty minutes of rhythmic running, everyone gathered in the main room, which was also lit by candles. Each person laid out his or her yoga blanket and began to do breathing exercises, followed by yoga postures. This was sacred time. Then the residents would meditate until seven forty-five.

After breakfast, everyone went to their jobs. Most of them worked within the ashram—Christopher, for example, worked in both the garden and the kitchen. After supper they gathered from seven fifteen to nine for chanting and inspiring talks. Everyone was asleep by ten. These disciplines set the rhythm for his days.

Within the first week, this community showed Christopher that groups could generate powerful energy fields. The residents formed an interconnected web, and their shared energy made all of the discipline much easier. Such a group, he realized to his satisfaction, lives the interconnectedness described by quantum physicists, ancient yogis, and Jesus.

Each of the six characteristics were present to some extent. Over all, it was a very good environment to experiment with, experience, and integrate the characteristics of energy in a group setting.

Christopher took the yoga-teacher training and massage certification courses that were offered to all residents. After nine months in the ashram, he began teaching yoga classes in the community. His classes grew as his ability to teach also grew. He tapped into the memories of his experience as a Franciscan monk teaching at the university.

Those in charge of the ashram's guest programs noticed Christopher's natural ability to teach. They asked him to lead a yoga program for guests at the Sumneytown facility. After just one experience, they scheduled him to lead programs regularly. His workshops always had waiting lists.

The workshops became Christopher's laboratory. In them he learned how participants create communities with unique ecosystems and energy fields. He learned how to uplift the workshop environment and energize the participants. He saw that energy and consciousness are entwined; when group energy is raised, so is the group consciousness. Then, whatever is blocking the energy is more easily seen and released. Personal growth breakthroughs were consistently occurring, and his method for achieving these ends was the application of the nature of energy as expressed in the teachings of Jesus.

At first he tried to script every minute of his programs. That was impossible. He couldn't predict what would emerge from any particular group field. Instead, he would prepare a plan, then throw it away and walk into each group field with an open mind.

He learned not to judge people who "blocked." Often, these people would inspire the whole group with their dramatic breakthroughs. One man showed up who was so somber that he seemed almost catatonic. Christopher wondered if he should ask for the man's medical records. But the next morning the man started to share. And by that evening, he had sixty people weeping with compassion and joy.

For openness, Christopher had to assure a safe environment. After all, he was asking his participants to break out of old patterns. So Kripalu provided trained, attentive staff, comfortable accommodations, and all meals. He enforced the spirit of confidentiality and compassionate listening.

He deliberately created interconnectedness by inviting participants to interact. Workshops always broke into small teams, so participants worked with each other. He struck a dynamic balance in scheduling—work, play, socialize, and exercise. He stimulated diversity by pairing up unlike people. He promoted a sense of possibility by believing in people's potential to reach the Light. In this environment, miracles happened.

But the workshops had a built-in limitation. They lasted only three to seven days. It was difficult for a brief experience to effect permanent changes. People would experience a peak "aha!" then gradually lose the insights and energy they had gained.

Christopher noticed that participants in the couples's workshops generally fared better. Couples reported that they not only retained the positive changes in their relationships but also gained new insights as they went ahead. He saw why: couples are actually group fields, partnerships that carry a shared energy when they leave the program. He realized that the group field itself can perpetuate a high-energy zone and be more in the Light.

Over the course of three hundred-plus workshops, he got to see what uplifts and depresses group energy fields. It didn't matter whether the workshop focused on stress management, personal growth, or relationship-building. High-energy group fields all shared certain characteristics—the same ones that describe the quantum field, the same described in the prakriti of ancient yogis. Any group field can develop the energy of Light. One only needed to adjust its culture.

Sometimes the participants in his workshops were CEOs and presidents of companies. Because these people were responsible for large and often dysfunctional organizations, they were invariably interested in Christopher's skill with group energy. They started asking him to bring his process out of the ashram—come run programs for their companies. He said yes. He could see that he was being handed a new opportunity, a chance to develop a group field that would outlast the brief time of a workshop, improvements that would sustain themselves. What would happen when a business organization integrated these characteristics of energy? He set out to get some answers.

In 1986 Christopher started a consulting firm. Its mission was to apply the energizing formula to help groups radiate at the highest level, where all things are possible. He knew that he had found his path.

All the marketing he needed for his new venture came from former participants in his workshops at Kripalu. Word-of-mouth quickly brought him a wide variety of contracts throughout the U.S. and even Iceland. The business groups he worked with ranged from aircraft manufacturers to restaurants. Christopher particularly enjoyed working with advertising agencies and TV broadcasting. He liked that these groups required awareness, creativity, and efficiency, and that they wielded such social power. Christopher realized he wanted to serve industries that shape consciousness.

He served hundreds of companies, working the trenches, doing consulting. A business's road to become more "spiritual" requires challenging work to break dysfunctional patterns that go against energy's nature. Leaders have to face their own energy-draining behaviors. They have to address conflicts. They have to retool systems that short-circuit productivity, creativity, and responsiveness. His work involved healing relationships and finding new ways to communicate. And yet he found that whenever a group aligns itself with the energizing characteristics, magic happens.

His reputation grew. He became known as a magician who could make a few changes and transform a business. He facilitated huge turnarounds in company fortunes. Many wanted to know how he was able to do this so consistently. He would say, "It's about becoming more aligned to the Light."

Christopher agreed to speak at a large business conference in Chicago. He walked onto a large stage to the applause of a full room. When the applause slowed, he went right to his point:

"All groups have patterns that shape the group field, the sustained energy of the group. These patterns reflect the true values and culture of the group, whether it's a family, a business, or a community. These patterns can either align with or oppose energy's nature. By changing the primary pattern that opposes the nature of energy, the most uplifting impact will result."

Then he introduced each of the six characteristics and their origins in spirituality and science. He also showed a process for transforming any group so that God's Spirit vibrates stronger within it. He finished to a standing ovation.

Afterwards, a man came up from the audience and introduced himself as Greg Henson. Henson said, "What you have uncovered could be very useful to the nations of the world. You do realize that, don't you? It could be a guide for global prosperity. I would like you to be part of a project sponsored by the U.N. Can we talk tomorrow?"

Without hesitation Christopher said, "Yes." He had an intuitive sense that he was about to make some life changes.

It was a brisk day in late October. The cold breeze from Lake Michigan whipped and swirled up the road. It was a short walk to the restaurant Christopher had chosen for his luncheon meeting with Greg. The U.N. under-secretary was already waiting for him when he reached the table.

Greg stood, and they shook hands. While they ordered lunch, they traded information about their personal histories. Then, when the menus had gone, Greg leaned over the table. In his precise British accent started describing the work of his committee.

"The U.N. is funding studies to investigate the prosperity of nations and the correlation of governance, culture, and its natural resources. What is the ideal governance that allows nations to prosper? What principles are true for all situations?" He received his cup of hot tea and squeezed a bit of lemon into it.

"So you can imagine how interested I am in your six characteristics. I'm wondering if this is the code." He stopped for a moment and looked at Christopher.

"Funny. I never thought for a moment that the code was in the gospels. The same code is etched in every atom of the universe. It appears you have uncovered the code for a prosperous environment."

Christopher smiled. "It's a code to a high-energy field. Everything is energy. Nations form massive energy fields, and they all resonate at different levels. The higher-vibrating ones are more prosperous. Their citizens are able to grow, like seeds planted in good soil."

Christopher recalled with happiness the first time he had ever heard the seed analogy.

"This is not my code. Jesus expressed it; so did yogis six thousand years ago. You can see it work on ecosystems and corporations. I would be very surprised if these six characteristics were not part of the most prosperous nations."

Greg leaned forward again. "The implications are staggering. We could show governments the optimal environment for prosperity and growth."

The waiter placed their lunches in front of them. Greg didn't stop to take a bite.

"We have gathered a lot of statistics. You will be assigned our two most competent staff. We will pay your consulting fee, and we will support your work with a strong network of cooperation. You can have an office in the U.N. building. There are apartments we can arrange for you within walking distance. Come and join us."

"Before I give you a decision," said Christopher, "one question. I had a premonition last night that your cooperation with the U.S. isn't very good. Is there any problem?"

Greg looked down on his plate. "When I mentioned that strong network of cooperation, I did not include the present U.S. administration. They have grown increasingly antagonistic. We have split over the war in Iraq, over the environment. Some close to the President are actively hostile."

Then Greg leaned back. "But don't let that stop you. After all, we are a sovereign nation that controls its own small patch of land in New York. Besides, this has a global implication. It will last far beyond the time frame of a U.S. administration."

Christopher was still, and then he closed his eyes for a moment. He recalled Isaac and Sivis and their manipulations. Then he thought of the potential good this could bring to the planet. "Okay, I will do it."

"When can you start?"

CHAPTER 16

Christopher arrived in New York on a cold day in January, 2005. His two assistants greeted him warmly at the airport. Prema Krishna was a woman from Bombay in her mid thirties, with dark skin and black hair that cascaded to her waist. She had striking eyes. Jean René from Paris was six foot tall and trim, with a radiant smile. Both were very knowledgeable about cultures and governance around the world.

Within a few days the three of them developed a strategy to look at the larger historical trends of nation growth and decline. It didn't take long to see the laws of nature actually ruling the laws of national success.

They posed two questions. What nation best embodied the nature of energy? And second, what nation dramatically violated this nature?

The answer to both questions was the same—the United States.

Christopher pondered this conclusion with Greg, Prema, and Jean. "It appears the founding fathers intuitively knew the code and wove it into the Constitution. The U.S. has succeeded because its framework mimics the nature of energy.

But the policies and actions of the present U.S. administration have opposed the nature of energy. Not surprisingly, the prosperity of the United States has declined rapidly. The huge deficit, the loss of global esteem, the rapid decline of the dollar, big business concessions, degradation of the environment—the facts are easy to read."

They agreed to discuss these preliminary findings with a few colleagues.

One week later, Greg came in the conference room with Christopher's team present. He was pensive, looking down on the table. "The funding for our project has been terminated. It seems that someone high on the appropriations committee wants to terminate our project before the results get out. The findings are so promising—and I guess threatening to the present U.S. administration. I don't know what to say."

Prema then spoke up. "My government will sponsor the project. India has a need to understand governance that enables its citizens to prosper."

Jean said, "The European Alliance wants this information. After all, they are totally occupied with framing a United Europe. Let us make some calls."

They both left while Christopher and Greg sat still.

Christopher blurted out, "I was actually beginning to imagine what it would be like to have all nations vibrating at a high level. No more poverty, famine, hunger, or lack of education. I thought that perhaps we could make a global leap into the Light. But now, this opposition."

Greg said, "It can happen. We just need to stay in truth and hold that vision. We have something devastating against this U.S. administration, and they just found out. Be careful, they are vicious. They will attack your character in order to deflate your message. They will plant nonsense in the media to defame you. I hope this doesn't get nasty."

Christopher nodded. "It was my premonition. I guess I'm meant to stir up something. It is so ironic. Here is an administration that claims to be religious but has actually taken this country farther from the teachings of Jesus than any other in the history of the U.S. Now the country's fortunes have shifted out of balance. An unprecedented proportion goes to a select few. The vast majority—who includes the unborn generation—must struggle with less and a growing debt."

Then Prema and Jean came in Christopher's office high-fiving each other. Jean said, "Our funding has not only returned, but it has increased. Also, we are scheduled to give a presentation in two weeks in the large auditorium. We should have a good attendance."

"That's terrific. How did you pull this off?"

Prema said, "It was easy. People are eager for some positive, constructive way to stand up to the United States."

Richard Rolando, a high-ranking member of the Federalist Society and advisor to the President, immediately recognized this new U.N. research as a threat—a public opinion nightmare at best. When he learned that Christopher Conrad was an American citizen, he was incensed. He believed that anyone who opposed the present administration was unpatriotic. Rolando also had a strong conviction that the country was better off being ruled by an elite group, an aristocracy whose existence was dependent upon it remaining in power. He was a ruthless strategist on retaining power.

Rolando took personal responsibility for neutralizing the study. If he could discredit this Conrad fellow along the way, all the better. The world is full of idealistic fools with no comprehension of the ruthless principles of power. That's fine—we have places for them, universities, think tanks, places where they can talk all they want with no results. But if one of these bright boys thrusts his ideas into the mechanism of power, he must be silenced.

It should have been easy. Most of the time it can be done with a few phone calls, twist a few arms, wipe out the project. But this approach had backfired. Opposition by the United States administration had done nothing more than create widespread interest in Conrad's upcoming presentation. The whole situation irritated Rolando to no end, like an invisible splinter.

Rolando himself attended the first presentation. The great hall was packed with representatives from businesses and governments throughout the world. Christopher stood at the bottom of the huge half-bowl auditorium, looking up at the diverse mix of representatives. It seemed that every race and religion was represented.

Before he began, Christopher mingled with the audience. A heavyset man stepped up and introduced himself. He had a full beard, tightly trimmed, and a perfectly shaved, gleaming scalp. His eyes were dark and humorless. "I'm looking forward to your talk," he said. "My name is Richard Rolando." He extended a sweaty hand with a limp handshake.

"Mr. Rolando!" said Christopher. "Finally we meet. I understand I have you to thank for the increase of funding and interest for this study."

Rolando tightened his brow. "The president is interested in your findings. I hope your report puts him in a good light."

"The report will shine a light of truth that penetrates through the smoke screens tossed up by this administration." Christopher smiled. "Give the President my regards."

Greg opened the presentation and introduced Christopher. The applause was widespread and enthusiastic. Christopher took center stage.

"Is there a code that can unleash the aspiring

potential of any nation? Greg Henson asked me to join with Prema here, and Jean, and as a team we set out to answer that question. My colleagues and I believe there is such a code, which we will present today.

"As a framework, we utilized the work I have done in organizational development. For there, too, is a code. As you shall see, it is the same code that is present in the Bible and that is etched into every atom of the universe, a code that even has spiritual implications."

He then explained each of the six characteristics from the view of science, ecology, organizational development, and spirituality. "Organizations that thrive and prosper have the six characteristics active in their culture. So it is no surprise to us that the nation most closely aligned with the nature of energy is also the most prosperous nation in the history of mankind—the United States."

Christopher waited for the buzz of reaction to settle.

"Before I show you the proof of this conclusion, I want to mention another aspect of our study, one that came to parallel this first in a rather startling way. From the beginning we set out another measure to test our theory. What nation that was aligned with energy had suddenly chosen to oppose energy's nature? And what have been the ramifications of this choice? We studied all nations. We eliminated those that had been struck by forces outside of their control—military invasion, natural disasters, that sort of thing. We were looking for the most vivid example of a society that had deliberately chosen to steer itself away from the natural patterns that support growth and prosperity. Here, curiously enough, the data forced us to the same conclusion we had reached with the first question. The most grievous example of a contemporary nation that has turned away from the natural principles of energy is the United States—and I should specify, the United States under its present administration."

A roar swept through the assemblage.

"In other words, our study shows that the present U.S. administration has taken that country farther from the nature of energy than any previous administration. The result is a reversal and sudden decline of the prosperity it previously bathed in."

He took a moment to study the audience. He spotted the scowling, bearded dome of Rolando and smiled. Christopher stared at him as his face got redder and his fists clenched. "The leaking of these findings has resulted in new sponsorship for our work, so I would like to thank the European Alliance as well as the governments of India and France. We hope that these findings will support global governance in a way that brings a higher energy, greater prosperity, and movement into the Light for all world citizens.

"We are not suggesting that governance should be modeled after the U.S. We are saying that each nation should look objectively at its policies and laws and see which ones align with and which ones oppose energy's nature. With this framework of understanding, each nation can make more intelligent choices about how best to serve its people and its future. Therefore, for illustration's sake only, let us look at how the U.S. integrated the natural principles of energy into its governance and culture, and then how the present administration has gone against these principles.

Intention and Alignment

"What gave the founding fathers of the U.S. the entitlement to begin this nation were the 'Laws of Nature and of Nature's God' as stated in the beginning of the Declaration of Independence of the Thirteen Colonies. I quote:

"'When in the Course of human events, it becomes necessary for one people to dissolve the political bands which have connected them with another, and to assume among the powers of the earth, the separate and equal station to which the Laws of Nature and of Nature's God entitle them…..'

"Even the lifeblood of currency that fuels the economic mechanism of the nation is imprinted on every coin and dollar: 'IN GOD WE TRUST.'

"The expression 'One nation under God' was added to the U.S. Pledge of Allegiance by President Dwight D. Eisenhower. Eisenhower said at the time, 'In this way we are reaffirming the transcendence of religious faith in America's heritage and future; in this way we shall constantly strengthen those spiritual weapons which forever will be our country's most powerful resource in peace and war.'

"The U.S. government acknowledges God's presence, but it in no way uses or abuses that connection. Church and state are separate for a reason. It becomes too easy to claim God's inspiration to excuse self-serving goals. Throughout the ages we have seen the abuse that occurs in the name of God: the crucifixion of Jesus, the Inquisitions, and the recent Jihad— all have been justified through the delusion of religion. The United States has wisely maintained that separation between church and state—has, that is, until this administration.

"The U.S. President and his administration have helped organize and form strong ties with the Religious Right. They claim God's guidance and inspiration in order to justify aggressive acts. His reelection was religious based, declaring moral values. I doubt that God, whose vibration is love, would attack another country on trumped-up charges of weapons of mass destruction and terrorist networks, killing over a hundred thousand people. But it has always been possible to delude people by saying that such violence is justified by the fact that the war is a holy war, or that the axis of evil must be destroyed. Or to delude people with frightening images, and color codes for terror alerts. Terrorists have a different delusion, that blowing oneself up—killing and maiming as many innocent people as possible—is also holy.

Diversity and Balance

"The Declaration of Independence says this: 'We hold these truths to be self-evident, that all men are created equal, that they are endowed by their Creator with certain unalienable Rights, that among these are Life, Liberty and the pursuit of Happiness.'

"The United States was founded on the principle of embracing diversity. Cuban-Americans in Miami differ from Mormon-Americans in Utah who differ from Silicon Valley–Americans in California. U.S. citizens are diverse in their thinking patterns, points of view, and cultural differences. Nations that encourage diversity become lands of opportunity. These countries embrace free speech, equal rights, and freedom of expression. They hold open a broad space, a foundation for exposing their citizens to diverse beliefs and preferences.

"The principle of tolerance must be upheld in a society that embraces cultural differences and outlooks. Most Americans now accept cultural differences, racially mixed marriages, and single-family households. Fifty years ago we were not so tolerant. We have prospered as we have become more diverse.

"The more tolerant a society is, the more likely it is to engender mutual trust and cooperation. Tolerance allows religions to disagree and yet flourish. It defends the rights of minorities.

"However, the United States' tolerance for diversity was severely tested by the Twin Tower collapse. The administration has reduced tolerance through its Patriot Act, its treatment of prisoners, its elimination of civil rights—the list goes on. This administration has reversed this nation's march toward tolerance.

Relational and Holistic

"Again, I state a principle: 'We the People of the United States, in Order to form a more perfect Union….' The very name of this nation is a mantra: the 'United States.' All its citizens are united, not only legally but also through the network of roads, railways, cables, air-waves, and systems of commerce bring the people into a working whole.

"And yet, this administration has divided its citizens more effectively than any other except during the American Civil War. Division seems to be this administration's deliberate strategy, applied through its fixation on non-essential issues such as same-sex marriage and the individual's right to die. The administration is deliberately fanning the flames of controversy over issues like these in order to deflect public attention from its failed policies."

Open and Flowing

"We live in an age when national walls have become porous. We now think in terms of global finance, global technology, and global information. Aided by cyberspace, investors roam freely, putting money into the economies of as many as one hundred eighty different countries. The investing arena has become a vast, open plain. As a result, financial activity is increasing. Openness is energizing our global economy.

"However, this administration has shut down its communication with other countries, just as it has clouded honest exchange with its citizens. For example, we were knowingly deceived about the cost of Medicare revisions. The administration cooked the books. Such behavior is not consistent with the American ideal of open government. Military advisors are dismayed that the administration is not open to their input, and this close-mindedness has resulted in stupid management of post-war Iraq. During its second term, the administration has become even more closed and insular than the previous four years. This trend is very dangerous when coupled with the government's so-called religious zeal."

Possibility and Uncertainty

"Uncertainty is the way of life. It is the deeper essence of our existence. Things that we take for granted as safe, secure, and permanent are actually illusions.

"The events of September 11 made these illusions very evident. As a global community, we were forced to grasp the unthinkable and confront uncertainty. Many people reevaluated their relationships and their priorities as life itself became less certain.

"But September 11 did not introduce America to the experience of insecurity. For example, as recently as the late eighties and early nineties, when many workers lost their jobs to downsizing, reengineering, and mergers, American business leaders viewed insecurity as a good thing—a sure sign that we were being active in a fast-paced, volatile global market. And yet, this administration has orchestrated waves of panic over insecurity, using its regular terror alerts and scenarios of doom, which somehow further justifies their actions.

Synergy and Love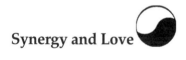

"Now, finally, this quotation: '...That to secure these rights, Governments are instituted among Men, deriving their just powers from the consent of the governed.'

"Synergy is an energy of exchange and relationship. It is the interface between relationships of two or more energies. Prior to this administration, the United States upheld its tradition of caring and justice toward its neighbors. But that freshness of international synergy has been greatly dampened. Synergy is also about the relationship among citizens. 'We the People of the United States,' goes the immortal phrase. What makes us a functional, non-manipulated 'we' is the tradition of truthful communication by the administration. Yet we have been fed more lies by this administration than by any other. Take, for example, the big lie about Iraq's weapons of mass destruction. What about other lies—global warming, social security…? The list goes on.

"Synergy involves support for all a country's citizens, but this support has decreased under the divisive tactics of the present U.S. Administration. Tremendous wealth has poured into the pockets of the top one percent in the country, while the debt to be paid by America's children soars. Thus, fiscal synergy has been severely compromised. Synergy also includes the relationship with the land, and it implies proper stewardship of the nation's resources. And yet, this administration has done more to turn back the progress made in our relationship to our environment than any previous administration. This deeply saddens me."

"The acts of the present administration present a clear warning to all nations who want their citizens to prosper: do not go down the road that is against nature's way. Do not go against the code given to us by Jesus, scientists, and sociologists. This U.S. administration's leadership claims to be 'guided by God,' yet its actions have strayed far from the teachings of Jesus, more than any other administration in the history of the United States. As a U.S. citizen, I am proud of my countries past and saddened and concerned by its present course.

"God bless the United States of America and all the nations of our planet. May we all move closer to the Light."

The auditorium exploded into applause. Richard Rolando, however, gave Christopher a scowling look as he rushed out of the auditorium.

Word spread about the U.N. study. Christopher was asked to speak at many venues. His schedule was booked for a series of talks, and he took two weeks to prepare the additional data coming to the team.

At his apartment he kept getting an email from some woman who had "urgent information about the administration's plans to invade Iran and Syria." At first he ignored them. But they persisted, and their claims grew more specific and more plausible. Finally he responded to emails. He set a time and place to meet with this stranger.

When he went to the restaurant down the street, he was greeted by a young girl in her teens. "Are you Melissa?" he asked. She smiled and nodded as he sat down. "You are much younger than I thought. Are you supposed to have some information for me about the administration?"

All of a sudden her sweet smile turned into a defiant stare. "Here's your information from the administration." She leaned over and said, "If you don't stop the U.N. project now there will be consequences."

Christopher looked on in disbelief and then started to laugh at the brazen child. She then leaned back and screamed, "Aaahhh!"

In a flash he was surrounded by three FBI agents. One big guy said, as the other two cuffed him, "You are under arrest for child molestation." They read him his rights. Christopher cried out, "This is a ridiculous set-up! I have done no such thing."

They pushed him out the restaurant door to a waiting squad car. "Move on, you creep."

For five hours he sat in a solitary cell. It was late that evening before he was allowed a call. He got Greg on the line, but it was too late—the papers and media had all learned that Christopher had been arrested on child molestation charges. Now the administration was doing what it did to all its opponents—discredit and attack, then use the media to generate spin. Christopher recognized these tactics in his memories of Sivis and Isaac. The attack simply further confirmed his claims about this administration.

It was an old pattern of manipulating the truth: attack the messenger to discredit the message. And it worked. Richard Rolando's staff mailed the newspaper clips to his upcoming sponsors. Quickly, people began canceling his speaking engagements.

Greg and his colleagues responded immediately with an investigation. Finally the scam was aired. It appeared that Melissa was a budding actress and her mother had been paid ten thousand dollars. Although the connection wasn't proven, many knew that the source of the bribe was Robert Rolando.

When the truth came forth, Rolando's plans back-fired for the second time; Christopher's persecution by the administration seemed to endear him to the public. He began to appear on talk shows. His straightforward illustrations about fundamental truths began to reach a larger and larger audience. He spoke as clearly as he could about administration policies that opposed nature's energy. At first, the right-wing talk shows invited him in order to discredit his findings. But the fact that his sources included the Bible, the U.S. Constitution, and fundamental discoveries in science would always silence them. Before long, the conservatives stopped inviting him onto their shows.

Christopher was a tireless advocate for Truth and Light. The fact that he was being tailed by the FBI and that his apartment had been bugged didn't deter him. He was committed to playing out his part as a bearer of Light.

Richard Rolando made it his personal crusade to silence Christopher. This entire failure had been a blight on his record, and it now stood in the way of his personal advancement. Every time he heard Christopher in the media, he felt it like a knife in his belly. So this time he tried a more sinister silencing technique.

Rolando had access to secret agents who knew how to eliminate people. In his vengeful mind Rolando wanted something painful, something that would not kill Christopher but would make him lose his mental ability. He wanted Christopher silenced but not as a martyr. One agent who was a chemist had just the potion.

The spies learned Christopher's routines. They learned, for example, that he stopped regularly at an espresso bar on the way to the U.N. So they planted an operative at the espresso bar to serve coffee. Mid-week, Christopher showed up. "Where is Wendy this morning?"

"She is on vacation," said the agent. While Christopher used the rest room, the agent dumped a vile of clear, tasteless liquid in his cup of espresso.

Christopher grabbed the cup. "Have a nice day."

The operative said under his breath, "Dude, you ain't ever going to have a nice day after you drink that."

The sidewalk was crowded as Christopher held his coffee in one hand and his briefcase in the other. He lifted his cup to take a sip, and someone knocked his elbow. "Excuse me," the passerby hurriedly said. Coffee splattered on the sidewalk.

He walked a little further and leaned against a building to catch some sun and watch the busy street. He raised his cup again, his elbow was bumped, more coffee spilled, as he turned he saw no one by his arm. A cold chill passed through him as he continued his walk. When Christopher crossed the street, a cab ran a red light and nearly hit him. His briefcase went flying, and the coffee got run over by the taxi's front tire. As Christopher recovered his briefcase, an Indian came out, apologetic. Christopher smiled, seeing his coffee in a puddle. "Well, I guess I wasn't supposed to have coffee this morning."

When Rolando learned that Christopher had not been hospitalized, he wanted to make another attempt. But then he was ordered by the administration to lay low. There were big things brewing.

The United States administration raised the terror alert to red. Then, shortly after, officials discovered high-grade anthrax in a Democratic senator's mail. Then a small bomb exploded in a Washington alley, hurting no one. No arrests were made in either incident.

Shortly after these "terror attacks," the U.S. government began pressuring for war on Syria and Iran, claiming that these "rogue nations" were responsible for the recent attacks. The U.S. began talks at the U.N., but everyone knew that the talks were a decoy—the U.S. had already begun deploying troops.

The President appealed to his religious supporters. "I have a mandate from God to end the war on terror by eliminating the axis of evil," he reiterated. Polls showed that citizens were willing to believe that another war was justified. Much of the delusion came from the proactive use of the media to sculpt a message. It seemed that more reporters than ever were on the payroll of the administration, and that the administration was actually crafting public information. Christopher refused to believe that it was necessary to continue to go down that same dark hole.

Christopher sat in the conference room with Greg, Prema, and Jean. "Now is our time to act," he told his colleagues. He was adamant. "The tremendous power of community can prevent this abuse. I tell you; last night I had a vivid dream. In the dream, we were all part of a team helping to assemble huge protests. The size of these protests dwarfed anything the world has seen before. I believe in the tremendous power of community. This power can overshadow any abusive power. This power of community can do anything, when it integrates energy's nature."

Christopher took advantage of the tremendous network encompassed by the U.N. He mobilized protests to be staged at every major city on the planet. The wave of response was global, fed by messages that saturated the Internet and the public media. Hundreds of thousands volunteered globally. Christopher believed that these people, too, believed in the power of the group field and were ready to stand in the Light.

They mobilized the protests to bring together community and to encourage the integration of the six characteristics in their structure and work ethic. Christopher personally trained the leaders of all the communities in the thousand locations throughout the globe. It was not just a U.S. community that was uniting; it was a global one.

Christopher worked tirelessly. His years as an organizational development consultant were paying off. He was able to orchestrate the simultaneous development of global communities with the support of the U.N. and his competent team.

He sat in the conference room at the U.N. with Jean and Prema. "Prema, call Munich and Bombay. They have questions about cable feeds for upcoming debates. It's amazing to see how these communities are integrating the nature of energy."

Prema responded "You made it easy for groups to develop these traits in their culture by providing simple tools.[67] Now all of the communities are practicing openness through active listening and honesty with each other. They resolve conflict. There are no secrets, no withheld information."

"Diversity is flourishing," said Christopher. "People are aligned to a common cause. There is a rich level of creative exchange. They are excited, elated. They are operating in the Light."

Prema said, "It's fascinating to see that these groups are thriving. They have become centers of hope."

Greg came in. "I just heard two TV broadcasts. Both of them commented on the rapid growth of these communities of Light. They are saying that this collective force has the power to shape policy throughout the world. Something is happening, and it's big."

"I know what you mean," said Christopher. "I feel it, too. Something is happening that is so much bigger than all of us."

Jean said, "It's the Hundredth Monkey Syndrome."

They all looked at each other with expressions of hope. "Critical mass," said Christopher. "Let's act as though this is true. If we strive with all our might, perhaps we will witness something the world has never seen before."

During the months leading up to the D-Day of global demonstrations, the communities of Light were

---

[67]   Check Your Alignment to the Nature of Light, Appendix C; page 447

all abuzz with excitement. Volunteers canvassed and rallied citizens, hooking them into involvement. Christopher's schedule of television and radio interviews never stopped. He thrived in all this activity. It felt so good to serve truth.

As the scope of their efforts grew, Christopher's team expanded. There were daily contacts with global communities, as well as media interviews and appearances. The core group enlarged to twelve.

One day they sat in the conference room for their morning brief. Christopher spoke. "I don't know what is happening, but it appears that the U.S. administration has been anticipating every single move we make." Everyone nodded.

Jean said, "I have charted the incidents of opposition to our work, and the pattern of resistance really shifted about two weeks ago."

Christopher said, "We are going to get this place debugged today. We will not have our normal discussion at this time. Please be discreet in your communications until we find out what is happening."

Then as they were leaving, June Das, one of the new members of the leading twelve, said, "Christopher, can I meet with you this evening? My time is committed to delegates from South America until seven o'clock."

"What is this about?"

She said, "Richard Rolando and the administration."

Later that day Greg came in. "The sweep of our offices, phones, and conference room came up empty. I suspect one of our staff."

Christopher said, "Two weeks ago, when this started, we had two new hires—James Gotel and June Das." Then he looked at the floor and felt some concern. "I'm meeting with June this evening. Something about our nemesis, Richard Rolando."

"Be careful," Greg said.

While he was walking to the quiet café where they were to meet, Christopher had an uneasy feeling. But an inner voice said, "Stay calm."

When he arrived, June was sitting at a booth. She signaled him. She looked nervous. He greeted her and asked, "June what did you want to discuss?"

Before she could answer, a big guy sat next to him with the muzzle of a gun protruding from his overcoat. "I will use this if you don't cooperate," said the goon.

Christopher took a deep breath and slowly exhaled. "Okay. What do you want?"

"Walk out quietly with us to that car parked outside."

The gun-toting behemoth sat in the back seat with Christopher. June took the front seat, whispering something to the driver as he whisked them off to an uptown apartment, where Rolando was waiting.

Richard Rolando sat in a big cushioned chair with a high back. "We have methods to make sure that your liberal ways will perish. Get real, my naïve boy. This administration knows how to sway opinions through the media. Look at how we play those religious fanatics. Ha Ha Ha! Our President is masterful. You think a few protests are going to stop this war? Ridiculous. There is far too much oil at stake. This administration has invested a fortune in two other wars, and now there is a lot more to take. The vault is open. You can't do a thing."

"I never heard you talk like this on *The News Hour*," said Christopher.

"I'm going to enjoy seeing you suffer!" cried Rolando with gusto. "Bawh ha ha ha! Don't think you are getting out of here alive."

Then Rolando ordered his goon: "Tie him up, and guard him in the next room."

While the goon was binding his legs and hands, Christopher heard Rolando give an order to June. "Get me a large vat of acid. Also, get me some surgical tools. I want to begin by removing his voice box." He hesitated for a moment, than said, "Oh yeah. Get some Drano, also. I don't want him to clog the pipes. Bhaw ha ha ha!"

Christopher lay bound on the bed. The goon was in a chair, and the door was closed. He remembered his message to stay calm.

Suddenly, in a blinding flash, a radiant being appeared. It was almost too bright to see, and yet Christopher perceived a human outline within that light. A voice from the radiance said, "Christopher you have much to do. The earth is ready to be in the Light."

Christopher's bonds fell away. He glanced at the behemoth, who was out cold. The angel opened the window. Down the fire escape he ran. When he reached the sidewalk, he turned. The angel of Light was no longer there.

From a pay phone, Christopher called Greg. Greg arranged through his U.N. connections to fly Christopher out of the country immediately, to Paris. There, Jean set up teleconferences between Christopher and the New York staff. In this way they coordinated the April protests.

Of course they tried to press charges against Rolando and his crew. But no arrests were made. Even so, they felt sure that Rolando's career was through. He had been pegged by the media as Christopher's failed adversary. He was portrayed as he truly was; self-centered, vengeful, and a liar. Now his own party was using him as the scapegoat, implying that he had acted on his own accord, when in reality higher authorities of the nation was in on the tactics he used.

The day arrived for the protests. Christopher was the keynote speaker for the demonstration in Washington DC. He was joined by numerous senators and members of congress who opposed this further use of force. Christopher stood on a raised platform with the Washington Monument and the U.S. Capitol in the background. He had two bodyguards with him. At ten in the morning, the sun shone as entertainers sang songs of peace and the crowd cheered. He walked past security to the steps and slowly ascended to the platform, where he took an empty seat. He had never seen such a vast crowd. Everywhere he looked was an ocean of people. The guy next to him elbowed him. "Hey, Christopher. They say that over a million are here in Washington for this event." Christopher leaned over and said, "It's ironic that the government was actually a catalyst for this type of gathering of humanity. The administration's practices have galvanized the globe in a stand for: 'No more war; be in the Light.'"

Christopher was introduced to an unprecedented storm of applause. By now, his face was familiar from the news and talk shows. He stood confident in his connection to the Light; he spoke slowly as his voice echoed out to the vast crowd. "There is a collective force that we harness when we empower any group field. Today we are tapping a world-wide group field that has the power to make global changes. We are saying NO to war and YES to the elimination of hunger, YES to education, YES to liberty, YES to global prosperity—for we are truly a global family."

After the applause, Christopher spoke again. "As a planet, we are ready to embrace the vision of peace and Light. Let us all unite with our brothers and sisters around the globe, this moment…. Let the vision come! Let us together as a collective force ensure that the tremendous resources formerly wasted in war will now be directed to the health and well-being of all the inhabitants on this planet."

In a Georgetown townhouse, a single shot was heard. It came from the house of Richard Rolando. The

TV was on, the live news covering the global protest. The announcer was saying, "Several hundred million people came together. The planet united as it has never done before. The global tallies are still coming in. It appears that the U.S. administration is standing down on its aggressive war posturing. Again, the force of political change lies with this unprecedented showing by the people of the world…."

On the floor in a pool of blood lay Rolando. Somehow, Christopher, while sitting on the platform, got a flash of the persona of Rolando, Sivis, and Isaac, all one in the same. Then he recalled a story Orion once told his sons: the beast returned a third time but killed himself because the environment was too pure—and he did not return again.

Christopher knew that the planet had made a shift into God's Light. He prayed for this new age being born, a new age ruled by governance of Light. These words came to him from the gospel of Thomas:

"The disciples said to Jesus, 'Tell us how our end will be.' Jesus said, 'Have you discovered, then, the beginning, that you look for the end? For where the beginning is, there will the end be. Blessed is he who will take his place in the beginning; he will know the end and will not experience death.[68]'"

THE END

68   Thomas:18

APPENDICIES

A P P E N D I X A

THE GOSPEL OF THOMAS[1]

These are the secret sayings which the living Jesus spoke and which Didymos Judas Thomas wrote down.

(1) And he said, "Whoever finds the interpretation of these sayings will not experience death."

(2) Jesus said, "Let him who seeks continue seeking until he finds. When he finds, he will become troubled. When he becomes troubled, he will be astonished, and he will rule over the All."

(3) Jesus said, "If those who lead you say to you, 'See, the kingdom is in the sky,' then the birds of the sky will precede you. If they say to you, 'It is in the sea,' then the fish

---

[1] Translated by Thomas O. Lambdin, selection made from James M. Robinson, ed., The Nag Hammadi Library, revised edition. HarperCollins, San Francisco, 1990.

will precede you. Rather, the kingdom is inside of you, and it is outside of you. When you come to know yourselves, then you will become known, and you will realize that it is you who are the sons of the living father. But if you will not know yourselves, you dwell in poverty and it is you who are that poverty."

(4) Jesus said, "The man old in days will not hesitate to ask a small child seven days old about the place of life, and he will live. For many who are first will become last, and they will become one and the same."

(5) Jesus said, "Recognize what is in your sight, and that which is hidden from you will become plain to you. For there is nothing hidden which will not become manifest."

(6) His disciples questioned him and said to him, "Do you want us to fast? How shall we pray? Shall we give alms? What diet shall we observe?"

Jesus said, "Do not tell lies, and do not do what you hate, for all things are plain in the sight of heaven. For nothing hidden will not become manifest, and nothing covered will remain without being uncovered."

(7) Jesus said, "Blessed is the lion which becomes man when consumed by man; and cursed is the man whom the lion consumes, and the lion becomes man."

(8) And he said, "The man is like a wise fisherman who cast his net into the sea and drew it up from the sea full of small fish. Among them the wise fisherman found a fine large fish. He threw all the small fish back into the

sea and chose the large fish without difficulty. Whoever has ears to hear, let him hear."

(9) Jesus said, "Now the sower went out, took a handful (of seeds), and scattered them. Some fell on the road; the birds came and gathered them up. Others fell on the rock, did not take root in the soil, and did not produce ears. And others fell on thorns; they choked the seed(s) and worms ate them. And others fell on the good soil and it produced good fruit: it bore sixty per measure and a hundred and twenty per measure."

(10) Jesus said, "I have cast fire upon the world, and see, I am guarding it until it blazes."

(11) Jesus said, "This heaven will pass away, and the one above it will pass away. The dead are not alive, and the living will not die. In the days when you consumed what is dead, you made it what is alive. When you come to dwell in the light, what will you do? On the day when you were one you became two. But when you become two, what will you do?"

(12) The disciples said to Jesus, "We know that you will depart from us. Who is to be our leader?"

Jesus said to them, "Wherever you are, you are to go to James the righteous, for whose sake heaven and earth came into being."

(13) Jesus said to his disciples, "Compare me to someone and tell me whom I am like."

Simon Peter said to him, "You are like a righteous angel."

Matthew said to him, "You are like a wise philosopher."

Thomas said to him, "Master, my mouth is wholly incapable of saying whom you are like."

Jesus said, "I am not your master. Because you have drunk, you have become intoxicated from the bubbling spring which I have measured out."

And he took him and withdrew and told him three things. When Thomas returned to his companions, they asked him, "What did Jesus say to you?"

Thomas said to them, "If I tell you one of the things which he told me, you will pick up stones and throw them at me; a fire will come out of the stones and burn you up."

(14) Jesus said to them, "If you fast, you will give rise to sin for yourselves; and if you pray, you will be condemned; and if you give alms, you will do harm to your spirits. When you go into any land and walk about in the districts, if they receive you, eat what they will set before you, and heal the sick among them. For what goes into your mouth will not defile you, but that which issues from your mouth - it is that which will defile you."

(15) Jesus said, "When you see one who was not born of woman, prostrate yourselves on your faces and worship him. That one is your father."

(16) Jesus said, "Men think, perhaps, that it is peace which I have come to cast upon the world. They do not know that it is dissension which I have come to cast upon the earth: fire, sword, and war. For there will be

five in a house: three will be against two, and two against three, the father against the son, and the son against the father. And they will stand solitary."

(17) Jesus said, "I shall give you what no eye has seen and what no ear has heard and what no hand has touched and what has never occurred to the human mind."

(18) The disciples said to Jesus, "Tell us how our end will be."

Jesus said, "Have you discovered, then, the beginning, that you look for the end? For where the beginning is, there will the end be. Blessed is he who will take his place in the beginning; he will know the end and will not experience death."

(19) Jesus said, "Blessed is he who came into being before he came into being. If you become my disciples and listen to my words, these stones will minister to you. For there are five trees for you in Paradise which remain undisturbed summer and winter and whose leaves do not fall. Whoever becomes acquainted with them will not experience death."

(20) The disciples said to Jesus, "Tell us what the kingdom of heaven is like."

He said to them, "It is like a mustard seed. It is the smallest of all seeds. But when it falls on tilled soil, it produces a great plant and becomes a shelter for birds of the sky."

(21) Mary said to Jesus, "Whom are your disciples like?"

419

He said, "They are like children who have settled in a field which is not theirs. When the owners of the field come, they will say, 'Let us have back our field.' They (will) undress in their presence in order to let them have back their field and to give it back to them. Therefore I say, if the owner of a house knows that the thief is coming, he will begin his vigil before he comes and will not let him dig through into his house of his domain to carry away his goods. You, then, be on your guard against the world. Arm yourselves with great strength lest the robbers find a way to come to you, for the difficulty which you expect will (surely) materialize. Let there be among you a man of understanding. When the grain ripened, he came quickly with his sickle in his hand and reaped it. Whoever has ears to hear, let him hear."

(22) Jesus saw infants being suckled. He said to his disciples, "These infants being suckled are like those who enter the kingdom."

They said to him, "Shall we then, as children, enter the kingdom?"

Jesus said to them, "When you make the two one, and when you make the inside like the outside and the outside like the inside, and the above like the below, and when you make the male and the female one and the same, so that the male not be male nor the female female; and when you fashion eyes in the place of an eye, and a hand in place of a hand, and a foot in place of a foot, and a likeness in place of a likeness; then will you enter the kingdom."

(23) Jesus said, "I shall choose you, one out of a thousand, and two out of ten thousand, and they shall stand as a single one."

(24) His disciples said to him, "Show us the place where you are, since it is necessary for us to seek it."

He said to them, "Whoever has ears, let him hear. There is light within a man of light, and he lights up the whole world. If he does not shine, he is darkness."

(25) Jesus said, "Love your brother like your soul, guard him like the pupil of your eye."

(26) Jesus said, "You see the mote in your brother's eye, but you do not see the beam in your own eye. When you cast the beam out of your own eye, then you will see clearly to cast the mote from your brother's eye."

(27) <Jesus said,> "If you do not fast as regards the world, you will not find the kingdom. If you do not observe the Sabbath as a Sabbath, you will not see the father."

(28) Jesus said, "I took my place in the midst of the world, and I appeared to them in flesh. I found all of them intoxicated; I found none of them thirsty. And my soul became afflicted for the sons of men, because they are blind in their hearts and do not have sight; for empty they came into the world, and empty too they seek to leave the world. But for the moment they are intoxicated. When they shake off their wine, then they will repent."

(29) Jesus said, "If the flesh came into being because of spirit, it is a wonder. But if spirit came into being because of the body, it is a wonder of wonders. Indeed, I am amazed at how this great wealth has made its home in this poverty."

(30) Jesus said, "Where there are three gods, they are gods. Where there are two or one, I am with him."

(31) Jesus said, "No prophet is accepted in his own village; no physician heals those who know him."

(32) Jesus said, "A city being built on a high mountain and fortified cannot fall, nor can it be hidden."

(33) Jesus said, "Preach from your housetops that which you will hear in your ear. For no one lights a lamp and puts it under a bushel, nor does he put it in a hidden place, but rather he sets it on a lampstand so that everyone who enters and leaves will see its light."

(34) Jesus said, "If a blind man leads a blind man, they will both fall into a pit."

(35) Jesus said, "It is not possible for anyone to enter the house of a strong man and take it by force unless he binds his hands; then he will (be able to) ransack his house."

(36) Jesus said, "Do not be concerned from morning until evening and from evening until morning about what you will wear."

(37) His disciples said, "When will you become revealed to us and when shall we see you?"

Jesus said, "When you disrobe without being ashamed and take up your garments and place them under your feet like little children and tread on them, then will you see the son of the living one, and you will not be afraid"

(38) Jesus said, "Many times have you desired to hear these words which I am saying to you, and you have no one else to hear them from. There will be days when you will look for me and will not find me."

(39) Jesus said, "The pharisees and the scribes have taken the keys of knowledge (gnosis) and hidden them. They themselves have not entered, nor have they allowed to enter those who wish to. You, however, be as wise as serpents and as innocent as doves."

(40) Jesus said, "A grapevine has been planted outside of the father, but being unsound, it will be pulled up by its roots and destroyed."

(41) Jesus said, "Whoever has something in his hand will receive more, and whoever has nothing will be deprived of even the little he has."

(42) Jesus said, "Become passers-by."

(43) His disciples said to him, "Who are you, that you should say these things to us?"

<Jesus said to them,> "You do not realize who I am from what I say to you, but you have become like the Jews, for they (either) love the tree and hate its fruit (or) love the fruit and hate the tree."

(44) Jesus said, "Whoever blasphemes against the father will be forgiven, and whoever blasphemes against the son will be forgiven, but whoever blasphemes against the holy spirit will not be forgiven either on earth or in heaven."

(45) Jesus said, "Grapes are not harvested from thorns, nor are figs gathered from thistles, for they do not produce fruit. A good man brings forth good from his storehouse; an evil man brings forth evil things from his evil storehouse, which is in his heart, and says evil things. For out of the abundance of the heart he brings forth evil things."

(46) Jesus said, "Among those born of women, from Adam until John the Baptist, there is no one so superior to John the Baptist that his eyes should not be lowered (before him). Yet I have said, whichever one of you comes to be a child will be acquainted with the kingdom and will become superior to John."

(47) Jesus said, "It is impossible for a man to mount two horses or to stretch two bows. And it is impossible for a servant to serve two masters; otherwise, he will honor the one and treat the other contemptuously. No man drinks old wine and immediately desires to drink new

wine. And new wine is not put into old wineskins, lest they burst; nor is old wine put into a new wineskin, lest it spoil it. An old patch is not sewn onto a new garment, because a tear would result."

(48) Jesus said, "If two make peace with each other in this one house, they will say to the mountain, 'Move Away,' and it will move away."

(49) Jesus said, "Blessed are the solitary and elect, for you will find the kingdom. For you are from it, and to it you will return."

(50) Jesus said, "If they say to you, 'Where did you come from?', say to them, 'We came from the light, the place where the light came into being on its own accord and established itself and became manifest through their image.' If they say to you, 'Is it you?', say, 'We are its children, we are the elect of the living father.' If they ask you, 'What is the sign of your father in you?', say to them, 'It is movement and repose.'"

(51) His disciples said to him, "When will the repose of the dead come about, and when will the new world come?"

He said to them, "What you look forward to has already come, but you do not recognize it."

(52) His disciples said to him, "Twenty-four prophets spoke in Israel, and all of them spoke in you."

He said to them, "You have omitted the one living in your presence and have spoken (only) of the dead."

(53) His disciples said to him, "Is circumcision beneficial or not?"

He said to them, "If it were beneficial, their father would beget them already circumcised from their mother. Rather, the true circumcision in spirit has become completely profitable."

(54) Jesus said, "Blessed are the poor, for yours is the kingdom of heaven."

(55) Jesus said, "Whoever does not hate his father and his mother cannot become a disciple to me. And whoever does not hate his brothers and sisters and take up his cross in my way will not be worthy of me."

(56) Jesus said, "Whoever has come to understand the world has found (only) a corpse, and whoever has found a corpse is superior to the world."

(57) Jesus said, "The kingdom of the father is like a man who had good seed. His enemy came by night and sowed weeds among the good seed. The man did not allow them to pull up the weeds; he said to them, 'I am afraid that you will go intending to pull up the weeds and pull up the wheat along with them.' For on the day of the harvest the weeds will be plainly visible, and they will be pulled up and burned."

(58) Jesus said, "Blessed is the man who has suffered and found life."

(59) Jesus said, "Take heed of the living one while you are alive, lest you die and seek to see him and be unable to do so."

(60) <They saw> a Samaritan carrying a lamb on his way to Judea. He said to his disciples, "That man is round about the lamb."

They said to him, "So that he may kill it and eat it."

He said to them, "While it is alive, he will not eat it, but only when he has killed it and it has become a corpse."

They said to him, "He cannot do so otherwise."

He said to them, "You too, look for a place for yourself within repose, lest you become a corpse and be eaten."

(61) Jesus said, "Two will rest on a bed: the one will die, and the other will live."

Salome said, "Who are you, man, that you ... have come up on my couch and eaten from my table?"

Jesus said to her, "I am he who exists from the undivided. I was given some of the things of my father."

<...> "I am your disciple."

<...> "Therefore I say, if he is destroyed, he will be filled with light, but if he is divided, he will be filled with darkness."

(62) Jesus said, "It is to those who are worthy of my mysteries that I tell my mysteries. Do not let your left (hand) know what your right (hand) is doing."

(63) Jesus said, "There was a rich man who had much money. He said, 'I shall put my money to use so that I may sow, reap, plant, and fill my storehouse with produce, with the result that I shall lack nothing.' Such were his intentions, but that same night he died. Let him who has ears hear."

(64) Jesus said, "A man had received visitors. And when he had prepared the dinner, he sent his servant to invite the guests.

He went to the first one and said to him, 'My master invites you.' He said, 'I have claims against some merchants. They are coming to me this evening. I must go and give them my orders. I ask to be excused from the dinner.'

He went to another and said to him, 'My master has invited you.' He said to him, 'I have just bought a house and am required for the day. I shall not have any spare time.'

He went to another and said to him, 'My master invites you.' He said to him, 'My friend is going to get married, and I am to prepare the banquet. I shall not be able to come. I ask to be excused from the dinner.'

He went to another and said to him, 'My master invites you.' He said to him, 'I have just bought a farm, and I am on my way to collect the rent. I shall not be able to come. I ask to be excused.'

The servant returned and said to his master, 'Those whom you invited to the dinner have asked to be excused.' The master said to his servant, 'Go outside to the streets and bring back those whom you happen to meet, so that they may dine.' Businessmen and merchants will not enter the places of my father."

(65) He said, "There was a good man who owned a vineyard. He leased it to tenant farmers so that they might work it and he might collect the produce from them. He sent his servant so that the tenants might give him the produce of the vineyard. They seized his servant and beat him, all but killing him. The servant went back and told his master. The master said, 'Perhaps he did not recognize them.' He sent another servant. The tenants beat this one as well. Then the owner sent his son and said, 'Perhaps they will show respect to my son.' Because the tenants knew that it was he who was the heir to the vineyard, they seized him and killed him. Let him who has ears hear."

(66) Jesus said, "Show me the stone which the builders have rejected. That one is the cornerstone."

(67) Jesus said, "If one who knows the all still feels a personal deficiency, he is completely deficient."

(68) Jesus said, "Blessed are you when you are hated and persecuted. Wherever you have been persecuted they will find no place."

(69) Jesus said, "Blessed are they who have been persecuted within themselves. It is they who have truly come to know the father. Blessed are the hungry, for the belly of him who desires will be filled."

(70) Jesus said, "That which you have will save you if you bring it forth from yourselves. That which you do not have within you will kill you if you do not have it within you."

(71) Jesus said, "I shall destroy this house, and no one will be able to build it [...]."

(72) A man said to him, "Tell my brothers to divide my father's possessions with me."

He said to him, "O man, who has made me a divider?"

He turned to his disciples and said to them, "I am not a divider, am I?"

(73) Jesus said, "The harvest is great but the laborers are few. Beseech the Lord, therefore, to send out laborers to the harvest."

(74) He said, "O Lord, there are many around the drinking trough, but there is nothing in the cistern."

(75) Jesus said, "Many are standing at the door, but it is the solitary who will enter the bridal chamber."

(76) Jesus said, "The kingdom of the father is like a merchant who had a consignment of merchandise and who discovered a pearl. That merchant was shrewd. He sold the merchandise and bought the pearl alone for himself. You too, seek his unfailing and enduring treasure where no moth comes near to devour and no worm destroys."

(77) Jesus said, "It is I who am the light which is above them all. It is I who am the all. From me did the all come forth, and unto me did the all extend. Split a piece of wood, and I am there. Lift up the stone, and you will find me there."

(78) Jesus said, "Why have you come out into the desert? To see a reed shaken by the wind? And to see a man clothed in fine garments like your kings and your great men? Upon them are the fine garments, and they are unable to discern the truth."

(79) A woman from the crowd said to him, "Blessed are the womb which bore you and the breasts which nourished you."

He said to her, "Blessed are those who have heard the word of the father and have truly kept it. For there will be days when you will say, 'Blessed are the womb which has not conceived and the breasts which have not given milk.'"

(80) Jesus said, "He who has recognized the world has found the body, but he who has found the body is superior to the world."

(81) Jesus said, "Let him who has grown rich be king, and let him who possesses power renounce it."

(82) Jesus said, "He who is near me is near the fire, and he who is far from me is far from the kingdom."

(83) Jesus said, "The images are manifest to man, but the

light in them remains concealed in the image of the light of the father. He will become manifest, but his image will remain concealed by his light."

(84) Jesus said, "When you see your likeness, you rejoice. But when you see your images which came into being before you, and which neither die not become manifest, how much you will have to bear!"

(85) Jesus said, "Adam came into being from a great power and a great wealth, but he did not become worthy of you. For had he been worthy, he would not have experienced death."

(86) Jesus said, "The foxes have their holes and the birds have their nests, but the son of man has no place to lay his head and rest."

(87) Jesus said, "Wretched is the body that is dependant upon a body, and wretched is the soul that is dependent on these two."

(88) Jesus said, "The angels and the prophets will come to you and give to you those things you (already) have. And you too, give them those things which you have, and say to yourselves, 'When will they come and take what is theirs?'"

(89) Jesus said, "Why do you wash the outside of the cup? Do you not realize that he who made the inside is the same one who made the outside?"

(90) Jesus said, "Come unto me, for my yoke is easy and my lordship is mild, and you will find repose for yourselves."

(91) They said to him, "Tell us who you are so that we may believe in you."

He said to them, "You read the face of the sky and of the earth, but you have not recognized the one who is before you, and you do not know how to read this moment."

(92) Jesus said, "Seek and you will find. Yet, what you asked me about in former times and which I did not tell you then, now I do desire to tell, but you do not inquire after it."

(93) <Jesus said,> "Do not give what is holy to dogs, lest they throw them on the dung-heap. Do not throw the pearls to swine, lest they [...] it [...]."

(94) Jesus said, "He who seeks will find, and he who knocks will be let in."

(95) Jesus said, "If you have money, do not lend it at interest, but give it to one from whom you will not get it back."

(96) Jesus said, "The kingdom of the father is like a certain woman. She took a little leaven, concealed it in some dough, and made it into large loaves. Let him who has ears hear."

(97) Jesus said, "The kingdom of the father is like a certain woman who was carrying a jar full of meal. While she was walking on the road, still some distance from home, the handle of the jar broke and the meal emptied out behind her on the road. She did not realize it; she had noticed no accident. When she reached her house, she set the jar down and found it empty."

(98) Jesus said, "The kingdom of the father is like a certain man who wanted to kill a powerful man. In his own house he drew his sword and stuck it into the wall in order to find out whether his hand could carry through. Then he slew the powerful man."

(99) The disciples said to him, "Your brothers and your mother are standing outside."

He said to them, "Those here who do the will of my father are my brothers and my mother. It is they who will enter the kingdom of my father."

(100) They showed Jesus a gold coin and said to him, "Caesar's men demand taxes from us."

He said to them, "Give Caesar what belongs to Caesar, give God what belongs to God, and give me what is mine."

(101) <Jesus said,> "Whoever does not hate his father and his mother as I do cannot become a disciple to me. And whoever does not love his father and his mother as I do cannot become a disciple to me. For my mother [...], but my true mother gave me life."

(102) Jesus said, "Woe to the pharisees, for they are like a dog sleeping in the manger of oxen, for neither does he eat nor does he let the oxen eat."

(103) Jesus said, "Fortunate is the man who knows where the brigands will enter, so that he may get up, muster his domain, and arm himself before they invade."

(104) They said to Jesus, "Come, let us pray today and let us fast."

Jesus said, "What is the sin that I have committed, or wherein have I been defeated? But when the bridegroom leaves the bridal chamber, then let them fast and pray."

(105) Jesus said, "He who knows the father and the mother will be called the son of a harlot."

(106) Jesus said, "When you make the two one, you will become the sons of man, and when you say, 'Mountain, move away,' it will move away."

(107) Jesus said, "The kingdom is like a shepherd who had a hundred sheep. One of them, the largest, went astray. He left the ninety-nine sheep and looked for that one until he found it. When he had gone to such trouble, he said to the sheep, 'I care for you more than the ninety-nine.'"

(108) Jesus said, "He who will drink from my mouth will become like me. I myself shall become he, and the things that are hidden will be revealed to him."

(109) Jesus said, "The kingdom is like a man who had a hidden treasure in his field without knowing it. And after he died, he left it to his son. The son did not know (about the treasure). He inherited the field and sold it. And the one who bought it went plowing and found the treasure. He began to lend money at interest to whomever he wished."

(110) Jesus said, "Whoever finds the world and becomes rich, let him renounce the world."

(111) Jesus said, "The heavens and the earth will be rolled up in your presence. And the one who lives from the living one will not see death." Does not Jesus say, "Whoever finds himself is superior to the world?"

(112) Jesus said, "Woe to the flesh that depends on the soul; woe to the soul that depends on the flesh."

(113) His disciples said to him, "When will the kingdom come?"

    <Jesus said,> "It will not come by waiting for it. It will not be a matter of saying 'here it is' or 'there it is.' Rather, the kingdom of the father is spread out upon the earth, and men do not see it."

(114) Simon Peter said to him, "Let Mary leave us, for women are not worthy of life."

Jesus said, "I myself shall lead her in order to make her male, so that she too may become a living spirit resembling you males. For every woman who will make herself male will enter the kingdom of heaven."

A P P E N D I X *B*

THE GOSPEL OF MARY[2]

Mary of Magdala was in charge of the close women disciples who traveled with Jesus, she was the first to see and believe in the risen Jesus. Unfortunately, the extant manuscript of the Gospel of Mary is missing pages 1 to 6 and pages 11 to 14 -- pages that included sections of the text up to chapter 4, and portions of chapter 5 to 8.

Chapter 4

(Pages 1 to 6 of the manuscript, containing chapters 1 - 3, are lost. The extant text starts on page 7...)

---

[2] Papyrus Berolinensis 8502 was acquired by a German scholar, Dr. Carl Reinhardt, in Cairo in 1896 (the codex is variably referenced in scholarly writings as the "Berlin Gnostic Codex", the "Akhmim Codex", PB 8502, and BG 8502).

. . . Will matter then be destroyed or not?

22) The Savior said, All nature, all formations, all creatures exist in and with one another, and they will be resolved again into their own roots.

23) For the nature of matter is resolved into the roots of its own nature alone.

24) He who has ears to hear, let him hear.

25) Peter said to him, Since you have explained everything to us, tell us this also: What is the sin of the world?

26) The Savior said There is no sin, but it is you who make sin when you do the things that are like the nature of adultery, which is called sin.

27) That is why the Good came into your midst, to the essence of every nature in order to restore it to its root.

28) Then He continued and said, That is why you become sick and die, for you are deprived of the one who can heal you.

29) He who has a mind to understand, let him understand.

30) Matter gave birth to a passion that has no equal, which proceeded from something contrary to nature. Then there arises a disturbance in its whole body.

31) That is why I said to you, Be of good courage, and if

you are discouraged be encouraged in the presence of the different forms of nature.

32) He who has ears to hear, let him hear.

33) When the Blessed One had said this, He greeted them all, saying, Peace be with you. Receive my peace unto yourselves.

34) Beware that no one lead you astray saying Lo here or lo there! For the Son of Man is within you.

35) Follow after Him!

36) Those who seek Him will find Him.

37) Go then and preach the gospel of the Kingdom.

38) Do not lay down any rules beyond what I appointed you, and do not give a law like the lawgiver lest you be constrained by it.

39) When He said this He departed.

Chapter 5

1) But they were grieved. They wept greatly, saying, How shall we go to the Gentiles and preach the gospel of the Kingdom of the Son of Man? If they did not spare Him, how will they spare us?

2) Then Mary stood up, greeted them all, and said to her brethren, Do not weep and do not grieve nor be irresolute, for His grace will be entirely with you and will protect you.

3) But rather, let us praise His greatness, for He has prepared us and made us into Men.

4) When Mary said this, she turned their hearts to the Good, and they began to discuss the words of the Savior.

5) Peter said to Mary, Sister we know that the Savior loved you more than the rest of woman.

6) Tell us the words of the Savior which you remember which you know, but we do not, nor have we heard them.

7) Mary answered and said, What is hidden from you I will proclaim to you.

8) And she began to speak to them these words: I, she said, I saw the Lord in a vision and I said to Him, Lord I saw you today in a vision. He answered and said to me,

9) Blessed are you that you did not waver at the sight of Me. For where the mind is there is the treasure.

10) I said to Him, Lord, how does he who sees the vision see it, through the soul or through the spirit?

11) The Savior answered and said, He does not see through the soul nor through the spirit, but the mind

that is between the two that is what sees the vision and it is [...]

(pages 11 - 14 are missing from the manuscript)

Chapter 8:

. . . it.

10) And desire said, I did not see you descending, but now I see you ascending. Why do you lie since you belong to me?

11) The soul answered and said, I saw you. You did not see me nor recognize me. I served you as a garment and you did not know me.

12) When it said this, it (the soul) went away rejoicing greatly.

13) Again it came to the third power, which is called ignorance.

14) The power questioned the soul, saying, Where are you going? In wickedness are you bound. But you are bound; do not judge!

15) And the soul said, Why do you judge me, although I have not judged?

16) I was bound, though I have not bound.

17) I was not recognized. But I have recognized that the All is being dissolved, both the earthly things and the heavenly.

18) When the soul had overcome the third power, it went upwards and saw the fourth power, which took seven forms.

19) The first form is darkness, the second desire, the third ignorance, the fourth is the excitement of death, the fifth is the kingdom of the flesh, the sixth is the foolish wisdom of flesh, the seventh is the wrathful wisdom. These are the seven powers of wrath.

20) They asked the soul, Whence do you come slayer of men, or where are you going, conqueror of space?

21) The soul answered and said, What binds me has been slain, and what turns me about has been overcome,

22) and my desire has been ended, and ignorance has died.

23) In a aeon I was released from a world, and in a Type from a type, and from the fetter of oblivion which is transient.

24) From this time on will I attain to the rest of the time, of the season, of the aeon, in silence.

Chapter 9

1) When Mary had said this, she fell silent, since it was to this point that the Savior had spoken with her.

2) But Andrew answered and said to the brethren, Say what you wish to say about what she has said. I at least do not believe that the Savior said this. For certainly these teachings are strange ideas.

3) Peter answered and spoke concerning these same things.

4) He questioned them about the Savior: Did He really speak privately with a woman and not openly to us? Are we to turn about and all listen to her? Did He prefer her to us?

5) Then Mary wept and said to Peter, My brother Peter, what do you think? Do you think that I have thought this up myself in my heart, or that I am lying about the Savior?

6) Levi answered and said to Peter, Peter you have always been hot tempered.

7) Now I see you contending against the woman like the adversaries.

8) But if the Savior made her worthy, who are you indeed to reject her? Surely the Savior knows her very well.

9) That is why He loved her more than us. Rather let us be ashamed and put on the perfect Man, and separate as He commanded us and preach the gospel, not laying down any other rule or other law beyond what the Savior said.

10) And when they heard this they began to go forth to proclaim and to preach.

APPENDIX

CHECK YOUR ALIGNMENT
TO THE NATURE OF LIGHT
Part 1:Group / Part 2:Personal

Part 1: Assess Your Group

Relational and Holistic

- This group uses work, play, learning, and social activities to create and maintain networks of relationships.

1	2	3	4	5	6	7	8	9	10

No such
activities

Abundant
activities

447

• This group feels like a healthy, high functioning inter-active community.

1	2	3	4	5	6	7	8	9	10

Not at all   *Extremely*

• This group taps the potential of the collective mind through the formal and informal exchange of information and ideas from every member.

1	2	3	4	5	6	7	8	9	10

Never   *Always*

Diversity and Balance

• This group includes a wide variety of personalities, cultures, and ages.

1	2	3	4	5	6	7	8	9	10

No   *Tremendous*
variety   *Variety*

• The diversity in this group is embraced and well inte-grated; it is a cohesive team.

1	2	3	4	5	6	7	8	9	10

No   *Completely*
integration   *integrated*

- This group's activity is balanced — neither overly stressful nor sluggish.

1	2	3	4	5	6	7	8	9	10

Out of
balance

Perfectly
balanced

Possibility and Uncertainty

- This group supports the growth and development of individuals and teams.

1	2	3	4	5	6	7	8	9	10

Never
encourages

Always
encourages

- This group recognizes the outstanding achievements of all its members.

1	2	3	4	5	6	7	8	9	10

Everyone is in
a negative box

No one is in
a negative box

- This group regards its uncertain future without stress and anxiety.

1	2	3	4	5	6	7	8	9	10

Future
seems bleak

Future
seems grand

Open and Flowing

- This group is receptive to viewpoints and ideas that challenge the status quo.

1	2	3	4	5	6	7	8	9	10

No
receptivity

Completely
open

- Communication channels are open in all directions throughout the group.

1	2	3	4	5	6	7	8	9	10

Open in all
directions

Blocked in all
directions

- When the unexpected happens, this group adjusts without stress or resistance.

1	2	3	4	5	6	7	8	9	10

Complete
breakdown

Stress-free
flowing

Intention and Alignment

- This group is guided by clear vision and core values.

1	2	3	4	5	6	7	8	9	10

No
vision
Clear
vision

- If a person or process fails to adhere to this group's vision and core values, those involved receive feedback that is constructive to align energies.

1	2	3	4	5	6	7	8	9	10

Never
Always

- Everyone is pulling together.

1	2	3	4	5	6	7	8	9	10

Very
aligned
Fractured

Synergy and Love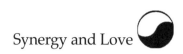

- This group has a loving, harmonious, uplifting energy.

1	2	3	4	5	6	7	8	9	10

Never   *Always*

- The interfacing of roles, responsibilities, and tasks is stress-free.

1	2	3	4	5	6	7	8	9	10

Never   *Always*

- You yourself are in alignment with energy's nature in your personal life.

1	2	3	4	5	6	7	8	9	10

Never   *Always*

Part 2: Personal Introspection

Relational and Holistic

- Do you reach out to others? Are you an introvert or extrovert? Are you shy and withdrawn? Do you take risks by extending out to others?

- Do you actively participate in a spiritual community, joining with others in praising our Source?

- Are you actively involved in webs of relationships through family, play, and social group endeavors?

- Do you participate in group problem solving and help others when they need it? At work and within sustained groups do you tap the power of the collective mind?

- Do you see that you are a part of a holistic web when you participate in a group? Are you aware of the repercussions of your actions within these groups?

Diversity and Balance

- What comments do you make or reactions do you have when your standards or beliefs are confronted? Are you open to different perspectives?

- Do you have friends and acquaintances who are very different from each other? Do you participate in a variety of groups?

- Do you often function with a high level of tension, always putting out fires?

- Do you often operate full of inertia, moving slowly, taking great effort to accomplish simple tasks, acting fearful and mistrusting?

- How often are you focused, centered, and at peace?

Possibility and Uncertainty

- How do you view your own prospects and possibility?

- Do you speak positively of others and make light of your burdens?

- Do you see the advantages of an idea first, before pointing out the disadvantages? Instead of looking for reasons why something can't be done, do you search for ways in which it can?

- Does fear prevent you from taking occasional risks and experimenting with things outside your routine?

- Are you sensitive to the internal communication of intuition? Do you use it as a guide for your decisions and actions?

- Do you do any practices like yoga or meditation to help still your mind and tune into that inner guidance of intuition?

Open and Flowing

- Do you tend to confine yourself to the four walls of your home? Do you often feel isolated and shut off from the world?

- Do you often judge and box people in negative packages? Do you believe people don't change?

- Are you receptive to others? Are you a good listener? Do you listen to other's viewpoints even when you disagree? Does your internal dialogue begin to respond before the speaker finishes?

- Do you forgive those who have wronged you? Do you hold resentments?

- Do you flow with unexpected occurrences or do you often shut down and react when things don't go your way?

- How open is your toleration window? Which behaviors shut it down and which ones open it up?

Intention and Alignment

- Do you spend time on a daily basis praising God?

- Do you hold an intention to bring Light into your relationships?

- Do you set goals and intentions to start each day?

- Do your words, commitment, and intentions align with your actions?

- Do the groups you're involved in have active core values that guide their actions? Are the groups aligned to these values?

- Do your groups utilize feedback if someone opposes the values of the group? Is there safety within these groups for this discussion to occur?

Love and Synergy

- How often do you feel the sensation of love and joy?

- Do you have harmonious relations or is there considerable conflict at work, and play, or within your family and social groups?

- Are you sensitive to the energy you put behind your words when you communicate?

- How closely are you in synergy with all six characteristics in your own personal life?

- What is your most significant behavior that opposes energy's nature?

- Are you taking action to shift this behavior at its roots?

Dedicated to the Light

ACKNOWLEDGEMENTS

Translating images and messages into this book was a collective effort— tapping a collective mind. Paul Wood, the Hawaii-based author and writing coach, served steadfastly as my mentor in the art of story writing. He guided me through this book's two-year development, and his talent is present throughout. Bill Greaves did a masterful job with the book's cover artwork and overall book design. Also, I am indebted to eight reviewers who made valuable contributions in response to their reading of the draft manuscript; these include Christine Warren, Tom Monahan, and Deanna Summers. Thank you.

CONTACTS

ORDERING BOOKS

Individual books can be ordered through bookstores or through the website listed below. Churches and non-profits can order cases of thirty-two books at a special discount by following instructions at this site.

THE AUTHOR

For the past twenty years Paul Deslauriers has worked as an organizational development consultant. He is the author of *"IN THE HIGH ENERGY ZONE: The 6 Characteristics of Highly Effective Groups."*

Contact the author, or provide feedback on the book by visiting the website listed below.

UPCOMING WORKSHOPS

The author gives lectures, half-day and full-day work-shops, and weekend retreats. For descriptions of his pro-grams, including locations and schedule, contact the website.

www.BearerofLight.com